Playing Dirty

San Diego Social Scene Book #3

Tess Summers

Seasons Press LLC

Published: 2018

ISBN: 978-1721833894

Published by Seasons Press LLC.

Copyright © 2018, Tess Summers.

Edited by Sandy Ebel, Personal Touch Editing

Cover by OliviaProDesign

This is a work of fiction. The characters, incidents, and dialogues in this book are of the author's imagination and are not to be construed as real. Any resemblance to actual events or persons, living or dead, is completely coincidental.

This book is for mature readers. It contains sexually explicit scenes and graphic language that may be considered offensive by some.

All sexually active characters in this work are eighteen years of age or older.

Playing Dirty

Cassie

I'm a career woman. I wear success like a second skin, and I'm rarely satisfied with anything less than the best. This includes my love life. If you want to date me, you better bring your A game because I don't play with the B team.

The only type of commitment I'm interested in is the one I have with my career. There is no man strong enough to tame me. Bold enough to rattle me. Or confident enough to win my heart. But then again, I have never met a man like Luke Rivas.

Luke

Cassie is one feisty, fiery, demanding woman who has enough confidence to intimidate even the bravest of men. She's driven, ambitious, and clearly has no interest in anything more than a casual fling.

But here's the thing. I want her, and once I have her, there will be nothing casual about it.

I will crack through that tough exterior she wears so well and bend her into submission. I'll make her break every one of her own damn rules just for me. And in order to accomplish just that...

I'm willing to play dirty.

Dedication

This book is dedicated to the people who, when life handed them lemons, decided to make lemon drop martinis with theirs.

Cheers.

Acknowledgments

Mr. Summers: Thanks for taking such good care of me all these years. You're my rock, and I love you.

Summers' children: Thanks for continuing to proudly tell people what I do for a living. All three of you are awesome; I don't care what your dad says.

Bad Girls' Club–expanded version: Y'all are the shit. Best beta readers on the planet. Seriously. Thank you, thank you.

Laura Giovanini: You are literally the definition of a *friend for life*. (40+ years!)

The amazing writing community-fellow authors, bloggers, readers, and industry counterparts: Wow. You are all amazingly generous with your support, advice, and time. Thank you for including me in the circle.

All my friends on social media: You make me smile every day. Thanks for being my friend even if you probably wouldn't say hi to me in real life. LOL

My real-life friends: Thank you for your continued support in this crazy new adventure. It means a lot.

My extended family: Thanks for buying my books even though you will never read them and for always showing up. Always. I love you for that.

Lastly, to my readers: I can't begin to express how humble it makes me that you read my work. Thanks for letting me continue sharing my stories with you. I hope to for a long time to come.

Table of Contents

Playing Dirty

Prologue

Cassie

"I'd love to take you out for a drink sometime."

They had just taken their seat at the restaurant bar when Dr. Rob Bennett made his declaration, his green eyes twinkling. The good-looking, orthopedic surgeon zoned in on Cassie Sullivan the minute she walked through the doors, approaching with a glass of white wine for her already in hand and a cocky smile on his lips that grew even bigger when she accepted the drink.

Rob's charm and confidence were working for him. The petite, dark-blonde found herself glad she hadn't bowed out of the Monday evening mixer her pharmaceutical company was sponsoring like she'd originally planned.

"Sure," Cassie smiled, "just say when." She wasn't the pharma rep for Rob's practice, so she didn't see a conflict going out with him.

"When."

She laughed out loud, fidgeting with the stem on her wineglass.

"Could you be more specific?"

"How about Friday night? We can meet at Oakwood for their Friday Whiskey Flights and Wings."

Whiskey and wings on a Friday night? What could possibly go wrong? Except Wake-Up Hungover Sans Panties Saturday.

"That sounds like fun. What time?"

His obviously groomed eyebrows drew together like he suddenly remembered something, and he shifted uncomfortably on the barstool.

"Um, how about seven?"

If she were gracious, she'd make an excuse and say Friday wouldn't work after all.

Except, she wasn't gracious. *He shouldn't have suggested it if he didn't mean it.* Besides, maybe he was going to reschedule whatever he obviously already had planned.

He texted her Tuesday night, flirting a little, but making no mention of meeting Friday. Same when they communicated on Wednesday, although he amped up his flirting, which she didn't exactly discourage. Rob was her textbook type—athletic build, not too tall but not too short, successful and driven, probably making as much money as she did. And green eyes.

Green eyes were her kryptonite.

Thursday found him casting his line to send a dick pic, but she didn't bite. *What was it with men's fascination with photographing their junk and wanting to show it off?* Yet still no mention of their whiskey and wings date, so she wasn't surprised when she got a text from him Friday afternoon.

Rob B: I am so sorry. I forgot my buddies bought me baseball tickets for tonight. Maybe we could have lunch tomorrow?

There were three things about the message that pissed her off. One, she knew he'd remembered he had plans the night he asked her out, so, two, why did he wait until the last minute to cancel? Was he waiting to see how easy she was before deciding which plans to go with? And three, *lunch*? *Really*? He wants to have *lunch* now?

On a Saturday.

Instead of taking her out Saturday night.

Fuck that. She didn't care how good looking he was or how green his eyes were.

You take the B team to lunch, you take the A-team out on a Saturday night. She was fucking A team material, dammit.

She replied: *Sorry, can't. Have plans.*

Rob B: Brunch on Sunday?

Hey, Dr. Asshat, eat a dick.

She hit the backspace before the send button and took the more polite route.

Cassie: No, busy. Maybe next time.

Rob B: When are you available?

She was sure he had 'better' plans on Saturday night and couldn't wait to hear his excuse.

Cassie: Saturday night.

Rob B: Great. How about seven o'clock again, same place?

Color her surprised.

Cassie: Sounds great. See you then.

**

Cassie's heels echoed off the wooden floors as she walked into Oakwood's bar area at seven fifteen. She had sent Rob a text to let him know she was running behind, so she'd meet him in the bar. Looking at the mostly empty tables, he was nowhere to be found.

Hmmm. He had responded it wasn't a problem she was going to be late, so she didn't think he would have just left. She walked up to the old-fashioned bar—the kind you'd see in a Western movie, complete with a bar-length mirror hanging behind it—and climbed onto a heavy, wooden barstool.

Maybe he's in the restroom.

A perky, redheaded bartender bounced over with a smile and asked what she'd like to drink.

"I'll have a Crown and ginger, tall, please."

As the woman gathered the ingredients on the other side of the counter, Cassie nervously traced her fingers on the scuffed mahogany while swiveling her seat back and forth. When the frosted bar glass was placed in front of her, Cassie jabbed the skinny red straw in the ice.

"There wasn't a guy here waiting for someone, was there? About five-eleven, athletic build, light brown hair, nice looking."

The bartender shook her head, swishing her red ponytail back and forth. "Sorry, hon, no one."

The drink was stronger than Cassie had anticipated, so she tried to nurse it, checking her phone, what seemed like every two minutes while perusing the walls adorned with memorabilia of famous people who'd visited the bar. When she'd almost finished her cocktail and run out of things to pretend to be interested in looking at, there was still no sign or word from Rob. The memory of the time her sister, Brenna had been stood up flashed to the forefront of her mind. Granted,

Brenna being stood up made it in the *Out and About* section of the paper, so at least there was the consolation of only the bartender knowing Cassie had been stood up and not all of San Diego.

Taking out her phone, she fired off a message: *Almost done with my drink. Should I just go?*

She'd give him five minutes to respond, then she was leaving if he didn't.

He immediately sent back a cryptic text.

Rob B: Be there soon.

What the hell?

Red eyed her near empty glass and asked if she wanted another.

"I'm not sure."

The woman gave a sympathetic smile. "What time was he supposed to be here?"

Cassie hesitated, then over shared. "Seven, but I texted to let him know I was going to be late. He said that was fine but made no mention of being late himself."

Red glanced at her watch and scrunched up her freckled nose. "Well, it's ten to eight now, hon." She must have sensed Cassie's indecision about what to do next because she said, "I've gotta grab a case of beer from the cooler, so no rush. Be right back."

The woman disappeared around the corner, and Cassie twisted in her seat, scanning the tables one last time before making up her mind she was outta there as soon as she could pay for her drink.

She heard the bartender say from around the corner, "Hey! Haven't seen you in a while!" and a deep male voice she recognized as Rob's respond, "Hey, Celeste. Just meeting a friend."

Rob came around the corner, looking hot in spite of his casual shorts, flip flops, wrinkled tee, and a baseball cap on backward. His appearance was a stark contrast to Cassie's high heels and perfectly pressed sundress—the dress she'd spent twenty minutes agonizing over before deciding to wear. Red rounded the corner with a case of beer in her hands and motioned toward Rob with her head.

"This who you've been waiting for?"

Cassie gave a meager smile when she nodded and felt oddly uncomfortable when the woman rolled her eyes at Rob with a smirk.

"Figures."

Celeste—Cassie assumed was her name since that's what she'd heard Rob call her—suddenly seemed less friendly toward Cassie when she took Rob's drink order, all but ignoring the pharmaceuticals rep now.

"How's Lauren?" the woman asked him, making sure to lean forward to show her ample cleavage while scooping ice for his drink.

"We broke up."

The barmaid eyed Cassie. "I wondered. Sorry to hear that." She proceeded to go down memory lane with him, leaving Cassie feeling like the third wheel. Apparently, the two went way back to his college days.

To Rob's credit, he really tried to include Cassie in the conversation, but between him canceling on her last minute yesterday, making her wait tonight for over thirty minutes with no explanation offered, and the reunion tour of memories with the Little Mermaid's stand-in behind the bar, Cassie was done.

"Hey, I need to close out my tab," she called out to Celeste as the woman made a drink for another customer.

Rob spun on his barstool to face her. "I just got here."

"Yes, I know," she said with a fake smile. She didn't try to disguise how she felt about that although she passive-aggressively pretended to. "I have some things I need to take care of. I could've taken care of them earlier had I known we weren't really meeting until eight."

He stood, pulled a money clip from his front pocket, and threw two twenties on the bar, still offering no reason why he was late.

"Let me walk you to your car, at least."

"No, you stay and enjoy your drink," Cassie smirked. "I'm sure you still have lots of catching up to do."

He shook his head and guided her by the elbow to the door without a second glance at the bartender.

"I'm sorry about Celeste. We used to work together a long time ago."

"I gathered that."

They started toward the parking lot, and Cassie noticed a group of women in standard little black dresses prancing up the sidewalk toward the bar, not so subtly eye him up and down. She didn't blame them—he *was* good looking. And successful. If he was good in bed that'd pretty much be her trifecta. But she got the feeling he was playing her for a fool about why he couldn't make it last night. And why was he so late tonight? Why didn't he tell her he was going to be late as well when she texted him she was going to be?

It was on the tip of her tongue to ask when she realized, she really didn't give a shit.

Opening the driver's door on her red Lexus LS 460, she tilted her chin towards him.

"Thanks for the drink, Rob. Have a great night," she said and slid onto the tan leather seat.

With his hands on the steel frame, he leaned down before she could close the door. His brown novelty t-shirt pulled tight at the chest, and she caught a whiff of his expensive cologne.

"Come on, let me take you somewhere else. I feel like we've gotten off on the wrong foot."

Cassie stared at him while contemplating her next move.

He smiled and with a wink, mouthed, "Please?"

His lips were really suckable when he pouted. And those fucking green eyes mesmerized her.

Snapping out of it, she asked sweetly, "How was the game?"

He furrowed his brow, "The ga--? Oh, it was good."

"Which game was it again?"

He'd recovered from his faux pas and didn't miss a beat this time. "The Padres."

Not many people knew Danny Roberts, second baseman for the Padres, was her brother-in-law for almost twenty years before he was killed in a car accident. Cassie still followed the team closely, so she knew they were in San Francisco last night.

It wasn't impossible he'd traveled the five hundred miles to the game. Looking at his handsome face and muscular arms, she was trying to convince herself he had until he added, "Ortiz pitched a helluva game, we should've won."

Unfortunately for him, Cassie knew Michael Ortiz was scheduled to pitch tonight after a last-minute roster change yesterday, and they went through six pitchers last night, trying to find a rhythm. Rob must've missed those little tidbits when he saw the score this morning. He probably never in a million years thought the dark-blonde followed baseball, anyway.

She pointed her finger upward in an *aha* manner, then started her sedan.

"I have an idea where we can go."

He stood up straighter, waiting to hear her suggestion, and she took the opportunity to close the door. Rolling her window down, she gave him a sweet smile.

"Well, where *you* can go, anyway."

He blinked at her, not understanding.

"For the record, Vaughn, Harris, Taylor, Dorn, and Cerrano all pitched like shit last night. The only one who was worth a damn was Cloney, and he was in a no-win situation by the time he took the mound. Ortiz pitches tonight." She started to roll her window up but paused for a second to add, "And Rob Bennett, you're a fucking asshole."

She shifted her car into drive and drove off without looking back.

Next.

Chapter One

Cassie

Cassie finished her walk down the makeshift aisle in the sand and turned to watch her older sister, Brenna make her way to where an anxious Lieutenant General of the United States Marine Corps, Ron Thompson stood in his dress blues, waiting for his bride. She chuckled, thinking of the fuss Ron made when Brenna insisted on a semi-traditional ceremony, whining he'd have to wear his uniform.

Watching Ron's face when her sister appeared on the aisle brought tears to her eyes. As he fidgeted while Brenna approached, there wasn't a thought in Cassie's head that Ron was nervous he was getting married. No, he was just in a hurry to get his ring on Brenna's finger and make her his forever. The way Ron looked at her sister, it was obvious she was the only woman in his world who existed.

The minister hadn't finished giving the instruction for Ron to kiss his bride when he had Brenna's face in his hands, staring into her eyes, then kissing her with such passion, *Cassie's* knees went weak.

Damn.

She glanced over at Ron's handsome, younger brother and best man, Greg in his tan suit and turquoise tie that matched Cassie's gown and wondered if he'd kiss like that. Maybe. When he smirked, winked at his date who was sitting three rows back and she blushed, Cassie knew there was no *maybe* about it. Too bad he was already spoken for.

Cassie gave Brenna the cascading, white and turquoise, calla lily bouquet she was holding as part of her maid of honor duties, then took Greg's offered arm to be escorted down the aisle behind the bride and groom. The other bridesmaid, Brenna's daughter, Danielle had healed nicely from her horrible car accident in May and was accompanied by Kyle Montgomery, the girl's Godfather and best friend of Brenna's first husband, Danny. Kyle's involvement in the wedding was all very soap opera-esque, something Cassie secretly loved. It was fun watching people who usually had a stick up their ass try not to appear scandalized when Kyle made his appearance at the pre-wedding festivities. Her parents, however, didn't bat an eye. Which made sense since Kyle was such an intricate part of their lives, both when Danny was alive, and maybe even more so once he was killed. Kyle had really stepped up to fulfill his role as Godfather after his best friend died, something Cassie appreciated and loved him for.

It was an intimate wedding held outside of Brenna—and now Ron's—San Diego beach house, so they didn't have far to go on the short, flower-covered runner. She smiled and squeezed Greg's arm before releasing it so he could walk back toward the guests and presumably, his lucky date.

The reception was being hosted on the patio, and Cassie had started making her way to the bar when Cooper Johnson stopped her. He was stationed at Ron's base, and if Ron's promotion ceremony pictures were accurate, the man could rock a uniform like nobody's business. But his more casual attire for the beach wedding worked, too.

"Cassandra! You look beautiful."

"Cooper, call me Cassie, please! Cassandra is just so... formal."

"I think it fits you. It's elegant. Classy."

It was all she could do not to snort out a laugh. She was many things—spunky, cute, a spitfire, a little mouthy perhaps—but classy and elegant were not words she would ever use to describe herself. Still, she knew how to be professional and was damn good at her job as a pharmaceutical rep, so she was comfortable in her skin.

Patting his cheek with her manicured hand, she smiled. "Aw, aren't you sweet? You obviously don't know me very well but thank you."

He leaned down and pressed his lips against her ear. "And how do I remedy that?"

Goosebumps ran down her spine, and she felt her nipples harden. Cassie searched his twinkling eyes as he pulled away from her. Was her mouth open? It might have been because he was smirking at her.

Brenna had told her Cooper insisted on getting Cassie's phone number right after a charity event they had all attended. He'd spent time at their table, and the two of them hit it off, she had thought like buddies—although there was no denying he was handsome. His dirty blonde hair with natural highlights and blue eyes screamed he was a California boy, through and through. His tall, tan, athletic body could easily be mistaken for a surfer's, not a Marine Captain's. Hell, he probably did spend time on a board catching waves. The toothpaste commercial smile was just the icing on the cake. The night of the charity auction, Cassie only had eyes for SWAT Sergeant Luke Rivas, so when Brenna told Cassie about Cooper's interest, she was certain Brenna had misunderstood, especially since he never actually called her.

Now, she wasn't so sure.

"Save me a dance," he said with a wink, then looked over her shoulder and straightened, taking a step back.

Luke appeared at her side and offered Cooper a smile and a handshake.

"Johnson. Haven't seen you since the auction. Anything ever become of that date?"

Cooper glanced over at Cassie when he answered. "Nah, we couldn't all be as lucky as you."

Her gaze went to the ground. Luke and Cooper had both auctioned themselves off at the Heroes of San Diego's Charity Auction last month, and she knew he was referring to the fact Cassie had bid on and won Luke's date for five hundred dollars.

A date that still hadn't taken place.

"I was pretty lucky, wasn't I?" Luke grinned, pinning Cassie with his gaze.

Really? He thought he was lucky? He sure has a funny way of showing it.

The smile on Cooper's face didn't reach his eyes when he said solemnly, "You were indeed."

Before turning on his heel, Cooper winked at Cassie and teased, "Make sure to save that dance for me."

At least she thought he was teasing.

A contemplative look crossed Luke's features as they watched Cooper walk off. He turned back to Cassie, a smile on his face and crinkle lines around his eyes.

Green eyes.

"How have you been?" he asked, gesturing for them to continue toward the house.

"I've been good, busy. How about you?"

"The same," he chuckled.

She wasn't sure what to say or how to act since she didn't know how he felt about her. Should she flirt? Or be the polite maid of honor and make insignificant chitchat while acting indifferent? She was interested in him but got the impression his feelings toward her were tepid, and a girl had her pride.

The awkward silence as they walked along the sand was finally broken when he quietly said, "You look really beautiful."

Cassie glanced up at him with a surprised smile. "Thank you. You look nice, too."

She wasn't lying. He *was* classically handsome, in a Latin lover kind of way and like he belonged on the beach in his khakis and blue linen popover shirt that showed off his tan.

They made it to the back patio where people were mingling and enjoying cocktails as the caterers set up for dinner. Taking in the scene, they watched an elated Brenna and Ron greet their guests under the twinkling lights strategically strung around the bricked pavers.

"I don't think I've ever seen a couple better suited for each other," he observed.

"They do bring out the best in one another," Cassie nodded.

"Being in love tends to do that to you."

She looked up at him and tilted her head. "It seems like you're speaking from experience."

Luke gave a whimsical smile. "I'm just observant."

"So, you've never been in love like that?"

He answered her question with a question. "Have you?"

"I asked you first."

There was a long pause while he considered his answer.

"I thought maybe I was, once. Turns out, I wasn't."

"Sounds like there's a story behind that." She was trying to draw more out, but he quickly shut her down.

With narrowed eyes, he shook his head, "It's in the past," then pressed the small of her back, urging her forward, letting her know that topic was closed.

She was intrigued, and Luke not wanting to talk about it only made her want to talk about it more.

She was obnoxious like that.

"So, what *do* you want to talk about?" she asked when they reached the back of the long line for the open bar. "Our date that's never going to happen?"

He raised an eyebrow. "And why isn't it ever going to happen?"

"I don't know, you tell me?" Cassie shrugged. "You haven't exactly been in a hurry to schedule it."

"Well," he smirked, "I've been waiting for you to call me, doll."

She opened her mouth, then closed it again with a frown. Why should she have to call him?

As if reading her mind, he continued in a gentle tone.

"The auction winner is supposed to make the first call. She's provided with her date's contact information but not vice versa. The committee wanted the ladies to feel comfortable providing as much or as little information about themselves as they wanted. The instructions were in your winner's packet."

Thinking about how annoyed she'd been he hadn't called, she felt a little silly and wanted to save some of her dignity.

"Well, last I checked, you already have my number. Unless you deleted it?"

"Of course, I didn't delete it." The thought seemed to surprise him. "I just thought I should wait to hear from you. I knew things with the wedding had to be keeping you busy and given how last time..."

Just then, someone tapped him on the shoulder, and he turned to find a few people from the fundraising committee for The Wounded Warrior Project.

Given how last time what? How nothing ever happened even though the one kiss they shared was the kind of kiss romance novels were written about? Given how he blew her off, repeatedly, even though he acted interested?

"Saved by the bell," she murmured as he excused himself to step out of line and talk with the group.

When Luke hadn't called after the charity auction, she honestly thought he still wasn't interested in her, that the chemistry they seemed to share had all been in her head or the result of too much alcohol. Granted, she knew he'd honor the charity auction date, eventually, she just assumed it would be obvious he meant it to be strictly platonic. Now, she allowed herself to feel the excitement she'd felt the night she bought his date. Maybe he was interested in her after all.

Once she got to the front of the line, she ordered a glass of white wine. While waiting for the bartender to return with her order, Cassie felt herself physically relax.

They'd pulled it off—a wedding and reception planned and completed in a month.

It helped her sister had some pretty good connections—being a famous screenwriter did have its perks—but the two of them along with Marlene, the jittery wedding planner, had organized, prepared, and executed a gorgeous wedding in less than five weeks' time.

A wedding her sister so rightly deserved.

"Fancy meeting you here." Cooper appeared beside her with a grin.

"Small world," she smiled brightly at him. "Did you cut in line?"

"Maybe we're just like-minded. And do I look like the kind of guy who would cut in line?"

"That's a scary thought," she teased. "And, yes, you do look like the kind of guy who would cut in line."

He clutched his chest as if her words wounded him, then quickly recovered when the bartender appeared, motioning he'd have one of the Scotch currently being poured.

He turned back toward her, chewing on a black stirrer straw he'd snagged from the cup full of them behind the bar.

"What's a scary thought? That you'd think like I do or that I'd think like you?"

"I haven't decided yet," she gave a small smirk and looked up at him through her eyelashes.

That caused him to break out into a big, perfect smile. "Let me know when you do."

"You'll be the first to know," she bantered back.

They got their drinks at the same time, and Cooper clinked his glass against hers.

"To the most beautiful maid of honor."

"Who didn't trip going down the aisle," she added.

"Were you worried?"

"Oh, yeah. I'm a klutz." She pulled up her chiffon dress to reveal her pink pedicure with no shoes. "I think that was part of the reason Brenna wanted us barefoot. It would lessen my risk of falling down and embarrassing her."

"I thought you seemed smaller."

"Yep," Cassie nodded. "I had some pretty high heels on the last time I saw you."

"Yeah, I noticed." There was no mistaking the naughty look in his eyes.

She gave a knowing wink and promised, "I'll have shoes on when we dance later," then turned to go mingle with the other guests.

Chapter Two

Luke

Brenna was a beautiful bride. Not only was she hot as hell to look at, but she was a beautiful person on the inside. Ron was one lucky bastard.

Cassie was the younger version of Brenna, minus the polish, and he loved that. He liked that she wasn't afraid to say *fuck* out loud or tell him exactly what she was thinking. That made her even more attractive as far as he was concerned.

He'd been looking forward to going out with her and was disappointed when she didn't reach out to arrange a time for their auction date, assuming she'd had a change of heart. He would have deserved that, in the most ironic way.

When she appeared at the beginning of the wedding to walk down the aisle, he was taken aback at how stunning she looked. He knew she was gorgeous, but damn, today, she was downright mesmerizing. From her blonde hair styled in an updo with wispy hairs framing her heart-shaped face to her baby blues, today the color of the ocean right after a storm. Her turquoise dress hugged her tight body, and her makeup was more dramatic than he'd ever seen before. He couldn't take his eyes off her the entire ceremony.

Apparently, he wasn't alone in that regard.

The fact he was jealous surprised him. He didn't usually get jealous. He'd always been the type to go after what he wanted and get it—with the one exception—so he never begrudged other people when they did the same. He actually respected it.

Not this fucking time though. He'd play dirty this time if he had to.

Maybe he was more ready for this date than he thought.

When his work phone started to ring, he cursed under his breath, "Goddammit."

He hadn't had much choice about being on call tonight; Nathan's wife was nine months pregnant and past her due date, so she was set to pop any time. Frank was gone for his monthly weekend with the National Guard, and Shawn's appendix burst last night, so Luke was the only SWAT sergeant left. He'd been silently praying for a quiet night, especially once he realized he might have some competition for Cassie. The universe seemed to have other plans.

After making his apologies to Ron and Brenna for his hasty departure, he sought Cassie out to say goodbye and hopefully prompt a quick discussion about when they were going to talk next.

When he explained he had to go, she seemed annoyed, at best.

"I can't figure you out," she mused from her seat at the head table. "You seem interested in me yet you didn't take tonight off work even though I'm assuming you knew there was going to be drinking and dancing tonight and that I was going to be here."

He kneeled so he was eye level with her. "It's not that simple. I traded weekends, so I actually *was* supposed to be off tonight but emergencies happened, and I was the last man standing. Actually, I was the *only* man standing. Believe me when I say, there's nowhere else I want to be tonight than here, ogling you in that dress. Unfortunately, a barricaded man with a gun decided to ruin that for me."

That drew a reluctant smile from her, and she softened her posture.

He felt safe caressing her elbow and asking, "Will you have dinner with me?"

She didn't hesitate in her reply. "I'd love to. When?"

He wanted to say *tomorrow* but thought that short of notice might reek of desperation. "Next Saturday?"

She seemed like she was about to agree, then stopped. "Wait, did you say dinner? I thought your date was walking dogs, lunch, and a tour of the SWAT station?"

"It is. But, I already have that date in the bag," he said with a wink. "Dinner is separate from the Heroes date, so you have to go out with me at least twice."

She pursed her lips. "Shouldn't we go on the auction date first? I mean, I paid good money for that. What happens if we go to dinner and have a horrible time? Then we'll still have the lunch date we'll both dread going on, so we won't ever schedule it, and eventually, we'll forget all about, and I will have lost out on a five-hundred-dollar date."

Luke knew she was teasing him, and he found her fucking adorable. He could flirt with her all night, unfortunately, duty called.

"Well, maybe we should start with a breakfast date then?" he countered as he stood up.

Her lips turned to a pout, thinking he was serious. He leaned down and kissed her cheek to growl in her ear, "Or better yet, we could end our dinner date with breakfast."

Her tiny gasp was the reaction he was hoping for, and he grinned before kissing her hand goodbye. "I'll text you about Saturday," he said with a wink, then turned to hustle to his car.

Chapter Three

Cassie

She watched Luke stride to the patio gate. The first time she ever saw him was from her sister's bedroom window on New Year's Eve day, getting out of his topless jeep in a tight grey t-shirt and mirrored aviator sunglasses. Cassie thought he was sex on a stick; that sentiment had not changed. The fact he was leaving to go be a badass kind of turned her on even more.

But she also liked the sweet side to him. The side that fostered rescue dogs like Brenna's lab, Zona. Actually, Zona was what brought Luke into her life since that's how he originally met her sister who in turn introduced them when they were splitting dog watching duties last January.

They'd hit it off or at least, she thought they had, but then he just disappeared, and she was not about to chase him. She fully endorsed Greg Behrendt and Liz Tuccillo's advice in *He's Just Not That Into You: If a guy wants to be with a girl, he will make it happen, no matter what*. When he didn't make an effort to see her, she conceded he didn't want to make it happen, and that was that.

Then she went to the Heroes of San Diego Calendar Event and Charity Auction in June, and he sat at her table. They flirted and drank, and when it came time for his date to be auctioned off, he whispered in her ear he'd make it worth her while if she won his date. That was all the encouragement she needed. When he was on stage, he blew her a kiss, and her competition all bowed out, and she got him for the bargain price of five hundred dollars. She would have gladly paid more.

But then she didn't hear from him again, just like in January.

Unlike a lot of women she knew, a guy didn't have to hit her over the head to convince her he wasn't interested. Also, unlike a lot of women she knew, she was never too broken up about a man's lack of concern. She reduced how she felt about it to one word—*next*.

Cassie had to admit though, she was glad to find out Luke wasn't blowing her off this time, they'd simply had a misunderstanding.

Although, frankly, she really hated poor communication. It was the kiss of death for even some of the best relationships. It had almost ruined Brenna and Ron's relationship before it even had the chance to get started. Cassie preferred the direct approach.

Unfortunately, much to her sister's chagrin, the direct approach tended to scare most guys off. That was fine with her, Cassie didn't want a guy to get too serious, anyway. The minute he started wanting more from her, she let him know it was never gonna happen. It wasn't that she didn't want a monogamous relationship, she just wanted one that didn't suffocate her. She liked her space.

Too bad there wasn't another man like Ron waiting in the wings somewhere. That would be the perfect relationship. Him being gone for weeks at a time and fabulous reunited sex when he returned.

Except if he was anything like Ron was with Brenna, he'd want to spend every possible minute with her when he was home on leave, probably even asking her to call in sick and spend the day in bed with him.

Oh, no, no, no.

Even in her daydream, the thought stressed her out.

Boundaries. A man needed to learn them and respect them if he wanted to be with her. The biggest ones—never, ever talk about the two of them getting married and having babies or her giving up her career. The gorgeous pediatrician she'd dated for almost a year made that mistake.

Cooper seemed to have decided to capitalize on Luke's departure and brought her another drink—the third one he'd put in her hand since Luke left. *Or was it the fourth?* She was a little worried walking in her heels at this point and voiced her concern when he asked her to dance again.

"Then take them off. Let's go for a walk on the beach, instead."

He really was a stunning specimen of a man. Broad shoulders, narrow waist, movie star looks, and man, was he smooth. Too smooth.

It was a perfect summer night in San Diego. She knew where a moonlit walk on the beach could lead, especially with her defenses down in her tipsy state.

"Okay, but so we're clear, we're just walking, not messing around."

That elicited a chuckle from him as he rolled up his pant legs and took his shoes off, and he wasn't at all convincing when he replied, "Of course."

Still, he was a perfect gentleman and only held her hand as the waves lapped at their feet on their romantic walk. Their conversation flowed easily, and Cassie found herself laughing out loud more than once. She didn't know whether she was disappointed or relieved he was behaving.

They stopped where the wedding arch still stood in the sand from the ceremony earlier, a testament true love did exist for some people. Cooper tilted her chin up and leaned down to gently kiss her lips. The soft kiss seemed purposefully intended to leave her wanting more. A move she was sure he'd perfected with the help of many women over the years.

"Go out with me. Tomorrow." His tone was urgent.

She didn't respond right away, so he continued, "I have to see you again, I feel this connection with you."

Her *player* radar had been quietly beeping all night around him, now it was blaring horns. Cassie had no problem with players when they were upfront about being one. She got the feeling Cooper was trying to sell her a line of bullshit, pretending to be more into her than he really was. Part of that, she suspected, was because he liked the idea of competing with Luke for her affection.

She knew Cooper would be fun to hang out with, but she was fairly certain he would lose interest quickly once he had conquered her. She knew his type—good-looking guy who thought he was God's gift to women. Unfortunately, those guys tended to be horrible in the sack—they were never called out for being selfish in bed, so they never learned how to properly please a woman. Pretty boy shoots his wad and is either asleep or dressed five minutes later, completely clueless or doesn't give a shit she's left aching.

Been there, done that. No thank you.

Now, Luke, on the other hand... She'd be willing to bet money he'd go all night and make damn sure she was satisfied—probably more than once—before he came. She'd only kissed him once, but, oh, baby, he definitely knew how to leave her wanting more.

So much more.

Technically, she didn't owe Luke anything, and it would be perfectly acceptable to go out with Cooper. Still, she wasn't sure how interested she was in the Marine.

"How about lunch on Friday?"

He smirked. Maybe he subscribed to the A-team/B-team theory too. "Sure, lunch on Friday sounds great." With a wink, he added, "But don't be surprised when you find yourself wanting to go to dinner, too."

That brought a smile to Cassie's face. She did like a man with confidence.

Chapter Four

Luke

Imagine his surprise on Friday afternoon to find Cassie having lunch with Cooper Johnson at the same bistro where he was meeting Hannah Flynn, the Commo, or Communications, Division's supervisor. He knew he had no right to be bothered seeing Cassie with another man, but fuck if he wasn't. Especially after the flirty texts he'd exchanged with her all week and how beautiful she looked in her plum colored dress and matching three-inch pumps that showcased her toned legs.

He wasn't exactly innocent. While his intentions concerning Hannah weren't amorous, he was pretty sure hers toward him were, and yet he still agreed to meet the pretty redhead for lunch. She did portray it as work-related, but he knew whatever information the 911 manager was going to provide could have been done electronically. Commo handled all communication with the general public--its most important function being 911 calls and dispatch operators who prioritized calls and sent officers where they were needed, in the order they were needed. Dispatch was his officers' lifeline, so he always made sure to be extra friendly and appreciative of their work. He realized he might have been *too* friendly and appreciative when Hannah started sending him flirtatious private messages over his mobile data computer in his work ride.

He reciprocated, even though he wasn't really interested. That probably made him a dick.

Even though Luke flirted with her, he knew better than to fuck her. He didn't need the headache in his professional life. He'd seen that shitstorm in fellow cops' lives, especially the idiots who were married and thought fucking around at work was a good idea. There was no way he was going to deal with the blowback of a scorned woman on the job.

He saw Cooper's hand above Cassie's ass while directing her to a nearby booth, and he clenched his jaw. They hadn't noticed him yet.

Luke debated about pretending he hadn't seen them and ignoring them, but he knew that would be impossible. His attention was going to be on what they were doing all through lunch, he was sure of it. Fortunately, they were seated over Hannah's shoulder, so it would at least seem like he was listening to her.

His phone buzzed in his pocket.

Cassie's face popped up on his screen before he clicked on her text.

Cassie Sullivan: Enjoying lunch?

The SWAT Sergeant wasn't even aware she'd noticed him. So much for his observation skills. Or maybe she was just that good at being discreet. He looked over, and she seemed completely focused on what Cooper was telling her. As she adjusted her long gold necklace, he saw her look down and suppress a smile five seconds after he'd sent his return text.

Luke: I'd rather be with you. Think Cooper would mind trading lunch dates?

How she managed to text him back without looking down was impressive.

Cassie Sullivan: Probably. He wants to have dinner tonight, too.

Luke tried not to snarl while reading, especially since Hannah was now telling a story about her yoga class. Ordinarily, thinking about hot women in yoga pants while they bent and stretched would have him with a chubby. The way his lunch date was swirling her straw and looking at him when she put it between her lips, he guessed that was her intention. Unfortunately for her, nothing moved in his pants.

God, he felt like a jerk for not paying attention to Hannah. She was hot, sweet, and not at all what he wanted. He wanted the petite dark-blonde a few booths over. Preferably naked. Possibly restrained. Definitely wet and panting his name.

Ah, there's that semi-wood.

Smiling kindly at his companion, he said, "I'm sorry to be rude, but I need to answer this text. My friends are going on their honeymoon and want me to watch their dog."

It was sort of true. Brenna had asked Luke to be her back up to take care of her Labrador mix, Zona, in case Cassie had an emergency. Cassie might have plans he needed to know about.

Like he'd been worried she had on New Year's Eve.

The night he saw her naked, and she still had no idea he had.

He was supposed to be the one staying with his former foster pup that night, but then the department had mandated everyone be available, so he had to cancel on Brenna. She asked Cassie to dog sit the lab instead, but once it became clear Luke wasn't going to be needed at work, he headed to the beach house. He had felt guilty, thinking Cassie had given up her New Year's Eve plans and was hoping to let her salvage them.

He walked in on her as she left the hot tub, soaking wet and not a stitch of clothing on. Okay, yes, he was a creeper and watched her dry off, then snuck out the door to pretend he'd just arrived.

They ended up hanging out all night, ushering the New Year in together with a kiss so hot, he wanted nothing more than to take her clothes back off and fuck her until morning. Luke was pretty sure she would have let him too, but he came to his senses and got the hell out of there.

He never pursued anything with her despite giving her the impression he was interested-because he *was* interested. Too interested, and that bothered him. At the time, he'd been unable to offer her more than a one-night stand, and she deserved better.

Now, he was ready to date—at least casually. In fact, he was looking forward to it. The little spitfire could be exactly what he needed to get back on the horse.

His fingers flew over his phone's keyboard. He'd already decided at Brenna's wedding he wasn't above playing dirty.

Luke: Tell him you're busy.

He looked over at the blonde beauty and their eyes connected. Her glossy wine-colored lips parted slightly, and her stare sent a thrill through him that led straight to his cock.

It was no longer semi.

She'd had him hard all week with their sexy banter back and forth over texts and private messages. Their exchanges had teetered on sexting but had never actually crossed that line.

Had—as in past tense. Her next text kicked it up a notch.

Cassie Sullivan: Well, I was planning on masturbating tonight.

He glanced over at Hannah to make sure she wasn't able to see what Cassie had written, then quickly responded:

Luke: Want some company?

Cassie Sullivan: Eight o'clock at the beach house. Bring Rex and food. Now, pay attention to your lunch date.

He'd try his best, but all he could think about was how hot she'd looked on New Year's Eve when she was wet and naked, and the possibilities tonight might bring.

Chapter Five

Cassie

Cooper was on his game at lunch, and he knew it. He seemed surprised when she turned him down for dinner, telling him she was busy as Luke had instructed. Maybe if she were five years younger, she might have been more receptive to the Marine, but she'd had too much experience, and *heartbreak* almost dripped from Cooper Johnson's lips.

The more he talked, the more she wondered if maybe he *wanted* to believe what he was saying. She knew better than to trust he could follow through.

Yet, he seemed so genuine. Bless his heart.

She wanted to tell him to slow down and get to know a woman. Implement a *no sex* rule for the first ten dates. If after the ten dates were up, and the sex was good, *then* start telling her how connected he felt, blah, blah, blah. None of that bullshit until then.

It struck her she should try practicing what she preached. Except, unlike Cooper, she wasn't trying to convince anyone she wanted a relationship. Because she didn't.

Still, maybe she'd implement the ten-date rule with Luke, or at least try.

She'd seen him in his SWAT gear in the pictures she found when she'd stalked him online. It made her panties melt. Today, he'd been in black trousers and a sage green shirt and tie that made his green eyes look even greener. But the gun and badge on his belt were almost like a siren's song. There was something incredibly sexy about a guy who kept people safe for a living and carried a weapon while doing it. She supposed it was probably because it translated to making her feel safe.

Okay, she'd be proud of herself if she got through the weekend without jumping his sexy bones.

**

The doorbell at the beach house rang at seven fifty-eight, and a barking Zona struggled to gain traction on the wooden floors while attempting to race to the door. Her bark turned into an excited whine when she saw Luke and her furry boyfriend, Rex through the side windows of the entry's nine-foot, alder wood double doors. Cassie cautiously opened the door and stepped aside, so as not to get run over by the two ninety-pound dogs, expressing their joy at seeing each other.

With a smile, she said, "Come in," then eyed the large, brown bag in his hand that said *Figurino's Italian Restaurant* on the side and bounced on her red-painted toes, squealing with delight. "Oh my God, that place is my favorite! Please tell me you got the ravioli."

"Oh, this isn't for us." Luke held the bag at shoulder height. "There's nothing in here but Rex's food. I was planning on ordering Chinese for us."

She knew by the smell emanating from the paper bag, he was a big, fat liar, but she played along, frowning. "Gosh, that's too bad. There's no telling what I would have done for Figurino's ravioli."

With eyebrows raised, he broke out into a wicked grin. "Oh, really? Is that so?"

Cassie bit her bottom lip while giving her own naughty grin. "Yeah. That's so."

He shook his head slightly, and in a low tone warned, "You're playing with fire, doll."

"I'll take my chances," she shrugged and turned toward the kitchen. The growl coming from behind her should have given her pause, but all it did was make her nipples stiff.

He had changed into more casual clothes than he'd been wearing this afternoon. The shirt, tie, trouser, gun, and badge look had been sexy in an authoritative I'm-in-charge kind of way, but his Levi's and navy-blue t-shirt, which showcased his chest and arms, worked quite nicely too.

A small gasp escaped her lips when she felt his hand hold her at the hip, trapping her against him so he could breathe into her ear, "There is ravioli; the question now is, how badly do you want it?" He gently squeezed before releasing his grip on her.

Oh, fuck. It was all she could do to not rub her ass against him like a cat in heat.

Ten date rule, ten date rule, ten date rule.

That had to be the craziest idea she'd ever had. That's how she knew it was precisely what she should do.

****

Luke

This woman might be more than he bargained for. She had the potential to make him do things he swore he never would do again. Still, he thought he was ready.

God, he hoped he was ready because if he blew it with her this time, he knew the chance of her giving him a third shot was nil.

After playing hot and cold with her at the beginning of the year until she finally quit returning his texts, he still hadn't stopped thinking about her. That both intrigued and dismayed him.

Intrigued him because she was one helluva chick who, in another life, would have given him a run for his money. Dismayed him because this wasn't another life.

Then he talked to her sister, Brenna who slipped and let out Cassie's little secret—she didn't do serious or want a real relationship. He got the impression Brenna thought those traits were faults, but as far as Luke was concerned, that made her perfect since he'd vowed to never do either again.

He saw her at the Heroes event, and when they clicked— *again*—he thought, *What's the harm in going out with her?* She didn't want anything more than he was willing to give. She wasn't going to fall in love with him and get hurt when he didn't love her back. Neither of them wanted anything long-term, just something fun that, hopefully, included sex.

Besides, the anonymous one-night-only thing had gotten old.

Now, here they were, alone at Brenna's beach house, where it had all started. Things were going to end a lot differently this time.

"How badly do you want it?" he asked, both of them knowing he wasn't referring to the ravioli he'd brought. A little whimper escaped from her lips, causing his dick to get hard.

He could only imagine the noises she was going to make later tonight.

Imagine his surprise at what she said next.

Chapter Six

Luke

He watched Cassie as she set the heavy, blue, stoneware plates on the island counter, keeping her gaze averted as he mulled over what she suggested.

"Ten dates, huh?"

She distributed the dishes and silverware, still not looking at him. "It's something I read about and thought it would be interesting to try it. I understand if you think it's a dumb idea."

Luke shook his head. "I didn't say that. It's just... unexpected. Here I thought I was going to help you masturbate after dinner," he teased.

She finally met his gaze, eyebrows raised in challenge. "Who says you still can't?"

Fuck, this woman knew how to push his buttons.

"Baby doll, that would guarantee a *one*-date rule wouldn't even apply."

She smirked as if proud of herself she knew how to turn him on.

He didn't know how to break it to her but just breathing in her scent did that. There was something about her that drove him crazy, from the first moment he'd met her. He couldn't help but stare at her luscious ass when she reached for paper napkins on the top shelf of the pantry.

"Well, then how about we have dinner and play the rest of the night by ear," she asked over her shoulder with a mischievous grin.

He took a steadying breath, not averting his gaze from her tight body. "That sounds like a good plan," he murmured then began taking the containers from the takeout bag. "So, no sex for at least ten dates. But what about other stuff?"

She slid onto the bar stool at the island, watching him open the containers' lids.

"What kind of other stuff?"

"Like, how many bases am I allowed before I'm thrown out?"

"I don't know," she snorted and handed him the serving spoon she'd gotten out earlier. "I mean, yes, I think there should be kissing and other... stuff. I don't want to set a hard and fast rule about what we can or can't do, other than sex. I guess if it feels right, we should do it."

He liked her answer until...

"But a blowjob is still considered sex, so there will none of that," she smirked, putting the garlic bread in a basket.

"Bill Clinton would have to disagree with you," he countered as he dished ravioli onto her plate and handed it to her.

"I think the blue dress indicated otherwise."

"Touché," he said with a laugh.

She moaned out loud when she took her first bite of food, and he gritted his teeth while groaning inwardly. His cock was all ears to the little noises she was making.

Fuck. Ten dates?

Her shy smile as she poured them both a glass of red wine answered his internal question.

Yeah, ten dates.

Something in his gut told him the wait was going to be worth it.

****

Cassie

She hadn't expected Luke to agree so easily to her ten-date suggestion. When he took a sip of his wine and watched her over the rim of his glass like he wanted to devour her, she gulped.

He was the sexiest man she'd ever seen. Not only was he breathtakingly handsome with his high cheekbones, square jaw, and piercing green eyes, but the way his muscles moved under his shirt when he simply lifted his glass made her squirm in her seat. His arms were magnificent. She could imagine how safe she'd feel being held in them.

Her thoughts turned a little dirtier as her gaze traveled from his shoulders to his hands and back up again. What would it be like to be pinned down by him?

Yeah, she was a dirty girl like that.

She remembered their one and only kiss on New Year's Eve and blinked a little longer than normal, thinking about the way he took control. At first, his lips were gentle yet demanding. When it escalated to tugging on her hair so her neck was exposed for him to kiss slowly, she had been putty in his strong hands. He knew it too, but didn't escalate things and instead, left right away.

Maybe getting to know each other better was going to be a good idea, because so far, he had confused the hell out of her.

The sound of him clearing their plates snapped her back to reality, and she refilled their wine glasses. He reached into the bag from Figurino's with a devilish smile.

"Dessert?" he asked.

Oh God. Muscles, green eyes, and dessert. That might be her new trifecta.

"I'm not looking for anything serious." Cassie wasn't sure why she blurted that out, maybe to remind herself.

Smiling, he kissed her forehead when he set her plate of cannoli in front of her.

"That's good, me neither. But I think we can become great friends and have some fun along the way."

She smiled shyly. "I think I'd like that."

****

Luke

Rex wasn't the only one who didn't want to leave.

Luke couldn't remember when he'd had such a great time with a woman.

Actually, that's not true; yes, he could. On New Year's Eve with the same gorgeous woman. Except his departure this time wasn't a panicked escape but a torturously teasing goodnight kiss that left him looking forward to the next encounter with her.

The fact he now knew they were on the same page helped. No relationships. No worrying about what the future held for them. Just a good time with no end game in mind.

He found himself still smiling as he and Rex drove home. Every now and then, he caught a whiff of her perfume on his shirt and would breathe in deeply as if etching the smell into his memory. It was a floral scent, and like her, it wasn't subtle.

Nothing about Cassie Sullivan was subtle.

She was direct and to the point, something he appreciated. He knew she wouldn't play games with him or leave him guessing what she wanted or even what she was thinking. When she was ready to move on, she'd let him know. Or if he was the first to feel like that, she'd appreciate him being upfront about it. He wouldn't have to pussyfoot around and worry about letting her down easy.

She was exactly what he was looking for, right now. His heart had finally started to heal, and he didn't have to worry about it getting torn to shreds again by her or breaking her heart while he got his shit together.

The situation was perfect.

He was even warming up to the ten-date rule. He liked the idea of getting to know her. She was someone he could see as a real friend in the future. Granted, a real friend whose brains he'd hopefully fuck out—repeatedly, but he knew when they eventually became just friends, she'd be cool about their prior sexual encounters. Maybe they'd even be confidants, offering each other dating advice. On second thought, he might be getting ahead of himself. The idea wasn't as appealing when he considered helping her with another guy.

Still, he was excited to get Date Two on the books, so he fired off a text to her while still sitting in his grey Challenger after pulling into the garage.

Luke: We're still on for dinner tomorrow, right?

Cassie Sullivan: I'm looking forward to it.

Luke: Me too.

Cassie Sullivan: Um, one problem.

Luke: ?

Cassie Sullivan: We never decided on a time or place. LOL

Oh shit, they hadn't.

Luke: Ha-ha. I guess I was busy thinking about other things.

Cassie Sullivan: Yeah? Like what?

Luke: Well, at first, getting into your pants.

Luke: Then keeping myself out of them.

Cassie Sullivan: You made it hard for me to think about other things too.

Luke: Glad to hear the difficulty was mutual.

Cassie Sullivan: It was hard, for sure. LOL

He'd take the double entendre bait.

Luke: I'm sure you noticed that wasn't the only thing hard. Especially, after kissing you goodnight.

Cassie Sullivan: You are an amazing kisser, btw.

Luke: That, doll, is definitely something that takes two to do. And you can be my partner, anytime.

Cassie Sullivan: I look forward to taking you up on that tomorrow night. Once you tell me when and where that is. (hint hint)

His cheeks hurt from smiling so much.

Luke: How about Danny's BBQ, 6 pm?

Cassie Sullivan: Can't wait.

Neither could he.

He'd gotten Rex settled down for the night and was in bed when he heard his phone ding. Was it too much to wish Cassie was sending him nudes?

His heart started to race when he saw it was a message from her.

Cassie Sullivan: Hey, I just wanted to thank you for such a great night. Glad we're hanging out.

He didn't know what to take away from that message. Was she thinking about him and sincerely thanking him for a fun night, or was she making sure he understood they were just *hanging out*, nothing more?

Maybe it was both.

Or maybe he could man up and stop trying to read into things like a goddamn school girl.

Luke: Me too, doll. See you tomorrow.

Cassie Sullivan: Sweet dreams.

Oh, she could count on that.

Chapter Seven

Cassie

She slid between the cool, cotton sheets of Brenna's comfy guest bed, fantasizing Luke was joining her. She hadn't wanted their night to end, and it was all she could do to mask her disappointment when he announced he had to leave.

Then came their goodnight kiss, and it was as hot as she'd remembered. She wasn't lying when she texted him he was an amazing kisser. He was. The man could write books on the subject. No one had even come to close to kissing her like he did.

She hoped he hadn't ruined her for future men.

I guess I'll have to keep him around a while.

At least for ten more dates, so she could see if he was as good at making love as he was kissing.

Oh, who was she kidding? There was going to be so much passion built up by their eleventh date they were not going to *make love*. They were going to have dirty, sweaty, monkey sex. Which would hopefully mean they'd have a twelfth and thirteenth date too.

At least.

Most surprising? The idea didn't freak her out.

Luke had been good all week about not being too clingy or needy. She really liked that about him. Although she liked it less when he had no problem getting up to go home tonight when she wasn't ready for him to. That was a new feeling. Normally, at the end of the evening, she was dropping hints or sometimes flat-out telling her date he had to leave. The pang of sadness instead of relief at seeing him go was unusual.

Wishing he was in bed with her? Not so unusual. She'd be the first to admit she liked a good sexscapade.

Wishing he was in bed to cuddle with her? That was a fucking anomaly.

There had to be a glitch in the Matrix or something because that shit didn't happen.

Hugging her body pillow, she decided she wasn't going to overanalyze it. They'd had a good time tonight, why spoil it?

**

She woke up the next morning and checked her phone.

Thank God there wasn't a *Good morning, gorgeous* text from him. He hadn't ruined it by starting in with that suffocating crap. Yet she found herself checking her phone throughout the day. It was a relief not to hear from him, but she kept her phone handy, just in case. He might want to change the time or location, so it was better to be safe than sorry. That was the only reason she was grabbing it immediately when she heard the telltale *ding* at four o'clock.

The *only* reason.

There was no gnawing pit in her stomach at the thought of him canceling their date at the last minute. Okay, even if there was, it was only because that would be rude to do.

She was *not* smiling when she read his text.

Sergeant Sexy: Is it bad that dinner is two hours away, but I'm already starving?

Cassie: Eat a sandwich to tide you over.

Sergeant Sexy: What?! And ruin my appetite for Danny's?! That's blasphemy, woman!

Cassie: We could meet earlier if you wanted.

Where the fuck did that come from? There was no way she could be ready any earlier than six. It wasn't like she'd already planned what she was going to wear after trying on twenty outfits or figured out how she was going to do her hair. Or painted her nails-fingers *and* toes. Or was having a glass of wine to calm her excitement.

Fine, that was exactly it, but there was no way *he* was going to know that.

Sergeant Sexy: I'm not even home yet, so I don't think I could get there before six. I'll grab a snack. Thanks for offering to be flexible though.

That didn't work. 'I'm not even home yet' was *her* line.

Cassie: Just thought I'd offer. I know how grouchy men can be when their blood sugar gets low.

She didn't quite know what to think about Luke Rivas or about being this excited to see him again so soon. That was a self-analysis for another time. Right now, it was almost time to start getting ready.

****

Luke

He could smell the barbecue before he even pulled into Danny's parking lot. He was in the Jeep tonight, enjoying the San Diego summer evening with the top off. When he walked into the restaurant and saw Cassie talking to a tall, good-looking man, his first instinct was to growl and mutter under his breath, "Who the fuck is that?" His second instinct was to ask himself, *Why the fuck are you jealous*?

He noticed the baby nestled into the man's core, facing Cassie and smiling and became envious of the guy for an entirely different reason.

Cassie gave Luke a big smile when he approached the picnic table next to the order window where she was standing. Seeing her so glad to see him made him relax. He leaned down and kissed her on the cheek, then offered the man his hand.

"Luke Rivas."

The dark-haired man shook Luke's outstretched hand. "Travis Sterling." He was dressed liked he'd come from the office despite having a baby in his arms.

"Travis is an attorney and his wife, Ava is my real estate agent. Brenna went to their wedding on New Year's Eve," Cassie explained.

Luke raised his eyebrows in recognition. "Oh. Congratulations, man." He gestured to the baby, "Looks like you've had a busy year."

Travis broke out into a big grin. "The best one of my life, so far. Hands down."

The girl behind the counter called out, "Sterling," then set two plastic bags filled with Styrofoam containers on the stainless-steel surface. Travis glanced at the counter.

"That's us. My wife is craving barbeque, and one thing I have learned is you don't keep a pregnant woman waiting for her food. It was nice meeting you, Luke. Cassie, I'll be sure to tell Ava you'll call her tomorrow."

"Take good care of your beautiful baby mama," Cassie told Travis, then grasped the baby boy's little fist and raised her voice an octave when she leaned down to talk to Travis' son. "And you let your mom get some rest, Alexander."

Travis chuckled. "Why do you think he's with me? I took him into the office this afternoon since it's the nanny's day off, and Ava's morning sickness is really afternoon sickness this time around. Instead, she calls me and tells me the baby's craving Danny's, so here we are."

"If mama ain't happy," Luke laughed, "ain't nobody happy."

"Ain't that the truth." Travis kissed the top of the boy's wispy haired head before adjusting the child's position to his hip. "You are way ahead of the game, my friend. It took me a while to figure that out."

Luke wasn't ahead of the game, quite the opposite in fact, but he simply nodded in agreement.

"Take care," Travis said before turning to grab his to-go order, his son looking over his shoulder at them and giving a toothless smile at Cassie when she waved goodbye dramatically.

"What a cutie," Luke murmured at Cassie's side.

She watched father and son walk out the door. "That kid hit the genetic lottery. There's no way he could be anything but adorable."

He looked over at her shiny, dark-blonde hair, perfect complexion, beautiful smile, and thought, *We'd have some pretty fucking adorable babies too.*

Where the hell did *that* come from? Better to not say that out loud. Even better not to think it again. Ever.

"Do you want to eat here or get it to go?" Her question snapped him back to the welcomed present.

"Do you have a preference?"

"Well, the Padres game starts in thirty minutes, we could plant ourselves in front of the TV while we eat?"

"That sounds like a great idea." He slid his arm around her waist and kissed her temple. "Your place or mine?"

"Pfft, Brenna's, of course. Unless your TV is bigger than hers."

"My place it is," he said, tugging her tight against him for a beat before releasing her.

Cassie rolled her eyes. "Of course, it is."

"Hey! A man really only needs three things to make him happy. A big TV, beer, and sex."

She didn't roll her eyes this time, but the look she gave him was the equivalent of an eye roll. He didn't let it bother him.

"Tonight, I'll be happy with TV, beer, barbeque, and maybe some heavy petting," he said with a wink as they made their way to the ordering line.

"Maybe," she smirked. "We'll see how big your TV is first before I commit to anything other than kissing."

He leaned down and whispered in her ear. "Baby doll, you'll be wet and begging, once you see it."

"I don't beg."

He chuckled and looked up at the overhead menu. "We'll see about that."

Chapter Eight

Cassie

Luke wasn't lying about his television. Good Lord, it was the biggest she'd ever seen. She wasn't complaining—especially once Astro's J.J. Matijevic got up to bat. That man was *hot* even if he had the wrong uniform on. A little young for her, but she could still appreciate a sexy, athletic guy.

Kind of like she was appreciating the one sitting next to her.

She was happy to learn Luke followed baseball and seemed to enjoy the game as much as she did. She glanced over at him as he took a pull from his beer bottle, the bottleneck dangling between his fingers. How did he make even drinking beer sexy?

TV, beer, and sex. He might be on to something. Their barbecue dinner was like the cherry on the sundae.

He caught her looking and furrowed his brows with a smirk. "What?"

"Oh, nothing." She bit her bottom lip, trying to keep her grin from spreading. "I was just thinking about how you weren't lying—your TV is awesome."

He leaned in closer to her. "Does that mean heavy petting is on the table?" he teased.

A coy smile escaped her lips. "Let's just say it's not *off* the table."

The smoldering look he gave her made her nipples stiff. She caught his lingering glance at her chest and the slight twitch of a smile on his face.

"Good," was his satisfied reply before he leaned back and stretched his arm along the couch cushions behind her.

Cassie rubbed her thigh against his. "Good?"

He made no attempt to intensify the touch, his eyes on the game as one side of his mouth turned up, and he affirmed with a nod, "Good."

She knew what he was up to. He thought he was going to make her beg.

I already told you, not happening, buddy.

Fighting the urge to scowl and cross her arms, she decided another tactic was needed. Two could play this game. Instead, she leaned over and kissed his neck, making sure to rub her tits against bicep and shoulder, before giving a breathy whisper in his ear, "Good."

Luke turned to her, cupping her cheek with a devilish grin. He was onto her. She couldn't miss the twinkle in his eye when he clutched the back of her hair before pulling her mouth slowly to his. She didn't hesitate to part her lips when his tongue began to seek hers, teasing at first, then he wrapped her hair around his fist and deepened the kiss.

Damn, can this man kiss.

Pausing for air, he gently pushed her back onto the couch and enveloped her body with his, resting most of his weight on his forearms but pressing his hips against hers. Cassie slipped her hand around his neck, her fingers skimming the short hair above his collar.

They angled their mouths for a deep kiss, and she was thinking she didn't give a damn about the ten-date rule when

Rex leapt from his dog bed by the fireplace and raced to the kitchen, barking excitedly.

Luke withdrew his lips from hers but was still positioned on top of her, and they both turned toward the direction Rex had disappeared, trying to determine what had disturbed the dog's slumber. She heard the door leading to the garage open and close, a bass voice greeted Rex, followed by heavy footsteps and Rex's toenails clicking across the tile. Luke sighed and hadn't quite managed to sit up when a gorgeous, bearded man with dark brown hair and three-quarter sleeve tattoos appeared in the doorway, flashing a grin and dimples when he saw the two of them sprawled on the couch.

"Sorry to interrupt." The deep voice held a hint of amusement while Luke's contained annoyance.

"What the fuck are you doing home, Ben? I thought you had a date."

Ben held his finger up, indicating to wait a minute, then turned back around into the kitchen, reappearing a minute later with a green beer bottle. Cassie noticed it was a different brand than they were drinking. Plopping down into the matching leather recliner, he let out a sigh as he twisted the bottle top off.

"Turns out she didn't know I had tattoos. Apparently, she" —he held up his hands to make finger quotes, holding the beer bottle in place in his large palm with his thumb and pinky— "isn't attracted to a man with tattoos."

"Ouch," Luke winced. "Sorry, dude."

The bearded man shrugged, put the bottle between his legs, and leaned forward to scratch Rex's ears with both hands. "Eh, she wasn't really my type either."

His twinkling eyes were blatantly on Cassie, almost as if sizing her up whether she'd be his type.

She was now seated upright, and Luke put a possessive arm around her shoulders. "Ben, meet my... friend, Cassie Sullivan. Cassie, Ben McCallister, my roommate."

She flashed him a smile and a little wave. "Hi, Ben. It's nice to meet you."

He winked, it was adorable. "Likewise."

"Back off, fucker," Luke warned.

With a smirk and the bottle against his lips before taking a swig, Ben needled, "I can't help it if I'm irresistible."

She got the feeling pushing Luke's buttons was one of Ben's favorite pastimes.

The bearded man looked at the game on the big screen, put his beer on the end table—on a coaster, she noted—then pulled the lever on the recliner so the footrest appeared.

"Ah, just in time to watch my Astros kick a little Padre ass."

Cassie snorted. "You wish."

"Please, I know."

Just then, the Astros' batter knocked one over the center fielder for a home run. *Talk about timing.*

Ben put his hands behind his head and crossed his ankles. The smug smile on his face said it all without him having to say a word.

"And here I was going to offer you some of our chicken and ribs." She gestured to the takeout containers on the coffee table in front of them where they'd spread their barbecue feast.

Luke picked up a drumstick with a grin, making a show of taking a bite.

"Oh, man, this is so good."

"Aw, come on," Ben whined, sitting up so the footrest disappeared. "It's not my fault my team is better than yours."

"It's only the bottom of the fourth," Cassie replied confidently. "Plenty of time for us to come back." She picked up a rib and tried as delicately as she could to eat it without making a mess while not using utensils.

"You guys suck. I hope we kick your ass," Ben said, flopping back against the chair cushion. That caused both Cassie and Luke to laugh out loud.

"Come on, buddy, I'm just having fun with ya. There's plenty, help yourself."

Ben was out of his chair the second Luke's words were spoken, scooping the containers' contents onto one of the clean paper plates on the table with a grin.

"Okay, I'm no longer rooting for the Padres' humiliation, just for them to lose," he said once he was situated back in the recliner with the plate on his lap.

"We're not gonna lose," she maintained mid-bite as the inning ended.

"Uh, yeah, you are."

Cassie swallowed her food. "Wanna bet?"

"Name the stakes, lady."

"Padres lose, I'll get you box seats next time the Astros are in town."

"Yeah, right." Ben narrowed his eyes at her. "And how would you manage that?"

Luke chimed in. "Danny Roberts was her brother-in-law. She's the real deal."

That caused Ben to arch his eyebrows. "No shit? What the hell are you doing with him, then?" He motioned his thumb at Luke. "Seems like you might have better options available."

"Actually, the box seats are my company's, but I do still know a lot of the players and staff. As far as other options—I wouldn't date a ballplayer if my life depended on it. All the ones I've ever known are unable to turn off the player status once they leave the field."

Ben snorted. "You think Luke isn't a—"

Luke coughed and interrupted his roommate. "Okay, so what if she wins?"

"Well, shit. I don't have anything like box seats to wager. How about an oil change and tune-up at my shop? I'll make sure your ride is in tip-top shape."

Cassie turned to Luke. "Is he any good?"

"Well..." Luke teased with a laugh before taking a serious tone. "Actually, his shops are some of the top-rated ones in San Diego County."

She was impressed. "Throw in a new brake job, and it's a deal."

"A new brake job? How much are these seats worth? My work's not cheap, ya know."

"Fine. I'll see if I can include a meet and greet with the team, too."

"Oh, just like that?" He eyed her suspiciously. "You can make a meet and greet with the team happen—no problem?"

"Kyle Montgomery and I are Godparents to my niece. He owes me a favor. Don't worry, I'm good for it. Besides, the Padres aren't going to lose." She didn't usually go dropping Kyle's name, but for some reason, felt compelled to make sure Ben knew she could back up her wager.

The mechanic didn't seem convinced and stared at her like she was trying to pull a fast one. "What kind of car do you drive?"

"A Lexus."

"How old?"

"A little over a year."

"And you already need new brakes?"

"Yeah, my job requires me to drive a lot."

Ben was contemplating the bet when a Padres' baserunner was thrown out stealing and quickly raised his bottle before she could change her mind.

"Alright, you've got yourself a bet."

****

Luke

It was weird, watching his best friend with Cassie. They were getting along like old pals, and Luke realized he liked the idea of Cassie meeting and hanging out with his friends. For the last few years, when it came to the women in Luke's life, his buddies' interactions with them consisted of appraising her at the bar before encouraging him to take her home, or Ben saying hi to her in the morning as she did the walk of shame.

There were never any repeat performers. After Adriana left, he was only interested in a good time, with the end goal being getting his dick wet. Seeing a girl twice gave her the wrong idea.

Meeting Cassie on New Year's Eve had hit him like lightning. Sure, he wanted to fuck her, but he found himself wanting to get to know her as well. No good was going to come of that, he'd been sure of it.

But waking up to women whose names he'd already forgotten by morning had started to lose its appeal. Call him old-fashioned, but meaningless sex had never really been his thing until he found a woman's body for the night provided him a temporary respite from the anger and heartbreak over what his life could have been.

He was drunk and laid a lot the first three years after his wife ran out on him.

Adriana had gotten pregnant, and he wanted to do the right thing. He wasn't sure if he loved her, but it didn't matter—he liked her enough, and they were going to have a baby. He was going to be there for his child, someday his children, and that meant having them under his roof with their mother.

He was happy about the new chapter in his life. When she first told him about the baby, he didn't think he was ready to become a father, but it didn't take him long to embrace it, even get excited about it. Adriana wouldn't move in with him unless they were married. He took her to the courthouse the next day.

One night, after a long SWAT standoff that didn't end well, he came home to discover his house completely empty. She'd taken everything and disappeared. An online check found his bank account drained and his credit cards maxed out.

His wife's betrayal was bad, but the worst was not knowing where his kid was. He needed to find her before his baby was born. The private investigator he'd hired found her back in her hometown in Mexico, no sign of his child. The P.I.'s questioning turned up she'd never been pregnant in the first place. It'd all been a lie.

He had no wife, no baby, no possessions, no money, and if Ben hadn't moved in with him so he could afford his mortgage along with the mountain of debt she'd buried him in, he would have had no home. He owed his best friend a lot.

But if the fucker didn't stop flirting with his girl, he was going to punch him in the throat.

His girl?

Borrowing a phrase from his twenties, he better pump his brakes. She wasn't his girl. He didn't want a girl. He'd better remember that.

Chapter Nine

Luke

The Padres' win had Cassie dancing to the kitchen for another beer. Ben shook his head in disgust until she left the room, then looked over at Luke with a grin.

"I like her. I think she'll be good for you."

"Slow down. We're just dating, nothing serious. We both want casual."

"My friend, you can both say *casual* all you want, but anyone with eyes can see there's something between you two."

"Jesus Christ, Ben. This is only our second date. Don't go marrying us off yet."

"Well, you can't exactly do that anyway, can you? Even if you wanted to."

"Even if he wanted to what?" Cassie asked as she came back carrying three beers. She handed one to Ben, then gave Luke a wanton look when she handed him his.

Damn, was she hot.

He ran his hand up the back of her tanned thigh and over her white shorts, stopping at her firm ass to give it an appreciative squeeze before she sat down next to him.

She looked back and forth between the two men, obviously expecting an answer to her question.

Luke and Ben stared at each other like idiots.

"He can't go surfing with me tomorrow, even if he wanted to." Ben offered.

"Yeah, I have to work."

"Not to mention he sucks at it," Ben added with a shit-eating grin.

Asshole.

She turned to Luke, having bought their story. "I didn't know you surfed. We should go this week, on your day off."

Ben chimed in, "You can go with me tomorrow if you want."

Luke had to give Cassie credit, she may be a flirt, but she knew where to draw the line—unlike his dumbass friend.

Putting her hand on his thigh, she replied, "No, I'll wait for when Luke can go."

He squeezed her shoulder, letting her know he appreciated that.

"You sure? I'm pretty good, I'd be happy to give you some lessons." Ben's grin let Luke know he was purposefully being a dick.

Luke flipped him off behind Cassie.

She felt the movement and turned to look over her shoulder, not in time to catch him in the act, then looked back at Ben, shaking her head. "No. Thanks for the offer though."

There was a lull in the conversation, and she leaned forward to start cleaning up the takeout containers. Luke pulled on her wrist. "Leave that, Ben will take care of it."

He half expected his roommate to protest, but Ben was a good sport.

"Yeah, it's the least I can do since you shared with me."

She patted the couch before standing. "I should get to Brenna's and check on Zona."

Ben smiled broadly. "Aw, how is Zona? You need to bring her with you the next time you come over. I'd love to see her."

"Yeah, you should bring her with you tomorrow when you come." Luke knew he was pushing his luck, suggesting they see each other again tomorrow, but he could always pass it off as teasing her if she bristled.

"I wasn't planning on coming over tomorrow."

"You weren't?" he feigned confusion. "I thought for sure you said you were."

"No. I thought we decided you were bringing Rex to Brenna's when you got off work so we could walk him and Zona together on the beach. And you were bringing me dinner with dessert."

Well played, Cassie Sullivan. Well played.

****

Cassie

Luke and Rex drove her back to the restaurant where she'd left her car, then followed her to Brenna's, citing it was dark, and he wanted to make sure she got inside safely. Never mind Brenna's neighborhood was one of the safest in San Diego. If the sexy SWAT Sergeant wanted to make sure she was safe and sound, who was she to argue?

After letting the dogs out and getting them fed, they sat on the back-patio loveseat, the warm ocean breeze causing her hair to blow in her face. Luke brushed it away, his thumb lingering to trace the bottom lip he was staring at.

"I've had a lot of fun this weekend."

"Me too," her words came out a whisper.

Holding her chin between his thumb and index finger, he smiled. "Good," he said in a soft voice before he brought his mouth down gently on hers,

She closed her eyes as he manipulated her lips with his. The moment was almost surreal; it was so romantic with the summer night air, the light wind, and the scent of the ocean mixed with Luke's masculine smell. His warm, muscular body hugged her close while his soft lips were on hers. She sighed with contentment when he broke the kiss and held her against him.

"I should go." The words vibrated through his chest against her cheek.

"Already?" She didn't even try to hide the disappointment on her face when she drew away from him.

"I work from nine to seven tomorrow." He looked regretful but quickly added, "I can be back here tomorrow by eight. I know it's a little late for you to have dinner, but if you can wait, I really will bring whatever you want when I come-including dessert."

She brought her hand to his cheek and kissed along his jawline. "Or you could stay and have an early breakfast with me before going home and getting ready for work."

Cassie didn't want the night to end. She loved being with him. She was practically throwing herself at him. This was not at all like her. Alarm bells should be going off in her head, yet, she was comfortable they weren't.

He shook his head gently and stood, drawing her fingertips into his fists, and pulling her up.

"I really do want to stick to ten dates, Cass."

"I do, too," she smiled, lightly swinging their entwined hands back and forth.

His look was skeptical. She slipped her fingers from his grasp and stroked his arms.

"Honest, Luke. I just want you to hold me tonight. That's it. Well, and talk, maybe kiss a little more."

He seemed to be considering her offer, and she was surprised when he shook his head and kissed the tip of her nose.

"I don't trust myself, doll."

She almost did it. She almost begged. The word *please* was on the tip of her tongue, but, luckily, her pride surfaced. Besides, she didn't know what she would do if she did beg, and he still rejected her.

"Okay," she agreed with a weak smile.

They walked to the front door of the beach house, and he whistled for Rex. The retriever stood at the bottom of the stairs but refused to come to him despite his commands.

"At least your dog wants to stay tonight." She tried not to sound like she was pouting although she was doubtful about how successful she was.

"I think Rex is smarter than me," he chuckled, then nestled his face in her hair and took a deep breath in. He held her for a few minutes, not in any hurry to release her. With his arms still holding her tight against him, he whispered in her ear, "I don't want to go either."

The solution seemed simple to her, and she murmured against his shoulder, "Then don't."

He sighed and pulled away, tucking some of her hair behind her ear. "I have to, Cass. If I stay, I'll want to make love to you."

Again, she didn't see the problem. "Then make love to me."

Luke closed his eyes and groaned. It was obvious he wasn't going to relent.

"Only eight more dates, doll," he murmured as he kissed her cheek.

She wanted him so badly, she didn't think she could wait that long. Luckily, her self-respect made her keep her mouth shut about telling him that.

With a meek smile, she managed, "See you tomorrow night, then."

He called for Rex, more sternly this time. The pup looked ashamed when he laid down and put his head on his paws, not obeying.

"Let him stay tonight." Cassie stroked Luke's elbow. "He misses his girlfriend. You can take him home tomorrow night."

She could tell he didn't like the idea of letting his dog win. She got the feeling he didn't like the idea of anyone disobeying him. That was probably a good thing when it came to his job. Or in his bed.

Whoa, slut, slow down.

Looks like BOB—her battery-operated boyfriend—would be making a booty call tonight.

Shit, did she pack it?

He kissed her again, his lips caressing hers with unspoken promises of things to come. When they took a breath, she found herself clinging to him.

It might not matter if she packed BOB. She was so turned on, her fingers would suffice.

It was like he read her mind because he was on the other side of the threshold when he growled in her ear, "No one touches that pussy but me, doll."

Who the fuck does he think he is?

Then he kissed her again.

Oh. That's who.

It was strange as hell she wanted to do what he said. She *wanted* to obey him.

Fuck. That.

That's not who she was. If she wanted to pleasure herself, she'd masturbate all goddamn night long if she felt like it. He had no right to tell her what to do. He had no control over her.

Yet she went to sleep without touching herself.

It was torture, too.

Chapter Ten

Luke

He'd noticed the way her breath hitched when he demanded no one touch her pussy but him, and he couldn't help but wonder—or was it worry—if he'd met his perfect sexual match. His cock was pissed at him all the way home, arguing, *Wouldn't the very definition of casual have meant staying when she extended the invitation?*

Maybe.

Or maybe this was casual with a twist. Delayed gratification if you will. A test of his self-control. But it was still temporary. The fact he was eager to see her again was only so he would be one date closer to the eleventh one.

Nothing more.

The little nagging voice in the back of his mind asked, *If it's just about sex, why didn't you take her up on the offer?*

The little nagging voice needed to shut the fuck up.

**

Ben was still up watching television when Luke walked into the living room.

"Hey, where's Rex?"

"He didn't want to come home," he said on an exhale as he dropped down on the couch.

Ben paused from taking a drink of beer. "But you did?"

Luke shook his head and mumbled forlornly, "Not really."

"She playing hard to get?" his roommate asked with a little too much glee for his liking.

Luke let out a whoosh of breath and ran his hands through his black hair.

"No, apparently, I am." Saying it out loud made him feel like a giant wuss. The look on Ben's face indicated he agreed with that assessment.

"What the fuck is wrong with you, man? Have you seen that girl? Her only goddamn flaw is she likes you instead of me, and I'm even willing to give her the benefit of the doubt since she met you first, she didn't know any better."

"Yeah, asshole," Luke snarled. "I've seen her. And touched her. And kissed her. And held her."

"So, what's the problem?"

"I don't know." His voice was agitated. "We're supposed to be getting to know each other before we sleep together. No sex until after at least ten dates."

"Whose idea was that?" Ben looked at him like that was the stupidest thing he'd ever heard.

"Hers, to begin with."

"But you agreed?"

"I liked the idea of getting to know her first..."

A look of recognition followed by triumph crossed the mechanic's face. "This is the chick who bought you at the Heroes' auction, isn't it? The same one from New Year's Eve."

"Yeah. So?"

"So, you've walked around here for the last month waiting for her to call you." Ben stood and headed toward the kitchen, snickering, "Keep telling yourself it's casual, buddy."

"Fuck off. We've only gone on two dates."

His roommate poked his head around the doorjamb. "Uh huh. And when are you seeing her again?"

Luke remained silent. At this point, it was his best recourse.

The kitchen light shut off and Ben reappeared, pausing on his way to his room, a more serious expression on his face.

"She seems pretty great, Luke. I'm glad you're giving this a shot."

The SWAT Sergeant shook his head. "I don't know what the hell I'm doing right now."

Ben threw his head back and cackled down the hall. "You're so screwed."

Yeah, he was. *But screwed in a good way or a bad way?*

He sighed and stood up with purpose. His friend was wrong. *They were just casual.*

****

Cassie

She woke up Sunday morning in a good mood, which was odd considering how sexually frustrated she was when she went to bed. Shuffling to the kitchen with bed head and still clad in her pajamas, she called for Rex and Zona while starting the coffee maker, then took them outside. She stared at the ocean, a smile on her lips as she waited for the dogs to sniff around. It'd been a great weekend.

She *almost* let herself predict what he was going to do to make her not like him as much but for once, decided to enjoy things and see what happened. She could do a lot worse than the walking sex god that was Luke Rivas. Actually, she had a hard time imagining anyone better.

Although she was a little dismayed at Ben's insinuation he was a player. She didn't get that vibe from him, and that worried her. She was okay with him being a player, she just didn't want to get blindsided by it, thinking he was something he wasn't.

Cassie shook her head. *Could you try to be happy and in the moment for a change?*

Brenna would be so proud of her.

The dogs came trouncing up, wet and dirty from running into the ocean, and she grabbed one of the outside towels to rub them down before letting them inside. The mindless task let her further contemplate the situation with Luke.

So, what if he is a player? He doesn't owe me anything.

We didn't say we were monogamous.

Hell, they weren't even having sex yet. But the idea of him sleeping with someone else while they were dating kind of pissed her off. Maybe that was why he wasn't in a hurry to get her into bed? He was getting his action elsewhere.

That asshole.

And to think, she didn't masturbate last night when he probably went on a booty call. Maybe with that woman he had lunch with on Friday.

"Jesus Christ, Cassandra Jo. Listen to yourself. You sound like a lunatic," she chastised herself as she threw the towel in the hamper and walked inside.

She really needed to find out what he was thinking in terms of their exclusivity.

After mulling things over while eating her cereal on the patio, she wondered how she was going to have a conversation with Luke about whether they were seeing other people without actually coming out and asking him.

Later, as she straightened up the house in anticipation of his arrival, she concluded maybe she didn't want to have that discussion after all. What if he did want to be monogamous already? One great weekend together was way too soon to come to a decision like that. After all, there was Ian, the real estate agent in Ava's office who had been flirting with her, not to mention the newly single Dr. Presley who'd made a point of letting her know his divorce was finalized. She shouldn't limit herself because she'd had *one* amazing weekend with a man. Right?

But, she didn't think Ian was even thirty yet. Way too young for her. And, did she really want to be the doctor's rebound fling?

Okay, so the idea of dating those two men wasn't that appealing. It didn't mean there couldn't be others. She should still keep her options open, Luke probably was.

Her thinking earlier she should talk to him about whether they were exclusive now seemed absurd. Thank God she'd had the day to think it through before she'd said anything.

It's only been two dates, for heaven's sake! They hadn't even made it to second base.

Besides, he was probably going to be a disappointment in bed.

Now, she'd gone too far. Even she couldn't believe that lie she was trying to tell herself.

****

Luke

The hostage situation was creeping up on seven hours.

Shit.

He was going to be late for his date with Cassie, if he even made it at all. He hadn't had a chance to text her all day and let her know what was going on. He slid his cell from his front pocket and quickly pulled up her number.

Luke: Can't really talk but wanted to let you know, on a SWAT call. Don't know when I'll be done. I'm so sorry.

Two hours later, his team had breached the building using tear gas and managed to rescue all the hostages without any casualties. The bad guy was on his way to jail and patrol was here to clean up the aftermath. That was his favorite thing he loved about SWAT. They got to go in, fuck shit up, and walk away without having to deal with the mess they made.

He finally had a chance to look at his phone again. Her missed texts made him smile.

Cassie Sullivan: Rex, Zona, and I will be waiting whenever you get here.

Cassie Sullivan: Don't worry about it being too late. We'll just order pizza.

Cassie Sullivan: No worries if you can't make it, Rex is fine here for the night. Keep me posted and let me know you're safe.

Luke: En route to the station now. I'll grab a quick shower and head your way.

Her response was immediate.

Cassie Sullivan: See you soon.

Not soon enough as far as he was concerned.

Chapter Eleven

Cassie

She could tell he was exhausted by the dark circles under his eyes and the smile that was slow to form on his lips. Cassie ushered him into the house and promptly instructed him to get comfortable on the couch in the family room that adjoined the kitchen. She stood behind him on the sofa and kneaded her fingers into his tense shoulder blades, causing him to moan with appreciation. Still rubbing his shoulders, she leaned down next to his ear.

"I'm going to call for delivery. What do you want on your pizza?" She caught his clean scent and gently kissed below his ear. "Or do you want something besides pizza?"

His low chuckle was barely audible, and she gasped.

"I swear, I didn't mean it like that!"

"No?" Luke grabbed her wrist and tugged her over the couch into his lap, laughing at her faux pas. His hand snaked around her hip as he held her against him. "That's too bad because I would very much like something besides pizza," he murmured into her hair, his eyes closed.

Cassie pulled back and looked at him, his eyes opening when she brought her hand up to stroke the side of his cheek.

She gazed into his green eyes, trying to figure out how he'd managed to make her care so much about him in such a short period of time. His stare back was so raw and genuine, it caused her to catch her breath. With an irresistible desire to feel closer to him, she leaned down and captured his lips with hers.

He let her control the kiss for a moment, then with a low growl, buried a hand in her hair to turn her in his lap so she was straddling him. She felt his hard cock against the heat between her legs and began to grind her hips against him, holding his face in both hands while he took charge of their making out.

"Fuuuuck," he groaned against her mouth and held her hips tight, pulling her deeper into him.

Their kisses became more frenzied, and she pressed her clothed chest against his. She needed to feel his bare skin against hers. The yearning to have him inside her was overwhelming her senses. She began to tug on his shirt and felt his hands go around her wrists, holding them in place. He broke the kiss and shook his head.

"Baby doll, I don't trust myself to be able to stop. I want you so fucking badly."

Being able to drive him crazy with lust made her feel like a goddamn goddess. Of course, she was equally crazed, but that wasn't the point.

She arched back to pull her blouse over her head and dropped it on the floor, meeting his hungry eyes as she slipped her hands around her back and undid her bra. Letting it fall down to her elbows, she leaned forward and pressed against his chest, shimmying the straps down further until the black lace garment was completely free from her body.

"We'll just go to second base," she breathed in his ear and slid her hands under his shirt, relishing the feel of his warm skin against her palms.

Luke reached behind his neck and tugged below the collar of his shirt, bringing it over his head in one motion, tossing it next to hers.

Cassie swallowed hard when she caught sight of his bare chest and chiseled abs. She'd seen them when he was on stage at the benefit, but there was no comparison to being up close and personal.

Very personal.

He caressed both her breasts in his hands, squeezing lightly while looking up at her, whispering, "God, Cass, you are beautiful." She gasped when he drew one nipple into his mouth and gently sucked. Switching to her other tit, he lavished his tongue around her areola, causing her skin to break out in goosebumps before he caught the tip of flesh between his teeth and tugged until she cried out. She felt him smile as he kneaded her other breast in his palm, then switched to attend to it with his mouth.

"I love your tits. They are fucking perfect," he moaned and squeezed them together, rapid-fire alternating sucking on her nipples.

With her fingers in his hair, she drew him closer to her, just as her stomach growled. Loudly.

He looked up at her in surprise, and they were both frozen in place, unsure of how to handle the situation. They burst out laughing at the same time. Luke lifted her off his lap and deposited her next to him on the couch.

"Let's get that pizza ordered, doll."

Cassie was about to protest when her stomach grumbled again. Giggling, she reluctantly agreed.

She slipped her blouse back on, but left her bra laying on the floor and went to grab her phone from the counter, turning back in time to see Luke reaching for his shirt.

"Oh, no, no, no," she scolded.

He furrowed his brows. "What do you mean, *no?*

"Sorry, babe, but I'm afraid you're going to be objectified until the pizza gets here."

He leaned back with a grin and laced his fingers behind his head. She didn't know if he was flexing his triceps on purpose or if it was simply a natural reaction to his arm position. Regardless, she needed to look away before she started to drool, so she started scrolling through her phone for the number to the local pizza place. Glancing back at him once the number started to ring, she caught her breath. He hadn't moved, but each time she looked at him, she couldn't get over how hot he was.

Like, smokin' hot.

So hot, alarm bells should be going off in her head. No guy was that gorgeous and not a player.

But the way he had looked at her before they started making out felt like it touched her soul, and she knew her feelings were not one-sided.

Holy hell, this was uncharted territory.

Just then, a voice on the other end of the line came on, giving her something else to concentrate on for the moment.

****

Luke

She got off the phone after ordering and came to sit beside him on the couch.

"How long before they get here?"

"They said thirty minutes."

"Good," he said before he pounced on her, pushing her backward on the couch and falling on top of her, catching his weight on his forearms.

He started kissing down her neck, wrapped his arms around her waist, and pulled her core tight against him. Cassie arched her back, molding her body to his while clinging to the back of his head with both hands.

"Luke," she gasped and wound her fingers through his short hair.

Sliding one hand under her top, he held the middle of her back firmly with his palm while the other hand edged her blouse higher so their skin was once again touching. He groaned at the contact and finished tugging the shirt over her head, eager to continue their bare connection.

She felt like fucking silk. Every inch was soft and smooth— a stark contrast to his rough and calloused hands. Her floral body lotion and lavender shampoo filled his senses. Everything about Cassie was feminine—from her petite frame to her soft hair to the curve of her neck. Her luscious tits beckoned him while his hands almost completely encircled her narrow waist before moving down to the flare of her rounded hips, not stopping until he was gripping her perfect ass with both hands. He could get lost exploring her body and not want to be found. It was amazing how perfect this woman felt in his arms.

Her fingernails tracing down his back made him pause his attention to her curves, and he groaned internally. How was he going to resist making her his tonight?

Just then the doorbell rang. Had it already been thirty minutes? Reluctantly, he moved off her, picking up his t-shirt, and pulling it over his head as he headed to the door. Her shirt was back on and she was setting plates on the granite island countertop when he returned to the kitchen with the piping hot pizza.

"Water, soda, or beer?" she asked, opening the refrigerator.

"A beer sounds good."

She grabbed a Pacifico for him and a Diet Coke for herself, sitting on the bar stool next to him. It was his stomach's turn to growl, and she giggled. They both moaned out loud when he opened the pizza box, and the smell wafted through the air.

"Tonight is a first. I've never had Marco's Pizza or Pacifico beer."

"I hope you like it. I eat Marco's whenever I stay at Brenna's, but I have no idea about the Pacifico. I think it's Ron's."

He unsuccessfully attempted to twist the top of the bottle while she plated their slices. Opening the drawers on the island, he asked, "Do you know where Brenna keeps the bottle opener?"

"In the drawer by the fridge. I'm sorry, I didn't realize it wasn't a twist off, otherwise, I would have gotten it for you."

Luke slid off the stool but trailed one hand along Cassie's waist, and with the other, moved her hair in order to kiss the back of her neck.

"It's okay, I got it," he murmured before pulling away and walking to the drawer by the fridge.

They took their pizza and drinks and sat back on the couch. Cassie flicked on the television, and they watched the end of a sitcom while they ate and talked.

Their plates were empty by the time the news came on. The lead story was the hostage situation. They sat in silence and listened to the reporter tell most of the facts correctly. Whether the press got the story right was always a hit or miss; he was glad tonight's was fairly accurate.

The news correspondent had just stated, "Now, back to you," in her glib voice when Cassie clicked off the remote and stared at him. He shifted uncomfortably in his seat while trying to figure out what was going through her mind. Suddenly, she launched herself onto him, knocking him backward on the couch cushion as she hugged him tightly.

"You're pretty incredible," she whispered with her cheek against his chest.

He stroked her hair, the scent of her shampoo wafting to his nose, and murmured into the top of her head, "So are you."

Cassie lifted her head to look into his eyes. "No, I mean it, Luke. What you do, how you risk your life to protect innocent people from bad guys, it's amazing." She put her head back down and sighed, nestling in closer to him.

"Thanks." He didn't know what else to say, so he kept stroking her hair in silence.

The toll of the events at work, along with his full belly of beer and pizza started to manifest itself in the form of heavy eyelids. Cassie's delicate, warm body on his provided the perfect blanket, and her soft, rhythmic breathing began to lull him to sleep. Luke didn't even try to fight it. He was far too relaxed and content to even think about moving, let alone leaving.

He was sure he fell asleep with a smile.

Chapter Twelve

Cassie

She woke up in the middle of the night on the couch, snuggled against Luke with her head on his chest, her hair stuck to her face from where she'd been laying on him, and a painful crick in her neck.

And yet she didn't want to move.

The soft snoring coming from him made her smile. His arm was firmly planted around her, and she knew if she got up or even adjusted her position, it might disturb him. She worried if that happened, he'd wake up and want to leave, and she was enjoying how good he felt next to her way too much.

But man, her neck hurt.

Moving as slowly as possible, she shifted her body so her back was to his side, his arm now draped over her hip. She didn't move slowly enough though because she felt him jerk, then he rolled to his side and drew her back against him tightly in a spooning position.

He whispered in her ear, "You okay, beautiful?"

She nodded while whispering, "Yeah," then gulped when she felt his cock harden against her ass.

He kissed her hair but his breathing soon indicated he had fallen back asleep.

She let out a contented sigh, allowing herself to relish how good it felt to be wrapped in his arms, safe and secure, and quickly nodded off again.

****

Luke

The sun in his eyes woke him. Why the fuck hadn't he closed his blinds the night before?

It took him a second to register he was not in his bed, those were not his blinds the sun was blaring through, and the soft pillow he was hugging was not a pillow at all but a beautiful woman.

A beautiful woman whose name he remembered when he woke up next to her, and he hadn't screwed her brains out the night before. How's that for irony? It was usually the other way around.

Inhaling the smell of her neck, he conceded, he liked waking up to her. Admittedly, he was going to like it more when he'd screwed her brains out the night before waking up with her in his arms and still remembering her name, but good things come to those who wait.

And she was worth the wait.

He wanted to say he was just now realizing that, but deep down, he'd known all along, which was why he'd agreed to the ten-date rule in the first place and probably why he bolted on New Year's Eve when he didn't have anything more to offer than a one-night stand.

She wiggled her ass against his morning wood, and he murmured in her ear, "Good morning, doll."

Her body went stiff as she gave a full body stretch before flopping over and snuggling back against his side, grumbling with her eyes still closed, "It's too early."

He chuckled to himself. *So, she's not a morning person.*

With a kiss to her cheek, he slid off the couch and covered her with a cream, cashmere throw he'd found in a basket by the fireplace, whispering, "I'm going to take the dogs for a walk." She whimpered when he left her side but fell back asleep after she rolled over and pulled the blanket up to her chin.

After using the bathroom, he stood at the patio door and quietly patted his leg to call the dogs. The three of them slipped outside and headed toward the water.

There was nothing like early mornings by the ocean to start his day right. Luckily, the community he lived in was walking distance to the beach, but it couldn't compare to walking out your back door and having the water right there. That was half the reason he usually stayed at Brenna's when he dog-sat Zona, instead of taking her home with him and Rex. Her hot tub didn't hurt either nor did her hot sister he hoped to run into whenever he had been there.

Now, he'd not only run into the hot sister, but he'd slept with her in his arms all night. That wasn't something he would have predicted a few months ago—hell, even a few weeks ago—but he was glad it happened.

The dogs had found a stick and were each proudly carrying an end while they trotted through the waves by the shore. He really wished he was in his running clothes instead of the last night's jeans and shirt. Maybe tomorrow.

Maybe tomorrow?! *Slow down, turbo.*

Cassie was drinking coffee on a blue patio lounger, still dressed in last night's clothes when he and the dogs arrived back at the house. Her hair was tangled and sticking up from her sleep the night before, makeup smudged, and she was blurry eyed. He grew up with a sister who wasn't a morning person either, so he knew not to be too cheerful yet.

Whispering, "Good morning," with a kiss on her cheek, he didn't wait for a response before heading inside for his own cup of coffee. Fortunately, she'd brewed enough to share. He came out with his steaming mug and sat in the matching lounger next to her, waiting for her to speak first. They sat there awhile until he heard her soft voice.

"I'm surprised you stayed."

He glanced over to find her staring at the ocean, blowing on the coffee in the mug she held between both hands. Not sure if his staying was a good thing or a bad thing, he remained quiet for an extra beat.

"Is that okay?"

She looked at him with a smile. "Of course. It was nice. Although, let's sleep in a bed next time," she suggested as she stretched her neck.

So, there was going to be a next time. That was promising.

"That'd probably be more comfortable," he said, returning her smile.

She was more awake and seemed less sullen, so he set his cup down on the side table between them and stood, gesturing for her to move forward so he could slip behind her. With her thighs between his, her back to his front, he wrapped his arms around her middle and put his chin on her shoulder. He felt her relax against him, and he closed his eyes briefly with a small grin, enjoying the warmth of her in the morning sun. They sat there silently, listening to the tide roll in, each seemingly lost in their own thoughts.

"So, if we have lunch and dinner today, does that count as two separate dates?" He knew he might be coming on too strong, but he got the feeling she was receptive to it.

Luke felt her head shaking, and she murmured matter-of-factly, "I can't today. I have a lunch meeting with a doctor's group, and I already have dinner plans."

"Oh, okay." He tried to mask the disappointment in his voice but didn't think he did a very good job. He shifted behind her, moving his hand from her waist to the top of her thigh.

Who was she having dinner with? He didn't like the idea of sharing her with another man. Still, he knew better than to ask. It was too soon to assume he had a right to know.

As if sensing he was upset, Cassie placed her hand on top of his and laced their fingers together.

"It's a company banquet tonight. I'd gladly skip it to have dinner with you, except I'm getting an award, so they'd kinda notice if I wasn't there."

He half expected her to invite him to go with her. He didn't know if he was relieved or disappointed when she didn't. Maybe a little of both.

"Congratulations. What's the award for?"

"Salesperson of the year."

"Wow, that's awesome, doll."

"Second year in a row." She said it boastfully, but he knew her bravado was teasing. Still, she should be proud of her accomplishments, they were impressive.

"Do you get a plaque and everything to hang on your wall?"

"Well, that and a nice bonus."

"Must be nice." He raised his eyebrows in admiration. "I only ever get a plaque and some bars for my uniform. Got any plans for the money?"

She shrugged. "Not really. It depends how much it actually is. With the last one, I was able to pay off my car, but this time, I'll probably just stick it in the bank."

"Well, if you decide you want to go crazy and buy a Corvette or something, I can help you test drive them."

She giggled. "I really want to sell my condo and buy a house. I'd love to have a little more privacy. Maybe get a dog."

That elicited a smile from him. "If you decide to get a dog, I can help you there too."

She squeezed their fingers together and leaned back harder against him. "Absolutely. I wouldn't dream of asking anyone else."

"There're some houses in my subdivision for sale," he teased. "One's a four-bedroom two doors down. We could be neighbors." He might actually like that, but he probably should dial it back.

She laughed and kissed his cheek, changing the subject.

"What do you want to do for breakfast?"

Yeah, no question, he needed to tone it down.

Chapter Thirteen

Cassie

She had just started her car when she heard her phone ding. It wasn't that late, but it was late enough only a handful of people would be texting at this hour.

A smile formed on her lips when she saw it was from Luke.

Sexy Beast: Hey doll. How's the banquet going?

Cassie: I was just thinking about you. It must be serendipity. It just ended.

Sexy Beast: Seren-what? Don't use such big words, I'm just a simple guy who plays with guns and works out all day.

She'd seen the results of his daily workouts last night. Thinking about his sexy body made her shiver.

Cassie: They really need an eye roll emoji. How was your day?

He sent an emoji of a face rolling its eyes.

Sexy Beast: Like this? Followed by one sticking its tongue out. *Long, I just got home myself.*

Cassie: Wow! You work a lot.

Sexy Beast: Business is definitely good. I'm not tired though. Where was your dinner? Want to meet for a drink?

The thought of seeing him shouldn't make her as giddy as she felt. She didn't get giddy over a man that was something other women did—not her. Yet her fingers were flying over the buttons.

Cassie: Downtown. I'm not tired either, so I could meet you at O'Malley's in 30?

Sexy Beast: Be there in 15.

She flipped the visor mirror open and reapplied her lipstick, then ran her fingers under her eyes to make sure there were no mascara smudges. Only after running a brush through her hair did she put the Lexus in drive, making sure to drive the speed limit.

She didn't want to appear too eager. At least not as eager as she felt.

****

Luke

He was out the door and on the road the second he sent his last text. He didn't want her waiting alone for long.

Wasn't he supposed to have waited three days after their first date before calling her or some shit like that? It's a good thing he never paid much attention to all the dating rules his sister had tried to explain to him when he used to actually date because he was pretty sure he'd broken them all by now. Asking to see her for the fourth day in a row? At nine-thirty at night, no less? With no advance notice?

He could picture his sister shaking her head at him right now.

He couldn't be fucking up too badly. Cassie had accepted his last-minute invitation with no hesitation, which was a surprise—a very pleasant one.

He could feel the looks he was getting from women as he walked through the place. He knew he was a handsome guy and kept in good shape, and there was no doubt he was an alpha male. In his experience, that was enough to get any woman he was interested in to go home with him for the night.

He was always upfront that it was only for one night, nothing more, but there had been several along the way who thought they could change his mind. There'd been too many who thought for sure after he'd had her golden pussy, he'd realize she was *the one.*

Maybe he just hadn't found the actual golden pussy yet, but he didn't believe there was such a thing as *the one.* However, he was willing to admit, Cassie might be pretty damn close. In a lot of ways, he wished he'd met her before Adriana. Back when he wasn't cynical and the possibility of a family and marriage were still options for him. Unfortunately, his wife robbed him not only of his money and possessions but also of his ability to dream of a future as a husband and father.

Maybe it was fate that brought him and Cassie together now. If they'd met when he still believed happily ever after could exist, he wouldn't have been willing to settle for anything less from her. Now, her fierce independence and unwillingness to settle down made her perfect.

He wondered how she was going to react to his control in the bedroom. The exchanges they'd shared so far seemed to indicate she'd accept his dominance. If not, he'd have to break his little filly until she did.

Actually, he was looking forward to that.

He felt a hand skim down his back and turned, expecting to see Cassie. Instead, a stunning raven-haired beauty with the most kissable lips he'd ever seen stood next to him, her hand still on his back. Her red lipstick matched her tight, mini-dress that left nothing to the imagination—there was no way she was wearing panties under it. She was hot and slutty and would have been exactly what he was looking for two months ago. Not now, though.

"Hi, I'm Amber."

He leaned away, resting his elbow on the back of his high-top chair to better look her up and down, and smiled. "Hello, Amber. That's a beautiful name. Not very fitting of you though with your black hair."

"I think my parents were hoping I'd look more like my mom."

"Ah," he replied. He couldn't help but notice her tits. They were big and perky and brazenly on display. Unquestionably, they'd be fun to slide his dick between and fuck.

She must have noticed his gaze because she leaned forward to give him a better view, one hand now rubbing the top of his thigh and the other gesturing to the empty chair next to him.

"Mind if I join you?"

"Actually, I do. I'm meeting someone."

That didn't cause her to back away from him in the slightest. If anything, she moved her hand to his inner thigh toward his dick and squeezed.

"It's a shame she isn't here." The way she rubbed against him suggested her words were insincere.

He gave her a wink. "She will be."

She reached into the top of her dress and produced a card with her name and phone number. "Well, if she doesn't show up, you know how to reach me." Her hand trailed down his inner thigh.

He took her card and slid it under his phone. "You'll be the first person I call."

Something on the other side of the table caught his eye, and he looked to find Cassie standing there observing them, her expression unreadable. She was in black, stiletto high heels and the black dress she must have worn to the banquet. It was sexy, in a conservative way, but a stark contrast to the red one Amber had painted on. Strangely, when it came to Cassie, he preferred that. There was no question she was stunning enough to turn heads, but she wasn't on display, begging to be noticed. Only he got to see what was under her dress.

He liked the idea of that, so without hesitation, he stood and handed Amber her card back.

"Looks like she made it."

He took the three steps to where Cassie was watching them. Normally, he towered over her, but in her four-inch heels, there wasn't as much of a height difference. With her face in his hands, he looked into her eyes then leaned down and kissed her thoroughly. It might have been a little obnoxious, considering they were out in public, but he wanted to leave her with no doubt he was glad to see her and had no interest in that woman talking to him. He pulled away, and she staggered a step, so he slipped his arm around her waist to steady her.

"Hi," he said with a knowing grin.

"Hi yourself," she said, placing her hand on his chest with her eyebrows raised. "That was quite the greeting."

"You're quite the girl," he replied unapologetically.

Amber had made herself scarce, and he pulled Cassie to the empty chairs at the high-top table.

"You look beautiful."

She eyed him suspiciously, like she didn't believe him, but simply said, "Thank you."

He gestured to the waitress, and asked Cassie, "What would you like?" when the woman appeared.

She ordered wine, and he ordered a beer, then asked her about her night. Somewhere in the middle of their conversation, he noticed he couldn't keep his hands to himself—she was like a magnet, pulling him to her. Whether it was to stroke her arm, or move her hair from her face, or hold her hand—he couldn't keep from touching her. The contact with her was both a way to make sure every man in the bar knew she was with him but also provided a sense of comfort that soothed his soul. He hadn't even realized he was doing it until she withdrew her hand from his to wipe some wine that had splashed when the server placed it on the table in front of her. He immediately felt the loss of her skin against his and wanted to remedy it as quickly as he could.

She looked down when he grabbed her hand again and ran his thumb over her knuckles but didn't say anything. Instead, she took a sip of her drink using her other hand.

"You know," she smiled, "we're supposed to be taking these ten dates to get to know each other, but here we are on Date Number Four, and I feel like the only thing I know about you is you like Italian food, dogs, baseball, and beer, and are an amazing kisser."

He smiled and leaned over for a lingering peck on her lips. He really liked the way she kissed, too.

"Well, we still have six dates, how should we rectify that?"

She sat up straighter and shifted in her seat. Obviously, she'd been giving this some thought.

"We should each come up with eleven questions to ask each other on every date."

He smirked and wrinkled his brows together in confusion. "Why eleven?"

She smiled slyly. "Because on our eleventh date, there are no more rules."

He liked the way she thought. "Okay, so tomorrow night, we'll each have to come up with eleven different questions. Do we have to answer the ones we ask too?"

"Hmm, I hadn't really thought about that? It would probably depend on the question."

He couldn't come up with an example of a question only one of them could answer, but he didn't want to dampen her spirits. Besides, she hadn't disagreed about their next date being tomorrow, so he didn't want to press his luck.

"I can still ask questions tonight, though, right?"

"Of course," she giggled. "I didn't mean we can only ask eleven questions of each other. I just thought it would be good to have specific ones with the purpose of getting to know each other."

"Isn't that the purpose of all questions?"

"I don't know. I think there's a difference between asking how your day went versus asking if you always wanted to be a cop."

He smirked. "Sounds like you already know what you want to ask."

She shrugged. "Maybe a few, but I really haven't given it a lot of thought, other than the actual idea of it."

He wasn't sure if he believed her, but he'd let it go for now. "So, how was the banquet? Are we going Corvette shopping this weekend?"

She smiled, picked up her black clutch from the table, and slipped her fingers inside it to pull out an envelope, handing it to him.

"No, but I might be a little more serious about my house hunting."

He peeked inside the envelope and his jaw dropped. "That's your *bonus*?" He'd only been teasing about the Corvette, but he might have been closer to the truth than he realized.

How much money did she actually make? He did alright, but she might be out of his league.

She shrugged as if trying to be nonchalant. "Selling drugs is profitable, what can I say?"

He handed her back the envelope. "Better not let anybody see that."

She slid it back in her purse, grinning. "I'll be careful."

"Make sure you let me walk you to your car."

Cassie tilted her head and smirked, "Were you worried I wasn't going to?"

He ignored the question and drew his brows in mock suspicion.

"Ya know, that's an awfully big check. I'm afraid I might have to frisk you in the parking lot to make sure the drugs you're selling are of the legal variety."

She pressed her tits against his chest when she whispered in his ear, "Will you use the handcuffs?"

Now she was speaking his language.

Six more dates.

Chapter Fourteen

Cassie

It'd been hard to say goodnight to Luke in the parking lot. She almost asked him to come back to Brenna's, you know, appealing to his sense of duty. It was dark out after all. Wouldn't he feel better, making sure she got home safely?

She couldn't do it though. Cassie couldn't be the damsel in distress. Her pride wouldn't let her. But man, she wanted to be a damsel for Luke. Every cell in her body was screaming for it, and that surprised the hell out of her.

She walked into Brenna's kitchen, tossed her keys on the dark granite counter, and dropped her purse on a bar stool. She couldn't stop thinking about how sexy he looked tonight in his grey Henley that showed off his defined arms and chest, not to mention his ass in those faded Levi's.

Cassie's first instinct when she saw him talking to the slut in the red dress was to turn around and leave with her player fears confirmed. Instead, she decided to see what he did once the woman offered him her card. He didn't pocket it, and he didn't give the skank his number in return. Instead, he politely laid it on the table. So, Cassie waited for what would happen next.

His reaction when he noticed her warmed her insides. She loved how he made her feel like she was the only woman in the room who mattered. Although she was one of the most competitive people she knew, years of watching her sister compete with cleat chasers for her deceased husband's attention made Cassie refuse to vie for a man's time and affection. Either he wanted to be with her or he didn't.

She couldn't help the corners of her mouth from turning up when she thought about how obvious Luke had wanted to be with her.

When she snapped back to reality, she realized she was standing in front of the refrigerator with the door open, staring into space.

"Oh my God, Cassandra. Get a damn grip."

Next thing she knew, she was going to be saying, "No, you hang up first," when they were on the phone. Good thing they mostly communicated over text.

Lying in bed provided no respite from her thoughts. If anything, it made it worse. She could almost feel his arms around her again. The warmth of his body, the smell of his skin, and his cock against her ass. She wondered if he was lying in bed thinking about her too.

Really? I wonder if he's thinking about me, too? What am I? Sixteen? Why don't I listen to some angsty love songs while I'm at it?

This was getting ridiculous.

She rolled onto her side and punched her pillow before plunking down forcefully. It was time for sleep; she didn't have time to worry about what Luke was doing or who he was thinking about. He probably hadn't thought twice about her since they left O'Malley's.

The *ding* of a text message quickly quashed that thought, and she eagerly grabbed her phone from the nightstand to see who it was from, letting out a giggle when Luke's picture appeared on her screen.

Sgt Studly: Goodnight doll.

With a broad smile, she laid the phone back on the nightstand without replying. She was afraid it would end up with *no, you stop texting goodnight first.* She was a thirty-four-year-old woman, there would be none of that.

Damn, that text made her giddy though.

"Who are you?!" she blurted out loud.

She sighed. She was Cassandra Jo Sullivan, and she really, really liked a guy for the first time ever. And she was going to own that shit.

****

Luke

He checked his work cell first thing when he woke up like he always did. Followed by a quick glance at his personal phone, which was a not-so-common thing for him to do first thing in the morning.

Luke hadn't expected to hear back from Cassie last night, but he thought he'd look again this morning, in case he'd missed her text. There was nothing from her, and he wasn't surprised. That wasn't her style.

Was he smothering her? That was the last thing he wanted. The idea of coming off as clingy or needy repulsed him. That was how desperate men acted, and he was far from desperate.

Except he really wanted to hear from her and couldn't wait to see her again.

It doesn't mean I'm desperate.

He shook his head in defeat as he tied his running shoes. Ben was right—he was so screwed. Hopefully, a run on the beach would help him see things more clearly. He leashed Rex, and they headed out the door and down the path to the ocean. The rhythmic pounding of his footsteps in time with the jingle of Rex's tags allowed him to contemplate what he knew.

One—he and Cassie obviously liked each other and had great chemistry.

Two—both of them said they didn't want anything more than a casual relationship.

Three—they seemed to be like-minded professionally. She would understand if he had to work a lot because she did the same thing.

Four—she was sexy as hell, and he couldn't wait to fuck her senseless.

Five—he was going to be open-minded and see what happened between them.

Oh, and six—he was still legally married to Adriana.

That damn number six.

He didn't think it was necessary to bring it up with Cassie at this point. He hadn't heard from his wife in over three years, after she took off with no warning, leaving him almost bankrupt and heartbroken over a child that never even existed.

Once he found out where Adriana was, and they didn't actually have a baby together, he tried serving her with divorce papers, but she refused to sign the acknowledgment forms she'd received them. Or the process server was trying to shake him down for more money he refused to pay. Either way, he was still married.

He thought about going to see her himself, but the cartel's control of the area she was from made traveling there too dangerous. Being a police officer came with an automatic bounty on his head if he were to cross the border, and he preferred to keep his head attached to his neck, thank you very much.

Since he'd filed paperwork to at least keep his accounts and mortgage from no longer being considered community property and she couldn't access his money or credit cards, getting divorced was no longer a priority for him. His attorney had said something about after she was gone for seven years, he could file without her acknowledgment or agreement. At this point, he was just planning on waiting it out, there'd really not been any reason to do anything else.

Until maybe now.

Not that Luke was planning on getting serious with Cassie, but he knew she might have a problem with him technically being married. He'd tell her when the time was right, but he was confident she'd understand.

He'd also made up his mind he wasn't going to ask to see her tonight or maybe even until the weekend. Although the idea of not spending time with her for three more nights was less than appealing, he needed to slow things down.

He could do it. He had willpower.

Hopefully, he'd get called out a lot for work, otherwise, he'd have to find ways to occupy his time other than being with Cassie. That might take some effort since the ways he usually kept busy involved women and alcohol. Maybe Luke would finally take Ben up on playing a pickup game after work with him and the guys from his shops. If all else failed, the garage could always stand to be cleaned out.

His Fitbit said he'd run two miles, a half mile farther from where he and Rex usually turned around on the beach to head home. The whole return trip back, he argued with himself about why not seeing Cassie until the weekend might be unnecessary and drastic. What was he hoping to accomplish by doing that?

He reached his doorstep drenched in sweat and Rex's tongue dragging with no more clarity about what he was going to do then when he'd started his run. Maybe he'd find the answers in the shower.

The water cascaded over his head while he contemplated his next move. The vision of her pretty face and pouty lips popped into his mind, followed by her hot, tight body. He smiled at the thought of her soft, round globes peaking over the top of her dress last night, and his fingers involuntarily flexed as he envisioned cupping them in his hands. Her tits were going to be his undoing. He couldn't wait to suck on them again and looked forward to running his cock into the valley between her peaks.

The image of that caused his dick to rise, and he started to stroke himself slowly as the hot water rained down on him. He wanted nothing more than her on her knees while she sucked him off.

Luke groaned out loud at the thought of her lips wrapped around his cock and started tugging his shaft faster. Leaning against the wall of the shower, he imagined her begging for him to come all over her face—it was *his* fantasy, after all—and envisioned pushing her head down on his dick while he furiously fucked her throat before his release. In his head, he heard her moans of desire as he pulled from her mouth and spurted all over her pretty, little heart-shaped face.

With a satisfied grunt, he came all over the tile floor, the image of Cassie's cheeks and chin glazed with his cum in his mind as rope after rope of semen spouted from his cock.

God, he fucking wanted that woman. The fact he liked her with her clothes on was a bonus. It could also be his undoing.

Sighing, he rested his head against the white, ceramic wall. He didn't know what he was going to do about seeing Cassie this week. The best he could come up with was he'd decide once he heard back from her.

He really wanted to get to Date Number Eleven, but he was willing to admit the anticipation was part of the fun. A small part of him also knew once they had sex, their relationship was going to go to a whole new level. Casual was going to be off the table.

He looked forward to that with both anticipation and trepidation. Cassandra Sullivan had the potential to knock him on his ass, in a way he hadn't thought possible. He needed to be smart about this, and trying to get too serious, too soon was a sure-fire way to fuck things up, not to mention spook her.

The sound of a message on his work phone prompted him to finish his shower. Getting out, he saw his team was needed to serve a search warrant and dried off quickly. He was dressed, his gear bag over his shoulder, jumping in the Jeep in less than ten minutes. Having to concentrate on the task before him was exactly what he needed right now to keep his mind off that sexy blonde.

Chapter Fifteen

Cassie

Her morning was booked solid with appointments, and she was up early to take Zona for an extra-long walk on the beach before she left for the day. The black lab mix spun in excited circles as she waited for Cassie to open the back-patio door that led to the beach. She wondered if Luke and Rex were out this early too and thought back to the other morning when he had stayed over. Their whole routine had felt so natural and right, she wouldn't mind doing that again soon.

She hadn't responded to Luke's text from last night yet but planned on reaching out before she left for work. Just thinking about hearing from him again made her heart happy.

Brenna and Ron were returning home that afternoon, so Cassie planned on coming back to the beach house after work to pack her things, catch up with her sister and new brother-in-law, and hear all about their honeymoon. They had driven the Pacific Coast Highway in the Corvette convertible Brenna bought Ron as an engagement/promotion present, eventually ending up in Napa Valley. Not Cassie's idea of a great time, but she also knew they weren't exactly staying in roadside motels along the way.

She hadn't decided what, if anything, she was going to tell her sibling about Luke right now. Brenna had been Team Luke since introducing the two on New Year's Eve, and Cassie didn't want to get her sister's hopes up unnecessarily until she had a better idea of where this was headed. She also didn't want to jinx it by talking about how good things were going between them. Maybe it would be best not to mention anything yet.

Inevitably, she would spill her guts if her big sister started questioning her.

She took too long on her walk with Zona, so she was running behind and didn't notice the autocorrect on her phone had altered her text message to Luke. Instead of *Good morning! I hope you had sweet dreams*, the text was changed to *Good morning! I hope you had sweaty dreams*. She didn't even realize she'd done it until he responded around lunchtime with:

Sgt Studly: While even in my dreams you get my heart pumping, there was no sweat when I woke up. Maybe you can make me sweaty when I see you again.

Cassie: OMG! Stupid autocorrect! I meant SWEET! LOL

Sgt Studly: Darn. I liked the idea of getting sweaty.

She responded with the eye roll emoji he had sent her previously.

Sgt Studly: When are you available to not get sweaty then?

Cassie: Well, I could get a *little* sweaty with you tonight? You get off work at 7?

She found herself disappointed he didn't respond again and experienced an unusual feeling of insecurity he didn't want to see her later. The idea of a man not wanting to see her had never bothered her before.

He didn't text back until she was walking to her car in the late afternoon on her way to Brenna's. By then, she'd changed his name on her phone again.

SWAT Hunk: Sorry I didn't reply sooner, was called to a scene. Tonight works. You want to meet somewhere around 8:30?

Cassie: How about my condo? I'll have dinner ready.

SWAT Hunk: I'll be there at 8:30. Text me your address.

She had a stupid grin on her face the whole drive to Brenna's, and try as she might, she couldn't stop smiling as she walked into her sister's house. Brenna and Ron were still in their honeymoon bliss, so Cassie thought they were oblivious as she packed her things and took them to her car. Things changed when she came back inside and sat down on one of the bar stools at the kitchen island.

It was her new brother-in-law who, with his arm on the back of his wife's chair, tilted his head and looked at her knowingly.

"Whatcha smiling about, Cass?"

She pursed her lips. "Am I smiling? I'm not smiling. How did you guys like touring the coast in the 'Vette?"

"It was great. Travis was diligent about the maintenance and took really good care of her; she still drives like a dream." His knowing look turned into a knowing smirk. The lieutenant general was not going to let her get away with changing the subject. "So, I was sitting on the couch when we got home, looking for the remote, and happened to find this in one of the cushions. Know anything about it?" He produced a bullet from his pocket.

Cassie swallowed hard as she weighed her options about what to tell them. Pulling her shoulders back, she plucked the ammunition from Ron's fingers.

"Oh, that's where I left that." She knew she wasn't fooling anyone, but she wasn't ready to talk about Luke yet.

Ron winked and said, "That's a pretty high caliber for you. I pegged you as more of a twenty-two kind of girl."

She had no idea what he was talking about, and both he and Brenna knew it.

She shrugged with an innocent half-smile. "Looks can be deceiving."

Brenna started to sputter, "What is going…"

Cassie shot them both a look that said, *drop it*, and Ron whispered something in his wife's ear. A smile spread across her sister's face, but Brenna didn't say anything more on the subject.

"Oh, I almost forgot! We got you something!" Brenna squealed and jumped from the stool to race to the garage. She returned with a bottle of wine and presented it to Cassie. "It's from our favorite winery we stayed at. We actually got you a case, but I didn't want to lug the whole thing in."

Cassie examined the label. "I can't wait to try it. Maybe I'll have some with dinner tonight," she said as she placed the bottle on the counter.

Brenna caressed her husband's cheek with a tender smile while speaking directly to Cassie. "It's not something you should drink alone."

Ron leaned down to murmur against his bride's lips, "Definitely not," before kissing her soundly. The two obviously were caught up in an idyllic memory the wine had spurred. Hopefully, it would reap the same results for Cassie tonight when she served it to Luke.

"Ahem. Okay, lovebirds, I have to get going." She grabbed the bottle off the counter and started toward the door.

"Wait! Let Ron put the case in your trunk."

The garage door started to rumble open as Cassie popped the latch on her trunk and waited. Ron easily carried the crate to her car, securing it once he set it in so it wouldn't slide around. He closed the trunk and kissed her on the cheek.

"Thanks for taking care of Zona," he said as he walked her to the driver's door and opened it for her. She was in her seat, the seatbelt fastened when he said smugly, "Tell Luke we said hi," then closed the car door before she could respond.

The glare she gave him as he stepped back when she started the car was more in jest than authentic, and she hoped her narrowed eyes conveyed, *You think you're so smart.*

The smirk on her brother-in-law's face seemed to answer her dirty look with a silent, *Yep, I do.*

Her scowl turned into a smile, and she blew him a kiss as she pulled out of the beach house drive. She knew there would be more questions in her future from Ron and Brenna about Luke, but she would worry about that later.

****

Luke

He arrived at Cassie's condo at eight-fifteen. He hadn't been sure how long it would take to get there, so he allowed himself some extra time, just in case. He definitely didn't want to be late. He was glad her condominium wasn't any farther from his house than Brenna's beach house.

He pulled up to a modern high-rise, exactly the type of building he imagined she would live in. The lobby was sleek and stylish with lots of stainless steel and leather, fitting for the professionals he envisioned as Cassie's neighbors. The doorman greeted him warmly when Luke gave his name, telling him Cassie had already called down to say she was expecting him and to please send him up.

Luke got on the elevator and pressed the button for the thirty-sixth floor like the doorman had instructed. The lift rose so quickly, his ears popped, and in what seemed like no time, the doors were opening. He looked to the metal sign on the wall for the direction of Apartment J. Of course, she would have a corner unit.

It didn't look like she'd changed out of her work clothes when she opened the door immediately after he knocked as if she were waiting by the door for him. That made him feel good, like she was anxious to see him. The feeling was mutual.

He slid his arm around her pencil-skirted waist and whispered, "Hi, doll," before kissing her softly. Her lips tasted sweet, like red wine, and he lingered at them longer than he had initially intended. He smirked when he pulled away to find her eyes still closed as if in a trance.

Yeah, I'm that good.

"How was your day?"

His question brought her back to reality, and she slowly opened her eyes with a smile.

"I had a good day. Really busy, but productive. Plus, I got to see Brenna and Ron, and now, I'm having dinner with you."

She led him by the hand from the entry down a short hall, her heels clicking on the wooden floor and pushed on a door leading to the sleek galley kitchen with grey cabinets, quartz counters, and dark stainless-steel appliances. Wonderful smells of something cooking greeted him when they walked through the swinging door. She gestured to the bottle of wine sitting on the counter next to one half-full and one empty wine glass and began to pour when he indicated he'd like some.

"Ron and Brenna brought a case of this back from Napa Valley, so I hope you like it because there's no way I can drink a whole case all by myself."

He brought the glass to his nose, then swirled the liquid around before slurping obnoxiously. He'd gone to a workshop at a winery once with a girl he had dated before Adriana, so he sort of knew what he was doing. Enough to impress the ladies, anyway.

Usually.

The bored look on Cassie's face indicated that was not currently the case.

"Do you like it or not?"

That brought a smile to his lips. He loved how unaffected she was by a lot of things most women would be impressed with. "It's really good."

"I think so, too. Dinner should be ready in..." She glanced at the timer on the oven. "Thirty minutes, but there are appetizers in the living room to start with."

"It smells delicious. What is it?" He tried to peek through the oven window with little luck.

"It's a casserole of some kind." She bit her bottom lip as if embarrassed. "I can't take credit for it. My housekeeper, Kristen prepares and freezes a few meals a week for me. All I have to do is put it in the oven when I get home."

She picked up her wine glass and started back toward the swinging door. He followed her into a modern living room with plush, light grey carpet and black and white leather furniture facing floor to ceiling windows on two of its walls. The view of the city was impressive.

He walked over and looked down. "Wow, Cass. This is beautiful."

She stood beside him and took in the view with him. "I think this is what I'll miss the most about living here."

They silently held their wine glasses, watching the city life move about below-the glass catching their reflection from the hued lighting of the recessed lamps. Luke slid his arm around Cassie's waist and kissed her temple.

"Why are you moving?"

She took a sip of the red wine before answering. "It's time. I'm ready for a house. Something a little bigger with more privacy and not as many restrictions. The building is in high demand, so I should be able to sell quickly and make a decent profit. Now, I need to find my dream house, which is proving to be easier said than done."

"Well, you're fortunate you can take your time and wait to get exactly what you want."

She tilted her head and looked at him a long time. "Some things are worth waiting for."

He didn't miss the double entendre. Staring into her eyes, he pushed her hair behind her ear.

"You're absolutely right. You'll know when it's meant to be."

Right then, he knew.

She was meant to be his.

Chapter Sixteen

Luke

Cassie's housekeeper was an excellent cook. Dinner was as good as he'd had at any five-star restaurant. He was elbows deep in sudsy water at the kitchen sink, sleeves rolled up and his big, silver watch temporarily sitting on the counter when she let out a gasp.

"I completely forgot to come up with questions to ask you tonight!"

"Me too," he smiled. "We're fired. I guess we'll have to wing it."

"Actually... We could cheat. I saw something in one of my magazines." Her voice faded as she began to rummage through what looked to be a stack of mail on the small desk off the side of the breakfast nook. She pulled a magazine from the pile and started flipping through it while he dried his hands on a dish towel.

"I think this was it." She stopped on a page and scowled.

He snatched the magazine from her hands and raised an eyebrow when he read the article's title, *How Sexually Compatible Are You?* He was grinning when he looked over at her.

"Oh, yes, we have to do this." Clearing his voice, he started "Question number one*: How do you feel about kissing?*

    A) It's overrated, but okay in moderation

    B) Keep your mouth to yourself

    C) I can't get enough."

They looked at each other. Based on the last week together, each knew the other's answer, and she giggled when they said in unison, "*C*." He handed the magazine back to her.

"You read the next one."

She scanned the pages, looking for where he left off and cleared her throat.

"Question Two: *Preferred form of birth control.*

A) Condoms only

B) The pill or other form of hormonal regulation

C) Spermicide

D) A combination of condoms and another form

E) Pull out and pray."

He paused, waiting to see how she answered first.

With some hesitation, she responded, "Well, I'm on the pill, so probably *D*."

Luke nodded in agreement although he wouldn't mind going bareback with her. He'd need to show her his recent test results first. It was his turn to read the next question, which segued nicely into that.

"Question Three: *Do you get tested for STDs?*

A) Yes, regularly

B) Yes, periodically or if I have a reason to be concerned

C) No, but I should

D) No, it's not necessary, I'm monogamous or celibate."

She was now the one who paused to see how he was going to respond. He knew his expression was pained when he answered.

"Well, it used to be *D*, but now it's *A*.

"Were you monogamous or celibate? What happened that it's no longer *D*?"

Her question was natural, given his response, still, he didn't want to talk about it, so his voice was gruff when he replied, "Monogamous. Then, she kind of destroyed me, and, uh, I no longer did monogamous." He hoped that was enough to satisfy her.

Cassie frowned, opened her mouth to speak, then closed it again. Finally, she said quietly, "Luke, I'm so sorry."

He looked down at the quartz counter and shook his head. "I didn't handle it very well." By *not handling it very well*, he meant, he had a lot of anonymous hookups, hence the regular testing and condoms.

She leaned over, put a hand on one of his cheeks and kissed the other. Normally, he hated people's sympathy, but he found hers comforting.

"I'm over it." Luke grasped her hand and gave a gentle smile. "I learned my lesson."

"What is that supposed to mean?" She narrowed her eyes as she withdrew her hand from his.

He needed to steer the conversation back to fun and sexy.

"So, what about you, baby doll? How often do you get tested?" He knew she understood what he was doing, and her expression was a mixture of amusement and annoyance.

"Well, I always get tested with my yearly physical, but since I haven't been in a committed relationship in a while, I get tested more frequently even though I'm always careful."

A pang of jealousy hit him. He didn't know if it was because of the idea of her being in a committed relationship with someone else or that she slept with other people. What did he expect? Her to wait for him to take her virginity? The caveman in him had to admit, the thought was appealing. But he also appreciated she seemed to know exactly what she was doing.

He motioned for her to continue reading.

She read the question silently, then blushed. He had to nudge her to ask it out loud.

"*How do you feel about oral sex?*

    A) I'll pass

    B) I'd rather give than receive

    C) I'd rather receive than give

    D) Giving and receiving are essential."

She had glanced nervously at him in between each letter choice, which only served to make him more curious, so he stood silently, waiting for her to respond. She smiled and hesitated. God, he hoped it wasn't *A* or *C*. He still ended up not liking her answer.

"*B.*"

Oh, no, baby doll, that's not going to work. He was going to be face first between those thighs of hers the second their eleventh date started.

"D," he said a little more sternly than he'd meant to. "Mind telling me why you'd rather give than receive?"

She shrugged, squirming a little and looking away. "I don't know. I guess I always worry about..."

He cut her off by gripping her chin so she had no choice but to look at him before she had a chance to finish her thought.

"Let's get one thing perfectly clear, Cass. I *will* be licking your pussy, and I will be licking it often because I love to, and when I'm licking your pussy, you will not be worrying about a fucking thing other than coming before I say you can. Do you understand?"

Her eyes were wide, and at first, he was worried he'd revealed too much, too soon. Then he saw the goose pimples on her flesh and her stiff nipples. She still hadn't answered him though, so he asked again.

"Do you understand?"

She licked her bottom lip, and her pupils dilated slightly.

"I understand," she whispered.

Oh yeah, they were going to work out just fine.

It was Luke's turn to read.

"Question Five: *Favorite position?*

    A) Missionary

    B) Cowgirl

    C) Doggie Style

    D) Reverse Cowgirl

    E) Standing

    F) Spooning

    G) Other."

They seemed to be alternating reading and answering first, so it was on him to respond. He chuckled. "Well, I like them all, but my favorite isn't listed."

She raised her eyebrows in encouragement for him to continue.

"It's kind of a combination between *F* and *C*. You'll be lying on your stomach, but not on all fours." He could tell she was trying to picture it. The look on her face told him she wasn't convinced. "Let's try it before you pass judgment," he advised with a wink.

That brought a smile to her face.

"What about you?"

She seemed to mull over her choices before replying.

"I guess it depends. I think with you, any position where I'll be able to look into your eyes and kiss you."

Fuck me. That made his cock jump. He stared at her, silently letting her know he was going to enjoy that, too. Reluctantly, he broke his gaze and gave the magazine back.

"Next question. *Do you consider yourself dominant or submissive? Both? Neither?*"

Even though it wasn't technically his turn to answer first, he didn't hesitate to respond.

"Dominant."

Cassie looked at him, almost defiantly. "*Equal.*"

He didn't know if she really meant it or if she was being a brat. Either way, her answer wasn't going to fly. He leaned his elbows back against the counter, crossed his ankles, and shook his head.

"No."

"No? What do you mean *no*? You can't say what I consider myself."

Luke stood up straight and raised one eyebrow at her.

"No, you are not my equal sexually. Outside of the bedroom, absolutely, but when our clothes come off, I will always be in control."

With a smirk, she started rubbing his cock over his jeans, standing on her tiptoes to whisper in his ear, "But if we weren't equal, I wouldn't be able to do this, just because I want to." She dropped to her knees in front of him.

He took a deep breath in, remembering all the times he'd jerked off, thinking about her in exactly this position. She looked up at him and licked her lips as she started to unzip his fly. It pained him to stop her, but he needed to lay the ground rules. He grabbed her wrist and tugged gently on her arm so she would stand. She had kicked off her heels earlier and was noticeably shorter.

"I'm in charge, doll. I'll let you know when you can do that."

Her indignant gasp turned into one of surprise when he reached under her skirt and slid her panties to the side, smirking when he found her drenched. Removing his hand, he took his wet fingertip and ran it over her bottom lip so she could taste herself, his face inches from hers.

"We're not equal, Cassie. Not here-not ever," he whispered.

Once he finished smearing her lip with her own juices, he ravaged her mouth with his, sucking and biting her lips before plunging his tongue inside. With his hands on her hips, he lifted her onto the counter, then broke their kiss to concentrate on bunching her skirt around her waist. With minimal effort, her panties were ripped off and tossed to the side. He glided a finger inside and began to finger fuck her slowly, whispering into her ear.

"I think you like me being in control."

She whimpered in response.

"You *want* me in control." He brushed her clit with his thumb, and she jumped. He started to fuck her faster, his thumb moving in circles on her pearl, and she began to moan while grinding against his hand.

"Let me see your tits," he commanded. "I want to watch them bounce as I finger you."

She obediently obliged like he knew she would, unbuttoning her blouse to pull her breasts out of her bra. He bent down to suck on her nipple, plunging two fingers deep inside her when he bit down. Her cry out made his dick harder. Her body was responding perfectly to his ministrations.

He could feel her getting wetter, and she began to tense. He grabbed her hair and pulled her head back, fucking her harder now.

Looking into her eyes, he growled, "Tell me. Tell me who's in charge."

She gasped and moaned but refused to give him the answer he wanted.

"Such a wet pussy," he teased as he slowed his frantic pace and stopped thumbing her clit.

"No! Please, don't stop!"

That elicited a small smile from him. "Do you wanna come?"

"Yes, oh God, yes!"

He flicked her nub once and whispered, "Who's in charge, Cassie?"

She was as stubborn as she was beautiful and shook her head, eyes closed tight.

"Baby doll," he warned in a low voice, his tone on the verge of menacing. He liked her being a brat—to a point. "Do I need to punish you to prove my point?"

Her eyes flew open, but her pussy grew wetter. She'd obviously never been with a man who could handle her. Until today.

"I will spank that beautiful ass until it's pink," he growled and gave her pussy a quick smack to drive his point home.

She jumped, then spread her legs farther.

He softly swatted her clit in repetition. "Who's in charge, Cass?"

She was panting now. Pushing her pussy against his hand, but obstinate in her denial of his authority.

Luke plunged two fingers deep inside her and curled them up, finding her pleasure spot. The wet sounds of her desire echoing throughout the sleek kitchen, and he began to use both hands—one to strum her and one to finger fuck her. He could tell she was on the verge of coming and stopped.

"Ohhhh," Cassie let out a low howl. "Please don't stop, Luke. I'm begging you, baby. Please."

He leisurely pulled her pussy lips apart and ran a finger up and down her slit without saying a word, ignoring her urgent attempt to grind against his hand.

"Who's in control here?" he asked again in a low voice.

"Oh God, you! You are!"

A small smile formed, satisfied with her submission. That was all he needed to make sure she understood he was in charge of her pleasure. He resumed fingering her and rubbing her pussy until she cried out, quivering around his fingers.

He didn't let her come down from her ecstasy before he spun her around and spanked her ass with quick bursts, then sank his fingers deep inside her again. This set off another orgasm, and as she lay panting against the counter, her pussy clenched around his fingers, he leaned down to whisper in her ear.

"I'm in charge, baby doll. Always remember that."

Even as worn out as she was, she raised her head to give him a look of defiance. Apparently, he was going to have to reinforce this-repeatedly.

Fuck, yeah. He looked forward to it.

Kissing her up and down her neck reverently, he murmured against her skin, "My tenacious girl. You'll learn."

He felt her stiffen like she wanted to argue, then sigh and relax in acceptance.

"That's my girl."

****

Cassie

Once her legs stopped quivering, she pulled her bra back up, buttoned her blouse, and mustered the gumption to stroke Luke over his jeans again. He was rock hard, obviously turned on by what he'd done to her, so she didn't understand when he grabbed her wrist, stopping her.

She felt tears prick her eyes. "Don't you want me?"

He brought her hand back to his cock—"Does that feel like I don't want you?"—then moved her hand away again.

"So, why won't you let me touch you?"

"Because if you touch me, I'm going to fuck you, and we agreed—no sex until after ten dates."

"But, we just..."

He smirked that infuriating smirk. "We just what, doll?"

"You...you..."

He leaned forward, putting his fingers in between her lips.

"I fingered that sweet pussy of yours, Cassie. I made you come all over my hand while I watched your tits bounce up and down."

She shuddered at his dirty words, pulling away from his touch—trying not to show him how much they affected her.

"Then, obviously our ten-date rule no longer applies."

"Oh, no, baby. That was only a preview."

With her hand on her hip, she raised her eyebrows. "So, why can't *you* have a *preview*?"

His grin grew wider. "I already told you, Cassie. When you touch me, I'm going to fuck you. We made an agreement—no sex until at least ten dates."

She squeezed his thigh while breathing into his ear. "What if I just teased you a little with my mouth?"

Luke put his hand on top of hers. "Because I know my limitations."

"What if I promise not to let you fuck me even if you begged?"

He chuckled softly and brought her hand up to kiss the inside of her wrist.

"I don't beg, doll. Ever."

She was pretty sure by the twinkle in his eye, he knew what she was thinking.

Challenge accepted, Sergeant Rivas.

Chapter Seventeen

Luke

He needed to go home in the next two minutes, or he was going to be balls deep inside Cassie within five. She was way too tempting, and she knew it.

"Do you want to sleep over? It can be like last time, we don't have to do anything," she cooed as she ran her fingertips over his chest.

Luke captured her fingers and brought them to his lips.

"You know I wouldn't be able to resist you tonight."

She brushed the hair around his ear with her other hand and looked up at him. "Who says you have to?"

He shook his head. The thought was enticing, but he was determined to see this through to the eleventh date before they had sex.

"Walk me to the door?"

She wasn't even subtle in her pouting. Another thing he loved about her. He pulled her close when they were in her entryway.

"Cassie, don't be mad at me. Only five more dates. I promise it will be worth the wait. I will make love to you all night long and the entire next day. Hell, we should probably plan on the whole weekend."

That made her smile begrudgingly, which she quickly hid. She shrugged her shoulders as if she were unimpressed.

"We'll see what happens, I guess."

Luke traced her bottom lip with his thumb while he stared at her mouth. Dipping his head, he captured her lip between his teeth, then nipped at her top lip before enveloping her mouth with his. She wound her arms around his neck, pulling him closer while pressing her tits against him. He could feel her need for him, and it only served to fuel his lust for her. He grabbed a handful of her ass and yanked her hips to his erection. This was getting dangerously close to the point of no return, and he needed to stop.

But she kept grinding against him.

Fuuuuck.

It took every ounce of his willpower to break their kiss, but he did. They were both breathing heavy, and he had to make himself look away from her tits heaving up and down. He pulled her tight against him instead and kissed the side of her head while he stroked her hair.

"God, I want you," he murmured.

"Then stay."

He pulled away, holding her at arms-length around her shoulders.

"Dinner tomorrow?"

He could see the conflict raging in her. She was mad he was leaving but still wanted to see him again. When she didn't answer, he opted to take the decision out of her hands.

"I'll pick you up at eight. Dress casual."

His stubborn girl shook her head. "I can't tomorrow."

He clasped her chin between his thumb and knuckle of his index finger, tilting her face to look at him.

"Cassie, this is killing me too. I want you so damn badly, my cock is literally aching for you, doll. Aching. If you think I don't want to stay, you're dead wrong. But I promise, when we do finally make love, you will be ruined for any other man."

Her expression was his undoing. Her big, blue eyes were brimming with tears, but she didn't look away when she whispered, "I already am."

Oh, fuck me.

Game over.

They stared at each other for at least five seconds. With every ounce of his resolve, he kissed her cheek and whispered goodnight, then quietly walked out the front door.

Chapter Eighteen

Luke

He hadn't even made it to the elevator when he asked himself, "What the fuck am I doing?" The most beautiful woman he'd ever met was practically begging him to sleep with her, and he left her with a kiss and a *see ya tomorrow*?

Idiot. It was Ben's voice he heard in his head before he turned around to make his way back to her welcome mat. It took her longer to answer this time, and her cheeks were streaked with mascara and tears when she opened the door.

Without a word, he was through the threshold, cupping her face in his hands, and kicking the door closed behind him. With the pads of his thumbs, he wiped her tears while looking into her eyes, silently searching for clarity—were they about to do the right thing? The only thing he found behind her baby blues was desire, and he finally allowed his to be unleashed.

Without warning, he slammed her against the wall in the entryway and ravaged her mouth. There was nothing tender about their kiss, and he felt her clawing against the material on his back, seeking purchase.

He pushed her skirt to her waist as he deposited her on the narrow entry table, then lifted the back of her right thigh around his hip, pressing the erection under his denim against her bared pussy—her panties still laying on the kitchen floor where he had dispatched them earlier.

Luke felt Cassie's fingers fumbling with the button on his jeans, heard the zipper being lowered, then felt his Levi's pool awkwardly at his feet, his boxer briefs tugged halfway to his knees. He released her thigh, toed off his shoes and bent sideways to gruffly free his legs. She began stroking his length when he stood up straight again and grabbed her hips, kissing her hard. Arching against him to line his cock up to her pussy, she panted, "Do you have anything?"

Shit.

He purposefully didn't.

He shook his head and muttered, "Fuck, I don't," and began to pull away, but she tugged him back by his cock.

"I'm on the pill, and I'm clean." She looked up at him in anticipation, breasts heaving, waiting for his response to her unspoken question.

"I promise, I'm clean. I can even show you the results."

That seemed to be good enough for her because she wrapped her legs around his waist and pushed his cock against her opening, tugging him closer by his shirt.

In one movement, his shirt joined his jeans on the floor. Luke slid his hands over her blouse, up her sides to her shoulders, and down the length of her arms until he had laced her fingers in his, then transferred her wrists to one of his hands. Holding her wrists above her head, he looped his other arm under her thigh and pulled her against him while he buried his face in her cleavage spilling out of her top. He pressed the tip of his cock against her, moving away every time she tried to maneuver him inside her.

Bringing his mouth next to hers, he murmured, "Did you already forget who's in charge, baby doll?"

She whimpered, "No. No, you're in charge," but continued to arch against him.

He chuckled as he released his hold on her wrists. "Leave them there," he warned, then gripped his cock to stroke her slit with it.

"Are you wet for me?"

"Yes. Oh, fuck yes, I am."

He pressed his cock harder against her, her pussy was soaked. She flexed her hips forward with her eyes closed.

Luke tsked and stilled his stroking.

Cassie's eyes flew open, and she stared at him soberly. "Luke—"

The look on her face cautioned him not to overplay his hand, so without another word, he thrust inside her warm, inviting pussy.

She felt like fucking heaven, but also like home. As if she was made for him.

"Oh my God, Cassie. Your pussy is so tight and wet," he growled as he drove his cock deep inside her. Each push caused her tits to jiggle, and he groaned at the sight.

Between the fact it'd been a while since he'd been with a partner, her bouncing boobs, and his cock riding bareback inside her exquisite pussy, he knew he wasn't going to last long if he kept up this pace. He started to slow, and she swallowed hard, shaking her head.

"No, please, Luke. Please don't stop."

Her hands were still above her head like he'd instructed.

"You're such a fucking good girl. Keep those hands right there."

He brought his fingers between their bodies and rubbed her clit in circles. She started to pant harder and cry out louder.

"That's it, baby doll."

He felt her pushing against his hand, so he increased the pressure and tempo until soon, it was almost a frantic pace.

"Come all over my cock, Cassie. Let me feel it, baby."

He felt her pussy grip his cock tight, then she brought her hands to his shoulders and lurched forward with a scream.

The look of ecstasy on her face while her cunt quivered around his dick made him grunt like a caveman while he continued to pump into her furiously. He felt his release all the way from his toes as he came deep inside her walls with a roar.

They were both gasping, his dick still buried in her pussy, and his forehead against hers.

"Holy shit," he heaved.

"That was... wow."

They stayed like that, catching their breath and basking in the closeness and afterglow.

He dropped her thigh and slid out of her as he began to soften, the remnants of their orgasms trickling down his balls and her legs as she slid off the table.

Grabbing his underwear from his jeans, he wiped her legs, then her pussy before he tended to himself.

"You're pretty fucking amazing," he said as he pulled her skirt back down her body.

"Are you upset we didn't wait?" she asked timidly.

"Oh, hell no. That was hot."

"It was," she smiled. "I just... I know you wanted to wait until after ten dates."

"Plans change. And if I recall, the ten dates rule was initially your idea. I'm still taking you on those five dates though."

"Just five? Then what?"

He scooped her up in his arms and headed down the hall toward what he assumed was her bedroom.

"Then we'll see what happens."

She wrapped her arms around him and nuzzled her face into the crook of his neck. He went to open a door and felt her head shake. "That's the guest room. The other door."

He opened the next door and stepped through the threshold, Cassie still in his arms like a bride.

Shit, a bride.

He was going to have to tell her about that. Soon.

But not tonight.

With his heel, he nudged the door closed and walked to the side of the bed where he gently set her feet down on a plush, cream throw rug.

He glanced at her made bed—throw pillows of varying sizes strategically placed—and briefly noted the rest of her room. It was a habit that came from years of constantly surveying his surroundings. Her bedroom was immaculate with expensive-looking cream colored shaker furniture and lime green and cream bedding. It was decorated much like the rest of her home, classy and elegant with touches of bold color and décor. Kind of like the woman herself.

He kissed her softly and a contented sigh escaped her lips when he pulled away.

"God, you know how to kiss," she purred, arms still looped behind his neck.

"Among other things," he added, sliding his hands down to grab her ass.

"Oh, yes. You do other things very well too."

Something had changed between them like he knew would happen after they'd had sex. His feelings for her were not fueled by a lust-infused haze. He wanted to hold her close and worship her body, slowly and sensually. She must have felt the shift too because she began to place deferential kisses on his neck and chest.

"You smell so good," she murmured between kisses.

"Eau de Sex," he teased and began to unbutton her blouse with care. He pulled the fabric apart to gaze at her when the last button unfastened. Her tits were spilling out of her black lace bra from when he had ordered her to show them to him earlier. Her stomach was toned and tanned, and her waist narrowed then flared at her hips, producing an hour-glass figure to drool over.

"God, you're beautiful," he whispered in awe.

She smiled and looked down like she was suddenly shy, eliciting an animalistic response from him. He was an alpha male, through and through, but he'd never felt so primal an urge to both revere and dominate a woman. Make her his, own her—body and soul—and make damn sure she knew it. He wasn't going to leave her with any doubt who she belonged to.

Unbuttoning her skirt, he tugged it down her hips until it fell in a heap on the floor, then moved his hands up her back to unsnap her bra and pull it away, dropping it next to her skirt.

He held her fingers as she daintily stepped over her discarded clothing. He couldn't resist twirling her around, slowly to admire her naked body.

She was fucking mesmerizing.

He sucked in a breath through his teeth and felt his dick getting hard again.

"Jesus Christ, Cassie. You are perfect."

There was no argument from her, which he appreciated, she just stepped toward him and rubbed her bare breasts against his shirtless chest, his cock pressing against her belly.

With one arm around her, he tossed her throw pillows on the floor and pulled back the covers. Luke directed her to the bed, and she wiggled between the sheets, making a production out of making room for him. Sliding beside her, he pulled her tightly against him.

"I think we should call in sick tomorrow," he murmured against her hair. He felt her stiffen, then she took a deep breath and snuggled in closer against him.

"Okay," she agreed softly.

He stroked her back until he felt the rhythmic breathing of her sleep. His eyes began to grow heavy, and he hugged her close. He was in deep.

Cassie Sullivan was like no woman he'd ever met.

Chapter Nineteen

Cassie

I think I'm in love with Luke Rivas.

There was no other explanation why Cassie not only agreed to call off work but actually *wanted* to in order to spend the day with him.

That shit didn't happen, in the history of *ever*.

It was still dark when she gingerly inched back under the covers after sending emails from the computer in her home office, canceling appointments and rescheduling meetings. The sexy SWAT Sergeant was still asleep, naked in her bed. His hard body was warm, exactly what she needed after sitting in her chilly office, and she burrowed next to him.

She felt his arms wrap around her. "Where have you been, beautiful?"

"Just clearing my schedule today."

He was slowly stroking her hair now. "So, does that mean I have you all to myself for the entire day?"

"I'm yours if you want me," she teased.

"Oh, Cassie, you have no idea," he murmured against her hair. "I might not give you back."

That made her smile. Then frown. What the hell was wrong with her? *I'm yours if you want me? 'He might not give me back' like he owns me? That excites me?*

Yeah. It did.

She'd gone on five freaking dates with this guy, had sex with him once, and she was calling in sick to work—something she never did even when she *was* sick. This was so not her.

As his hand moved up her side and began to caress her breast, she realized that might not be such a bad thing. He massaged her breast and squeezed, pushing her tit up to his waiting mouth. His tongue swirled around her nipple, sucking the peak until she moaned. His focus was completely on her. When she tried to reciprocate, he pinned her to the bed.

"Let me concentrate on you, doll," he growled in her ear.

She arched off the bed, parting her legs involuntarily at the mere thought, and moaned, "Ohhh."

She'd never had a lover place so much emphasis on her gratification. It was strange and wonderful. She'd had partners satisfy her, but she'd never been with someone who seemed to get as much pleasure giving as he did receiving. It was as if her body was Luke's only concern, and he wouldn't let her worry about anything but what he was doing to her.

And what he was doing to her was mind blowing, like he'd been making love to her his whole life. He was that attuned to how her body responded to his touch. If she thought he ruined her for any other man before, she was completely wrecked beyond repair now.

It terrified her to allow herself to be vulnerable and not in control all the time, but there was no one she'd ever trusted more. She remembered how content she was last night, snuggled against his hard body. He'd held her so close as if to say, *I'll take care of you*. She had never felt safer in her life.

His whole demeanor screamed there was nothing he was afraid of. His confidence in being able to deal with anything thrown his way was a source of comfort. She knew he'd always protect her and not just physically. He would treat her heart with care, too.

She'd dated plenty of alpha males, but there was something about this one that had her wanting to submit to him. That also had never happened before. All of it was new and exciting, and scary as hell.

In love after five dates? The sheer premise was ridiculous.

But God help her, she'd never felt like this before, and if this wasn't love, then what the hell was it?

****

Luke

He could still taste her sweet pussy as he watched her once she'd fallen back asleep after their morning sex and felt a little melancholy.

Why hadn't he been more cautious before he met her? If he had, he'd be free to imagine a future with her. As it stood, his marriage was like an albatross hanging around his neck. Worse, he didn't foresee a way to remedy it for another four years when he could get an uncontested divorce. He and Cassie weren't even close to having the marriage and kids talk, but he assumed she wanted children someday. Probably before she was thirty-eight, the soonest he'd be able to marry her, assuming he was correct about how old she is. Not to mention, he didn't want to wait until he was thirty-nine before becoming a dad.

He had a lot of regrets about how stupid he'd been with Adriana; how could he not? After she'd duped him and stolen everything, he felt anger and embarrassment, coupled with distrust of the female species in general. It had been humiliating having to file a police report. He was a cop for Christ's sake, he should have known better.

What was coursing through his veins right now felt more like hopelessness and anger at how unfair it was he'd finally met someone he'd been waiting his whole life for, and Adriana was still ruining his chance for happiness.

At the time, the idea of becoming a father was all he could see, hear, or care about. Finding out he wasn't ever really going to be a dad was what crushed him the most. Looking back now, he could only shake his head at his impatience and gullibility.

That bitch was still affecting his ability to be a father. Whether it was with Cassie or someone else. If he were being honest with himself, only Cassie would do. Although he was sure he could find a woman to take the job who wouldn't care if he married her, that wasn't the type of woman he wanted to be the mother of his children, and it wasn't how he wanted to do things. Dating, engagement, marriage, babies. Call him old-fashioned, but that's what he wanted—in that order.

He hadn't done it right the first time, and it never sat well with him.

Holding Cassie against his chest as he languished in the misery of his own making, he came to a decision. He was going to try serving Adriana with papers again, and if she still refused to sign, he was going to Mexico himself. The cartel be damned.

He looked down at the beauty in his arms. Some things were worth waiting for.

And worth the risk.

Chapter Twenty

Cassie

She woke to Luke's body pressed against her back, his fingers stroking her stomach while he kissed her shoulder. When he noticed she was awake, he softly asked, "Baby, I gotta go take Rex for a run. Do you want to come?"

She rolled onto her back and opened one eye to look at him.

"Do we have to run? Can't we just walk?"

That made him laugh out loud, and he leaned down to kiss her forehead.

"We can walk."

"Great. I'll even buy breakfast." She sat up and swung her legs to the side of the bed. "Okay, give me ten minutes."

Her hair was pulled up, she was dressed in her grey yoga pants, baby pink t-shirt, and Skechers walking shoes, and they were sitting in Luke's Jeep fourteen minutes later.

"I really didn't believe you when you said ten minutes," he teased.

She shrugged. "I'm only high maintenance some of the time."

He leaned over the console and kissed her cheek. "But you're beautiful all the time."

She gave him an impish grin. "I would say, *you should see me in the morning*, but I guess you already have."

"I certainly have and let me tell something." His expression and tone were somber. "You are gorgeous when you're sleeping."

"Did you creep on me while I was sleeping?"

He put the car in reverse, backed out of his parking space, and deadpanned. "I like that you're a heavy sleeper. You didn't even stop snoring when I felt you up in the middle of the night."

"I don't know if I'm more upset you're lying about me snoring—which I do not do, by the way—or that I slept through getting fondled by you."

They were pulling into traffic when he replied, "I'm just teasing-about feeling you up. Trust me, doll, you wouldn't sleep through that. The snoring, however..." He was grinning ear to ear.

Cassie smacked his arm. "Shut up! I do not snore!"

"You know what they say about denial."

"Keep it up, and you're buying your own breakfast," she warned.

"Okay, okay! You were dead silent all night. Like a delicate flower, perfectly still."

"Now *that*, I believe because I *am* a delicate flower."

He slid his hand between her legs, rubbing where her legs met in a V. "Delicate flower indeed."

She bit her bottom lip and opened her legs slightly, whimpering, "Ohhh."

He smirked and continued moving his hand up and down between her pussy lips.

"You probably should stop," she whispered, "or I'm going to have a wet spot between my legs."

"I could clean you up with my tongue if you'd like."

She spotted the tent in his pants and squeezed his bulge. "I think we'd end up making a bigger mess."

He was slipping his hand under her waistband when she heard a "Whoop whoop," and noticed red and blue lights behind them. He casually withdrew his hand from her pants and adjusted himself in his jeans as he pulled the Jeep over to the right. The police car pulled in behind them.

Luke kept his hands on the wheel as the officer took his time walking to the driver's window. Normally, Cassie was a bundle of nerves when she was pulled over, but Luke simply waited patiently, his expression almost bored, until he muttered, "Shit. I don't know if I have my ID."

Now she was worried. The good-looking blonde approaching the car had the typical cop look—short haircut, mirrored sunglasses, muscular build, and judging by his scowl, he was the no-nonsense type.

"Good morning, sir. Do you know why I pulled you over?"

"Because you smelled donuts?" Luke laughed and brought his arm up to grasp the man's hand.

"What's going on, Sarge?" The man asked with a laugh. His dimples were adorable.

"I didn't know you were working days, Corey. Just on my way to take Rex for a run."

"Walk," Cassie muttered under her breath.

Luke looked at her and chuckled. "I mean walk."

"You off today?"

He gripped her thigh. "Yeah, took the day off to spend with my beautiful girl."

The handsome, young officer leaned down, tipping his sunglasses down his nose to appraise her from where he stood.

"Smart man." Then reached across Luke with an outstretched hand. "Corey Young, ma'am."

"Cassie Sullivan. And please, don't call me ma'am."

"Yes, ma'am," he chuckled. She raised her eyebrows, and he laughed nervously. "Sorry, I probably can't promise you that."

"Your mama raised you right," she smiled. "I get it."

"Reinforced by my training officers at the academy."

She leaned over and patted Luke's cheek. "San Diego's finest have such manners," she cooed.

The look he shot her suggested his thoughts were anything but polite.

Officer Young must have noticed the feral look too because he coughed and said, "Well, I'll let you two be on your way."

"Thanks, Corey."

The young, uniformed man hesitated before walking away. "And Sarge?"

"Yeah?"

"Try to keep it between the lines from now on."

Luke grinned unabashedly. "Sure thing, man."

Young tapped the hood and walked away without another word, and Luke had his hand between Cassie's legs again.

"See what you made me do?" he murmured

"Nope." Cassie shook her head and pushed his hand. "You're not blaming me for your poor driving."

He sighed dramatically and pulled his hand back to put the car in drive. "Fine. But I am blaming you for the huge hard-on I'm always walking around with."

"Blame?" she giggled. "I'm not taking the blame—I'm taking the credit for that."

He glanced at her several times with a smile as he drove, finally shaking his head in defeat.

"You're something else, Cassie Sullivan."

****

Luke

Their walk was fun and easy. Rex loved Cassie to the point Luke was a little jealous of how much his dog paid attention to her instead of him. She giggled when she noticed Luke's frown at Rex's focus on her as they walked along the beach.

"He associates me with Zona."

"No," Luke shook his head, "he's a smart dog and recognizes a beautiful woman to fawn over when he sees her."

"You trained him well," she teased. "Is he your wingman?"

He stopped walking and gripped her around the waist, his hands sliding down to cup her ass and pull her against him.

"I don't need a wingman. Not anymore." He dipped his head to kiss her, the waves crashing onto the surrounding shore.

Shit.

He pulled back and looked down. "Too soon, too fast?"

She hesitated before shaking her head. "Normally, I would say yes, but it doesn't feel like it's too soon. Is that crazy? We haven't even been dating, what, two weeks?"

He shook his head. "It's not crazy. When it's right, it's right." He wanted to say so much more but opted to hold off.

One side of her mouth went up. "How am I supposed to know if it's right? I've never felt like this before."

Luke kissed her cheek by her ear before murmuring, "That's how you know it's right."

Arching back to study his face, her blue eyes serious, she curved his cheek in one hand and whispered, "I think I..."

He waited, and when she didn't finish her thought, he prompted her. "You think you...?"

She blinked and her face relaxed. With a pat on the cheek, she gave a fake grin. "I—I think—I think I'm hungry."

That was *not* what she was thinking, but he'd let it go. For now. He tugged her hand and started walking.

"Well, let's get Rex home and fed so we can go to breakfast."

The look of relief that he was dropping it was apparent on her face.

Don't get too comfortable, baby doll. This discussion is far from finished.

****

Cassie

Luke took her to a little diner down the road from his house. After the waitress in a tight, pink uniform took their order, he turned his attention back to Cassie.

"Are we counting today as a new date or a continuation of Date Number Five?"

"Does it matter?" she smirked.

"For some reason, it does."

"Why?" Cassie felt a twinge of panic but tried to keep her voice light and teasing. "Are you planning on breaking up with me on date eleven now, instead of sleeping with me?"

He placed his hand on top of hers on the oak resin tabletop and squeezed. "I don't see that happening any time soon."

"But you do see it happening?" She hated how needy she sounded.

"Only when you finally get sick of me." He sat back and reached for his coffee, eyes intently on her face.

"Oh." She was suddenly very interested in the little dessert menu at the edge of the table by the wall.

"Do *you* see that happening?" he asked in a low voice.

The vulnerability in his tone struck her as she flipped the laminated sheet over, pretending to peruse the available pies and cakes. She felt cocky at the sudden shift in power that had transpired in a matter of seconds. The question was, what was she going to do with that unexpected control?

With great power comes great responsibility. Doesn't the saying often associated with Spiderman go something like that? She wouldn't necessarily classify the revelation Luke Rivas was feeling vulnerable about their relationship as *great power,* but she wasn't going to abuse it. She put the menu back where she found it, looked him square in the eye and smiled.

"Not a chance."

The smile he gave her made her want to crawl over the table and into his lap to emphasize she meant it. She knew being exposed wasn't something Luke allowed very often, and she felt honored he'd let his guard down with her.

The server appeared with their breakfast. She set the plates down, along with the check and disappeared.

As Cassie began buttering her fluffy pancakes, he asked, "You didn't answer me. Does today count as Date Six?"

She poured syrup over the hotcakes. "I think so. Don't you? It feels like a new date."

He took a bite of toast and grinned. "But with the same ending."

"Well, hopefully, they'll be some twists to last night's ending," she flirted.

"Oh, there will be. You'll never be bored, doll."

The power had once again shifted. Her alpha was back.

"Aren't we supposed to ask each other questions on each date?" He was cockily grinning as he took a bite of bacon.

She smiled at him, shaking her head in amusement. "I'm assuming you have some in mind?"

"A couple."

"Shoot. I can come up with some on the fly, I'm sure."

"What's your full name?"

She quirked her eyebrows. "You know my name. Cassandra Jo Sullivan. What's yours?"

"Luke Santiago Rivas." He laid his Spanish accent on thick, rolling his r's and enunciating the pronunciation.

"I like it," she smirked at him. "It's distinguished, yet sexy.

"That is the perfect definition of me. Distinguished and sexy."

Cassie made a show of rolling her eyes. It was her turn.

"How old are you, oh sexy and distinguished one?"

"Thirty-five. You?"

"Thirty-four."

He smiled like she'd confirmed something for him.

"Next question. When's your birthday? When will you be thirty-five?"

"Not until May eleventh."

He jerked his head back. "Mine's the ninth. We should have a party to celebrate."

"I don't know," Cassie grimaced, "I don't think two Tauruses make a good match."

"Why not?" he asked with a frown.

"Come on. Two bulls? Butting heads?"

He typed something into his phone and tutted. "It says here when two Tauruses are in a relationship, it's rock solid. They are fiercely committed and passionate, value the same things, and will have a long, loyal love."

That surprised her. "Oh. That's good to know, I guess." Somehow, she wasn't entirely convinced and did her own Google search. "It also says we could get stuck in a rut, we're both stubborn, and it could be war with neither willing to compromise."

His look was one of amusement, and she scowled, "What's so funny?"

He grabbed her hand, stroking her knuckles with his thumb. "Cass, does that sound like us?"

She pursed her lips and took her hand back. "Well, not the rut part. But I could see the stubborn and unwilling to compromise part. I know I can be pretty damn willful, and I suspect you could have a tendency to be pig-headed on occasion."

He was still smirking. "I'm not worried."

Exasperated, she sighed. "Fine. Whose turn is it?"

"Yours."

She looked at him reflectively. "Hmm. Do you have siblings?"

"An older sister. She lives in Florida, but just got divorced not too long ago, so she might be moving back to Cali with my two nephews."

"How old are they?"

"I'm not sure." He furrowed his eyebrows. "I think something like sixteen and ten."

"Oh, rough ages to move."

"Yeah, I think that's why she hasn't done it yet. But really, is there a good age to haul your kids across the country, away from everyone they know?"

"No, probably not," she conceded. "But I think some ages are easier than others."

"That's true. I guess we'll see what happens. What about you? Is Brenna your only sibling?"

"My only one. My parents tried for a lot of years before getting pregnant with me. That's why we're over ten years apart. It sucked growing up. It was almost like I was an only child, but it's been amazing as an adult."

"My sister is only two years older, and there were many times growing up I wish I'd been an only child," he laughed.

"Are you close now?"

"I love her more than anything, but she went off to the University of Florida when I was a junior in high school, met her ex her freshman year, and never came back. So, we're kind of the opposite of you and Brenna. We were close as kids and have grown apart as adults."

"Do you miss her?"

"Sure, especially when she went through her divorce. I really wanted to be there for her and the boys, but it was hard being so far away."

She shuddered. "Divorce sucks. Watching Brenna go through hers was heartbreaking. I can't even imagine having to go through that, especially if there are kids involved."

Luke's expression changed briefly, but before she had a chance to ask him about it, he was asking his next question.

"Did you go to college?"

"I did. UC San Diego. Brenna said she'd pay for my schooling if I stayed here, so I did. It was a pretty easy decision, Danielle, my niece, was only like four, so I wanted to be close. What about you?"

"I joined the Marines fresh out of high school. Did two tours, and when my time ended, I didn't re-up. Instead, I came home and was fortunate enough to get hired right away by San Diego PD."

"Do you like it?"

He looked at her like she was crazy for even asking. "I fucking love it." He took another bite of bacon, then asked, "What about you? How d'you come to be a pharma girl?"

She rolled her eyes at the name. "I was planning on going for my Ph.D. and becoming a pharmacist, but after I graduated with my bachelor's, recruiters were pounding on my door. The promise of six figures when you're twenty-two is pretty hard to say no to."

He snorted. "Pretty hard for a thirty-five-year-old to say no to as well."

"I was really lucky, no doubt about it."

"I don't know if luck has anything to do with it," he disagreed. "It sounds like you're pretty great at what you do."

"I can't take all the credit, my company makes it easy with all the research and development they do. They're able to roll out new drugs regularly."

"Just what the world needs," he mocked.

She felt her hackles rise and threw her napkin on her finished plate. "Tell that to the mom beating cancer because of our drugs, or the dad who doesn't reject his new liver, or—"

Wiping his mouth with his napkin, he cut her off. "Whoa, whoa. I was just teasing. I'm in no way against Big Pharma. I totally understand the need for it."

That soothed her feathers. "Sorry, I guess I get a little defensive."

Luke stood and picked up the check, offering her his hand. "No need to be defensive with me, Cass. I'll always be in your corner," he said as he kissed her cheek once she stood.

"Thanks," she smiled and reached for the check. "I believe I said I was buying breakfast."

He pulled the slip of paper out of her reach. "Yeah, no can do, doll."

"Luke, I'm not sure if you realize this, but I make a shit-ton of money. Probably way more than you do."

He pressed against the small of her back and urged her toward the front of the restaurant.

"Well, I don't give a damn how much money you make. I have a pair of balls, so I'm buying."

She shook her head and muttered, "You know, the whole premise of a man always buying was because men traditionally made more money than women."

He stopped her before they reached the register. "You know the whole premise of why I will always buy is because I fucking take care of what's mine."

It was so Neanderthal-like, and yet she felt herself getting turned on. She didn't know if it was his claiming her or his declaration that he takes care of what's his, maybe both. Regardless, it was sexy.

Maybe it was because she'd never dated a Taurus before.

Chapter Twenty-One

Luke

Spending the day playing hooky with Cassie was better than he'd imagined. Morning sex followed by a walk on the beach with his dog, then breakfast where they talked nonstop. With a little afternoon delight at her place and a nap. He needed the rest, sex with Cassie was mind-blowing. She seemed to be submissive by nature, at least with him. Judging by her initial insistence they were equal, he assumed she'd never been with a man strong enough to tame her.

He was taming her all right.

She woke up from their nap to find his face between her legs. He knew the second she was fully awake because she went from being compliant and wanton to self-conscious and unsure and tried to scoot away from his mouth. Luke grabbed the backs of her thighs and tugged her pussy back to his face.

"Excuse me, I'm not finished with you yet."

She was tense and rigid and tried pushing his head from between her legs.

"It's just that... I don't think..." Her protests were replaced with a low moan when he spread her pussy lips apart and plunged his tongue inside. He momentarily replaced his tongue with a finger in order to correct her.

"*It's just that* you taste so fucking good, *I don't think* I'll ever get enough of your cunt." He dipped his mouth back to suck on her clit while he continued fingering her, then lifted his head to resume admonishing her. "Don't ever think I don't love this, Cassie, because I do. Your pussy is fucking beautiful."

He stroked one finger down her ass crack. "And I'll be having this ass sometime soon, too."

She froze.

Idiot. He scared her with that admission. He knew he needed to ease her into that. He wasn't going to let her think about it and dove back to pleasuring her.

As he licked and sucked, he felt her holding back, so he paused and kissed her inner thigh, asking, "What's wrong?"

"I told you, this makes me uncomfortable. I know I get really wet, and that can't be..."

He was in action before she could finish her thought, hovering over her body and completely enveloping her frame with his. Kissing her mouth thoroughly so she could taste herself, he pulled his lips away and murmured, "How do you taste, doll?"

She refused to answer and tried to kiss him again instead. He jerked his face back.

"How do you taste?" he asked more insistently. They weren't going any further until she acknowledged his question.

"I don't know. I taste different."

"You taste fucking delicious."

She gave a small smile. "Really? You like that?"

"Like it? Are you kidding me? I fucking love it."

"But I get so... wet. Isn't that a turnoff? Especially when you're doing... that."

"Are you serious right now?" She was batshit crazy, there was no other explanation. "Do you have any idea how hot that is? Your body's telling me you like what I'm doing. Your soaked pussy is like a fucking round of applause. I could lick you all day long."

She smiled and murmured, "Oh my" and ran her fingers through his hair with both hands, drawing his face back to hers.

Luke kissed her again, her body relaxed and pliant now. He slithered down her body, stopping to suck on her nipples until she moaned and bowed her back off the bed, then kissed down her core to settle back between her legs. Stroking her slit, he asked, "Now, where was I?"

She spread her legs wider and whispered, "I think there."

"That's my girl," he murmured into her labia before running his tongue up and down. Cassie gasped and pressed against his mouth. He tried not to smile.

Swirling his tongue around her clit, he slid one finger inside, then two, finding her G-spot. He wiggled his fingers in time with his tongue until she cried out, her pussy making the most delightful sounds with the added wetness from her orgasm. He looked up at her with a devilish grin.

"Hear that? A fucking round of applause."

She lay panting and quivering but breathlessly whispered, "Bravo, Sergeant Rivas."

He smirked and pushed his fingers deeper inside her. "What's that? Encore?"

"Oh my God," she moaned. She let him continue for a moment before pushing his head away. "No more! Mercy!"

"Mercy?" he asked, pausing his ministrations.

"Yes, mercy. Please."

"Mercy?" he repeated as he began fingering her again.

"Yes, Luke!" She squeezed her legs together, giggling loudly. "Stop! I can't take it."

He pulled his hand away and chuckled. "I think we just found your safe word, doll."

Chapter Twenty-Two

Cassie

"Safe word?" she squeaked.

She'd heard of safe words, read about them in her dirty books, but never in a million years did she think she'd have the need for one.

"Why would I need a safe word?" her voice went up an octave.

He touched the tip of her nose with his finger. "Because, Cassie, even though I am the one in charge, you always, always have the final say. From now on, anytime you say *mercy*, things will come to a stop."

"But I say that in jest sometimes," she frowned. "Like, I might not really want you to stop when I say it."

"Did you want me to stop just now?"

"Well, yes. But sometimes I might not."

He furrowed his brows. "Hmm, then we'll need a different word."

"How about red?" she suggested. It seemed to be a standard safe word in the books she'd read.

She jerked her head back. *Wait!* Did she not only agree to use a safe word but come up with one, too?

"Red works."

She pushed him down on the bed and mounted his stomach, leaning down to kiss his chest as she glided her wet pussy over his left hip and down his thigh so she was straddling his leg. She firmly stroked his shaft while kissing his stomach.

"Green, Mr. Rivas?" she murmured against his skin.

He wound her hair in his fist and directed her mouth to his dick.

"Green, Ms. Sullivan. And you can call me Sir."

Yeah, doubtful.

He thrust into her mouth and grunted, "Suck my cock, slut."

What did he call me?

Using her hair as a guide, he moved her mouth up and down his shaft, occasionally pushing her head so he was deep in her throat.

"That's it. Take it. Take all of it like a good little whore."

No one had ever dared speak to her that way-in or out of the bedroom. She'd never been so turned on in her life.

"Mmm, yes, Sir," she said after slurping off him and stroking his slippery shaft. She cupped his balls and he groaned, "Fuck, yes," urging her mouth to them. Cassie circled her tongue around his sac, then sucked one nut into her mouth. She started to stroke his shaft as she tugged his skin between her lips, releasing him with a *pop!* before drawing in the other.

His cock was hard as steel, precum leaking from the tip. She smeared it around with her thumb, and he drew her mouth back to his cock where she began to suck and stroke like a woman on a mission, which she was. A mission to taste his cum.

He abruptly pulled her off him.

"What's wrong?" She was worried she'd hurt him somehow.

"Not a goddamn thing," he growled. "Other than I'm ten seconds away from coming down your throat."

Cassie cocked her head and resumed stroking him slowly. "Maybe you aren't aware of how this works. There's this end goal people like to achieve..."

Luke burst out laughing and pulled her wrist to position her on all fours. Grabbing the back of her neck, he pressed her head into the pillows with one hand and smacked her ass with the other.

"Naughty girl," he said in between swats. "Your ass looks so nice in this shade of pink. It matches your beautiful pussy." He then tenderly caressed her bottom before covering her body with his, taking care to keep his weight on his forearms. He began kissing the back of her neck, which was her undoing. She rubbed against him, trying to convey her want without words.

Wrapping his arms around her front, one hand around her neck beneath her chin and the other across her tits, he continued kissing her neck as he thrust himself deep inside her needy pussy. She arched back, compelling him farther inside her and reached behind his neck to pull him closer to her. It was like she couldn't get close enough to him.

They moved in time together, both moaning and panting. Their bodies caressed each other since their hands were occupied. She'd never felt this connected to a man before; their rhythm seemed to match their desire.

He continued to thrust inside her, his speech incoherent with lust until they came simultaneously. It was the most euphoric orgasm she'd ever experienced. He must have felt the same because his words only became intelligible when he hugged her body tightly against him while they came down from their high.

"I love you so goddamn much," he panted in her ear.

He immediately froze, obviously not intending to say that out loud. She wasn't sure how to react now. She knew she loved him too, but it seemed like he was regretting letting that slip. Should she pretend she didn't hear him?

That was what she was going to do until he flipped her on her back and gazed into her eyes.

"I know it's way too soon to be saying it, but I'm head over heels in love with you, doll."

She stared at him, speechless. She hoped her eyes were conveying what she couldn't find the words to say. He leaned down and kissed her gently. When he pulled away, she finally found her voice.

"I love you, too. This is crazy, we barely know each other, but when I'm with you, everything seems right with the world."

He smiled. "Yeah, exactly."

Luke continued looking into her eyes, the depth of his feelings coming through loud and clear, and it caused her to tear up. She was on emotional overload.

He gathered her into his lap, holding her close to his chest. "What's wrong, baby?"

"Nothing. Not a thing. This is all so new. I've never felt... How I feel... it's a little overwhelming."

She felt him smile against her hair. "Let's be overwhelmed together."

"Okay," she laughed as the tears spilled onto her cheeks.

He drew her away from his chest and wiped her eyes. "Feel like grabbing something to eat with me? I have to go let Rex out, then we can get whatever you feel like."

She nodded, then leaned against his chest again. "I wish we could bring Rex back here, but my building doesn't allow pets."

"Why don't you pack a bag and stay at my place tonight?"

"What about Ben?" she asked.

"What about him?" he snarled.

"I don't want to intrude."

Luke chuckled. "He won't care. He'll be glad to see his prediction came true."

Cassie frowned. "What was his prediction?"

"That I was going to fall hopelessly in love with you. Actually, I think his words were, *You're so screwed.*"

"That's not very nice," she giggled.

"Oh, he meant it in the nicest way," he assured her.

She wasn't convinced but decided to take his word for it. Besides, Luke Rivas was in love with her, so who cared?

Chapter Twenty-Three

Luke

Having a lot of sex with someone you're in love with is pretty fucking awesome. He highly recommended it. He and Cassie had been fucking like rabbits since their fifth date, and it only got better each time.

Date Number Eight was later tonight. He hadn't taken her anywhere fancy yet, and he was remedying that by escorting her to Evangeline's at six-thirty. A few nights ago, while they had pizza at his house, he had asked her to go on Friday and was surprised at her reaction as they cleaned up the kitchen.

"Why?" she asked, sealing the leftover pizza in a plastic bag.

He scowled, "What do you mean, *why*?"

Cassie placed the bag in the refrigerator and closed the door. "Why do you want to go to Evangeline's? It's expensive, impossible to get in without a reservation, and they have a dress code."

"I have a reservation, I'm not worried about the cost, and I feel like dressing up and showing you off." He wrapped his arms around her waist and murmured in her ear, "I'm pretty sure the dress code doesn't apply to underwear, so feel free to wear some risqué lingerie if you'd like."

"Maybe I won't wear any at all," she purred as she ran her fingertip across his shoulder.

His dick jumped up and screamed, *That works for me!*

Cassie was the walking definition of his idea of sexy, something his cock took notice of basically every time he laid eyes on her. He loved it when she talked suggestively, especially since she was so receptive to following it up in the bedroom. His girl was definitely not all talk. She walked the walk. Actually, it was more like she strutted it, which was even better.

"You might get fingered under the table if you do that," he warned.

"Promise?" she whispered breathlessly in his ear.

That decided it, he was marrying her. If only he fucking could.

"Would that turn you on?" he asked. He really wanted to know if she was serious or simply teasing him. "Me sliding my fingers inside your pussy under the table at a fancy restaurant? Having to be quiet while I make you come in front of everyone?" He rubbed his hand between her legs as he spoke, feeling the heat generating from her sex.

Her nipples were visibly stiff under her gray UC San Diego t-shirt, and her breathing was coming in shorter breaths.

He kissed her neck, his hand still massaging her pussy over her yoga pants. "Would you like that, baby? Hmm?"

Her smile was naughty, and she bit her bottom lip but didn't answer him.

He stepped back to emphasize his shock with an incredulous smile. "You dirty, dirty girl. You *would* like that!"

"Would you? Like that?" she asked shyly.

He put his hands around her waist, moving them down to squeeze her butt. "Would I like to finger fuck you in a restaurant, under the table? Hell yeah, I would."

She whimpered either at the scene he'd set or his hands on her ass, he wasn't sure which.

"No, I mean, would *you* like to be touched, you know, in public?" she asked in a small voice.

"Oh, Cassie, I would love to fuck you senseless somewhere in public. Discreetly, of course. I probably shouldn't get arrested for public indecency. I think the department frowns upon that."

She laughed. "Yeah, I think my work does too. But that's not what I meant. Well, kinda, sorta it is. What I meant was would you like to, you know, get a hand job in public?"

"Like in a restaurant?"

"Yeah."

"With my cock out and everything?"

"Well, yeah with your cock out." She scrunched up her nose. "It's kind of hard to give a good hand job with it in your pants."

"Depends on the pants."

She shot him a look. "Are you planning on wearing sweatpants to Evangeline's?"

Chuckling, he responded, "Well, no, of course not. Slacks would require strategic napkin placement though. I think it'd be easier for a woman not to get caught if she were wearing a skirt and no panties."

With a shrug, she stated, "So go commando, too" like it was the obvious answer.

"Miss Sullivan, are you suggesting we perform lewd acts in a five-star restaurant?"

"Of course not, Sir!" She feigned being scandalized at the suggestion, then gave him a devilish grin.

He did like she called him Sir. His cock did too.

****

Cassie

She opened the front door to her condominium and gasped. She'd never considered a man beautiful before, but that was the first word that came to mind when she saw Luke standing in front of her in his black suit, crisp peacock blue shirt, and matching tie. The color of his button-down made his eyes appear even greener than normal. One hand in his pocket caused his jacket sleeve to push up, revealing his platinum-colored watch worthy of being called arm porn. The man rocked a suit like a GQ model.

"Wow, Mister Rivas, you look sexy."

He grinned. "I have to step up my game if I'm going to be seen with you." He blatantly looked her up and down. "Speaking of sexy. That dress…" He gave a low whistle.

With a coquettish smile, she looked down and smoothed the mint green fabric. "This old thing?"

He was leering at her like a wolf about to pounce. "Yeah, that."

She loved that he made her feel so desirable. "Thanks, I'm glad you like it" Cassie grinned, then grabbed her purse from the small table next to the door. "Shall we go?"

Luke stepped away from the doorjamb to let her through and lock her unit. His hand on her back, he directed her to the elevator where another couple also waited. Once they all entered the crowded car, Luke stood behind her and lightly traced a finger up and down her ass. She knew he was checking for panty lines and tried to contain her smile.

The elevator was exceptionally quiet for as many people as it contained. The melodic sounds of what once was a hard rock song came through the speakers as they descended to the lobby. The *ding!* alerted the passengers the sliding doors would be opening, and as everyone exited the car ahead of them, Luke growled in her ear, "Good girl."

She knew exactly what he was talking about, but looked at him over her shoulder and teased, "Why, Mister Rivas, whatever do you mean?"

He ran the palm of his hand firmly down her ass. "You know damn well what I mean," he snarled through gritted teeth and squeezed a handful of flesh as they stepped into the lobby.

The smirk on her doorman's face told her the ass grab did not go unnoticed. She didn't really care, she loved the possessiveness of it. It made her feel special.

Yeah, an ass grab just made her feel special. Who'd a thought?

She looked up at him out of the corner of her eye.

But, come on, look at him. There wasn't a woman alive who wouldn't love that.

"You really do look stunning tonight, baby doll," he told her as he opened her car door. "I need to take you out more often."

She waited until he came around and got in the driver's side before replying, "Just so you know, as much as I loved getting ready tonight and as delicious as you look in that suit,

I'm just as happy staying at home in my jeans with you and Rex, watching a game, and eating takeout."

He gave a closed-lip smile and squeezed her thigh. "I love that too, just so *you* know."

The drive in his silver muscle car was brief, but he kept his hand on her thigh the entire time until he got out to hand his keys to the valet, then held her hand to accompany her inside.

The maître d' escorted them immediately to their table once Luke gave his name. As they weaved through the dining room, she heard a deep male voice call out, "Luke."

She and Luke turned at the same time to see who had recognized him. He gripped her hand and steered her to a table with several couples. The man who had called for Luke stood. He looked familiar. She figured out why he was familiar when Luke released her hand to shake his and smiled.

"Hey, Chief." He then nodded at another man seated farther down the table, "L.T."

The chief's body language was welcoming. "How have you been? I haven't seen you working out at the station lately."

"Yeah, with all the callouts we've been having, I've been really tired after work."

The man was stealing glances at Cassie as Luke spoke, something Luke must have noticed. He slid his arm around her waist. "Todd, this is my girlfriend, Cassie Sullivan."

Cassie pulled out her A-game work charm—the stuff usually reserved for doctors who needed convincing to prescribe her company's drugs.

"Chief Pearson, so nice to meet you," she gushed while stepping toward him and extending her hand.

The twinkle in the older man's eyes was apparent, and he grasped her hand between both of his. "The pleasure is all mine, Ms. Sullivan." He directed his next words at Luke but kept Cassie's hand between his and continued to look at her. "I hope Ms. Sullivan has something to do with why you haven't been around after work lately."

Luke gave a sly smile and placed his hand on the small of her back. "She might be."

The chief noticed the maître d' waiting patiently nearby. "I don't want to keep you. We'll talk soon. Ms. Sullivan, it was nice meeting you. Have a nice evening."

They were seated right in the line of sight of his boss' table, and she sighed heavily once they were situated.

"What's wrong?" he asked with a slight frown.

She discreetly nodded to the party of important people merely yards away. "That probably means lewd acts are off the table tonight."

He chuckled. "Definitely *off*, maybe still under," he teased. "Hopefully they'll leave soon."

Just then she heard her name. She looked up to see a man approaching their table and muttered under her breath, "Oh, fuck."

****

Luke

He heard Cassie grumble, "Oh, fuck," and felt her tense up as a short man in his forties, dressed in a navy suit that made him look like he had borrowed his father's, stood before them.

"Cassandra!" the man exclaimed with a smarmy, fake smile.

"Dr. Szolowicz." She tried to make her tone airy and light, but Luke knew her too well.

"Did I see you talking to Chief Pearson?"

She cocked her head and looked at him suspiciously. "Yes?" The *why?* was unspoken but implied by her inflection.

"I didn't realize you knew him."

"Actually, I don't. My boyfriend does." She looped her arm around Luke's bicep and looked up at him with an adoring smile.

Luke stood and extended his hand. "Luke Rivas."

"Dr. Michael Szolowicz, partner, San Diego Oncology Specialists."

Way more information than Luke wanted or needed. He noted the man made sure to mention *doctor* and *partner* and internally rolled his eyes as he sat back down.

"Oh, so you know Cass through work."

Cassie gave her best fake smile. "Yes, Dr. Szolowicz's medical group is one of my new clients although he's been somewhat reluctant to meet with me."

"I've had a really busy schedule. Please call my assistant on Monday. I'll make sure she knows to find some time on my calendar for you."

"That would be great, doctor. I appreciate it."

Luke now understood why she was salesperson of the year. While he wanted to tell this little prick to go fuck himself, Cassie was gracious and fed his oversized ego.

"Yes, I'm sure you do. Enjoy your meal." And without another word, he turned on his little heel and left.

"What a fucking douchebag," Luke muttered once he was out of earshot.

"Yep. But, hey, at least he's giving me an appointment now. I have you to thank for that. Well, your connection to the chief, anyway."

"Really? You think that's why?"

"Oh, I have no doubt. It's well known Michael Szolowicz is all about making sure he knows the right people. I guess he never thought I could do anything for him before, so he didn't waste his time meeting with a nobody-sales rep. I mean, I still can't do anything for him socially, but I'll let him think I can," she chuckled mischievously.

"What about your connection to the Padres?"

"I don't think he knows about that, and I've never really had an opportunity to bring it up. Trust me, there's no shame in my game. I'll find a way to slip in Danny was my brother-in-law, not that I'd lift a finger to help him with anything Padres related, but I'll need that connection once he realizes I'm worthless as far as the chief goes."

"I wouldn't say worthless. I consider Todd a good friend even if he is my boss. He's really looked out for me, and he appreciates I bust my ass for his department."

"Yeah, but that's you."

He tucked her hair behind her ear as he looked into her eyes. "Doll, that's you, too, by extension of me. I'm pretty sure you've figured it out by now I'm not going anywhere."

She gave a shy smile and lifted up from her seat to give him a peck on the cheek. "Good. I'm not either."

Luke lowered his lips gently to hers. It wasn't obnoxious, but it was definitely something the clientele at Evangeline's would notice, which only spurred him to extend the kiss a few minutes longer.

"I'm glad we have that settled," he smiled against her lips as the back of his fingertips caressed her jawline.

A quiet, polite cough drew his attention away from her lips, and a waiter stepped forward to take their drink order, immediately followed by another waiter telling them about the evening's dinner specials, and yet another arriving to take their food order.

The entire time, his hand stroked her inner thigh under the tablecloth. Cassie appeared completely focused on the wait staff even as she spread her legs when his fingers started making their way to the apex between her thighs. He could feel how hot her sex was, and it fucking made his dick hard.

They were alone at their table, and he smiled while he asked her thoughts on the Padres' chance at the post-season, all the while stroking her wet cleft. He tried to look like he was interested in the nonsense she was stuttering when he dipped his finger inside her.

"So, um, yeah, I think if the pitching staff keeps... oh!"

He smiled devilishly.

"What about the pitching staff?" He flicked her button with his thumb while sliding in another finger.

"Well, um, they need to stay, um, healthy and, um..."

He stroked her in and out, his hand drenched.

The waiter appeared with their drinks, and Luke didn't stop finger fucking her. He even picked his glass up with his other hand and took a sip while he finger-banged her under the tablecloth.

The waiter walked away, and she gripped his bicep while leaning her face against his shoulder.

"Luke, I'm going to come," she gasped in a whisper.

"I know," he growled and increased the pace.

He felt her tighten around his fingers, and she let out a little whimper as her cunt milked his digits.

Nonchalantly, he withdrew his hand from her quivering walls and brought his fingers to his nose and lips, drawing the tip of one into his mouth while he stared at her with a grin.

"So fucking delicious," he murmured.

"Oh my God," she gulped. "I can't believe you made me do that."

"Believe it, doll. All before the appetizer even got here."

As if on cue, a new server appeared with their order of calamari. She dished some fried squid on a plate and set it in front of him, "For you, Sir," then dished a smaller helping on another plate for herself.

As if his cock wasn't already hard, her little proclamation of *Sir* turned it to steel, and he snarled through clenched teeth, "I am going to fuck that little pussy so deep and hard."

She smirked. "God, I hope so. Sir."

Check, please.

Chapter Twenty-Four

Cassie

She wasn't brave enough to return the favor of masturbating him under the table—she was worried it would be too obvious—but she did tease and talk dirty in his ear. Then gave him roadhead on the drive home.

They walked into Luke's house through the door leading from the garage and discovered Ben was making dinner.

"What are you doing home?" Luke asked. "I thought you were having dinner with what's-her-name."

"Change of plans." Ben scowled at them both as he stirred the contents of the saucepan on the stovetop.

Cassie set her purse on the counter and asked gently, "Wanna talk about it?"

"Nope. You guys can go. I'll take care of Rex."

"See ya later, dude." Luke ushered her out the door by her elbow, barely pausing so she could retrieve her clutch.

"Don't you think we should stay and be with him?" she asked, stumbling over her feet as he tugged her back through the garage to his Challenger. He opened the passenger door, and she slid inside.

"Fuck no. When Ben says to leave him alone, you leave him the hell alone."

She quirked her eyebrow at him before he shut her door. "Is that a guy thing?"

He rounded the front and got in the driver's side. "Eh, to an extent, yes, but with Ben, especially. He's very introspective. He's probably going to spend the whole night analyzing how much effort this girl is worth so he can decide how he wants to proceed."

"What do you mean, *how much effort she's worth* and *how he wants to proceed*?"

Luke shrugged. "It's simple. Does he like her enough to continue pursuing her even though something obviously didn't go right tonight? If he decides she's worth it, he'll keep trying. If he decides she's not, he'll cut his losses."

"What makes her worthy?"

"Lots of things. Her personality, looks, brains, body, sex appeal, how she is in bed. Is she high maintenance? Stuff like that. If he thinks she is, he'll try harder. If not, he'll move on."

"Wow. It's that easy?"

"Most of the time, yeah." His tone was unapologetic.

He grabbed Cassie's hand and kissed her knuckles with a wink. "But now and then, a woman comes along and knocks you on your ass, and you'll move heaven and earth to be with her."

She hoped he was talking about her, it seemed like he was.

"I'd hate to think you'd ever have to reduce yourself to a pros and cons chart to decide if you wanted to be with me. If that ever happens, do us both a favor and just don't."

Luke squeezed her hand. "Not a chance."

****

Luke

He got home the next morning to find Ben sweaty in running clothes, downing a sports drink. Rex's tongue was hanging out when he greeted Luke with a slobbery kiss; he'd obviously just drank water.

"You're home early," Ben said between gulps.

"Yeah, I've got some things I need to do today."

Luke started toward the hall leading to the bedrooms when Ben called, "You tell her yet?" His tone was aggressive.

Luke was feeling just enough testosterone in his veins to take the bait and turned. "Tell her what?" he snarled. He knew exactly what Ben was referring to.

"That you're fucking married."

Luke folded his arms across his chest and widened his stance. "No, I haven't yet. You have a problem with that?"

Ben stepped toward Luke, snorting in disbelief. "Yeah, I have a problem with that. She's a cool chick, and you're playing her dirty by not being honest with her. She deserves better."

If Ben hadn't been his best friend, Luke would have lunged for his him, instead, he clenched and unclenched his fists hidden under his elbows.

"Don't fucking tell me what she deserves."

"Well, someone needs to be looking out for her because it sure as hell ain't you."

Luke grabbed Ben by his sweaty t-shirt. "I don't know what the hell is wrong with you today. You obviously are looking for a fight, so I'm betting it has nothing to do with me. But hear me now. I love that woman, and I am *not* playing her dirty. I know I need to tell her, but I can't..." He abruptly let go of Ben's shirt and retreated down the hall.

Ben followed him. "Hey, man, I'm sorry. I didn't know..."

"Fuck off," Luke snarled from inside his bedroom, poised to slam the door. His roommate kept coming down the hall and stopped in front of Luke's door before he banged it closed.

"No, seriously. I didn't realize you were in that deep with her. I'm just projecting my own shit. I'm really sorry." He offered his hand in a grip as if he wanted to arm wrestle.

Luke glared at him for a moment, then grasped Ben's hand. The mechanic pulled him for a bro hug. Smirking while they patted each other's backs, Luke asked, "Did you say you were projecting?"

They pulled apart, and Ben looked unperturbed. "It's a thing, look it up."

"I know it's a thing. I'm just wondering where you heard it."

Ben shrugged. "I'm getting in touch with my feelings."

Luke rolled his eyes. "Good luck with that."

The younger man's expression turned serious.

"What are you going to do about telling Cassie?"

"I'm going to serve Adriana divorce papers again, and if she still won't sign, I'm going down there myself and make her."

Ben let out a low whistle. "Wow, you *are* in love with this girl if you're willing to risk your head, literally." Luke nodded in agreement but didn't say anything further. Ben clapped his hand on Luke's shoulder. "Well, I got your back, bro, if you need me to go to Mexico with you, I'm in." He pronounced Mexico with a Spanish accent.

"I'm hoping it doesn't come down to it, but I might take you up on that," Luke said, his tone a little defeated.

"Lemme know when," his roommate called over his shoulder as he walked away.

Luke's formerly euphoric mood after another night with Cassie was sullied, and now he was grumpy and needed to burn some energy. He threw some workout clothes in his gym bag and headed to the weight room at the station. Hopefully, he'd run into the chief since his boss had noticed his absence at the gym lately.

Chapter Twenty-Five

Cassie

Luke had been called out for the last couple of nights, so she hadn't seen him since the morning after their date at Evangeline's.

She missed him, and sent him a text late Monday afternoon, telling him exactly that.

Cassie: Am I going to see you tonight, handsome? I miss you.

Sgt. Orgasm: I'm en route to a barricaded subject. Not sure how long I'll be.

She replied with a needy: *Come slip into bed with me when you're done. I don't care what time. I'll leave the door unlocked.*

She didn't hear back from him. Takeout from her favorite Chinese restaurant, followed by a pint of Talenti Sea Salt Caramel ice cream was her consolation for eating by herself two nights in a row.

It was funny, she used to cherish her alone time, safeguarded it, actually. Now, she wanted to spend all her free time with Luke. She hadn't even seen Brenna since the first day her sister and Ron returned from their honeymoon. Her niece, Danielle, had sent her a text that morning. She was coming to San Diego the following weekend, and all Cassie could think about was whether she should bring Luke to the family dinner Brenna was sure to have. It took her all of three seconds to determine, of course, she should.

Even though he hadn't responded, Cassie took extra care getting ready for bed that night, making sure her legs were smooth, and there was a little dab of perfume on her neck.

Yeah, I'm wearing perfume to bed, what about it? You know what I'm not wearing to bed? Clothes.

She was happy with her decision when she woke to the sound of her front door opening, followed by heavy footsteps that were attempting to be quiet. She tried to suppress her smile when she heard his boots hit the floor, followed by the rustling of clothes being shed. He slid between the sheets and groaned when he found her completely nude. Wrapping her in an embrace, his bare chest against her naked back, he kissed her neck. He held her close and tight, breathing in deep like he was smelling her before letting out a contented sounding sigh. With an arm under her and draped around her chest, his other hand caressed from her cleavage and under her boob, down her side, and casually traced circles on her stomach. She stroked his forearm at her chest with her fingertips.

"Hi, doll," he murmured against her neck.

"Hi, baby," she replied in a soft whisper.

"You don't know how badly I've needed to hold you. Thank you for inviting me over."

She wiggled her bum against the erection in his boxer briefs. "Thank you for *coming* over."

His index finger stroked her slit, up and down. "I won't be the only one coming tonight," he growled.

She arched against him, pushing against his cock harder and whimpering softly.

He continued, "You're already wet for me. Such a good girl." Luke dipped a finger inside her. "Mmm, so wet and ready. Does my little slut want this cock?" He pressed his steel rod against her ass, and she reached behind her, trying to free his dick from his underwear.

He pulled his hips back, out of her reach, and she whined, "Aww."

"You'll get my cock when I say you can," he warned in her ear.

God, she loved his dirty talk and dominance. He turned her on so much. Everything about him did—his masculine, woodsy scent, deep voice, large calloused hands, green eyes, and oh-so-yummy fat cock, to name a few things.

"Okay, Sir," she said in a soft voice.

He groaned in response and pulled her back close. "You have no idea what you do to me."

Cassie shifted her hips, not-so-subtly rolling them against his hard cock. "I actually have a pretty good idea," she quipped.

That caused him to chuckle and smack her bare ass.

She reached behind his neck, drawing his face close to her so she could kiss his jaw. "Please, baby. I've missed you so much. I need you inside me."

Those were apparently the magic words. He tugged his underwear down his legs, slid his cock between her legs, and aligned himself with her entrance before thrusting himself deep inside her.

She closed her eyes at how good he felt and let her body move in rhythm with his. He took his time, his cock slowly pushing deep inside her wet pussy and withdrawing just as slowly before sliding back in again. It was like he wanted to make sure he felt every inch of her. Like he was savoring her.

It wasn't lost on her how he could go from alpha dom to reverent lover in minutes. She loved both sides of him. But either side, he was always in control.

Always.

And she fucking loved that. She didn't think she'd ever admit it to him out loud. Her obstinacy in giving him her submission was part of the game they played. But he knew he had it. He had all of her—heart, soul, and submission; her deference to him unlike any man she'd ever known. Her father and Ron came close, but that wasn't really the same.

She shuddered at the intensity of her feelings. They were definitely making love tonight, and Cassie had never felt closer to him. She clung to his forearm, still holding her tightly around her chest and met his every thrust, arching back against him.

Luke rolled her onto her back, resting his weight on his forearms. His cock stationary inside her while he brushed her hair across her forehead and stared into her eyes.

"I love you so much." His incredulous tone suggested he was amazed at how much.

"I love you, too." It seemed an inadequate way to express the depth of her feelings.

He leaned down and kissed her as he began to move his cock inside her again. She kissed him back while rolling her hips to meet his.

It was nirvana, and she felt a sudden gush of wetness between her legs.

"Baby doll, did you just squirt?"

Instantly embarrassed, she stammered, "No, I don't think... I mean I've never. I—"

He cut her off. "That's the sexiest thing I've ever felt." Picking up his pace, he groaned, "So. Fucking. Sexy."

She was on the edge of coming, and Luke's grunting signaled his impending release. He put his thumb to her clit. "Come for me," he commanded as he thrust in hard. That set her off, and she bowed off the bed as her climax wracked through her body and cried out his name. Luke roared when he burst. She felt jet after jet of cum hit her womb, triggering another mini-orgasm for her.

She was trembling long after she caught her breath. Luke lay motionless, his face buried in her neck, arms enveloping her, seemingly equally overwhelmed. Finally, he began to soften, and when he slipped out of her, he raised on his elbows, hovering over her to look into her eyes.

"That was fucking incredible. I wouldn't be surprised if we made a baby."

Record screech.

She talked herself down from the proverbial ledge before she started to hyperventilate. *No, he was just being dramatic. He didn't really mean that.*

"God, let's hope not," was all she could muster.

She immediately felt the shift in him, and he rolled off her and headed to the bathroom without another word.

Jesus Christ, was he serious? Does he want a baby?

No. No, no, no. No babies.

He didn't say anything else about it, but something about the way he held her for the rest of the night felt different, and not in a good way.

Good grief, how did that go from the closest she'd ever felt to a man to this? Was this the beginning of the end? Already? They'd barely gotten started. The thought devastated her. Yet, she didn't know if she was willing to have kids even for Luke.

A tear escaped out of the corner of her eye and slid onto the pillowcase by her ear. Could she be a mother if it were Luke's baby? Was this the deal breaker she had always maintained it was? More tears wetted her pillowcase, and soon, her hair was sticking to her damp face.

She just didn't know.

Chapter Twenty-Six

Luke

Last night's lovemaking session with Cassie had been mind-blowing. The intensity of the feelings and emotions they exchanged was fucking epic. The kind of shit he expected when babies were made. It had touched him to his core.

He should have kept his dumb mouth shut, but he wasn't thinking straight. Clearly.

Luke didn't really want to have a baby with Cassie before they were married or even engaged. He was determined to do things the old-fashioned way this time—but damn, her reaction bothered him.

Her body had gone rigid when he said he wouldn't be surprised if they'd made a baby, and her breathing became shallow like she was on the verge of a panic attack. Did she not want kids at all? Or was it because their relationship was new, and they weren't technically committed to each other? He could understand the latter, but the former worried him. He thought about it all night. If she didn't want babies that didn't necessarily mean he didn't want to be with her. He fucking loved her, but it did make him pause with the need to talk to her. Last night, while they were naked in bed, was not the time to have the conversation.

The way she refused to look at him across the breakfast table made him think maybe now wasn't the right time either.

Yeah, fuck that. This discussion needed to happen, or it was going to eat at him all day.

When they were both finished with their eggs and pancakes, he cleared their plates, then took her hand and led her to the couch. Once she was seated, he scooted the ottoman so he was sitting between her legs and grabbed both her hands. She still didn't want to make eye contact, but he was making it difficult for her not to.

"Baby doll, I wasn't serious about what I said last night. I just meant, whatever happened between us was special. I didn't mean to upset you or scare you."

She nodded her head as her bottom lip trembled, tears filling her eyes.

"But I have to know. Was it the thought of having a baby *right now* what troubled you, or was it the thought of having a baby with me—period?"

"I don't know," she choked out.

That caused him to take a deep breath. "Okaaay," he said slowly as he released it.

She laid her hand along his jawline and finally looked at him willingly.

"Luke, before I met you, I didn't want babies or marriage, doing holidays and vacations together... none of it. I didn't fall in love. That's not what I was looking for. *You* are nothing like I was looking for, and you have thrown me for a loop. I'm just getting used to being in love and wanting to share my life with you. You kind of freaked me out with the babies thing."

He smiled, in spite of how he was feeling. "I noticed."

"You can't blame me." She took her hand away from his face and frowned. "What happened between us last night was intense, then you go and throw, *I hope we made a baby* at me. How the hell did you think I'd react?"

"Okay, first of all, I never said, *I hope we made a baby.* While, yes, I want to have a baby with you—lots of them, actually—I don't want to do it until we're ready. And we need to be married first. I meant last night was fucking amazing, it felt like something special happened. Making a baby made sense."

She sat staring at him for a moment before speaking. Her voice was an octave higher than usual.

"Lots of babies? I'm trying to come to grips with *a* baby and now you're throwing *lots* at me? And... married?" Cassie shook her head as if trying to clear it while taking a deep breath.

He held her face between both his hands and scanned her eyes with his.

"Make no mistake, I'm marrying you someday, Cassandra Sullivan." He leaned down to kiss her tenderly, leaving her no opportunity to argue. They came up for air, and with a smirk, he murmured against her lips, "Knocking you up on our wedding night is negotiable."

He just needed to not already be married so he could make that happen.

****

Cassie

She was freaking the hell out.

Luke wanted her to have his babies.

Wasn't that like her number one rule-no babies?

He also said he was going to marry her.

Now, that idea turned her on a little.

He knew it, too.

"Mmm, Mrs. Cassie Rivas. I like the sound of that," he said as he kissed her neck, his arms wrapped around her waist.

She did, too-damn it. Tilting her head to give him better access and running her fingers through his hair, she pleaded, "Luke."

"Hmm?" he asked as kept nuzzling her neck.

"I can't think when you kiss me like that..."

He smiled and moved his hands down to squeeze her ass. "Tell me you like the sound of it, too," he murmured against her skin.

"God, I do," she confessed breathlessly.

He jerked his face away from where he'd been kissing, his eyebrow quirked as he looked down at her. "Yeah?"

Damn him for lowering her defenses.

"Yeah."

"Fuck yeah," he exclaimed with a grin, then kissed her lips softly as if to seal the deal. "I planned on asking you a little better than that."

"What?" She felt her chest constrict. "Wait! No! I didn't mean to make you think I was saying yes right now! That wasn't really a proposal, right?"

"Well, um, I guess not?"

"You're freaking me out again, Luke Rivas." She pushed at his chest, trying to get out of his grasp.

"Fine." He rolled his eyes and sighed dramatically, pulling her back close to him. "It wasn't a proposal—yet. I'll surprise you when we're ready. I'll even have a ring and everything," he smirked.

She let out a sigh of relief, then continued teasing him. "Besides, you have to save up for a while-remember, two months' salary."

"Really?" Luke blanched. "Two months? Who the fuck came up with that rule?"

She burst out laughing at his distress. "Probably the jewelry companies," she said as she kissed his cheek. "Just so you know, I would never wear something ridiculously big and that expensive."

Cassie was fucking talking about engagement rings.

Engagement rings.

For her.

She shouldn't be doing that. It wasn't fair. He deserved babies like he wanted, and she wasn't sure she could do that. Not even for him.

Chapter Twenty-Seven

Luke

Wednesday morning, he was on the phone with Mike Randall, a new private detective who came highly recommended. Things were still dangerous in Sinaloa, and Luke knew this was going to be expensive. Hopefully, Adriana was still in her hometown, and the information Luke had from the previous PI's work would provide assistance. He needed his wife to sign the divorce papers like yesterday.

His marriage and the fact he'd been omitting its existence in his conversations with Cassie was looming large over his head.

He was going to tell Cassie, he just wanted the divorce process started when he did. It seemed like it would soften the blow, somehow. But the longer he kept it from her, the more he knew he was skating on thin ice. The feeling of dread had settled into his stomach, and it became his mission to get divorced as soon as possible.

He was grateful for all the overtime he'd been working. It gave him a legitimate reason to avoid Cassie. She knew something was wrong, and he hated lying to her when she would ask him about it.

Lying and omitting facts were two different things, he reasoned when his conscience called him a hypocrite.

Besides, he *was* going to tell her. Just not yet.

Their next date would be Date Number Ten. Their ten dates had become a big deal in his mind, regardless that they'd already had sex. It was as if on the eleventh date, he was somehow getting boyfriend tenure.

He needed tenure with her. Especially when he told her about Adriana.

****

He didn't know whether to be jealous, pissed, or curious at Ben's comment a week later as Luke prepared omelets for both of them.

"Saw your girlfriend yesterday. She came into the shop to collect on our bet and get her oil changed after she scheduled a brake job," Ben said nonchalantly as he sat down by the counter where Luke was chopping green peppers on a small, white cutting board.

"Oh yeah? She didn't mention that." Granted, he'd been doing his best to avoid her this last week, so it would have been hard for her to discuss it with him.

"I think she was discreetly trying to pump me for information about you. When was the last time you saw her, anyway?" Ben said while reaching over and snagging a piece of ham that had been sliced to go into the omelet.

"A week ago."

Ben raised his eyebrows at Luke's answer. "I'm willing to bet you haven't told her about Adriana yet."

"What makes you say that?" Luke snarled as he cracked eggs to whisk in a bowl.

Ben shrugged as he attempted to steal more ingredients. "She was asking how long I've known you, how long we've been roommates, if I've been tempted to adopt any of our fosters, things like that. If she knew about Yanna, she wouldn't be asking. Plus, you've been dodging her, which is fucking stupid, by the way, and the only thing that makes sense is you haven't told her."

Luke both loved and hated Ben knew him so damn well. Right now, he was feeling like the little boy in front of the principal, accounting for offenses he knew better than to commit but couldn't help himself. He set the pan on the stove with a little more enthusiasm than necessary.

"No, I haven't told her. I know I need to, and I am going to. I don't want to scare her off. I want to be able to say that it's simply an issue with paperwork being processed when I tell her."

"So, basically, you're planning on hiding out for another four years?" Ben was not cutting him a break today.

Luke wanted to be defensive but knew he had no right to be.

"Actually, I hired a new guy who is heading to Mexico Friday. I'm hoping by next week, I'll have something more concrete."

"That's great, man." Ben seemed genuinely happy for him while he poured his second cup of coffee. "Why you ever married that bitch..." His friend stopped short, horrified. "Shit, dude, I'm sorry. I know why."

Luke gave a sad smile. "Don't worry about it."

"I'll be glad when you are out of her grip and can start living your life again."

The sergeant sighed and poured the ingredients into the hot pan. "You and me both, brother. You and me both."

"You better lock Cassie down soon, my friend."

An actual growl came out of Luke's throat. "Why do you say that?"

"Well, aside from every man with a working dick at the shop being interested in her, including my customers, she's a cool chick with a hot—"

Luke cut him off, pointing the spatula ominously at his friend. "You fucking finish that thought, and it will be through broken teeth."

"I was gonna say hot car. She's got a hot car," Ben smirked and took a sip from his mug.

"Uh huh." Luke returned the smirk, then let the gravity of the situation take hold. With a frown, he carefully flipped the omelet. "I know I need to make things official with her, but I feel like I can't until I tell her about Yanna."

"I get it, bro. I do. And for what it's worth, I think you're right about holding off. Alls I'm sayin' is, don't wait too long. You need to get that shit taken care of."

Luke didn't know if Ben meant his divorce or claiming Cassie as his, but it didn't matter either way. He needed to get both taken care of. Like yesterday.

****

Cassie

She hadn't seen Luke since their marriage and babies talk eleven days ago, and his texts had been brief and to the point. He even declined her invitations to come over, regardless of what time he finished work. He always had an excuse—he had to go home and let Rex out, he had reports to write, he had workers coming to the house in the morning, and last night's excuse, he was too tired.

If she were more insecure, she would be worried their conversation was the reason. Thank God she was totally secure when it came to all things Luke Rivas.

Yeah, right.

Cassie went so far as to get her oil changed at Ben's shop, hoping to run into Ben and somehow get him to spill what was going on with her Sergeant Orgasm. She hated wondering if he'd really been working like he said he had or if he was blowing her off.

She even changed Luke's name back to plain old *Luke Rivas* in her phone, trying to distance herself from the little white picket fence fantasy she had briefly imbibed. Luke was obviously having second thoughts if he'd even been sincere in the first place, and she needed to get her head straight about him.

She was turning into someone she didn't like. Insecure. Questioning herself. Was she being too clingy? Or not giving him enough attention? Maybe he wasn't interested now that he knew how she felt about babies. Maybe he'd met someone new?

Ohmygod! This obsessive shit is exactly why she didn't do serious, lovey-dovey relationships.

Thank God, her niece, Danielle, had arrived in town, and Cassie now had something else to focus on. If Luke didn't want to spend time with her that was fine. She had better things to do, anyway.

She dressed for Brenna's Saturday night impromptu party in honor of Danielle in jeans and a fitted, grey University of Arizona tee to show her niece her support. Dee was about to start her junior year at her dad's alma mater. Danny Roberts had been an outstanding second baseman at the U of A and was drafted his junior year. He met Brenna two years later after he'd been called up to the majors and was starting at second base for the Padres. Kyle Montgomery, Danielle's Godfather, had played shortstop. Kyle was the first person Cassie saw when she walked into Brenna's beach house kitchen.

"Cass!" he exclaimed as he picked her up and swung her around in a big hug. The house was buzzing with people, something that hadn't occurred since before Danny's death. She loved Ron had brought her sister back to life.

Friends of both Ron and Brenna as well as Danielle meandered from the kitchen into the adjoining family room and spilled out onto the patio leading to the beach on the Pacific while the two of them stood at the island counter in the kitchen. He helped himself to a beer in the fridge and poured her a glass of Riesling from a bottle sitting in a red and blue tub of ice next to the refrigerator.

Kyle handed Cassie her drink, and with her thumb, wiped the red colored lipstick from his cheek where she'd kissed him. "How have you been? You seemed like you were up to something when I saw you at the wedding."

Kyle gave a guilty smile. "I've been fucking great."

She raised one eyebrow. "Anything you'd like to share with the class?"

Shaking his head, he couldn't seem to stop smiling when he replied cryptically. "Not yet. Hopefully, soon."

"Aw, come on, Kyle. Give me a hint."

He tapped her nose with his index finger. "Not a chance, sweet pea. I'm not jinxing it."

"Fine," she pouted. "Have your secrets."

Leaning back with his elbows on the counter, he gave her a knowing grin. "Speaking of secrets, your sister tells me you have a six foot one of your own."

It was Cassie's turn to smile as she brought her wine glass to her lips. "Maaaybe."

"Well, well, well. I never thought I'd see the day. Is he coming later? When do I get to meet him?"

She shook her head, trying to hide her frown. "No, I think he's working tonight."

"You *think* he's working?" Kyle asked incredulously.

"Well, I haven't really talked to him very much this week." *Or last week*, but Kyle didn't need to know that.

"You haven't talked to him much this week," he stated flatly. "But Bren tells me this is serious?" Kyle stood up tall and gave her a look that was something between pity and condescension, so she found herself scrambling to explain.

"He's on the SD SWAT team, and they've been really busy. We haven't had a lot of time to talk."

"Hmph, I see," The former shortstop nodded, grabbing a tortilla chip from a blue, glass bowl on the counter next to a dish of salsa. She knew he was placating her, and for some reason, it really pissed her off.

"Why are you being like that?"

He paused from taking a pull of his beer and frowned. "Like what?"

"Like an asshole."

Her outburst seemed to surprise him, and he lowered his bottle as he contemplated his response. Her reaction sort of surprised herself. She was always very accommodating to Kyle, and he'd never been anything but kind to her.

"I'm not trying to be an asshole."

"Then why do you have that smug look on your face?" she accused.

He tried to look innocent, like he had no idea what she was talking about.

"I never thought you, of all people, would ever put up with that."

"Put up with what? How is understanding a man has been busy working putting up with anything?" Her tone sounded way too defensive even to her own ears.

With raised eyebrows, Kyle threw the mantra she liked to quote back at her. "If a man wants to be with you, he will make it happen. No exceptions."

"Oh, Jesus Christ, Kyle," she seethed, spilling her glass on the counter when she set it down too hard. "This isn't the same thing. This is two, busy professionals trying to have a relationship. That takes some understanding and flexibility. If you were in a relationship, you'd get that."

"Hey, I'm sorry." He brought his hands chest high in the universal *I surrender* gesture. "You're right. I'm talking out of my ass. Don't be mad at me."

The truth was, she wasn't really mad at Kyle, he was only saying out loud what she had been considering over the last week. She felt embarrassed someone else was also thinking it and had to rationalize it to him like she had been doing herself.

"I'm not mad," she said in a low voice, looking past him at the cupboards.

He bent his knees so his face was at the height of hers. "No?"

"No. I'm sorry I yelled at you." She finally looked at him, tears threatening to fall from her eyes.

"Oh, Cass. I'm so fucking sorry. Don't listen to me, I'm an idiot." He set his bottle down and pulled her in for a long hug. "Don't cry, baby girl. It'll be okay," he whispered in her hair.

Feeling the tears wet his navy polo shirt, she let out a long sigh once she stopped crying. Kyle laughed, then briefly hugged her tighter.

"Love is definitely not for wimps."

She had to agree. No, it most definitely is not.

The theme from the television show, *Cops* started blaring from her back pocket, and she loosened her hug from Kyle to retrieve her phone. It wasn't the most original ringtone for Luke, but she liked it.

"Is that him?"

"Yeah," she murmured as she looked at his smiling picture on her phone

"Invite him over," he mouthed.

She shook her head while answering, "Hi there!" and headed toward the guest room to talk to him in a quieter place.

****

Luke

Just the sound of Cassie's voice made his mood lighter and brought a smile to his lips.

I've missed her so damn much.

Luke had wanted to take her up on her invitation and crawl into bed with her every night she asked, more than anything. Last night, in particular, but, the murder-suicide call he was on had drained him. The week, in general, had kicked his ass even before his team showed up last night to the nondescript suburban home where a man was possibly holding his ex-wife hostage. He knew before they breached the front door they were too late. Every fucking call for over a week had been a shit show, so between work, hiring his new P.I., and worrying about how Cassie was going to take the news about Adriana, he was spent. He needed to be thinking straight and on his A-game when he was with Cass, or he'd end up spilling his guts.

He was willing to take his chances tonight though. He needed to wrap his arms around her and hold her close until morning, maybe even noon. Being with her soothed his soul; he even slept better when he was next to her.

"Hi, baby doll," he responded to her greeting. "It's good to hear your voice. I've missed you so damn much." There was a pause on her end, and when she replied in a soft voice, it sounded like she was sniffling.

"I've missed you too."

"Hey, you okay?"

Silence.

"Babe?" he asked quietly.

"I'm fine," she squeaked out.

"I'm on my way over."

He heard her take a deep breath, and her voice was stronger when she told him, "No, I'm not at home. I'm at Danielle's party."

He waited for her to invite him over.

"I don't know how late I'll be. Maybe we can catch up tomorrow," she stated coolly.

He deserved this. Of course, she was upset he hadn't attempted to see her for almost two weeks. He'd hated it, too and knew he was a chicken shit for the way he had handled things.

"Why don't I come there?"

"No, that's okay. I'm sure you're tired."

Oh, his proud, little, stubborn girl, throwing his excuse from last night at him.

"I'm not tired, actually. I was able to sleep late today and even got a run in with Rex. Let me get changed, and I'll head that way."

"No, really. It's fine," she said with finality.

The fuck it is fine. He understood she was mad, and he worried maybe he'd made a big mistake being away from her for so long.

"What's going on, doll?"

"Nothing. I, um... You don't have to..." She let out a deep sigh. "Let's just meet for lunch tomorrow at The Pier. Say noon?"

"Yeah, okay. Sure." He didn't even try to hide his bewildered tone.

"See you tomorrow then."

It seemed like she was about to hang up, so he urgently called out, "Cassie!"

"Yeah?"

"I love you, doll."

Her pause was too long for his liking before she finally replied, "Love you, too," then hung up.

He tossed his phone on the bed, then started pulling on a pair of jeans. There was no fucking way he was waiting until tomorrow to see her. Besides, he remembered Brenna had sent him a text earlier this week, inviting him tonight. He had been on his way to serve a search warrant and forgotten all about it until Cassie told him where she was.

It would be rude not to show up to his future sister-in-law's party after she invited him, right?

Chapter Twenty-Eight

Cassie

She shouldn't have told Luke not to come, but she was feeling vulnerable after her conversation with Kyle and trying to regain some semblance of her pride. Now, all she could do was feign a smile as she talked to other partygoers, all the while wishing Luke was there next to her.

Cassie missed the smell of his subtle aftershave and soap, the way the lines around his green eyes crinkled when he smiled, his deep voice, and how he always had his arm around her waist or shoulder whenever they were together.

Was it too late to call him back?

With a sigh, she conceded she wasn't that desperate. It was a big enough blow to her self-esteem when he didn't want to come over each time she asked despite her almost begging. Besides, Kyle was right. Luke sure as fuck wasn't putting much effort into being with her, and she was worth the effort, goddammit. She needed to remember that.

Cooper Johnson definitely seemed to think so. He looked hot as hell in the light blue Henley, showcasing his tan, blonde hair, and blue eyes, not to mention muscles that would make most girls go weak in the knees, and he'd been eye-fucking her all night. Frankly, there was no one she felt safer flirting with than Cooper. He knew where he stood with her, so she thought he was harmless. Still, she had to admit, it was a much-needed ego boost after Luke's rejection, so she didn't exactly discourage him, but she didn't encourage him either.

Okay, so maybe not discouraging him was technically encouraging him.

Tomato, tomahto.

Cooper's charm and deliberate bad jokes were at least making her laugh, something she hadn't done for ten days. Still, when she caught him staring at her tits as they sat around the fire pit on the patio drinking, she felt a little guilty like maybe she was leading him on. Cassie tugged her neckline up as she leaned forward.

"You do know I'm dating Luke exclusively, right?" she quietly asked him.

"I know, and I'm trying like hell to respect that," he smirked as he brought his eyes to her face. "Promise me if you're ever *not* dating him, you'll give me a shot. Deal?

With a grin, she raised her glass. "Deal."

She knew deep down, the Marine was a good guy, and if he ever did decide to settle down for real, whoever he chose would be one lucky woman. Cooper flashed his boyish grin at her, and Cassie understood why Brenna and Ron liked him so much.

"Glad that's settled."

A deep voice behind her made her heart sing. "What's settled?"

Then she remembered she was mad and tried to contain her smile.

****

Luke

He had to tamp down his jealousy when he stood in the doorway and saw Cassie sitting with Cooper by the fire on the patio, a huge smile on her face. His girl should only be smiling at him like that, not some other guy. Taking a second to collect himself, he made his way to them as Cassie raised her glass and announced definitively, "Deal," which seemed to please Cooper.

Luke tried to keep a growl from escaping his throat when he asked what they'd settled. Her panicked eyes and stuttering to answer when she turned around to look at him weren't helping him feel good about things. He pinned her with his stare, eyebrows raised.

"If I'm ever single, we'll go on a date," she sheepishly replied.

Yeah, Cooper didn't need to worry about that. It wasn't happenin'. She wasn't ever going to be single again, not if he had anything to say about it.

Luke put his hands on her shoulders and leaned over to kiss her cheek, then came around the bench to sit next to her.

"Sorry, buddy," he laughed as wrapped his arm around her waist. "She's off the market." Her body was rigid next to his.

"For now," Cassie murmured under her breath. She said it so softly, he wasn't sure if she meant for him to hear it or not. Regardless, he wasn't letting her get away with it.

"For always. You're not getting rid of me that easily, baby doll," he growled low in her ear.

"Hmph," was her challenging reply.

He'd show her *hmph*. Holding her chin between his thumb and index finger, he tilted her face toward him and looked into her beautiful blue eyes.

"I'm sorry it's been so hectic. I've really missed you."

Her eyes softened, and Luke leaned in for a tender kiss.

Cooper's baritone voice interrupted them. "Okay, well, see you guys later. I'm going to go mingle with the single people."

Cassie stood up and hugged Cooper tight. "It was good seeing you, my friend. Take care and keep in touch, okay?"

A small smile formed on the Marine Captain's lips, and he gave her a wink. "Count on it."

He turned to Luke and shook his hand firmly with a smirk. "Rivas, good seeing you. Take good care of our girl."

*She isn't our girl. She's **my** girl.*

Borrowing Cooper's words, Luke grinned back. "Count on it."

Luke settled in next to Cassie again. He could tell by the way she didn't melt into him like she usually did, she was pissed. He couldn't blame her.

"I promise I'll make my absence up to you this weekend."

Ignoring his pledge, she blustered, "What are you doing here? I told you not to come."

Nobody but his command staff tells him what to do, but Luke decided to take a more contrite approach and not blurt out that tidbit. Yet. He stroked her cheek with the back of his fingertips.

"I came to see you, Cass. I've missed you and needed to kiss your sexy lips."

Her eyes shone with sarcasm when she looked up at him. "Sure, you did."

"What the fuck's that supposed to mean?" he snarled. This was not how Date Number Ten was supposed to go. This was the Tenure Date.

"I don't know," she shrugged. "What's changed? You haven't wanted to see me for the last week and a half. *Now* you need to see me? When I told you *not* to come? You sure you're not too tired?" She put air quotes around *too tired.*

"No, I'm not too tired. I told you, I've been busy with work."

"Whatever." She tried to shrug his arm off of her.

That pissed him off. "I guess it's a good thing I came tonight, otherwise, you might have gone home with Cooper."

Her body froze as she let out a small gasp, then shoved him away from her.

He knew instantly he had fucked up. *Shit, wrong thing! Wrong thing!*

"Are you fucking kidding me right now?" she spat out in disgust. "I'm not the one who went MIA after his alleged love confession. You don't get to turn this around on me, Luke. *You're* the one who didn't want to see me. I'm supposed to sit home and wait around for when the desire to be with me again strikes your fancy? Fuck you."

She got up and stormed off to the kitchen. He saw Cooper watching their exchange with interest, but the man didn't go after her. Which was a smart move on his part. The way Luke was feeling right now, he wasn't above a good fight. But goddammit, not with her.

He followed her into the house where she was cleaning the kitchen with gusto. She heaved the garbage out of the can and tied it closed with force. He'd smile if he didn't think it'd piss her off more if she caught him. Trailing her into the three-car garage where she was taking the trash, he opened the lid to the larger barrel for her to deposit the bag without any acknowledgment from her.

She turned to head back to the house when he grabbed her by the elbow and tugged her toward him. She didn't fight him, but she didn't help him, remaining silent as the grave. He held her by both elbows and scanned her face. She was doing her best to appear bored, but he could see the pulse in her neck beating fast.

"I shouldn't have said that about Cooper, I'm sorry. I was totally out of line."

"Damn right you were," she scoffed.

"I'm sorry I've been so busy." His voice softened, and he let go of her elbows to stroke her upper arms. "I've missed the fuck out of you but work really has been hell."

She closed her eyes tight for a moment as if absorbing what he was telling her. Opening her eyes, she looked defeated.

"I'm the one who's sorry. You don't owe me anything. I know you were busy with work, and the last thing you need is me laying on the guilt trip about not seeing me."

He didn't like her martyred tone. One arm slid around her waist while the other brushed the hair from her face.

"Don't be sorry, baby. I'm an asshole. I do owe you, and I should have done a better job of being with you." His lips hovered over hers. "It wasn't because I didn't want to though," he whispered before capturing her mouth with his.

The worry about hiding his marriage, missing her, wanting her, coursed through his veins and poured through his kiss. He needed this woman like he needed oxygen. He wouldn't make the mistake of staying away from her again.

With any luck, the private investigator he hired would have his divorce papers signed by Monday, and there'd be nothing left hanging over his head.

At first, she returned the kiss with fervor, but then she pushed him away, hitting his chest with her tiny fists when he wouldn't release his hold on her. He saw the tears in her eyes, and it hit him. He'd made her feel vulnerable. *Cassie Sullivan isn't used to being vulnerable.* That wasn't something he could take lightly.

Luke held her tight against him and murmured in her hair, "I'm sorry. I should have tried harder. I promise it wasn't because I was regretting anything between us or having second thoughts. I was busy, that's all there was to it."

He could feel her shoulders shaking as she quietly cried. He felt like such a fuck for making her cry, and all he could do now was hold her. He breathed in the scent of her shampoo and closed his eyes, relishing the feel of her in his arms. He didn't like that she was crying, but he liked that he was with her while she did.

She took a shuddering breath, then began to strike him against his shoulders, hard.

"You asshole! You don't get to just disappear on me like that!"

Holding his arms up to defend himself, he exclaimed, "I know! I know! I fucked up, Cass. I don't know what else to say, other than *I'm sorry* again." He tentatively reached for her. "So, so sorry, baby doll. I love you, let me make it up to you?"

She arched away from his grip and narrowed her eyes. "How are you going to do that?"

Luke pulled her close, not caring she wasn't exactly willing as he encircled her waist with his hands. "You'll see. Give me another chance."

When she said with a completely even tone, "Okay, but only because you have a big dick," he knew he was safe to kiss her again.

"But blue balls," he muttered before digging his hands into her hair and drawing her face to his.

****

Cassie

Luke's aforementioned big dick was pressed against her stomach as he continued to kiss her. She could sense his relief when he possessively held her tight against him. He seemed like he was genuinely worried about losing her.

As he lifted her up under her ass, she wrapped her legs around him, and he walked out the side door of the garage and proceeded straight to his car, only pausing to get the fob out of his pocket and unlock the doors before gingerly depositing her in the passenger seat.

"We'll get your car tomorrow."

"I need to send Brenna a text. I don't want her to worry."

He nodded, closed the door, and came around the front of the car so she could continue.

"Except I don't have my phone."

Cassie opened her door, and before Luke had a chance to object, got out and made a beeline for the front door of the beach house. He could make it up to her after she'd properly said goodbye to everyone. Besides, it felt like she gave in too easily. She didn't want him to think she was a pushover, even though she was one when it came to Luke Rivas. How he did it, she wasn't sure. His green eyes must contain some magic in them.

She forgave him the second his deep voice said he was sorry. Actually, it was relief more than forgiveness she was feeling. He still wanted to be with her, and she was thankful.

Thankful?

What. The. Fuck.

He totally blew her off for the past eleven days, and she felt *gratitude* because he still wanted her when he finally decided to show up?

His palm was firmly planted against the small of her back as they walked back into the party through the front door. His commanding presence next to her made her feel safe, and she admitted it, his apology was what her heart needed to hear.

He whispered in her ear, "Hurry and get your things, doll, I need to hold you."

At that moment, Cassie felt so wanted and loved by him. She was happy, giddy even, and conceded, yes, she was *grateful* he was a part of her life.

But she was going to make him wait. Not necessarily suffer, but she wasn't rolling over that easily.

Maybe Luke Rivas was finally going to know what it was like to beg.

Chapter Twenty-Nine

Luke

Instead of collecting her things and leaving, Cassie dragged Luke by the hand to introduce him to everyone she knew at the party. A man he recognized as baseball legend, Kyle Montgomery lit up with a broad smile when they approached him.

Cassie tried talking baseball, but he didn't seem interested in chatting about the sport that made him famous. Instead, he focused his attention on Luke, going from pleasant gentleman to overprotective big brother in a heartbeat, eyeing him up and down as he took a swig of beer.

"So, Cass says you've been too busy to call her this week." It was a statement, not a question, and one that dripped with censure. Disapproval was not something Luke was used to, personally or professionally, but the retired shortstop was giving it to him in spades.

The little smile she was unsuccessfully trying to suppress seemed to indicate Cassie loved it. He was going to spank her little ass pink for this later.

"It was a pretty shitty week for SWAT, no doubt, but I should've done a better job of making time for my girl." He drew her close. "I definitely fucked up, but it won't happen again." He bit his tongue when he almost called Kyle, *sir*. The look on Kyle's face made Luke feel like he was being reprimanded by one of his commanding officers in the Marines. Fortunately, like his COs, Kyle appreciated Luke's honesty and willingness to own his mistakes, so the man lightened up. They ended up having a great conversation about

San Diego politics, and the things Luke had to endure as a police officer.

Cassie excused herself to go talk with ladies she knew. Before unwrapping his arm from around her waist, Luke squeezed her hip, a warning she was in trouble later. Hearing her giggle as she walked off, he wondered, *was it really punishment if she looked forward to it?*

He couldn't wait to find out.

Luke found her in the kitchen, alone, refilling her wine glass. Running his hand discreetly over her ass as he came up behind her, he whispered, "Are you almost ready to go?"

She gave a mischievous smile. "Almost."

He crowded her into the corner of the cabinets, pressing his erection against her. "You're playing with fire, doll."

His cocky little minx just grinned. "I seem to recall you've told me that before."

"Little girl..." he growled.

"Yes?" she asked sweetly.

"You have no idea what you're getting yourself into, baby." His tone was ominous.

Cassie traced her index finger across his chest. "Oh, on the contrary. I think I do."

"You sure about that?" He grazed his thumb over a diamond-pointed nipple jutting out from under the big red A on her t-shirt.

Her whimper made his cock so hard, it was going to punch a hole through his zipper. He hovered his mouth over hers and murmured, "The things I'm going to do to you when I get you home, baby doll..."

She kissed his cheek and skimmed her fingertips in a circular motion around the hair at his neckline. Standing on her tiptoes, she pressed her tits against his chest, and breathed in his ear, "Promise?"

Luke sucked a breath through his teeth. With his hands on her hips, he held her tight against him and whispered back, "Can we go now? Please?"

A satisfied grin spread across her beautiful, heart-shaped face, and she teased, "Since you asked me so nicely."

He bent down and kissed her mouth without hesitation, tangling his fingers in her silky hair and tugging it into his fist. She clung to his neck and pulled him closer. The urgent way she returned his kiss was dizzying.

"Alright, alright. Get a room already."

They broke apart at the sound of Brenna's voice chastising them. Looking at Cassie's sister with her hands on her hips and an eyebrow raised, but a small grin on her face, made him chuckle with embarrassment.

Cassie peeked over his shoulder at her sibling. "Like you have any room to talk."

"Okay, I'll give you that." Brenna grinned like only a newlywed can. "But we behave in other people's homes!"

"That's only because you two never leave your house!"

Luke took a more sheepish approach. "Sorry, I haven't seen her in ten days, I got a little carried away."

"Eleven," Cassie softly corrected.

Shit. How did he go eleven days not seeing her?

Oh, that's right. He was hiding from her. Scared he'd spill his guts about his marriage.

Just a few more days, Luke. You can do this. Keep it together until you get the paperwork filed. Then you can come clean.

In the meantime, he was going to have to find ways to occupy their time so he didn't even have a chance to act suspiciously.

He had a few ideas in mind how he planned on doing that.

Chapter Thirty

Cassie

Luke insisted she ride with him even though it was going to be a pain in the ass tomorrow to come back and get her car. But the smoldering look he gave her as they approached his Challenger made her suddenly not give a damn about the inconvenience. They would worry about it tomorrow.

The sexual tension between them was palpable. When he put the car in the direction of his house, she looked over at him.

"We're going to your house?"

"Ben is away for the weekend, and I don't want to leave Rex alone for the night."

"No, you can't leave him alone. Is Ben gone for business or pleasure?" She was grasping for anything mundane to talk about, trying to diffuse the sexual tension in the confined space.

"Do you really want to talk about my roommate's weekend getaway plans, right now?" he asked with a small grin as his hand firmly began to rub her slit through her jeans.

"No," she giggled, "I guess not." All she could think about was having his throbbing cock deep inside her. She took off her seatbelt and leaned over the console, intent on unbuttoning his jeans and sliding his shaft between her lips as he drove. He grabbed her wrist and stopped her from touching his denim.

"Uh uh, baby doll. You're not getting this cock until you take your punishment."

With a gulp, she asked, "Punishment?"

One corner of his mouth turned up. "Punishment. You didn't think you were getting away with what you did tonight without having your ass spanked, did you?"

Well, yeah, she did.

"I'm a grown woman, you can't spank me."

His raised eyebrows and subtle smirk suggested, *Wanna bet?*

"You know your safe word, doll. Otherwise, yeah, I'm turning your bare ass over my knee and spanking it 'til it's pink."

Did her lady parts start to tingle more? What the hell was that about?

Cassie buckled her seatbelt and sat back, crossing her arms over her chest.

"We'll see about that."

Pushing her legs apart so he could resume caressing her over her jeans, Luke chuckled. "There's an awful lot of heat being generated here." He undid the button and lowered her zipper before sliding his hand under the waistband of her panties. Running a finger up and down her soaked folds, he flicked her clit, then dipped inside her.

She was such a shameless slut when it came to him. She should be squeezing her thighs together, instead of spreading them so he could have easier access. Fuck this man turned her on.

"Mmm, so wet for me," he murmured as he plunged his digit in and out of her.

She let out a whimper when his palm put pressure on her clit, and she found herself pushing against his hand.

The car slowed down as they maneuvered the streets in his subdivision. He hit the button for the garage door and withdrew his hand from her pussy. It was all she could do not to beg him to keep going. Luke closed the garage door and turned the engine off. He turned to look at her, and she could feel his entire being was in Alpha Dom mode.

"Go into my room, undress, and wait for me. Be kneeling by the bed when I come in."

She snorted internally, thinking, *kneeling, yeah sure.* Shouldn't she be thinking *yeah sure* to all his demands? Instead of saying anything, she gulped and nodded her head.

"Good girl," he whispered with a slight smile before getting out and coming around to open her door. Helping her out of the car, he murmured in her ear, "What's your safe word, Cass?"

"Red," she uttered softly.

"Red," he affirmed. Tilting her chin up, he kissed her lips tenderly, then rested his forehead against hers, caressing her jawline.

"I'll never hurt you, baby doll."

"I know," she said so quietly even she had a hard time hearing her words.

He reached down and grabbed a handful of flesh from her ass.

"Bedroom. Naked. Kneeling. Now," he snarled as he swatted her bottom.

With one last look at him, she made her way into the house and into his bedroom.

Luke

He came in from the garage, let Rex out, fed him, washed his hands, and removed his shirt before walking into his bedroom. His cock was hard in anticipation of seeing his beautiful girl, naked and kneeling in submission.

He should have known better.

She was naked, but instead of kneeling, she was sitting on the edge of his bed, her legs crossed in seductive defiance. It was all he could to suppress his chuckle at her deliberate rebellion.

"Tsk tsk. Naughty girls get punished, good girls get orgasms," he said as he approached her.

She shrugged, pretending to be unimpressed, as usual.

"So, if I would have been kneeling, you wouldn't spank me?"

"Now, I didn't say *that*..." he laughed quietly. He sat down next to her and placed a bed pillow on his lap, then patted it. "Come on."

With only a bit of hesitation, she crawled across his lap, bare bottom up. He stroked her beautiful, round butt reverently, sliding his hands between her toned thighs, and casually inserting his ring finger into her slick cunt.

"So beautiful," he moaned.

She relaxed into the pillow, her face on the comforter before he delivered five quick blows to each cheek. Her only response—after jumping at the initial swat—was to flinch in anticipation. After landing the last strike, he caressed her reddening ass with care. When he stroked her inner thighs, he found they were wet with her excitement.

"Green, doll?"

"Green," she purred.

A smile involuntarily formed on his lips, and he spread her ass apart, fingering her pussy with his thumb. Was what he was doing technically *thumbing* her? The heat coming from her tight entrance, along with her soft moans made what it was called irrelevant.

"Such a good girl, to lie here and take it," he praised as he slid his wet thumb from her pussy and up her crack. Circling her back door, he spread her wetness before breaching her star. He felt her tense up, and he paused.

"Color, Cass," he demanded.

She hesitated, then he felt her relax. "Green."

He moved his thumb in and out of her asshole slowly as he began to tend to her pussy and clit with his other hand. She moaned, and he withdrew his thumb to release a set of five more blows to her ass without stopping his attention to her pussy. She gasped, soaking his hand that continued to finger fuck her, while he tended to her pink ass with care.

"Such a good, little submissive slut," he lauded as he began to fuck her faster and deeper. "Mmm, keep that ass in the air for me, baby doll."

The wet noises from her dripping pussy being fucked by his hand filled the room.

Whack! Whack! Whack! Whack! Whack! Whack!

His hand slapping her bottom echoed with her moans off the walls.

Whack! Whack! Whack! Whack! Whack! Whack!

"That's it, take it like a good whore."

She cried out something unintelligible, then Luke felt her tight cunt clench around his fingers as her body began to convulse on his lap. She gasped and cried out more. He'd never seen her jerk so much, and it felt like her pussy was contracting around his digits.

Her body stopped twitching, and except for her heaving chest, she laid perfectly still in his lap, her face pressed against his bed. He leaned over and rubbed her ass in circles as he kissed it, murmuring, "So beautiful."

She didn't move her face from where it rested when she uttered, "That was the best fucking orgasm I've ever had."

With a grin, he bent over to kiss her cheek. "That's because you secretly love being submissive."

She sat up quickly, a solemn look on her face. "No! Well, I mean, obviously, yes. It's just... I've never wanted to be, you know, before. Only with you."

Although he already knew she'd never been with anyone strong enough to handle her, his ego quadrupled in size.

"It's because I'm your man, and your body knows it belongs to me."

"See? Shit like that. I don't fucking belong to anyone, but goddamn, when you say it, it turns me on so much. It shouldn't excite me like it does."

He winked at her. "It's because it's true."

She stared at him for a long time before conceding, "I guess it is." She didn't seem happy about that revelation.

"I'll take good care of you, doll. I promise."

She tossed the pillow spotted with her juices, straddled him, and grabbed his face with both hands while looking into his eyes. "You better," she murmured before nipping his bottom lip.

"I will," he said solemnly while grabbing a fistful of hair to hold her head in place as he took control of the kiss.

Cassie started to grind her naked hips on his hard cock under his jeans. She reached between their bodies for the jean's button.

"Can we finally take these off?"

He smirked as he undid the button and zipper, and she lifted her butt so he could slide them down his hips. He held her at the small of her back with one hand while trying to pull his Levi's completely off with the other. A feat made harder as Cassie grabbed his face with both hands again and kissed him passionately as she resumed rolling her hips over him.

"I missed you so much, baby," she gasped desperately when they came up for air.

Looking up at her, Luke pushed her hair behind her ear. "I missed you too, doll."

His palms firmly grasping her underneath her shoulder blades, he thrust his cock deep inside her womb. They moaned in unison as he filled her pussy.

Cassie wrapped her arms around his neck and began to ride him slowly. She was breathtaking—uninhibited with her wild hair, flushed cheeks, and swollen lips from his hard kisses. Luke lifted her luscious tits, kneading and squeezing them before drawing a nipple between his teeth. She bent back with a moan, offering her firm, pale globes to him.

He lifted her off him and steered her onto her stomach. She tried to get on her hands and knees, but he slipped the pillow under her tummy before pressing on her back, guiding her body down and pushed her legs together.

"This is the position you told me about. Your favorite."

"It is," he responded as he slid behind her, aligning his cock with her entrance, and pushing inside.

"Oh. My. God," she moaned. "That feels so fucking good!"

Luke chuckled in her ear, "That's why it's my favorite."

He rhythmically began to move in and out of her, fucking her at a steady pace while trying to keep his orgasm at bay, which wasn't easy. It had been eleven days since he was inside her, and he could feel her getting wetter with each stroke.

"Ohhhh, yes, Luke. Just like that. Your cock feels amazing, baby," she crooned.

He didn't need any encouragement, but she kept providing it.

"Oh, God, yes! Fuck me, baby. Please!"

"Faster, Luke, oh yes!"

And finally, "Oh, don't stop! Please don't stop! Yes! Yes! YES!"

As her pussy quivered around his shaft, he drove into her hard and fast, his release not far behind hers. He held her by her hips while he came inside her, plunging in deep one last time before stretching his body out fully over hers. His fingers entwined with hers, and he dragged her hands over her head as he completely enveloped her body with his, careful to distribute his weight on his forearms.

"I love you, Cassie Sullivan," he panted in her ear while he tried to recover. "Don't ever doubt that for a second. You're my girl. Always."

She kissed his arm, probably because that was all she could reach with how he had her pinned.

"I love you, too, Luke Santiago Rivas. I like being your girl."

He rolled over, pulling her with him. She adjusted her position so they were chest to chest.

"I'm sorry I was such an ass," he confessed, then wanted to punch his own face.

Fuck! He didn't need to open that can of worms.

Cassie didn't miss the opportunity either.

"What's been bothering you?" she asked gently as she lowered her head on his chest.

Luke shook his head subtly. "I told you, doll. Work has been crazy."

She raised up on her elbow, looking directly at him for a few beats, obviously unconvinced.

"I tell you what. If you promise to quit lying to me, I'll promise to back off until you're ready to tell me what's going on with you. But under no circumstances are you allowed to fall off the face of the earth again. That I can't handle."

"I swear, I'm not going anywhere. You're stuck with me. Just give me a few more days to get things sorted out. I promise I will tell you everything."

"Should I be worried?" she asked cautiously.

He pulled her back against him. "Cassie, no. Not at all."

That seemed to placate her, for now, and she relaxed her head back on his chest, lightly drawing imaginary shapes on his pecs with her index finger.

"Don't disappear on me again, Luke Rivas. I don't think my heart could take it."

Talk about a punch to the gut.

He tightened his arms around her and vowed, "Never again."

His heart wouldn't be able to take it either.

Chapter Thirty-One

Cassie

She woke up as dawn began to break, wrapped in Luke's strong arms, and smiled. It was going to be a beautiful Sunday.

She carefully eased out of his embrace so she didn't disturb him. Finding the shirt he had worn last night, she pulled it over her head and breathed in deep—it still smelled like him. After using the bathroom, she headed to the kitchen to start the coffeemaker. Rex followed her, happy someone was up to let him out.

Cassie piled her hair on her head with a hairband from her purse, grabbed her phone and a cup of coffee, and went outside to sit on the patio and enjoy the quiet of the morning. When her mug was almost empty, Luke appeared in the doorway in his boxer briefs and adorable bedhead, coffee cup in hand. She wished she could take a picture of him at that moment. This was the side of Luke Rivas only she got to see. Okay, Ben did too, but it wasn't the same.

He stepped outside with a smile and, instead of sitting in his own chair, slid behind her on the lounger she was sitting on.

His chin on her shoulder, he murmured, "Good morning, doll. You sleep okay?"

"Mmm, like a baby. You?"

"Yeah, I always sleep better when you're next to me."

That little admission made her heart happy. How silly was that?

Rex came bounding up, wiggling with excitement to see more people awake who would be willing to play with him.

Luke laughed, ruffling the dog's head playfully. "Okay, buddy, we'll go for a run." He shot Cassie a look. "Er, walk."

She smiled, thinking of the last time they took Rex for a walk on the beach. She could get used to this routine.

Is this what they called *domestic bliss*?

Heaven help her.

****

Luke

They spent the morning together until he had to leave for work. Cassie invited him to come to her place once he finished, but he declined since Ben wasn't returning until tomorrow.

"I really wish my condo was a more dog-friendly place," she lamented.

He shrugged, noncommittally. "We'll make it work."

God, he hoped he heard from Mike Randall soon.

Luke wanted nothing more than to suggest they buy a place together. Somewhere that had enough room for dogs and babies with an office for her, a man cave for him, and a hot tub. They were going to have a hot tub. He was dying to fuck her in one ever since he saw her getting out of Brenna's, naked on New Year's Eve.

He was going to buy one of those plaques to hang outside their door: *Luke and Cassie Rivas*. He'd coach their sons' little league teams and go to every one of their daughters' dance recitals or games or both. Their kids would grow up with dogs and learn the importance of...

What. The. Fuck?

He really needed to learn how to dial it in. She hadn't even agreed to marry him yet, let alone have his babies.

Chapter Thirty-Two

Luke

He heard from Mike Randall early Monday afternoon. He'd located Adriana, and she agreed to sign the papers with some conditions.

Of course, she had conditions. She was probably going to try to squeeze more money out of him.

"There are some things I need to discuss with you in person, Luke." Mike's voice was somber.

"I don't care what her conditions are, just get a bottom line from her, Mike. Whatever I need to do to get this over with."

"We'll talk Wednesday when I get back," was the P.I.'s vague reply.

Luke didn't care if he had to sell his house and give her everything, he was finally going to be free of all things Adriana. The relief he felt was liberating.

He was going to start living again. Beginning now.

He fired off a text to Cassie.

Luke: Date Number Eleven tonight. Let's celebrate!

Hot and Beautiful: Sounds great! Where?

He burst out laughing when he saw her name on his phone. She must have changed it when he wasn't paying attention.

Luke: Hot and Beautiful, huh? I can't say I disagree. That was hilarious, btw. Dinner at my place tonight. 7:30 work?

Hot and Beautiful: I'm glad you're not mad I messed with your phone, and I'm happy you laughed.

I'll be there at 7:30! Should I bring dessert?

Luke: Doll, you are dessert.

****

Cassie

She arrived at Luke's at seven twenty-five, and even though he promised she was dessert, she had stopped on the way to pick up a Nothing Bundt Cakes lemon-flavored cake. She knew Luke's favorite was lemon, and for some reason, the idea of pleasing him made her happy.

Cassie sighed. She was so over-the-top in love with that man it was ridiculous.

She let herself in, calling out, "Knock knock!"

Luke came around the corner, barefoot with a dish towel thrown over his shoulder, dressed in faded Levi's and an untucked, azure blue button down.

"Hi, doll!" He greeted her with a chaste kiss on the lips.

"Hi, handsome," she said through her smile as she stared up at him.

He grinned and took her hand to lead her into the kitchen.

She set the cake on the counter and said, "It smells good. What are you making?"

With a chuckle, he confessed, "It's from Figurino's, I didn't cook."

"Of course not, what was I thinking?" she teased.

"Hey! I can cook!"

Cassie shot him a look. "Really? When have you ever cooked anything but breakfast?"

He pulled her to him in an embrace. "How about I make breakfast this weekend?"

Trying to contain her smile, she nodded. "I think I'd like that."

"Good," he said as he guided her to the table. "Let's eat."

Luke had gone all out. There was a bucket of ice with champagne chilling and glasses empty and waiting to be filled. The table was covered with a linen cloth, candles, and a bouquet of roses adorning it. The plates and silverware even all matched, and he'd set the table properly.

Cassie was impressed.

"Wow," she said while inching her chair forward after he'd pulled it out for her.

"I'm glad you like it," he replied, dropping a kiss on her nose.

"I love it. All this because we made it through ten dates?" she called after him as he walked toward the kitchen. He reappeared with a covered plate, setting it down in front of her.

"Just because we couldn't wait to get naked with each other doesn't mean Date Eleven is any less important."

Why he was obsessed with the eleventh date thing, she had no idea, but she understood it was important to him, so she tried not to discount it. He was still standing by her side.

"Well, we made it. Should we open the champagne and toast?"

"In a minute."

He hadn't returned to the kitchen to get his plate, and she cocked her head curiously.

He pulled the cover off her plate, and she gasped. Instead of Figurino's ravioli and salad on her plate, there was a red rose with a box containing a shiny diamond. Tears instantly filled her eyes, and she looked at him frantically.

He can't be asking me this already. It's too soon.

It had been fine when they were talking hypothetically, someday off in the future. But not this very moment.

He dropped to his knee in front of her.

He's actually doing this.

"Cassie, I didn't need ten dates to realize I wanted to spend the rest of my life with you, but I thought I might need ten to convince you. You make me so happy, doll. I can't imagine my life without you in it. I know it's only been like a month, but I know I love you and want to marry you, and I don't want to wait. Cassandra Jo Sullivan, will you marry me?"

She should have burst out an enthusiastic *yes!* after that proposal. Instead, she burst into tears.

"You can't be doing this, right now. How can you want to marry me? I don't even know if I want to have kids. I thought I'd have more time to figure this out."

Still kneeling, he stroked her shoulder. "Oh, doll. I want to be with you no matter what. If you decide you don't want to have kids, we'll be the aunt and uncle who spoils our nieces and nephews rotten and have lots of dogs."

She shook her emphatically. "No, I know how important children are to you, Luke. That wouldn't be fair. I love you too much to deprive you of that."

He wiped her tears with his thumb, then tucked her hair behind her ear and smiled meekly. "Then have my babies, Cassie Sullivan."

"I can't promise you that, Luke."

"Not ever?"

"I don't know. I've never thought about it before you came along and turned my world upside down," she whispered.

"So, you have thought about it?" he teased.

"Only when you freaked me out telling me we made a baby," she confessed.

"And what did you think? Was the idea so bad?"

"It wasn't *so* bad, but I have to be honest, it isn't something I can see myself doing." His face fell, so she quickly added. "But I've never had a reason to before."

"Now you have a reason?" he asked hopefully.

"You could say that," she said with a small smile.

Luke sighed. "I did this too soon, didn't I?"

With a grimace, she replied, "Yeah, I think so."

"How about this," he suggested diplomatically. "Take the ring..." She started to shake her head, and he put his hand up in a gesture for her to stop. "Take the ring, wear it on your right hand for now, or put it in your jewelry box if you'd rather, but take it, and at least tell me you'll think about it. Just don't tell me no. I'll wait."

"I don't know if I can ever give you the answer you want," she told him truthfully.

Luke shook his head. "Promise me you'll think about it." He stood, pulling her up with him. "I would love for you to be my fiancé, Cassie Sullivan," he whispered in her ear as he hugged her tight, "but I will wait as long as you need to decide to become Cassie Rivas."

The doubt loomed large in the back of her mind. As much as she wanted to be with Luke, she didn't know if she could pull off the wife and mother thing. Fortunately, he seemed to understand he needed to back off and wasn't pressuring her, giving her plenty of time to decide.

****

Luke

What the hell was I thinking, asking her to marry me so soon?

After he'd hung up with Mike this afternoon, he decided he wasn't waiting anymore and went and bought her a ring. He didn't tell anyone what he was doing, probably because he knew they'd think he was nuts and try to talk him out of it.

Luke knew it was rash, and he didn't give a damn at the time. It was right, he knew it in his soul. She was perfect for him. Not perfect in a put-her-on-a-pedestal way, he knew she had faults. Perfect in the sense she made him want to be a better man. Perfect because he knew life with her would never be boring.

He slid the round, one-and-a-half carat ring on her right ring finger.

"Do you like it? We can exchange it if you want something different, it won't hurt my feelings."

She held her hand at arm's length to admire the ring.

"It's beautiful Luke, classy but not gaudy. It's exactly what I would have picked."

He was beaming with pride. The minute he saw it, he knew it was the one. It was simple, but the color and the cut were flawless, and it wasn't obnoxiously big, but big enough to let people know he wasn't a cheap ass. Still, he made sure he could exchange it if she didn't like it.

He couldn't, however, return it for his money back.

It didn't matter. She was going to be his wife. She didn't say yes today, but she was going to someday, he knew it. He could wait.

Cassie slid it off and handed it to him, shaking her head. "I can't wear it, though."

Luke placed it back in her hand and closed her fist around it. "You don't have to wear it yet, hang onto it for when you're ready."

"What if I'm never ready?"

He didn't answer, simply slowly captured her lips with his, taking his time to kiss her thoroughly.

Cassie sighed with a smile when they broke the kiss. "Best. Kisser. Ever."

"Just think, when you say yes, it would guarantee you get to kiss me for the rest of your life," he smirked and continued, "Are you ready to eat?"

"You're impossible," she scolded. "I'm not sure if I can eat right now, but I'll try. Can we still have champagne?"

"Why not? We're still celebrating."

She tilted her head. "What are we celebrating?"

"You didn't say no," he said with a wink.

Chapter Thirty-Three

Cassie

Lying in bed early the following morning, Luke teased, "I had planned on calling in sick to work and lying around in bed the entire day posting *we're engaged!* all over our social media accounts."

"Aw," she said, rolling over, kissing his cheek, "wouldn't that let everyone at your work know you weren't really sick? Good thing I didn't say yes, I saved you from getting written up."

"Yeah, well when you do agree to marry me, we're posting that shit everywhere—even in the newspaper. I'm getting a t-shirt in every color that says, *Cassie Sullivan is marrying me.*"

She giggled. "Do they still post engagements in the newspaper?"

"Fuck if I know. I'll put it on a billboard if I have to, start a Twitter campaign."

"Oh my God, you're a nut!"

He nodded in agreement with her assessment. "That's what you and Ben are always telling me."

"Speaking of Ben, did he make it back from his trip?"

"Yeah, but he decided to stay at her place last night. I think he's got it bad for her."

"Ooooh, Ben's in looooove. That's awesome!" She really was happy for him.

"Yeah," Luke chuckled, "never thought I'd see the day. But I think he's known her since they were kids and always had a thing for her. He's been very tight-lipped about the whole thing, which is how I know it's serious."

"Two of San Diego's most eligible bachelors off the market!" she teased.

"I don't know how eligible we were. A girl would have been crazy to want to be with either one of us just six months ago. We didn't have our shit very squared away."

"But you do now?"

He kissed her sex hair. "Four right angles square, doll. Don't you worry."

She hugged him tight, then sighed, "I probably should go home and get ready for work."

"That's something else I want to talk about soon."

She got out of bed and kissed his cheek. "One thing at a time, Rivas," she advised, dodging his hand with a giggle when he tried to swat her butt as she darted toward the bathroom.

Dressed in last night's clothes, she walked into the kitchen to find him standing at the counter in his boxer briefs, reading his phone and drinking a cup of coffee.

"Okay, I'm off to do my walk of shame," she announced. "Do you want to come to the condo for dinner tonight?"

He looked at her thoughtfully. "We need to talk about our living situation."

She really didn't want to have this conversation right now. Why did he always have to do things with guns-a-blazin'? Trying to quell the rising panic she unexpectedly felt, she kissed him quickly on the lips.

"Later. I need to go home now and get ready for work. I have morning meetings."

Before he even had a chance to respond, she was rushing out the door.

****

Luke

Ben said he was going home before heading to his girlfriend's, meaning he could take Rex for a walk and feed him, so Luke showered at work, stowed his gear in his locker, and went directly to Cassie's. He was there by seven-twenty. The delicious aroma of Kristen's casserole emanated from the kitchen when he opened the front door.

"Damn that smells good," he called out, announcing his arrival.

She opened the swinging kitchen door and greeted him with a smile. "Hi, handsome."

"Damn, Kristen knows how to cook," he said as he approached her. His lips hovering over hers, he greeted her, "Hello beautiful," then planted his lips on hers. When they pulled apart, she led him into the kitchen.

"How was work?" she asked as she opened the refrigerator to pull out a beer and handed it to him.

He twisted the bottle top and tossed it into the garbage can. "Well, I'm here on time, so no callouts. That's always a good thing. How about you?"

She grinned, cutting cucumbers for the salad she had started making. "Another day, another dollar."

"Or in your case, several hundred of them," he teased.

She threw an oven mitt at him. "Hey! Don't hate me because I make a ridiculous amount of money. I could put in a good word for you if you want," she smirked.

"Can I play with guns all day?" he asked, pausing to take a swill of beer.

"Mmm, probably not."

"Then I'll stick to fighting crime and suppressing evil for paltry pay."

"Suit yourself," she said with a nonchalant shrug, tossing the ingredients together in a large, glass bowl. She set the tongs down, her face turning serious. "So, are you ready to tell me what's been bothering you?"

A smart man would have recognized right then was the time to tell her about Adriana. Apparently, Luke wasn't a smart man.

"Tomorrow, doll, I'd much rather enjoy my time tonight charming you into marrying me."

She looked at him suspiciously as the timer for the oven went off.

Saved by the bell.

****

Cassie

They had just finished dinner, when Luke got a text from Ben, explaining he hadn't even left his shop yet. Something about having to tow someone from the freeway, so he hadn't been home to let Rex out.

"Wanna go with me? Pack a bag and go to work from my place tomorrow."

"I can't spend the night. I'm meeting my realtor, Ava here early in the morning so she can give me an idea of what I could list it for."

A smile spread across his face. "Maybe I should schedule her to come by my place, too."

Panic rose up in her chest again. "Why?"

"We should move in together, Cass. Soon."

"You can't sell your house! What about Ben?"

"Hell yes, I can sell my house. Ben will be happy to have his own place again."

Cassie tilted her head. "So, why doesn't he already?"

Luke was visibly uncomfortable. "He helped me when I was in a financial jam. I promise I'll tell you all about it tomorrow."

"I'm holding you to that, Luke." She noticed he had become a master at changing the subject and putting off telling her anything. Her patience was wearing thin. "You're not getting out of it, so you better not have any callouts, emergencies, flat tires, or heart attacks. You're telling me everything."

"Everything." He held his hand to his heart and promised, "Tomorrow night. Scout's honor."

Chapter Thirty-Four

Luke

He took a deep breath of the ocean air when they walked to his car on the way to let Rex out. He insisted she ride with him even if it meant he had to drive her home later. He'd never looked more forward to a meeting than the one he had with Mike tomorrow. He couldn't wait for when he was free of this shit hanging over his head, and the only thing he had to worry about was convincing Cass to marry him.

Soon.

They pulled onto his street, and it took a moment for him to recognize the bright blue Kia Rio with Sinoloa plates was in his driveway, not his neighbors.

As it turned out, tomorrow was a day too late to talk to Cassie.

*****

Cassie

"What the hell?" Luke snarled when he pulled into the drive, and instead of opening the garage, parked next to the blue car she didn't recognize with a Mexican plate. He was staring at his front door where a young, pretty Hispanic woman stood in a rose-colored, stylish peasant dress with a wide brown leather belt around her waist and matching sandals.

"Luke? Who is that?"

He didn't answer at first, his eyes still on the dark-haired beauty standing on his doorstep. Eventually, he drew his eyes back to Cassie.

"Luke?" She asked again.

"She's my wife," he answered quietly as his eyes fell to his lap.

She felt her heart drop into her stomach, her palms instantly sweaty.

"Your—your wife? You mean your ex-wife, right?"

He looked up at her, shame written all over his face.

"I can explain, Cass. It's not what you think."

Folding her arms around her middle, she snarled, "Start talking."

His attention was diverted back toward the house, and he took in a sharp breath.

"Oh my God," he hissed.

Stumbling out of the car, the color draining from his face, he stared dumbfounded at the woman standing at his door, a little boy about two or three now visible behind her skirt.

Cassie got out of the car too, walking around the front of the hood to stand next to him. His hands were shaking, and he gulped before taking steps toward the house.

When he was about five feet in front of the woman, he asked in Spanish, "Is that..."

The little boy—who was the spitting image of the man who'd just asked her to marry him a day ago—clung to the back of the woman's leg, peeking up at Luke with a curious look.

"This is our son, Lucas," the woman replied, also in Spanish, as she pressed on the boy's back to bring him in front of her.

Luke remained frozen in place, tears in his eyes, and whispered, *"El es hermoso." He's beautiful.*

Cassie didn't think they knew she could understand them. One of the benefits of being a *guera*—slang for *white girl*—who spent her junior year of college in Spain was people usually underestimated her ability to understand Spanish. She'd learned to perfect the blank look of incomprehension. Pretending to be oblivious had benefitted her more than once.

He kneeled down, smiling at the boy through tears, talking softly in Spanish. "Hello, Lucas." Glancing up, he asked, "Does he—does he know I'm—"

The woman didn't answer him, instead casting her brown eyes at Cassie. She continued speaking Spanish. "Who is this?"

Luke barely looked at Cassie, responding gruffly, *"Mi... amiga." My friend.*

What happened to wanting to marry me? Shouting it from the rooftops?

"Your friend? *Your friend*?" The woman started shuffling toward her car with the boy in tow. "Lucas and I need to get going. I don't want to interrupt time with your *friend*."

He reached up and grabbed the woman at the elbow, his eyes pleading. His next words in Spanish hit Cassie squarely in the gut.

"No! Don't go, please! She's no one important. I'll call her a cab."

A smile formed on the dark-haired woman's face.

"I thought you should meet your son at least once before I signed your divorce papers." The woman's tone was almost defiant as she produced a bundle of paperwork from her big leather bag.

Still kneeling, Luke took them from her, ripping them in half.

"We'll obviously need to revisit these."

Cassie fought to keep her expression neutral even though she wanted to drop into a heap on the ground and sob hysterically. Part of her wanted to wrap her arm possessively through his, but she knew that wouldn't accomplish anything except her humiliation when he chose his wife over her.

His *wife*. He had a son and a wife. A family. The family he so desperately wanted, and she was reluctant to commit to giving him.

Her head was spinning, *talk about getting blindsided*. She suddenly realized, she didn't belong here. That became even more apparent when Luke tentatively offered his finger for the child to grasp in his small fist. Lucas kept his eyes on his finger in Luke's hand.

Luke was beaming like she'd never seen.

"Hi, buddy, I'm your papa," he uttered softly while moving the little boy's hand in tiny circles.

Lucas slowly looked up at Luke, staring at him intently before flinging his arms around his father's neck and hugging him fiercely. Luke stood, holding the boy tightly, tears openly streaming down his face as silent sobs racked through his body. He pulled Adriana in with one arm and whimpered, "Gracias," over and over into her hair.

It would have been a heart-warming scene to anyone else watching it unfold.

She wanted to be happy for him, but she'd admit it, she was selfish and couldn't be, not with what it meant for her and Luke. It was as if he'd forgotten Cassie even existed while the bottom of her world collapsed.

Adriana looked over at her standing on the fringe of this family reunion that obviously had no place for her and smiled triumphantly.

Ben pulled up on his motorcycle, his face shell-shocked when he cut the engine and took in the scene.

Cassie wanted to run crying to Ben and beg him to get her out of there, but she wasn't about to give them the satisfaction that she was destroyed, so instead, she sauntered over to where he remained on his bike, still seemingly trying to absorb what was happening.

With a meek smile, she asked, "Do you think you can take me home?"

He continued to stare at Luke and his family and nodded once without looking at her, finally glancing back after she swung her leg over the seat behind him.

Only when her hands were firmly around Ben's middle, and he had started the engine again, did Luke look at her. The expression he wore as he watched her was one she'd never seen on him before.

Guilt.

With her fingertips, she brushed away a tear that had escaped and stared at him, trying to etch every detail in her mind of him with his arms wrapped around his wife and child.

It would help bring her back to reality when she tried to convince herself later tonight and for the next decade, he had really loved her.

She kissed Ben long on his cheek, then with as real a smile as she could gather, whispered in his ear, "Let's go."

Yeah, it was petty and immature, but when she looked at Luke again, the transformation on his face from guilt to rage made it worth it.

Without another word, Ben hit the throttle, and she held on tight as he left rubber on the asphalt. They were off with flair, which seemed a fitting way to leave behind the only man she'd ever loved.

Her heart was shattered, but she managed to dig deep and muster up the only word she could think of.

Next.

Chapter Thirty-Five

Luke

He had a pit in his stomach the whole drive to Cassie's place. He'd gotten Lucas and Adriana situated in the guest room and made the excuse he had to go into work—even taking his gear to make it believable. Also, because he wasn't sure he trusted Adriana with his things, not to mention he didn't want his guns out with Lucas around. His personal guns were secure in his gun safe bolted to the floor in his closet.

He needed to see Cassie again—he owed her that much— and knew he needed to handle her with kid gloves, or she was liable to slam the door in his face. He couldn't let her walk away. She was his forever, the kind of woman who came around once in a lifetime, but he had no idea how he was going to keep her. Or if it was even fair to ask her to stay with him. Or if she even would want to, now that he had a son, and, well, a wife.

Fuck. He should've told her about Adriana when he had the chance.

Luke was going into an unknown situation he wasn't prepared for, and he had no strategy about dealing with what was coming next. That went against the nature of every cell in his body. He always had a plan.

Parking on the street next to her building, he took a deep breath before getting out of his Challenger. On the elevator ride up, he realized he should have brought Figurino's ravioli. He was not above bribery at this point.

Cassie's red eyes when she opened the door made his heart drop to his stomach. He hated seeing her cry. She looked so vulnerable, which made him fall in love with her even more. All he wanted to do was wrap his arms around her and tell her everything was going to be all right.

Except he knew it wasn't going to be. Things were never going to be the same again.

She didn't say anything, just stood there staring at him.

"Can I come in?" he asked hopefully. She still didn't speak and stepped aside to let him pass. He walked inside, feeling very much like a visitor. He'd always felt comfortable and at home here, but now, it was as if he didn't belong. It sucked.

"Thanks," he murmured once she'd closed the door behind him. He went to caress her arms, but she twisted out of his reach.

"Don't," was all she said as tears filled her eyes. He watched her close her eyes and take a deep breath as if willing them to stop. Which they did.

He'd never met anyone quite like her. *Obviously, since I'm head over heels in love with her.*

He was pleasantly surprised when she gestured to the living room instead of tossing him out.

That was a good sign, right?

Pointing to the couch, she whispered, "Have a seat," but remained standing, hugging herself as she looked out her floor-to-ceiling windows at the city.

Okay, this wasn't so good.

He sat on the edge of the couch, refusing to get comfortable. The awkward silence was almost painful, the only sound the squeaking of the leather as he adjusted his seated position. He knew he needed to start explaining, but he didn't even know where to begin.

Finally, she turned and asked, "What do you want, Luke?"

"To explain."

Her face void of emotion, she huffed, "Um, I don't think there's really much to explain. You have a wife and a son you kind of forgot to tell me about when you asked me to marry you."

His head was spinning. He willed his crisis management training to take over but was coming up empty. Leaping to his feet, he went to stand a foot in front of her.

"It's not what you think."

"Really?" her voice got louder. "Because *I think* I saw a beautiful woman at your house who you, yourself, told me was your wife, holding a little boy who is the spitting image of you while you held both of them, after ripping up divorce papers. I *heard* you tell her I was just your friend, that I was no one important."

"How did you--?"

She began to speak rapidly in Spanish. She spoke so fast, he almost had a hard time keeping up with what she was saying. He caught, *"A year of college abroad... Madrid... asshole,* and, *grew up twenty miles from the Mexican border, of course, I can speak fluent Spanish."*

Looking at her in her black yoga pants and University of Arizona sweatshirt she was swimming in, he realized he'd never noticed how tiny she really was. Her big personality made up for her petite stature, but right now, she seemed vulnerable and hurt, and it was all his fault.

He grabbed her hand and pulled her to the couch where he tugged her to sit down next to him before turning in toward her.

Taking a deep breath, he whispered, "You are important to me. But tonight, meeting my son..." His voice cracked, but he continued, "I had no idea he even existed, Cassie. None. *I'm a dad!* I'm a fucking dad! It knocked me on my ass, and at that moment, I would have said anything to keep her from running away with him again."

He then told her everything, including how devastated he was when he was told Adriana was never pregnant, and why he'd wanted to wait to tell Cassie until he had the divorce papers in his hand. By the end, she was weeping with compassion for him and nodded in understanding when he pressed his forehead against hers and whispered, "I have a son, Cass."

"I know. But where does that leave us? I don't think I fit in your life anymore. You need to get to know your son, he should be your priority. If we're meant to be, someday we'll be together. If not..." she let her voice trail off.

Part of him was relieved she was the one suggesting it and not him. Still, he was heartbroken at the thought of not being with her and wondered if she proposed the break because she didn't want to be a stepmom and doing it this way was easier.

Tears openly fell on his cheeks when he replied, "I don't want this to be the end of us. But I know I can't ask you to stay with me, given the circumstances."

He wanted to. God, did he want to, but it wouldn't be fair. He had no idea how he was going to get Adriana to give him a divorce *and* custody of Lucas. He wasn't going to do anything to jeopardize having his son with him, but he wanted Cassie too. He was such a selfish bastard.

Her reply of, "I understand," hurt. Deep down, he wanted her to fight for them, and the fact she was willing to give up so easily confirmed what he already knew. Now that he had a son, she wanted to bolt.

He closed his eyes tight. He fucking loved this woman to his core, but he had to let her go. Lucas had to be his priority right now. What he said next would haunt him every sleepless night of his life.

"I think I need to try to make it work with my wife, for the sake of my son."

Chapter Thirty-Six

Cassie

She felt like she'd been gutted. The only thing she had left was her pride, so she squared her shoulders and put on her best *no big deal* face even though she was dying inside.

"Yes, of course. You should do that. You should be a family." She nodded her head as she stood. "I hope it works out for you. I know how important having a wife and child is to you."

She turned toward the door, assuming Luke would follow her out. He grabbed her elbow, and she jerked violently away from his touch. "Don't you dare," she managed to snarl without sobbing.

He looked devastated.

Good. Fuck him.

"I love you so much, doll. Please don't ever doubt that for a minute."

She let out a mirthless laugh. "Yeah, you love me so much you're going to make things work with your wife. Please, just go." Cassie could feel her bottom lip quivering, but there was no way she was going to let him see any more of her tears.

"Cass..."

"Please," she eked out.

He hesitated, like he wasn't going to honor her request, then leaned down and kissed her cheek, and she closed her eyes tight.

"I will always love you, Cassie Sullivan," he whispered in her ear.

She felt the tears streaming down her face but refused to wipe them away or open her eyes until she heard the door close. She made it to her bedroom before collapsing in a sobbing heap on the floor.

**

She remembered crawling into bed at some point although her sense of time all but vanished for the next four days until she finally emerged from under the covers Sunday evening, knowing she had to go to work the next day and face the world.

Luke had texted her repeatedly to check on her. Fortunately, her phone had died, so she didn't get any of them until she had cried herself out and decided to get on with her life. There was no point responding by then.

It was weird walking into work Monday morning and seeing everyone going about their daily lives while hers had been destroyed. The world hadn't actually stopped turning after all.

Over the next several days, she wavered between being on the verge of tears and being pissed off. Everything reminded her of him, from the fucking songs on the radio to the dinners Kristen left her.

And Figurino's? Yeah, thanks for ruining that for me, too, asshole.

Logically and even emotionally, she understood why Luke chose Adriana and Lucas over her, but it didn't make it hurt any less. She knew time healed all wounds, but as she sat sobbing in her shower Friday morning before work after having a dream about him, she had a hard time believing it was ever going to get easier.

Her job and her family turned out to be her saving grace. Her sister even skipped traveling to D.C. with Ron the week after their breakup in order to be with Cassie. The pharmaceutical rep threw herself headfirst back into work, keeping long hours and collapsing into bed so exhausted, she had no choice but to sleep. On the weekends, she was at Brenna's.

Ron came home the second Thursday and announced to his wife he had to leave for the weekend.

"I'm sorry, darlin'," he murmured as he nuzzled her neck from behind. "I'll make it up to you, I promise."

Ugh. Cassie wanted to puke at how in love they were.

"I think Cass and I will take the 'Vette to Palm Springs for a spa weekend," her sister announced to both her and Ron.

That was news to her. Cassie's expression must have given away her surprise.

Ron smirked with one eyebrow raised. "That sounds like fun, but I need to get the oil changed first. I'll see if Ben can get me in tomorrow before I leave."

Turns out, Ben could.

Cassie got a call from Brenna late the next morning.

"Hey, sis. What are you doing, right now?"

"I was headed to the office to do some paperwork. I finished the last of my appointments about fifteen minutes ago."

"Any chance you can pick Ron up at the auto shop and take him to the airport so he can catch his flight? They were able to get the car in for an oil change and service, but it's going to be awhile before they can finish it, and I'm stuck at the vet's office with Zona."

"How are we going to get your car later?" Cassie asked, dreading the thought of running into Ben. She knew she looked like shit these days.

"Pick me up around one, then we'll stop at the shop before going to your house on our way out of town."

Getting out of town was exactly what she needed right now, so she focused on that.

"Tell Ron I'm on my way."

****

Luke

He was meeting his former roommate that Friday for happy hour. Ben had graciously moved out the day after Adriana and Lucas showed up. His friend had gotten an apartment with a month-to-month lease, since he wasn't sure where things were going with his girlfriend, and he wanted to leave himself options.

Between losing Cassie and no longer having Ben to talk to everyday, Luke was feeling desolate. He'd lost count of how many texts he'd written to Cassie but never hit send. He wanted to share all the wonderful things he was learning about his son with her. He'd write the message, sometimes even including pictures, then he'd hover his finger over send and talk himself out of pushing the button.

She didn't want kids, he was sure she wouldn't be interested in learning Lucas was able to say dog in English correctly or any of the other little things about his son Luke thought were amazing, so he always pressed *delete* instead of *send*.

Things at home were odd, at best. He and Adriana were strangers who only had their son in common anymore. Lucas was well cared for by his mother, but Luke's heart soared when the boy showed an obvious preference for him over Adriana.

There was nothing like hearing, "Papa!" when he walked in the door at night, followed by his legs being slammed into by thirty-five pounds of force. Lucas was his father's shadow when Luke was home. The boy obviously adored him and often tried to mimic whatever he was doing. Whether it was sitting on the couch cheering for the Padres or brushing his teeth—his son wanted to do it, too.

But he fucking missed Cassie every single second of every single day. There was no comparison to her company. Watching baseball without her was especially tough.

"Things will get better," Ben offered when Luke lamented his situation to his best friend in the restaurant bar. "If it's any consolation, I saw her today. She looks about as good as you do."

"You saw her?"

"Yeah, she picked up Ron after be brought in his Corvette to be serviced. Something about Brenna and Cassie taking it on a road trip this weekend."

"I wonder where they're going, and who's watching Zona." A wave of sadness hit him for an entirely different reason than missing Cassie. He was no longer going to be asked to watch his former foster pup, and he loved that dog.

"I think it's a quick girls' weekend." Ben was a great friend and tried to change the subject. "How're things going at home? Things going okay with Adriana? Are you still trying to make it work with her?"

Luke sighed. "I don't know. It sounds great in theory, but..."

Ben filled in the rest. "But there's that pesky problem of being in love with someone else."

"Exactly." Luke gave a humorless laugh. "But I gotta tell ya, being a dad is the best thing to ever happen to me. I look at him sleeping and am in awe he's really there. I can't believe how much I love him already, and I'm having a hard time not wanting to strangle her for keeping him from me for over three fucking years. To her credit, she's remorseful. She cried the other night and told me how sorry she was, she knows what a mistake she made."

"That's good. Right? Why do you have that look on your face?"

Luke grimaced. "Because after I hugged her and thanked her for telling me that, she started stroking my dick."

"Oh shit! Did you fuck her?"

The SWAT sergeant shook his head. "No, which pissed her off. I know it's only a matter of time before she pushes the issue again."

"So," Ben shrugged, "fuck her."

"You're an asshole. It would complicate things in the long run. Besides, I don't even know if I could get it up, I'd be thinking about Cassie the whole time."

Again, his former roommate shrugged like the answer was simple. "So, close your eyes and pretend she's Cassie. Just don't say the wrong name when you bust a nut."

Luke couldn't help but chuckle. "Fuck you."

Even if he wanted to, Luke could never pretend his wife was Cassie. Cassie had her own unique scent and touch. Her hair always smelled of lavender, and her perfume intoxicated him. Her skin was like silk, like her hair was when he had it fisted in his hand while she sucked his cock deep in between those luscious, kissable lips. Her tits were the perfect size for his hands. Actually, her entire body fit his perfectly. And the little noises she'd make when he was seated deep inside her...

Great, now my dick is getting hard.

"I miss Cassie so much, Ben. I'd give anything to have her back." Even Luke didn't miss the desperation in his own voice.

"So, get her back." His friend seemed to think all the solutions were simple today.

"Even if by some miracle, Yanna gave me a divorce and custody of Lucas, I don't think Cassie would be interested anymore. I've got a lot of baggage now, and my son has to be my priority."

"Have you talked to Adriana about a divorce?"

"The first night. I tore the divorce papers up when she arrived, but when we were talking later, I suggested revising them. She said if she wasn't married, she'd have to return to

Mexico with Lucas. The threat wasn't very thinly veiled. I'm going to bide my time, for now."

"What about fighting her for custody? Getting Lucas one hundred percent of the time?" his friend asked bluntly.

"I've thought about it, but I don't think a judge would grant me custody when I've only known my son two weeks. Besides, I don't want to keep him from her, he needs his mother in his life. But if we have joint custody, I worry she'd take off again to spite me."

"What about Cassie? Couldn't she be his stepmother?"

"She doesn't want kids." Luke sadly shook his head and took a pull from his beer. "Besides, she's never going to forgive me; I broke her fucking heart."

"Along with yours," Ben murmured, doing his best to be supportive.

The cop let out a long breath and ran his fingers through his hair.

"I'm so fucking lost without her, it's not even funny."

His best friend looked at him sympathetically. "I wish I had the solution for you, brother."

"Yeah, me too," he responded in defeat.

****

Cassie

While sitting in Brenna's kitchen one afternoon almost a month later, she reflected how easily Luke seemed to have moved on with his wife and child. On one hand, she was glad he hadn't tried to get in contact with her. His words would have only served as a sadistic torture—comforting in a sad, pathetic way by letting her know he still cared about her but reminding her she couldn't have him. On the other hand, it hurt at how effortless it had been for him to forget about her.

It was serendipity she was thinking about that when, out of the blue, her sister said, "Cooper wants to know if it's okay to call you."

She thought about it a long time. What was the point of moping around over Luke anymore? They weren't getting back together. If he had wanted to be with her, he would have found a way by now.

If a man really wants to be with you, he'll make it happen, no matter what.

He hadn't made it happen.

"I'll send Cooper a text this week."

That brought a smile to her sister's face. "Good. I think it's time for you to get back out there."

"It's only been a month, Bren."

"About as long as your relationship lasted. I think there's a rule—you can't mourn for longer than you dated."

She knew her sister was trying to be light-hearted and cheer her up, and she even knew Brenna had a point, but for some reason, the realization of how little time she'd actually had with Luke hurt, and she lashed out.

"We were together longer than a month, thank you very much. And I thought we were in love; he even asked me to marry him. Something most people think is kind of a big deal."

The look on Brenna's face made Cassie feel terrible as did her sister's unnecessary apology.

"Oh, honey, I'm so sorry." Her sibling came around the island and hugged her. "Of course, it's a big deal. I wasn't trying to be insensitive. I hate seeing you like this, and I don't really know what to do. You're supposed to be my badass little sister who doesn't fall in love or take any shit. I've never had to deal with heartbroken Cassie before. I'm sorry, this is all uncharted territory for me."

Cassie snorted. "How do you think I feel?"

"Well," Brenna smirked, "you look good, anyway."

"Thank you." With a sigh, Cassie squeezed her older sister tight. "For everything. I'm sorry I snapped at you."

"Don't give it a second thought. Don't ever forget how amazing you are, okay?"

They pulled apart, and Cassie smiled. "I'll try not to. Thanks for the reminder."

"That's what big sisters are for."

Chapter Thirty-Seven

Luke

He had lunch with Ben again. His friend was the only one he trusted to confide in.

"I've thought about texting her," Luke confessed. "Maybe I could introduce her to Lucas, see if she's interested in getting to know him."

"And what if she is?" His friend looked at him skeptically. "You're still married. I thought you were going to try to make it work with Yanna?"

"We both know that was a crock of shit." Luke was exasperated. Ben, of all people, should know better.

"Maybe you should sleep with her, man."

He closed his eyes. "She came on to me again the other night."

"Okay, well, that's a start."

"I couldn't get it up," he confessed.

"Is that new?" Ben chuckled.

"Fuck you." Luke grinned, wadded his napkin up, and threw it at the mechanic, then quickly shook his head with a frown when the gravity of the situation struck him. "I don't know what to do. I want my girl back, but I can't lose my son. Why can't there be a simple damn solution?"

"Well," his friend grimaced, "I debated about telling you this, especially since you seem so down, but I owe it to you. Your girl is bringing me all kinds of business—of the Marine variety."

"What do you mean?" Luke snarled.

"Well, you know her brother-in-law has been bringing his sweet 'Vette in, then some other jarhead showed up the other day in his vintage Gran Torino. It was fucking beautiful, man, like Starsky and Hutch. You should have seen it..."

"The Marine, Ben. Get to the part about the Marine."

"Oh, yeah, sorry," the mechanic chuckled. "Anyway, he mentions Ron referred him, so I don't think much of it until Cassie comes into the lobby, and he says, *My ride's here.*"

"Whoa, whoa, whoa." Luke sat up straight in his seat. "Cassie picked up some guy from your shop? What was his name?" He already knew the name but needed it confirmed.

"Cooper... Johnson. I remembered it because it reminded me of Cooper Tires."

"Did you talk to her?" he asked, probably a little too eagerly.

"Fuck yeah, I talked to her. You aren't the only one who misses her, ya know."

Luke sighed, his tone melancholy when he replied, "I know. Did she..."

"Ask about you? No. But that's probably because of the guy. I could tell there was a lot more she wanted to say."

He knew his friend was trying to make him feel better. Luke was almost afraid to ask the next question because no matter how Ben answered, it was going to suck. He did, anyway.

"How'd she look?"

His best friend eyed him for a beat before answering, "Fucking radiant, man."

Luke winced and closed his eyes. While he wanted to be happy for her, the truth was he had been holding onto the glimmer of hope there was still a shot for them, somehow, someway. He knew she was going to move on, he practically forced her to with his bullshit lie, *I need to try to make it work with Adriana.* Maybe this was the gods' way of letting him know he needed to do just that.

Chapter Thirty-Eight

Luke

The call from the secretary of the Heroes of San Diego planning committee was a surprise.

"Hey, Frannie, what's going on?" he greeted the older lady who seemed to be connected to half of San Diego.

"Luke, my dear, how are you?"

"I'm doing great. To what do I owe the pleasure?"

"Some unfortunate business, I'm afraid. I was making follow-up calls with all the winners from the auction event, and it seems you have not honored your commitment, Luke Rivas."

That caught him off-guard. He didn't like being accused of not keeping his promises.

"Well, I don't know if the winner is interested in going on her date with me, Fran," he confessed.

"Strange, I talked to her this morning, and she said the same thing about you."

"Huh. Okay—"

She cut him off, "Look, Luke. I don't know what's going on, and if I'm being honest, I don't really care. What I do care about is being able to truthfully advertise next year one hundred percent of the auction winners had a fun date with their hero. So, I'm going to need you to make that happen for me."

Luke didn't know much, but he knew the last person in San Diego he wanted to have pissed at him was Francine Ericson, Federal Court Judge Robert Ericson's wife.

"I'll take it care of it, Frannie," he promised before hanging up.

****

Cassie

She was expecting Luke's call after hanging up with Francine Ericson but didn't anticipate it would come so soon. She let it go to voicemail since she was a little busy peeing on a stick. Cassie listened to his message while she paced her condominium, waiting for the results of the test she just took.

"Seems I owe you a date," his deep voice said with a chuckle.

Simply hearing his voice should not make her feel this happy. Especially since her gut was filled with dread when she glanced at the thermometer-looking thing sitting on her bathroom counter.

Chapter Thirty-Nine

Cassie

The two little pink lines appearing on the stick was the ultimate irony. Or God's cruel joke. She was in her car, headed to Brenna's before the pregnant lines mocking her life even reached their full shade of pink.

"Oh, honey. What are you going to do?" her sister asked sympathetically.

Cassie took a deep breath. "I don't have any idea, Bren. This is the cherry on the shit sundae that is my life right now."

"Well, I can tell you if you decide to keep this baby, you need to start looking at it as a blessing. This negative energy will affect her. She will feel everything you're feeling."

"In that case, I definitely shouldn't keep it 'cuz this kid would be screwed," Cassie groused.

"Would it really, Cass?" Brenna softened her tone. "Let's look at this objectively. You're freaking loaded, more than capable of providing for a baby as a single mother. Your kid will be gorgeous and talented. You've got a great support system, including a baby daddy who would be active and involved in his child's life, and a sister who would be the most doting aunt on the planet. Which, oh, by the way, the house next door is for sale. And you can't see it yet because the hurt is too fresh, but that baby was made in love."

"This baby was made while I was living a lie. It'd be nothing more than another obligation to Luke now," she choked out as tears started streaming down her face.

"Oh, little sister." Wrapping her arms around her shoulders, Brenna hugged her tightly. "Luke was an idiot, I can't even defend what he did, but don't ever doubt he loved you. Maybe you didn't get the ending you wanted, but this baby might be exactly what you need."

The Rolling Stones' "You Can't Always Get What You Want" immediately began rattling around in her head. *Damn you, Brenna.*

Wiping her eyes as she pulled away, Cassie asked, "So, you think I should have it?"

"Oh, no," her sister shook her head, "don't put that on me. This is a deeply personal decision. It will affect your life far more than it will mine. Only *you* can make this choice because you're the one who has to live with it whatever you choose. However, I will say this, I think before you decide anything, you should talk to Luke."

"I'm not talking to him until I've decided," Cassie's tone became defensive, "and only if I decide I'm keeping it."

There was no judgment in Brenna's voice when she replied, "That's your right, honey, but I think you'd regret it someday if you didn't talk to him."

"Fuck my life," Cassie said as she buried her head in her hands.

"It's going to be okay, little sister, I promise." Brenna rubbed the middle of Cassie's back in broad circles. "Do you know how far along you are? How much time do you have to make a decision?"

"I'm at least eight weeks since the last time we were together was the night he asked me to marry him, but I guess I could be as far along as eleven weeks."

"So, you still have some time to decide. Are you leaning one way or the other?" Brenna delicately asked, hugging Cassie around the shoulders again.

Cassie shook her head sadly. "I'm so fucking shell-shocked by this, Bren, I don't even know which way is up right now."

"There's no rush, honey. You've still got plenty of time."

"Plenty of time for what?" Ron asked as he came into the kitchen from the garage. He was obviously coming from work since he was dressed in his fatigues.

Brenna brought her hand to her chest in surprise. "I swear to God that damn new garage door opener is so quiet, I never know when you've gotten home anymore!" she admonished Ron as if him arriving without them hearing was his fault.

"You want me to call the company and see if they can install a noisier one?" he asked sarcastically, then kissed his wife hello on the lips, not waiting for a reply to his hypothetical question.

"Hey, Cass. Everything okay?" he asked, eyeing her with concern as he set his gear down.

She shot a panicked look at her sister. Brenna read her mind, replying, "She's still upset about Luke. I said she's got plenty of time to heal before she starts dating again."

The Marine general looked at his sister-in-law thoughtfully. "I thought you went out with Cooper already?"

"No, he needed a ride from Ben's shop while his car got worked on, so he took me to lunch. I'm not ready to date yet. He was cool about it."

"Don't rush it, Cass. You've got all the time in the world. Unless…"

Don't say it, please don't say it.

"Are you worried about your biological clock ticking?"

Once again, her sister swooped in to save the day. "Don't be silly, babe. That's not even on her radar right now."

"I was just askin', I didn't know," Ron defensively teased with eyes wide and eyebrows raised as he opened the refrigerator and pulled out a Pacifico beer bottle. He opened the top and wrapped an arm around his bride as he took a swig. The two of them were a perfect unit together, so much in love. It was almost a crime it took them so long to find each other.

Maybe she'd find her own Ron Thompson someday although that was probably going to have to wait until she was in her fifties after her kid was in college. She didn't think she'd want to date anyone seriously until then.

The thought startled her. *Well, I guess that answers that.*

"Actually, Ron, you're going to be an uncle."

Chapter Forty

Luke

The minute he saw Cassie's name on his phone, his heart started hammering in his chest. Fortunately, he'd just arrived at work and was alone in his Jeep, so he could talk without anyone overhearing him. He'd called her two days ago, so he was beginning to wonder if he was ever going to hear back from her. After the way they'd left things and hearing she was dating Cooper, it wouldn't have surprised him if she'd ignored him altogether.

He hadn't brought himself to change her *Hot and Beautiful* name, but he did disguise it to *HBD Sullivan*—short for *Hot and Beautiful Doll Sullivan*. Luke was a little surprised she was calling instead of texting.

"Hey, doll."

Her voice was soft when she greeted him, "Hi. It's Cassie."

Her voice soothed his soul, and he tilted his head back against the seat rest with his eyes closed.

"I know. I'm so glad to hear from you. How have you been?"

"I'm okay," she said politely. "How are you?"

He wanted to tell her *miserable*—because he was without her—but decided against it.

"I'm doing great. I love being a dad."

She didn't acknowledge his response, instead getting to the point. "So, about the auction date."

"Yeah, about that. Frannie Ericson is ready to have my hide for not having taken you out yet. I'm sorry I haven't done that.

"Listen, Luke," her voice turned somber, "we don't have to do the whole station tour and dog walking thing if it's going to cause trouble for you. I completely understand, and we can skip it. I'll tell Fran we had a fantastic time. I should have told her that to begin with, but she caught me off-guard with her phone call. If you don't mind, I would at least like to have lunch though. There's something I need to discuss with you."

That piqued his interest. "Don't be ridiculous, Cass. I owe you this date, and I'd love to go on it with you. You tell me what day and time work for you.

"Is tomorrow too soon?"

"Doll," he chuckled softly, "today wouldn't be too soon to see you."

"Oh, could you really do today?"

Now he was really intrigued. "I'm at your disposal, Cass."

"I can meet you at the station in an hour, but I'm not really dressed to walk dogs."

"We can do that another time. Text me when you get here, and I'll meet you in the lobby."

He heard her take a deep breath before replying. "Great. See you then.

"I'm looking forward to it."

Luke laid the phone on the passenger seat and gripped the steering wheel in both hands, wondering if he was setting himself up for further misery seeing her again. He missed her so fucking much, there wasn't a day he didn't wake up with an ache in his heart only she could fill. But she was no longer his, and he was pretty sure the only thing lunch was going to do was torture him with what he couldn't have.

Things had started to crumble with Adriana since his last sexual rebuke of her. She was actively passive-aggressive toward him, and Luke knew it was simply a waiting game at this point for her to name her price for a divorce He was willing to give her anything she wanted as long as he got custody of his son, but he could stick it out with her for as long as he needed if it meant being with Lucas.

He wanted desperately to have Cassie meet his little guy. Maybe she'd change her mind about kids once she met him. But then again, maybe it'd only solidify her feelings.

When she appeared in the station's lobby in her royal-blue sundress, strappy nude kitten heels, and blonde hair cascading around her shoulders, he conceded his best friend was right, she looked fucking radiant.

Cooper Johnson must agree with her, he thought bitterly. He wanted to punch every bastard who slyly gave her a second look as she walked toward him with a small smile.

"Hey," he said stiffly. It was awkward trying to act respectfully when what he wanted to do was pull her into the nearest empty office and kiss her head to toe.

"Hi," she responded shyly.

Luke had never seen her shy. "You look beautiful," he murmured. Unable to resist, he leaned down and kissed her cheek, catching a whiff of her perfume. The scent went straight to his cock. Or maybe it was the feel of her silky skin against his lips that caused things to stir in his pants. Or her spectacular tits. He needed a distraction, otherwise he was going to have full-blown hard on in about five seconds.

"Ready to get started on your tour?"

She took a deep breath. "As I'll ever be!"

He watched her smile and decided she might be acting a little too cheerful for the Cassie Sullivan he knew. He was glad the awkwardness seemed to be mutual.

They chatted politely as they toured the halls, but after five minutes they were laughing and teasing each other like nothing had changed until he absent-mindedly reached for her hand when leading her to the garage, and she naturally took it. Her touch was what he'd been missing in his life; her hand fitting perfectly in his sent a wave of calmness over him.

He realized what he'd done and let go like he'd been shocked.

"Sorry about that," he said with a cough as he opened the door leading to the armored vehicles.

"It's fine," she whispered softly, her voice tinged with sadness when she walked past him.

It isn't fine. Fucking things will never be fine again without you.

"So, I hear you're dating Cooper Johnson?" He was a glutton for punishment right now.

Cassie tilted her head like she was surprised he knew about her and Cooper.

Like my best friend wasn't going to tell me, he admonished in his head.

"How's married life?"

Ouch. He may have winced at her question. He noticed she didn't answer his.

"Never better. I love being a dad," he replied as he directed her to the nearest truck.

She stepped inside the vehicle with S.W.A.T. boldly displayed in yellow lettering on the side and looked around with polite curiosity before turning to him.

"Do you have pictures?"

"Of Lucas?" He wasn't expecting her to be interested, so the question surprised him.

"Yeah. If you don't mind, I'd rather skip the ones of the happy family."

That was fine because he didn't have any of those anyway, only of Lucas. The son he barely knew, Adriana had cruelly reminded him last night.

"No judge would give you custody of him," she warned when he broached the divorce topic.

Luke knew she was right, but it only strengthened his resolve to stick with the status quo. He had nothing but time anymore.

Cassie's smile was genuine when he showed her the pictures of his little guy on his phone. It dinged as she was scrolling through the ones of Lucas at the zoo, and she abruptly handed it back to him with a frown. He saw he had a text from Adriana.

"I'll text her back, later," he told her as he clumsily shoved the phone back in his pocket.

"No, it's okay," she said with a tinge of bitterness in her voice. "Don't ignore your wife on my account."

Her unpleasant reminder that they weren't together and his anger they never would be caused him to lash back.

"You're probably right. Feel free to text your boyfriend while I answer my *son's mother's* text."

Her face went visibly white, and he felt like the world's biggest asshole.

This isn't how things were supposed to be between them.

****

Cassie

Why the hell did he have to look so good?

She saw him the second she walked through the police station's sliding doors before he noticed her coming in the lobby. He must have had court today because instead of his usual fatigues, he was in black slacks, pink shirt, white, pink, and black striped tie, and shiny black shoes with his gun and badge displayed prominently on his belt.

Real men definitely wear pink.

Real men who are married with children, that is, she reminded herself.

She couldn't help the warm feeling in her stomach when he flashed his smile at her, his green eyes crinkling in familiarity. Cassie took a deep breath and offered a much weaker smile than his. She tried to shake his hand, but he ignored her and leaned down to kiss her cheek in greeting. His familiar scent was like a warm hug.

"You look beautiful, Cass," he said softly.

"Thanks. You look nice too.

"Thanks," he replied with a wink like he already knew he looked good.

Things between them were uncomfortable for all of five minutes until he teased her about not being a morning person. After that, they quickly fell into an easy banter back and forth.

Then the text from his wife brought them back to reality. He'd chosen Adriana over her. It still stung, but she thought she had been coming to terms with it, then just like that, the pain was as strong as the night he ended it.

They had a hard time recovering from their petty exchange in the garage but managed to be civil as they drove to lunch together. She still wasn't sure how she was going to tell him she was pregnant.

"Now, Frannie can't be mad at me." His attempt at small talk brought her back to the present.

She tried not to appear deflated that was why he had agreed to see her. Cassie had been a goddamn obligation, nothing more.

"I'll be sure to tell Francine I had a lovely time," she murmured, blinking back tears while looking out the window at the passing buildings. Weren't they head over heels in love with each other a month ago? She realized she had secretly hoped he'd been miserable without her and profess his undying love and regret they weren't together, then promise her he'd fix it.

Pathetic.

Luke gave no indication he was anything but content with his married life. He was living the life he had wanted, the one she had been unwilling to commit to.

Oh, the irony.

They decided on the same bistro where they had secretly texted each other while dining with other people. That felt like a lifetime ago.

"Shall we?" Luke gestured toward the hostess stand. She'd made a reservation after hanging up the phone once he agreed to meet today.

Smiling warmly at the hostess, she announced, "Sullivan for two."

The young girl scanned her list. "Ah, right this way, Mrs. Sullivan."

"It's just Ms.," Cassie corrected, then closed her eyes tight. It was a simple mistake, and she should have let it go, but somehow, with this man who had obliterated her heart standing next to her, it escaped her lips.

"Oh, I'm sorry! *Ms.* Sullivan, please follow me."

Now, she felt petty and small. *Great.* Exactly how she wanted to start this little tête-à-tête.

Luke slid into the booth across from her and smiled, obviously trying to cut the tension between them. "You really do look great, doll."

She ignored his pet name for her and put her napkin in her lap, replying. "Thanks, Luke. You never did tell me, how's married life?" Yeah, she went there, right out of the gate.

It didn't faze him though because he said with a goofy smile, "Lucas is incredible, he already has learned so much English. They're such little sponges at this age, ya know? I'd love for you to meet him."

She didn't acknowledge his comment about meeting his boy. Their waiter appeared with waters, both of them declining anything else when the young man asked to take their drink orders. The server left, and she shrugged with indifference.

"I'm glad things are working out with your family."

"Things are working out with my son, Cass. *My son.*"

"Aren't you trying to work things out with Adriana?" *No sense in beating around the bush.*

His hesitation said it all, and she quickly blurted out, "Never mind. It's none of my business."

Luke grabbed her hand and squeezed, staring into her eyes. "We're trying to get along, but we don't share a bed or even a room. My sex life consists of my hand getting a helluva workout in the shower, thinking about you."

She withdrew her hand from his with a small smirk. His admission shouldn't make her this happy. They sat in awkward silence before he reached for her hand again.

"So, what did you want to see me about, doll?"

She hastily removed her hand from his grip. "Please don't call me doll."

He sat up straighter, placing his napkin in his lap with a frown. "I don't know if I can promise that, Cass. I mean, I'll try, but it's probably going to slip out." He paused briefly then tried again, "So, what did you want to see me about?"

She took a sip of her water, avoiding his gaze and picking up her menu to peruse it. "Let's order first, okay?" When she snuck a glance at him, he was eyeing her suspiciously as he opened his own menu.

"Yeah, sure. Do you know what you want?"

She knew exactly what she was going to order. The same thing she always did—sesame-crusted salmon over asparagus with mashed potatoes—but she pretended to be fascinated with the entrée selections, hoping to avoid his scrutiny.

Cassie didn't know if she could do this today.

You have to.

Fuck you, conscience.

He closed his menu and set it aside, watching her closely as he did. She set hers aside too. With the universal, *we're ready to order* message sent, their waiter appeared immediately.

Luke ordered steak like she knew he would, and she ordered the salmon.

She'd stalled long enough and reached in her purse for her phone, hoping to pull up the sonogram pictures the doctor had emailed her while at her appointment without Luke noticing what she was doing. With a deep breath, she started to form the words on her lips, then dropped her phone back into her purse.

Maybe after lunch.

She sat up to find him staring at her with a soft smile.

"I wish things could be different, baby doll," he murmured quietly. She opened her mouth to tell him not to call her that, but he cut her off, shaking his head. "I know, I know, but I can't help it."

Having no idea what to do with that, she reached for her water, taking a long drink before setting it down with no still idea how to respond.

"I'm pregnant," she blurted out.

Hi, pregnancy brain, Cassie Sullivan, nice to meet you.

The unflappable Luke Rivas sat there stunned like he was processing her words over and over, then scowled. He barely contained his snarl when he told her, "Congratulations."

Not quite the reaction she was expecting from him. She wasn't sure how she thought he was going to respond but never envisioned him being angry with her. His next statement cleared up why, although it took her a second to put it all together.

"Is Cooper excited?"

She furrowed her brows. "I haven't told him yet—I haven't told anyone except Brenna and Ron. I thought you should be the first to know."

Slowly, a huge smile of realization spread across his face. "It's mine?"

Did he really ask that?! Who else's would it be? Oh...

She nodded once, and he ran his fingers roughshod through his hair, still smiling, asking incredulously, "Are you serious?!"

"Of course, I'm serious," she said in clipped tones. What did he think, she was playing some kind of sick joke?

He failed to notice her brusqueness while he thoughtfully scrubbed his jaw. "Holy... This is so awesome." He went to get out of his seat, then seemed to think better of it, and stayed put. It was obvious his brain was going a mile a minute with all the questions he began to pepper her with.

"How far along are you?"

"Eleven weeks."

She saw him doing the math in his head, his smile grew wide again, and he reached for her hand, rubbing his thumb along the webbing between her thumb and index finger.

"I *told* you we made a baby that night!"

She shook her head and rolled her eyes, pulling her hand away and putting it in her lap.

"It wasn't necessarily that night. If you recall, there were several nights to choose from that week." She knew in her heart he was right though.

"Oh, I recall, doll." His grin turned salacious. "Pretty much every time I'm in the shower."

Smoothing the napkin on her legs, she couldn't help the corners of her mouth lifting.

"You're impossible."

"Are we having a boy or a girl?"

"I don't know yet, it's too early." Her nervous fidgeting transferred to lining up her silverware in front of her.

"How did this even happen? I thought you were on the pill," he asked, still stunned.

"I was, faithfully, so I have no idea. The doctor said it happens, especially with how often we were intimate."

"You told her how often?!"

"Well, I didn't volunteer the information, geez. I answered her question when she asked."

"Oh," he chuckled.

She fished her phone out of her purse and brought the sonogram pictures up before handing it to him.

"Is this our peanut?" he asked in amazement, studying the screen in front of him.

"He's more like the size of a raspberry, but yes, that's him."

He looked up from the screen with an accusing expression. "I thought you said you didn't know the sex?"

"Well, I don't officially. I just don't like calling him *it*."

"So, *he* could really be a *she*," he stated optimistically as he handed her back the phone.

"Yes."

Unable to contain his grin, he took a sip of his water. "I can't believe this. Wait 'til I tell Lucas. He's going to be so excited. He's going to want to help us pick out toys and clothes when we go shopping."

Those words felt like a stab to her heart, and she shot him a pained look. It was like he'd gotten so caught up in the news, he'd entirely forgotten their fucked-up situation. She could tell the minute reality set in by the look on his face. He scrubbed his face with his hand.

"Shit, I'm sorry," he muttered. "I got ahead of myself."

"Don't worry about it," she said with her hand on her stomach. "We'll get a schedule figured out. Lucas can still do all that with you."

"What's that supposed to mean?" he growled.

"It means, just that. When the baby gets here, we're going to need to establish a custody agreement. I'm assuming you want to be a part of this." With tears in her eyes, she shrugged her shoulders. "If not, that's okay, I'll manage. Obviously, I hope you'll want to be a part of your child's life, but if you choose not to be, we'll be alright."

He snarled at her suggestion he wouldn't want to be a part of his baby's life. "I'm not fucking going anywhere, doll. I take care of what's mine."

"Yes, I know. You're very good at meeting your obligations."

Luke grabbed her elbow across the table. "Is that what you think? I view this as an obligation? This is a goddamn gift. The universe is saying you and I were meant to be together."

Cassie shrugged out of his grip. He didn't get to choose her now because she was pregnant.

"As far as you and me... well, there is no *you and me* anymore. You're already married, remember? Giving your marriage a shot."

He blanched. "Don't do this to me, Cass. Don't throw that in my face now. I've been miserable without you, but I did what I had to for the sake of my son. I don't blame you for being angry, but please don't torture me for trying to do the right thing."

She reached into her purse and pulled out the box with her engagement ring.

"I wanted to give this back to you," she said as she handed it to him across the table.

He looked like she'd slapped him and pushed it back toward her. "No. It's yours, I bought it for you."

She shook her head, more emphatically this time. "Etiquette says to return it."

"Etiquette? You think I give a fuck about etiquette right now? It's your ring, Cassie, I bought it for you. I don't want it.

I still hope you'll wear it someday, but either way, I don't want it back. It's yours."

She slipped it back into her purse and patted her stomach. "I'll give it to him when he decides to get married."

She knew he was seething, but he said nothing more than a terse, "Whatever you want."

Their food arrived, and they remained silent until their server left. She could tell his mind continued to race. He cut his steak while asking, "So what does this mean, Cass?"

"I guess this means you're going to have two children with two different women," she said snidely.

Her bitch switch had been flipped. *Ah, pregnancy hormones, gotta love 'em.*

He looked so sad when he asked, "What if I ask you to wait for me?"

Setting her fork and knife down forcefully, she glowered at him.

"How can you even ask me that? You're *married* and last I knew, trying to make things work for the sake of your son. Then you find out I'm pregnant and suddenly, you want me to wait for you? No thanks. I'm not interested in being your second choice, and damn you for even suggesting it."

Her outburst didn't seem to insult him. "You know I want to be with you, Cassie," he said quietly.

"I do?" Her voice was loud enough for other diners to look their way, so she toned it down to a hiss. "Because I haven't heard from you in over a month after you told me you were going to try to make it work with your wife."

"And you also know why I said that. It was a mistake to lie to you, Cass, but you know why I did it. It wasn't fair to ask you to be with me while I figure things out with Adriana. I have to be smart about this and patient. It's the only way I'm going to get Lucas. He's what matters most."

She'd only taken a few bites of her food, but suddenly felt sick and jumped up, tossing her napkin onto the table. With her hand on her belly, she said wryly, "I wondered where we would rate in your life," before rushing to the bathroom.

How appropriate Cooper was there with friends from work when she walked out of the bathroom. It was purely coincidence, she hadn't texted him, just pretended to in order to save her dignity when Luke exchanged texts with his wife at the station.

She didn't know how she was going to sell this. She wasn't dating Cooper Johnson, but she sure as fuck wasn't going to tell Luke that. Yet if she acted like she was, Cooper might be confused and not play along or worse, freak out, thinking a pregnant woman was interested in him.

Taking a deep breath in, she greeted the Marines at their table with a friendly hello and leaned down to kiss Cooper on the cheek. He smiled when he put his hand on her hip from his chair and asked what she was doing there, then waved to Luke when she told him who she was having lunch with.

"Well, I'll let you get back to lunch. I just wanted to say hi."

He stood and kissed her on the cheek. "Great seeing you, Cassandra."

The scowl on Luke's face as she returned to their table told her she had been successful in making him believe she and Cooper were an item.

It was a hollow victory, but at least her pride remained intact.

****

Luke

He watched her briskly make her way to the restroom, then surveyed the untouched food on their plates. He wasn't hungry anymore. He'd managed to say the wrong thing, again.

She'd just broke the best news to him he could have ever received, and he couldn't even wrap his arms around her and hold her in celebration. He was in a no-win situation.

If he asked Adriana for a divorce, there was a good chance she'd bolt to Mexico with his son, and he'd never see Lucas again. While the woman he was in love with was carrying his baby and had moved on with someone else.

When he watched Cassie leave the bathroom and make a beeline toward the front of the restaurant, he thought she was leaving without telling him goodbye. Once he saw where she was headed that might have been his preference.

Cooper Johnson better hope to never run into Luke in a dark alley. He'd beat the fuck out of that jarhead for having what should have been Luke's.

Cassie appeared at the table, paler than before.

"I don't think I'm going to be able to eat lunch," she stated unapologetically as she sat down.

"Did you tell him we were coming here?" Luke snarled.

She looked over at the Marine's table. "What? No, of course not."

He didn't know if he believed her but decided to drop it. There was no point arguing about it.

With a nod toward her lunch, he asked, "Do you want to get it boxed to go?"

She shook her head. "No, I think my days of eating fish are done, at least until the morning sickness passes."

"You probably shouldn't eat a lot of fish, anyway. I remember reading about mercury in it or something."

She gave him a placating smile. "Salmon is okay. But it doesn't really matter right now, anyway," she said with a wrinkled nose as she looked at her plate and pushed it away.

Luke picked it up and brought it to his side of the table, covering it with his napkin, then moved to sit next to her. He needed to touch her, fuck everything else. With one arm draped on the back of the booth behind her, he ran his fingers over the back of her hand before entwining it with his. She seemed to lean into him momentarily before catching herself and stiffening.

"You're just as important to me as Lucas is. I'm sorry I've not been able to show you that, but you are." He dropped his hand to her belly, it felt softer than the last time he'd touched her. "You and our little raspberry."

She let out a laugh, which turned into a sob. "It doesn't matter anymore, Luke. Just be there for the baby, okay?"

He held her in his arms, half expecting her to bristle against his touch. Instead, she did the opposite and melted into his embrace. He noticed the Marine looking at them but didn't give a fuck.

"I'm sorry, Cass. I've messed this whole thing up from the beginning. I should be marrying you tomorrow instead of you going home to Cooper, but I'm not sorry we're having a baby. I'm fucking ecstatic."

He felt her smile. "Brenna said you would be."

"Brenna's a smart woman, you should listen to her."

She pulled away from him and stared into her lap. "She also said I should date Cooper."

That elicited a scowl from him. "Okay, maybe you shouldn't listen to *everything* she says. What's he going to do when he finds out you're pregnant with *my* baby?" The question came out more accusatory than he intended, but Cooper Johnson getting to be the one to take care of her felt like a kick in the gut.

"I'm sure he'll be nothing but kind."

He knew he had no right to say what he was about to say, but he did anyway. "I don't like you seeing him."

With a look of incredulity, she huffed, "Huh, well you don't have any say in who I date these days."

"I do have a say in who is around my baby,' he snarled.

"Really? You're going to go there?"

"Cassie..." he softened his tone to plead his case.

She interrupted. "Are you getting divorced, Luke?"

"Yes, of course."

"Are you getting divorced *any time soon*? Like before the baby is born?" she clarified.

"It's not that easy."

"It really is that easy. You're the one making it complicated. As Lucas' father, you have rights like you'll have rights when this baby is born."

"Those rights don't do me any good if Lucas is in Mexico."

Her smile was sad. "Well, at least you won't have to worry about that with our baby. But I also get a say in who's around him, and I'm not thrilled about the prospect of your wife caring for him when he's with you. Maybe I'll request supervised visits since she's such a flight risk to Mexico, I wouldn't want her taking off with my child, too."

His stomach dipped. "You wouldn't do that."

She shrugged. "Probably not. But don't you dare tell me who I can or cannot see while you sit playing house with your happy family. I'm just getting used to this Mama Bear business, you don't want to see what I'm capable of when my cub is bigger than a raspberry," she warned.

His baby doll was going to be his baby mama bear. It was the most inopportune time for his dick to get hard, but the realization did exactly that.

"God, I love you."

"No," she glared at him, shoving him out of the booth, then scurried out behind him, poking his chest with her finger. "You don't get to say that to me anymore, Luke. You made your choice, and it wasn't me."

Borrowing a move he'd perfected over the last few years, she threw a hundred-dollar bill on the table and left without another word.

Chapter Forty-One

Cassie

She brushed the tears away from her cheeks while brusquely walking to her car. Damn Luke Santiago Rivas to hell. She had told herself she was done crying over him. She was blaming it on the pregnancy hormones, *not* because he made her toes tingle at his slightest touch, and it felt like her heart was breaking all over again.

She heard someone calling her name behind her. "Cassie, wait!"

Turning around, she watched as Cooper jogged after her in the parking lot. She hesitated, she wasn't in the mood for his attempt to comfort her, but out of politeness, waited until he caught up with her.

His face visibly was concerned when he rubbed her biceps and asked, "Are you okay?"

Cassie took another swipe under her eyes with her fingers and gave him her best attempt at a smile. "No, but I will be."

"Want some company?"

Her bottom lip began to tremble as she nodded her head. He brought his arms around her in a warm embrace.

"Hey," he whispered. "I'm here. It's okay."

Her eyes were closed, but she heard footsteps of someone running and knew it was Luke when they stopped suddenly a few feet from them.

His voice was contrite when he asked, "Can I talk to you, Cassie?"

Cooper pulled away and bent down with a questioning look.

She knew if she said no, the two men would get into a pissing match—the last thing she needed right now.

"It's okay," she whispered to her friend.

"I'll call you later," the Marine said as he reluctantly released her and began to walk away.

"I promise I won't take much of your girlfriend's time," Luke said caustically.

Cooper paused and turned back toward them, jerking his head. "My girlfriend? You think we're together?"

Fuck.

The blonde man must have noticed her look of panic because he made his best attempt at a recovery.

"Well, er, good. I'm glad you, uh, know," then awkwardly directed at Cassie, "I'll see you later, sweetheart."

The amused look on Luke's face let her know he wasn't buying it. Before he could say anything, she turned to walk away.

"I really can't stay, Luke. I'm late for an appointment."

He grabbed her by the elbow and spun her around, with a gruff, "Bullshit."

"Excuse me?" she asked, trying to jerk out of his grip. He reluctantly let go but pinned her in place with his glare.

"Bullshit, Cassandra Jo Sullivan. You scheduled at least a few hours for our date, and we didn't get through half that. You're not late for anything except running away from me."

She placed her hands on her hips. "Did you just full name me, Luke Santiago Rivas?" She couldn't help but laugh since she'd done that in her mind to him moments earlier. Of course, she was damning him to hell at the time but, hey.

He didn't hide his own grin. "Whatever works, doll."

"What do you need, Luke?" Her tone turned more serious.

"Well, first, you dropped this," he held her folded hundred-dollar bill out.

"That was for lunch."

"I told you before, I take care of what's mine."

This made her fume. "Well, you don't have to worry about taking care of me, since I'm not *yours*." Her anger was like water off a duck's back for him.

"Well, that baby you should be feeding is mine, so..." he declared as he tucked the money in her purse, leaving no room for further argument.

Whether it was because she was too tired to fight anymore, or she genuinely was appreciative, she wasn't sure as she said with a polite smile, "Thank you," and left it at that.

They stood in awkward silence before she spoke again. "I really do need to get going. I wanted to go to the grocery store since my food options seem to be dwindling by the day and take a nap before I have to go to a work dinner tonight."

He was a little too nonchalant when he asked, "Can I go with you?"

That surprised her. "To the grocery store? Don't you have to go back to work?"

"I'm taking the afternoon off. I'm going to use some of my much-accumulated personal time to get used to the idea of being your Baby Daddy. So, let me go with you, or do you think your *boyfriend* will mind?"

"Okay, fine." She let out a heavy sigh and rolled her eyes. "I admit it—I'm not dating Cooper. But why do you want to go to the grocery store with me?"

"A couple of reasons. One, to make sure you're feeding my baby healthy things and not junk." She shot him a look of exasperation. "And two, because it will let me spend time with you. I'll take that however I can get it."

She teared up again, and he looked horrified. "What?! What did I do?"

"Stop being nice to me. I'm trying to hate you right now."

He slid his hand around her waist with no hesitation. "No can do, baby doll. I won't let you hate me," he murmured in her hair, then gave her a long kiss on her head before slowly releasing her.

"I wish you would," she whispered. "It'd be so much easier that way."

"No, it wouldn't, and you know it. We're having a baby, Cass. We need to be on each other's team."

"I don't know how to do that with you any more."

He guided her toward her car. "Well, let's start with groceries."

****

Luke

He stopped pushing the shopping cart and stared at her incredulously.

"How can you *not* want to know? Think about how much easier it will be to prepare for its arrival."

"Stop calling the baby *it*."

He laughed. "That's also why I wanna know! How about if they tell me, then when your Type-A personality takes over, and you need to get shit done before it gets here, you'll ask me. *Maybe* I'll tell you."

They resumed walking down the aisle with Cassie shaking her head with a smirk.

"You think you know me so well. You don't know."

Luke pulled a box of Life cereal from the shelf and shook it at her before putting it in the cart. "I know you like cereal for dinner because you're too impatient to cook anything."

"Everyone knows that." she scoffed.

"I know not feeding your caffeine addiction during this pregnancy has probably been harder for you than morning sickness. Your favorite color is blue, you say your favorite author is Stephen King, but the only thing I've ever seen you reading are romance novels. You don't easily forgive people who have wronged you, but you're fiercely loyal to the people you love," he put his hand on her stomach, "and you are going to be the best mama bear with our little cub."

She stood glaring at him. Twice she opened her mouth as if to speak, then closed it. Finally, she took over pushing the cart and mumbled, "You think you're so smart."

That elicited a loud laugh from him as they continued towards the fresh vegetable section.

"You know you love me."

"I love you like a friend," she said very matter-of-factly as she surveyed the produce.

He patted her back. "Sure, doll. Sure."

Without even looking at him while she inspected peppers, she asked quietly, "Are you going to ask Adriana for a divorce?"

He stood next to her, picking up a red pepper.

"I have to be smart about it but, yes, eventually. I meant what I said. I do love you and want you to wait for me. Don't give up on us, Cass."

"I think I have to, Luke," she said in a low voice, looking up at him. She set down the yellow pepper she'd been holding as a single tear slid down her cheek. "I can't do this. Being with you like this, like a couple—feels so natural. It's not fair to me. You're going home to your family tonight, and I'm going home alone. You're someone else's husband, whether you're together as man and wife or not doesn't matter. You're not mine. Yes, you're the father of my child, so we'll always be connected, but we need to stop this. My heart can't handle it."

He nodded reluctantly in understanding as he absent-mindedly turned the bell pepper over and over in his hand. She was right, it wasn't fair to her; it wasn't fair to him to be without her either, especially since she was carrying his child. But until he was free to fight for her, he'd have to accept that even though a part of him was dying not being able to hold her.

"I hate this," he whispered.

Cassie plucked the vegetable from him and put it into a plastic, produce bag—spinning it closed before placing it in her cart.

"Me too," she said matter-of-factly. He realized she was dismissing him when she turned to him with a fake smile. "Thank you for coming with me, but I've got it from here. I'll be in touch about things."

"Can I at least go to your appointments with you?" he asked hopefully.

She mulled over his request as she moved along the aisle. "Yes. I'll let you know when the next one is, okay?"

He wanted to tell her he loved her and was going to find a way for them to be together again, but until he could back that up, it wouldn't be fair to say it, so he simply leaned down and kissed her cheek.

"Take care of yourself, doll. Let me know if you need anything, please? Anything. Even if it's pickles and ice cream at three in the morning, all you have to do is say the word, and I'll be at your doorstep with Haagen-Dazs and Vlasics.

That drew a small smile, and she patted his hand. "Thank you. I hope things work out for you, Luke. I'll text you."

He knew that was his sign to go, but he couldn't bring himself to leave, desperately trying to think of something else to say to keep him there with her even for only a few more minutes.

"I can't believe we're having a baby," he said with a big smile.

"It took me a little while to come to terms with it, too."

"How long have you known?" Keeping her talking was working, she hadn't shooed him away yet.

"I took a home test last Thursday and went to the doctor today. I called you when I was finished with my appointment."

"I wish I could have been there with you," he murmured.

She smiled politely but didn't respond further.

It was time to go. He couldn't put it off any longer.

"Please let me know when your next appointment is, doll."

"I will. Take care."

With that, he reluctantly left her looking at the spinach. At least she was eating healthy.

Chapter Forty-Two

Cassie

The next month flew by, the holidays passed in a blur. She still felt sorry for herself when she was alone in bed, unable to sleep, picturing Luke with his family at Thanksgiving or on Christmas morning as Lucas unwrapped his gifts from Santa. Meanwhile, she didn't even bother with a tree.

Next year, she thought. Every holiday after the baby was born was going to be a big deal, so she was going to cut herself a break until then.

She heard from Luke every Monday morning like clockwork, asking how she was feeling and if she needed anything, then inquiring about her next appointment. The tone of his texts or calls was always polite and friendly, but never suggestive or even flirtatious.

Their exchanges usually went something like this:

Luke Rivas: Good morning! How are you feeling this Monday?

Cassie: I'm fine, thanks. You?

Luke Rivas: I'm great. Another busy week ahead.

Everything okay with the baby? Any concerns? Do you need anything?

Cassie: Everything seems to be right on track. I will keep you posted if something changes.

Luke Rivas: Be sure to let me know when your next appointment is.

Cassie: Of course.

Luke Rivas: Have a great week.

Cassie: You too.

They could have been talking about a car for how impersonal they were; except the man who sold her the Lexus had been far more engaging when he followed up with her after the sale.

The impassive nature of Luke's texts made her wonder if things with his wife were working out. She especially liked to torture herself, wondering if he and Adriana were being intimate. It had been almost three-and-a-half months since she and Luke had sex. She was kidding herself if she thought he wasn't sleeping with his wife.

Hell, Cassie had thought about propositioning Cooper the few times they'd had lunch or dinner. Not because she wanted to date him, she was just that horny. She couldn't imagine Luke was any less horny, and he had a *wife living* with him. The wife he was trying to reconcile with even if he said it was only for the sake of his son.

As Brenna would say, it wasn't very Christian of her, but she really hated Adriana Rivas. She didn't deserve Luke after what she'd put him through. It wasn't fair she got to be with him every night with her child while Cassie would never get the same opportunity with her baby.

Part of Cassie wondered if Luke ever really wanted to divorce Adriana since he never did in all the years after she left him, and now Lucas was a convenient excuse not to. Cassie's pregnancy complicated his life, sure, but the fact he hadn't been willing to divorce Adriana and fight for Cassie told her all she needed to know.

Buying the house next door to Brenna proved to keep her exceptionally busy. Ava Sterling had sold her condo—in a day—

so Cassie was now dealing with home inspections on both the buying and selling end of things. Not to mention all the other things that came with being a new homeowner—everything from working with architects and designers, buying furniture to be delivered when she moved in, to simply establishing the utilities for her beach house in her name.

Her own beach house. That was crazy!

Almost as crazy as decorating a nursery. She would never have imagined it yet here she was, buying baby furniture. Alone. It was bittersweet. She was starting to get excited about being a mother, something Luke had wanted so badly, and now, they weren't together.

Her new place was a four-bedroom, two-story beach house similar to Brenna's, but in need of updating. Cassie was okay with that since it meant she was going to be able to remodel it to her specific tastes, and she got it for a song. She had contractors lined up ready to start the day after she closed.

The biggest selling point was its location. Being next to Brenna when she was about to become a mother provided her with a sense of peace—she wasn't all alone in this, help was right next door.

Luckily, the condo's buyers were not going to be moving in until late spring and agreed to let her rent it back for a month once they finally closed, so she didn't have to stay at the beach house while renovations were being done. Brenna had offered to let Cassie stay with her and Ron, but Cassie didn't want to intrude on the newlyweds. She'd stay overnight with them here and there if she were at her house working late but not for an extended period of time.

The condo needed minor repairs before closing, so she went to the hardware store for materials and ran into Ben, of all people.

"Well, well, well.... Look who it is and more beautiful than ever." She recognized his baritone voice before she even turned around from the plumbing supplies she was currently perusing.

"Mr. McCallister. Well, I do declare, as I live and breathe," she teased, fanning herself and using her best Southern drawl impression. "Why, whatever are you doing in these here parts?"

With a grin, he leaned down and kissed her cheek. "Hi, sweet thang. I live around here now. How are you?"

"I'm okay." She put her hand on her visible bump. "Pregnant and exhausted but surviving. How are you? How are things going with the ladies?"

"You know I don't kiss and tell, Missy." Ben winked that adorable, charming wink of his. "But I'm doing well. I'm glad to see you are too." He tilted his head at the plumbing package in her hands. "What are you up to?"

With a heavy sigh, she explained. "I sold my condo and have to fix a couple of things before I can close on it."

"Congratulations! Are you staying in town?"

Cassie knew he was probably probing her for Luke's sake, worried she was going to skip town with his best friend's baby like Luke's wife had.

"Actually, I am. I bought a place on the beach next to my sister."

"Niiice. So, I'll be first on your list to call for housesitting, right? It always pissed me off when Luke got to—" He stopped abruptly. "I'm sorry. Is it okay if I talk about him?"

Her laughter suggested how ridiculous he sounded. Patting her belly, she teased, "Well, we obviously have a history, I think it'd be pretty silly to pretend we don't."

"Okay, good. I was worried. I'm not allowed to talk about you with him."

"What do you mean, you're not *allowed* to talk about me?"

"Well, not *you*, in general. *You* if you're, you know, out with someone else."

He must have been talking about the time she picked up Cooper at his shop. She nodded her head in agreement.

"I understand that. I mean, I'd prefer not to hear all about his domestic bliss if you don't mind. But given our circumstances, he and I are connected for life, so there's no use pretending he doesn't exist."

Ben snorted. "There's definitely no domestic bliss although he does love being a dad. He's really excited to do it again. From the start, this time. He doesn't want to miss anything with... Him? Her?"

"We'll know next week."

He nudged her with his elbow. "I'm going to be a kick-ass uncle, ya know."

"I have no doubt." she chuckled. "Maybe you'll even get baby fever yourself."

Expecting him to scoff, she was shocked when he shrugged with a grin and with his steel-booted toe, tapped the bottom shelf filled with bins containing white plastic casings of varying sizes.

"Maybe."

"Ben McCallister, are you becoming domesticated?" she teased as she clutched his elbow.

"I plead the fifth." He tried to change the subject by taking the package from her and turning it over. "So, what repairs are you doing? Do you need any help? I'm pretty handy when it comes to fixing things."

She grabbed his arm around his bicep. "Oh my God, Ben, I would love you forever. I have no idea what I'm doing! I was going to go home and watch YouTube videos to try to figure this out," she confessed.

His deep, booming laugh echoed off the metal shelves in the aisle and gestured toward the cash registers. "Come on, mamasita. I've got you covered."

****

Luke

The bellman in Cassie's apartment was busy with a Girl Scout troop when Luke marched into the building and made his way to the bank of elevators. It was probably because he acted like he belonged there and his face was familiar, coupled with the older man's preoccupation with the eight young girls' animated cookie sales pitch that Luke made it to Cassie's apartment without her receiving notice he was coming.

Knocking loudly on her door, he waited only a few seconds before brusquely rapping his knuckles again hard against the wood.

Her tone was annoyed as she came toward the door, yelling. "I'm coming." then he heard her mutter softly, "Jesus, relax."

That made him briefly grin, in spite of himself.

She yanked the door open, her scowl turning into a look of surprise, then bewilderment.

"Hi?" The greeting was in the form of a question. He barged in without being invited. She closed the door behind him with a sarcastic, "Come on in."

She'd barely gotten the lock latched when he whirled around at her.

"You have a doctor's appointment this week to find out the sex of the baby?"

The bewilderment remained in her expression. "Yes."

"Mind telling me why I have to learn about this from my best friend?" he accused. "When were you planning on telling me about it? An hour before, hoping I wouldn't be able to make it?"

"Are you fucking for real right now?" She stared at him in disbelief. "You... You're fucking with me, right?"

"Why didn't you tell me?" As he towered over her, the desire to touch her clashed with his anger as he tried to control both.

"I *did* tell you, asshole."

Dressed in a pink flowing top and black stretch pants, she started waddling toward the kitchen, and he stood frozen. This was the first time he'd seen her obviously pregnant. His anger instantly dissipated, replaced with regret and sadness.

Cassie came back with her phone and started forcefully scrolling on the screen. Shoving it at him, she declared, "See? Right here. I told you the time, date, and place."

He took it from her, biting back his smile when he looked at the screen. "Uh, Cass? You didn't hit *send*, doll."

She snatched it from him, shaking her head when seeing the pending text.

"Shit. Damn pregnancy brain," she muttered.

The phone in his pocket chirped. He pulled it out and laughed. It was her message.

"Thanks."

"There, now you have it. Anything else you need to bark at me about since you're here? I'd hate for you to have to make a second trip to barge into my place and yell at me, uninvited and unannounced, I might add."

He brushed against her as he headed toward the kitchen. "As a matter of fact, there is."

With a heavy sigh, she followed him. "What now, Luke?"

"You let Ben fix your faucet?" He started inspecting her faucet, looking for any mistake his friend hopefully made while he helped her.

"Among other things."

"What the hell does that mean?" he roared.

"It means," she planted her hand on her hip, unimpressed with his tirade, "I let Ben fix my faucet, among other things."

He was hanging on by a thread. He'd had lunch with Ben this afternoon and had worked himself into a fit, thinking about Ben helping her instead of him, not to mention he didn't even know she was moving before today. Then he learned about her appointment, and he almost came unglued right at the restaurant table. Ben had managed to calm him down, but the minute Luke left lunch, he started to get upset all over again. He left work an hour early, hoping to catch her at the condo.

The oversight about actually sending the appointment text soothed him a little, but he was still mad about her asking Ben for help. Whether she was pushing his buttons on purpose with her, *among other things* didn't matter. It was working.

"What kinds of other things?" he snarled.

The glint in her eye told him the button pushing was on purpose, and he gripped the edge of the countertop tightly.

"I don't know, things that needed to get done before the sale..."

"And that's another thing. When were you planning on telling me you were moving?"

"I dunno," she shrugged nonchalantly. "When I actually moved, I guess."

"You don't think that's something I should probably be made aware of?"

He could tell she was starting to get mad, which part of him took delight in. He'd rather have her pissed off than not giving a shit.

"Who the hell do you think you are?" She thrust her finger into his chest. "You don't get to come barreling into my home, yelling at me about having someone help me with things I needed to have taken care of. Demanding I keep you informed of my every move. Sorry pal, you lost those privileges when you chose your wife over me."

Luke grabbed her finger, and the two stood staring at each other in a Mexican standoff. He noticed her chest heaving and groaned internally. Her tits were getting bigger, too. Unable to resist, he kissed her wrist tenderly.

"Goddammit, Cass, I didn't choose her over you. It will always be you, doll."

She closed her eyes and let him continue kissing her. He could feel the goosebumps covering her skin and pulled her into him. His mouth captured hers, and after a momentary, token resistance, she succumbed to him. Their tongues tangled until they were angling to deepen the kiss, his arm wrapped around her waist, arching her back so she was completely enveloped by his frame. Cassie mewled when he pressed his cock between her legs. The heat from her pussy was like a flame, and his cock was the moth being drawn to it.

She began to subtly grind against him. Luke pulled her shirt over her head, then freed her heavy tits from the confines of her bra. He wanted to stop and stare at them in amazement but worried any discontinuity would break the spell she seemed to be under. Instead, he began suckling one nipple while pinching and rolling the other. Cassie gently tugged the hairs at the back of his neck, holding him where he lavished her deprived tits with much-needed attention.

She reached down to unbutton his jeans, and his throbbing cock started to sing the hallelujah chorus when her petite fingers encircled the head and began to stroke his shaft. Luke groaned into her chest, sucking her pebbled peaks with ferocity. It'd been so long since he'd felt her touch and his cock was weeping with joy. At this rate, he was going to come in her hand like a pubescent schoolboy.

Gently tugging her black pants over her beautiful belly and down her thighs, he lifted her on top of the counter and continued removing them. To his delight, he found she wasn't wearing panties. He spread her legs wide and ran his index finger up and down her soaked slit. With both hands, he pulled her pussy lips apart and dipped his head down to lick her labia using long strokes of his tongue. She bucked her hips against his face, and he slid one finger inside her tight little hole while his tongue began to alternate flicking her clit and sucking it. Her little pearl was rock hard in his mouth, and she spread her legs further apart. Bowing against his mouth, she started to moan.

"Yes, baby. Right there. Oh, fuck, Luke, yes. Right there. Don't stop, please don't stop!"

He replaced his mouth with his fingers and began to polish her nub while he continued finger fucking her. Her pussy started to quiver around his digits while she gasped for breath and raised her hips an inch off the counter.

"That's it, baby," he purred in encouragement. "Come for me. Come all over my hands."

Her frustration was evident in her cry. He could tell she was so close but seemed to be giving up, sliding her thighs together.

"Keep those fucking legs spread," Luke snarled as he yanked them apart again, then pushed his jeans all the way off. He slid inside her pussy with one thrust, her desire helping his cock find its way deep inside despite how tight she was. They moaned in unison as he began to move his hips.

What was happening between them was carnal, and as much as he hated their reunion sex was lust-fueled instead of loving and passionate, it might be exactly what they needed.

He plunged inside her cunt, manipulating her clit as he did. Cassie bent off the counter while he strummed her jewel faster.

"You're so tight. Your pussy has missed me."

"Yes! Oh, fuck yes, it's missed you so much," she panted, moving her hips in rhythm with his.

"Are you going to come all over your baby daddy's cock?"

"Mmm hmm," she whimpered.

"Take my cock, doll," he growled. "Take it all."

Luke started to fuck her faster while rubbing her clit with a frenzy.

Her pussy gripped his dick, and she bowed off the counter, her mouth in the shape of a silent 'O.' Suddenly, she let out a long moan. "Ohhh, fuuuuck, yes!" and her body began to shudder.

As her orgasm racked through her, he held her hips tight and seated himself deep inside her, grunting his release.

With his cock still buried inside her, he stared in wonderment as she laid before him—rounded, pregnant body, sex hair, and flushed skin. Luke leaned down and kissed her mouth, looking into her eyes while murmuring against her lips, "You're the most beautiful woman I've ever seen."

She gazed back with a smile, her fingers entwined in his hair. "You're the sexiest man I've ever seen. I've missed you so much, Luke."

His softening cock slid out of her, and he grabbed a towel to clean her gently before scooping her up and carrying her pliant body to her bedroom. There, he pulled back the covers and laid her carefully on the bed. She moved to the middle, beckoning him to lie down next to her.

Instead, he knelt on the floor and brushed the hair from her face. "I wish I could, doll, but I have to get home."

She sat up like a shot.

"You mean you're not staying?"

"I can't, Cass. You know that."

"Are you kidding me? You're still going home to her? You're going to leave me here alone, again?"

He didn't want to leave her. There was nothing he wanted more than to hold her in his arms all night, talking about nothing and everything, then wake her up with his face between her legs. But he couldn't—not yet.

She started to sob. "I am so fucking stupid. Nothing has changed, has it? This was you, getting your rocks off, nothing more." Her bottom lip quivered, and he tried to put his arm around her, but she pushed him away. His little mama bear lifted her chin defiantly even though her lip still trembled.

"Get out." He was reluctant to move, and she shouted, her outstretched arm gesturing toward the front door. "I said, *Get out!*"

"Cass...."

"Get the fuck out of here, Luke. I can't even stand to look at you. This isn't good for the baby."

He couldn't argue with the *not good for the baby card* she played, so he had no choice but to head toward the door. She followed behind, tying her robe closed as she carefully kept her distance.

As he stepped out the front door, she pulled off one last parting shot.

"I don't want you at my appointment. I'll let you know how it goes."

Spinning around to look at her standing in the doorway, he implored, "Cassie, no. Please."

"Fuck you. Go home to your *wife.*" She closed the door in his face and immediately threw the lock.

He willed himself not to pound on the door again and demand she talk to him. He'd give her time to cool down.

And he was going to that appointment.

Chapter Forty-Three

Luke

"I'm sorry, Mister Rivas. Ms. Sullivan rescheduled her appointment."

"For when?"

The lady behind the desk who was the spitting image of his grandma looked sympathetically at him. "I'm sorry, sir, that's confidential. You're not approved to share that information with."

"That's my baby." Luke was seething. "I have a right to—"

"Mister Rivas, please. I would tell you if I could, but I could very well lose my job if I did. I'm sorry, there's nothing I can do. Maybe get in touch with Ms. Sullivan?"

He nodded with a gruff, "Yeah, I'll do that."

A new tactic was needed. If ever there was a time to play dirty, this would be it. He looked at the older woman, flashing his most charming smile at her, the one that usually had a woman taking off her clothes, and glanced at the name placard on her desk.

"Phyllis, please," he beseeched her.

He could see her conflict, but she stood strong. "Mr. Rivas, I can't."

"I'm begging you. I would never disclose you told me."

He turned his head, his hand pretending to pinch the top of his nose between his eyes as he sneakily yanked an eyebrow hair so tears were filling his eyes when he met her gaze again. He could see her resolve weakening.

"I'm sorry, sir. I wish I could help you. You seem like a nice man."

"I really do love her, ya know? I just want to be a part of her life." That part was true. He nodded his head sadly, then turned on his heel and headed toward the door.

The gray-haired woman called after him, "Mister Rivas! I think you dropped something," and pushed an appointment card off the desk to the floor.

He bent over and picked it up, glancing at the date and time of Cassie's new appointment and gave the receptionist a smile. "Thanks. Wouldn't want to lose that."

"Good luck, Mister Rivas."

His hands were shaking, he was still so angry with Cassie. He sat in his Jeep in the parking lot and fired off a text to her.

Luke: I was just informed you rescheduled the sonogram.

He was surprised she responded before he even put the vehicle in drive.

HBD Sullivan: I told you not to come. I'll let you know what we're having.

Luke: This is bullshit, Cassie. I have a right to be there.

HBD Sullivan: Nah, you're needed at home.

Luke punched the steering wheel. *Damn that woman for being so hardheaded.*

He'd fucked up by sleeping with her. He shouldn't have done it, he knew that now, but at the time, all he could think about was her silky skin on his, her delicious lips on, well, everything of his, and getting his cock deep inside her heavenly pussy. It was fucking glorious even if it was short-lived.

Now, she thought he'd used her. Which, if he was being honest with himself, maybe he had. He'd wanted her so badly, he hadn't cared about the consequences.

Well, he was caring now.

Somehow, he'd make this right and give her the pound of flesh she was demanding, all before her sonogram appointment. He had to, there was no other way around it. He needed to be with her like he needed air. So help him, he'd find a way to have both Lucas and Cassie in his life.

Chapter Forty-Four

Cassie

She felt guilty finding out the sex of the baby without Luke there. Brenna's silent disapproval as they sat in the waiting room didn't help matters. Cassie almost rescheduled in order to give Luke the opportunity to attend but in the end, decided not to. She was still angry with him and wasn't willing to play nice yet.

He texted every day, sometimes two or three times—always in the morning to ask how she was feeling and ask her forgiveness, and often later to tell her something about his day or that he was thinking about her.

Damn him. He was making it hard for her to stay pissed. She needed to hang on to her anger. Sometimes, it was the only thing that got her through the day without breaking down.

Other than the text about the sonogram, she hadn't responded to him since their fight after they'd slept together. She didn't know why she thought sex was going to make him stay with her—at least for the night—but she did and was crushed when she realized nothing had changed.

"Do you want to have a gender reveal party?" Brenna's question brought Cassie back to the present.

"What? God, no! I don't want to do anything like that. I don't even want a baby shower."

"Too bad," her older sister said emphatically. "You're not denying me that.'

Cassie leaned back with a sigh in her uncomfortable tan, fake leather seat. There was no point in arguing with Brenna—

she could be as stubborn as Cassie when she wanted something.

"And you're doing a housewarming party, too. Separate from the baby shower."

"Now, *that* you cannot make me do."

"Oh, yes I can. I'll have everyone at my house first, then we'll go traipsing over to your place."

"Ya know, if I had known you were going to act like this, I would have moved further away."

"You love me," Brenna grinned as she flipped through a complimentary magazine.

Cassie couldn't deny that and grabbed her sister's hand. "I do. Thanks for coming with me today. I really appreciate it."

Brenna squeezed her hand. "I'm honored you let me be here." The unspoken admonishment of not including Luke hung heavy in the air, and Cassie looked at the ground trying to keep from tearing up.

Her sister tried to lighten the mood. "Let me take you to lunch after this, then we can go to my place and video chat with Dee and tell her the good news."

"I'm so tired, Bren..."

"You gotta eat, honey. I promised Lu..." Brenna shook her head. "I promised mom and dad I would make sure you were taking care of yourself."

"Let's see how I feel after this, okay?" She'd let her sister's collusion with Luke slide—for now.

Brenna patted her hand. "Okay." Her placating smile turned genuine as she looked past Cassie. "I thought you said you didn't tell him the day."

Confused, Cassie turned toward her sister's focus. Luke was striding toward them, holding Lucas' hand, a masculine-looking, black diaper bag draped over his broad shoulder. She was pretty sure every woman in the waiting room was swooning.

"I didn't," she responded. She felt a combination of happy, mad, and relieved to see him.

He sat down next to her with a sheepish smile, drawing Lucas into his lap.

"That's a dirty trick, bringing your son with you, Mister Rivas," she murmured while looking at his beautiful little boy.

He handed Lucas a book he'd pulled from the black bag. "I know, but I'm done playing fair. Desperate times call for desperate measures," he replied softly, then louder, and in Spanish, introduced his son to Cassie and Brenna.

Luke's mini-me turned charmingly shy and burrowed his head into his dad's shoulder, occasionally peeking over at the women with a small grin, then quickly hiding his head again when they'd return his smile.

"Cassie va a ser tu madrastra algún dia." *Cassie is going to be your stepmother someday.*

She was shocked he was telling Lucas that.

Luke softly patted Cassie's belly and continued, "Ella tiene a tu hermito o hermana en su barriguita." *She has your little brother or sister in her tummy.*

The little boy's eyes went wide in wonderment as he stared at Cassie's round belly.

"Luke, should you be telling him this?" Cassie asked, barely moving her lips as she smiled at mini-Luke.

The gorgeous man grabbed her hand and kissed it, not letting go once he brought it away from his lips. "Yes. I should have done it the first night he arrived."

Cassie had no idea where all this was coming from or what it meant as far as Adriana was concerned, but obviously, questioning him in front of Lucas was not the appropriate time to find out.

Brenna's Spanish was rusty, but judging by her blue eyes as wide as Lucas' brown ones, she understood the gist of what Luke had said.

"You've got a lot of explaining to do, Rivas," Cassie quietly warned then started talking to Lucas in Spanish. The little boy's face lit up when he realized Cassie spoke his native language, and he started to warm up to her even going so far as to tentatively touch her stomach and ask how his little brother or sister was in there.

"*Cassie Sullivan*," a woman in teal scrubs holding a clipboard called from the side of the lobby.

The younger Sullivan sister took a deep breath, then stood, motioning for her entourage to follow. The ultrasound tech smiled at the brood behind Cassie and said, "You've got some backup today."

"I hope that's okay?"

"Of course. It's a big day for your family."

Cassie surveyed the group. *Her family.* "Yeah, it is. More than you know."

Chapter Forty-Five

Luke

He couldn't stop smiling. He'd just heard his baby's heartbeat and was waiting for the doctor to get a look if they were having a boy or girl.

Pointing to the monitor screen, he tried explaining to his almost-three-year-old what he was seeing. Luke knew Lucas didn't understand but could still sense the excitement and happiness in the room. That was what Luke wanted, his son to understand the love flowing between them. He hoped Lucas felt included in that dynamic.

Cassie was fucking amazing with his son. To ease Lucas' concern, she held his hand and told him the doctor was tickling her with the ultrasound wand. That elicited a giggle from the boy.

"You were in your mommy's tummy once, too," she explained.

"Like his little sister is in yours now," the doctor added.

He and Cassie froze, staring at each other while they processed the news they were having a little girl. The doctor gestured to the screen where their little girl—now bigger than a raspberry—was displayed.

The woman in the white coat drew an imaginary circle on the monitor and said, "No little boy parts. Congratulations, Mom and Dad. You're having a girl."

Luke leaned down, cupping one side of Cassie's face in his hand while he pressed his cheek against hers, tearfully whispering. "We're going to have a little princess."

Her eyes were wet when she murmured, "A little girl."

Brenna stood on the other side of the table, tears streaming down her cheeks when she leaned over and hugged them both. "Congratulations you guys. This is so exciting! I'm really happy for you."

"Everything looks great, so far, Cassie," the doctor interjected as she threw her disposable blue gloves in the stainless-steel trash can. "Call my office to schedule your next visit in two weeks," she instructed, then excused herself. Luke lifted Lucas up, setting the boy on his hip while explaining he was going to have a little sister.

"You're going to be a great big brother," Brenna told him in stilted Spanish as she stroked his arm.

"¿La Madrastra Cassie, mi hermana y la tía Brenna van a vivir con nosotros y mamá?" *Are stepmother Cassie, my sister, and Aunt Brenna going to live with us and mama?*

Cassie shot Luke a look of worry. Of course, his son didn't understand the dynamic. He had never seen his father and mother interact as a couple, but he was witnessing his papa and Cassie holding hands and whispering words of comfort to each other. Obviously, he thought that would translate to include his mother.

"Tia Brenna lives with her husband in their own house," Luke explained in Spanish, then looked at Cassie sheepishly before saying, "And someday you, me, Cassie, and your little sister will live in a different house." *I probably should have talked to her about that first.*

To his amazement, she didn't balk.

"What about mama?" his son asked in a small voice.

"Mama will have her own house where you will visit her. We'll be in a new house by the water."

Lucas did not like that idea and started to cry. "I want mama to live in the new house with us! She'll be sad by herself."

"You'll go visit her all the time," Luke assured his son as he hugged the boy tight to his chest, calming him down. Looking over Lucas' head, he addressed Cassie who was sitting up and pulling her blouse down after wiping the goo from her stomach. "Um, I need to talk to you about this, later. But it's very possible Lucas and I, uh, might be homeless shortly."

She looked at him with a sly smile as she hopped off the table. "As long as you don't mind sharing a room with Lucas, you're welcome to stay in the guest room at the condo if you need to."

"Any way I can upgrade to the master bedroom?" Luke asked hopefully with a grin.

"Don't push it or you'll be staying in Brenna's guest room."

"Hey! Don't I get a say in this?" her sister asked in mock indignation, then in a stage whisper added, "You two are welcome anytime, Luke."

He didn't take his eyes off Cassie. "Maybe Lucas can have a sleepover with Tia Brenna very soon so his papa can show Madrastra Cassie how sorry he is."

Brenna smirked, but Cassie remained unaffected, nonchalantly responding as she walked out the exam room door, "Lucas' papa needs to get out of the doghouse first, then he can worry about sleepovers."

Luke picked up the diaper bag in one arm, shifting Lucas to his alternate hip before following, loudly calling after her,

"I'll gladly serve my penance, doll. Whatever it takes, however long it takes. As long as I'm serving it under the same roof as you and my kids, I don't care."

She slowed her stride and turned around to look at them. "You mean, *our* kids, right?"

Luke was pretty sure this was what it meant when people said someone was beaming. He was on fucking Cloud Nine.

"Yes, of course."

Chapter Forty-Six

Cassie

"If you're going to fall asleep, at least wait until after lunch," her sister teased.

Cassie knew Brenna was dying to talk about Luke. Cassie purposefully didn't invite him and Lucas to lunch so the two sisters could dissect what the hell just happened. But once she got situated in Brenna's warm car, it became harder and harder to stay awake

"I'm sorry, Bren. I'm exhausted and feel like I don't know if I'm coming or going right now."

"Let's order takeout from the Chinese restaurant around the corner from the house. You can prop your feet up on my couch and relax. I don't want you to get too overwhelmed. A lot happened this morning."

"You're telling me," Cassie grumbled.

"Are you okay? With... well, all of it?"

"I'm thrilled I'm having a little girl although a boy would have been fine too. I don't really care as long as she's healthy. As far as Luke and Lucas... Let's just say, I'll believe it when I see it."

"You don't think he's really going to ask Adriana for a divorce?" Brenna prodded.

Cassie burst into tears.

"I don't know. He shows up out of nowhere and drops this into my lap, typical Luke Rivas style. Am I supposed to be happy? Angry? He doesn't give me time to process things. First, we're in love, and he asks me to marry him, then the next thing I know, he's living with his wife and son and *trying to make it work.*" She put air quotes around *trying to make it work.* "Then he's at my condo last week, going all sexy alpha-male, and I end up sleeping with him, only for him to say nothing's changed between him and his wife. Now, he..."

"*He did what?!*" Brenna interrupted.

"Yeah. I thought I told you that was why I was mad at him and didn't invite him today. Which, by the way, how did he find out the day and time?"

"I swear, I didn't tell him, Cass. I have no idea how he found out. But he did what?!"

"Yeah, we slept together. It was a mistake." She shrugged, too tired to try to figure out how he found out or tell her sister much about last week's encounter with Luke. "

Brenna continued the recap of the morning's events, "And now he wants to move in with you and bring his son."

"Like I said," Cassie sighed, "I'll believe it when I see it. He hasn't wanted to be with me since Adriana showed up, what's different about today from yesterday? He just woke up and thought, *I'm going to ask my wife for a divorce today*? I have a hard time believing he's really going to do it."

Her sister pursed her lips. "He found out he was having a daughter today, that's what's different. He was pretty excited. I think he seemed sincere."

"We'll see," she replied with a shrug of the shoulders. "Besides, do I really want to have a relationship with someone who only wants to be with me so he can be with his daughter?"

"He'd want to be with you, no matter what, Cass."

"Hmm..." She shook her head slowly. "I don't know if I believe that. He only decided he wanted to be with me once he found out I was pregnant. Before that, he was going to make it work with his other baby mama."

Brenna looked at her skeptically. "I don't think that's true. I think your pregnancy spurred him to do what he's wanted to do even before he found out you were pregnant."

"I don't know what to think anymore, Brenna," Cassie sighed in resignation. "I'm not even convinced he's going to leave her." Truth was, Cassie didn't want to get her hopes up. She didn't think she could handle having them quashed again.

Brenna cocked her head. "Do you think she loves him? Do you think that's why she came back? Or do you think it was for money?"

"I only know what she did to Luke before Lucas was born, and she kept Lucas away from him for over three years. I have to wonder why she decided to show up now."

"He served her with divorce papers in Mexico, right?" her sister asked as she slowed for a stoplight.

"I guess. But why didn't she just sign them there? Why did she come back? Was it because she developed a conscience or because she saw an opportunity to get more money out of him? Or maybe she realized she is still in love with him, who knows."

"I highly doubt that's it." Brenna made a face. "If she really loved him, she wouldn't have left him in the first place, ya know?" She accelerated off the light. "But let's think positively and say she developed a conscience about keeping her son from his father. A divorce settlement will be a small price to pay if he can get custody of Lucas and be done with this, once and for all."

"Let's hope so," Cassie sighed. She wasn't convinced it was going to be that easy but agreed, she needed to think positively. "That is if he even actually asks her for a divorce. I'm still skeptical," she murmured as she put the passenger seat back and closed her eyes.

Cassie dozed until they arrived at Brenna's beach house. Luke's Challenger was in the driveway when they pulled in. Cassie had woken up disoriented when the car slowed down, wondering if she was imagining it being there until Brenna said softly, as if to herself, "I guess he decided to come today."

They walked into the house through the garage to find Luke with his son sitting at the kitchen island, talking to Ron. Well, Luke and Ron were talking, Lucas was happily munching on cookies, swinging his legs on the barstool as he did.

"Madrastra Cassie! Tia Brenna!" the little boy squealed, and before Luke could stop him, he jumped off the stool and hugged each woman around one leg at the same time. The little guy was already finding his way into her heart.

"Hi, buddy," she said quietly in English as she stroked his hair.

Luke must have noticed her look of exhaustion because he was at her side before she even had time to greet him.

"Madrastra is tired and needs to lie down for a little while," Luke told his son in Spanish, then addressed Cassie in English, "Why don't you rest in here," he suggested as he guided her to the guest room.

Cassie leaned against him for support as they walked and whispered, "What are you doing here?"

"I came to drop Rex off, remember?" he replied as he helped take her shoes off. "Rest for a while and we'll talk when you wake up, okay?"

If she wasn't so exhausted, she would have argued and been unable to fall asleep from the questions seeing him brought. As it was, she was out as soon as her head hit the comfy pillow. She vaguely remembered feeling little hands stroke her face and give her a sloppy kiss on the cheek before she fell fast asleep.

****

Luke

While they were at Cassie's appointment, Brenna had told him Rex could stay with her until he had resolved things with Adriana. Knowing Rex was safe and being taken care of was one less thing he'd have to worry about.

He didn't waste any time and picked his dog up while he knew Adriana was still at the classes she was taking at the community center on Fridays. Rex and his son were the two things he cared most about getting situated right away. If Yanna agreed to his terms, his intention was to let her stay in the house and buy all new furniture and clothes for Lucas.

Apart from his clothes, tools, guns, and weight set, Luke was going to leave everything else. If Cassie didn't agree to let him and Lucas move in with her, he was going to rent a furnished apartment in Ben's building.

"Together again," Ben had teased when Luke called him the day before to ask about his complex.

"Not quite," Luke corrected. "And no offense, but I'm really hoping not to be your neighbor."

"Yeah, I don't blame ya. I'd rather live on the beach too."

"She doesn't live on the beach." Ben knew where she lived since he'd been to her condo, so Luke didn't understand why he'd say that.

"Not yet, but her new place is right next door to her sister's."

"No shit?" He had no idea that's where she was moving although the thought of her being so close to Brenna comforted him.

"Did you really not know that?" his former roommate chided.

"I knew she was moving, but I didn't know where, and for the record, I'd live in a fucking shack as long it was with her."

"The record is noted. And fortunately for you, that's not gonna happen. I still can't believe you knocked her up, fucker. Am I going to have a niece or a nephew?"

"I find out tomorrow."

"Are you hoping for a boy or a girl?" Ben asked.

"I don't care as long as it's healthy."

"Yeah? So, when you find out you're going to have another boy, you won't be disappointed?"

"Okay, maybe a little," Luke confided. "I'd love to have a little girl. But if we're having a boy, it's a good reason to try again."

"You probably should work on getting her to forgive you before you go planning more kids."

"Yeah, yeah. I know. She will," he responded confidently.

"I hope so, for your sake, brother."

"Me, too," Luke sighed nervously. He refused to even think about what he would do if she didn't forgive him.

"Keep me posted on what you find out," Ben said.

"I will," Luke promised before hanging up.

Chapter Forty-Seven

Cassie

Someone was stroking her arm and whispering, "Cassie, time to wake up, doll" when her eyes fluttered open.

"Let me rest a little while longer," she moaned in disagreement.

"Come on, baby, you need to eat."

She deduced Luke was the offender trying to rouse her out of this comfy bed. Why was he there? And more importantly, why was he trying to make her get up?

A little voice called out, "Madrastra, despierta." *Stepmother, wake up.*

The events of the day came back to her in a flash. She felt Luke's lips on her ear.

"Cassie, baby, you need to eat something so Brenna will let me take you home and put you in your own bed."

"Alone," she grumbled as she sat up.

"No, baby, we're going to take you home, okay?"

"Fine, but I'm going to *bed* alone," she corrected.

His tolerant smile when he responded, "Of course" suggested he was placating her.

Still, he was true to his word. After feeding her the Chinese food Brenna had picked up earlier while everyone else had pizza, Luke and Lucas took her back to her condo. There Luke put Lucas down in the guestroom, promising, "It's just a nap until I take him home," then came back to sit on the end of the couch where she was currently lying, propping her feet into his lap so he could rub them for her.

"Thank you for being so great with Lucas," he observed as he kneaded the pressure points on her feet. It felt heavenly. Feeling herself relax, she laid her head on one of the throw pillows resting against the arm of the couch.

"He's a wonderful little boy, Luke. He's lucky to have you as his father."

"He's going to be an awesome big brother to Claire."

Nodding with her eyes closed, she opened them suddenly and lifted her head slightly, propping up on her elbows.

"Wait, who's Claire?" She had an idea who he was talking about by the sly smile on his face.

"I thought maybe we could name our daughter that."

"Why Claire?"

"Well, so our kids' initials would match ours. L and C. Claire was my grandmother's name."

She actually liked the name Claire, and his reasoning was adorable, still she knew better than to give in too easily. This was a bargaining chip.

"I'll think about it," she said noncommittally, leaning back against the cushion.

"That's all I can ask."

Cassie knew he was going to make it difficult for her to stay mad at him, but she was determined to make him work for her forgiveness. *Damn, this foot rub is a nice start.*

"The contractors are actually ahead of schedule. It looks like I'm going to be able to start moving boxes into the beach house by this weekend. If you want to move your things into the house guest room instead of the condo's, we can maybe go shopping for furniture for Lucas' room on Saturday. I'm assuming you're not going to want to share a room with him if you don't have to?"

His smirk suggested she was the only person he was planning on sharing a room with and moved his fingers in circles up her calf, lingering right below her knee, not going any higher. His caress was firm yet tender, and all she wanted was for him to keep moving his hands north.

Damn him and his alpha maleness for making her lady parts tingle. Which wasn't hard these days. Sleeping with Luke last week had only served to make her more horny, not less.

"Whatever you say, doll. You're the boss."

That made her sit up straighter, something he noticed because he chuckled, "Don't get any ideas. You know what I mean."

She slumped back against the cushions in defeat, but quickly added, "I don't know what you're talking about."

Again, with his smirk. "Sure, you don't."

Chapter Forty-Eight

Luke

He left Cassie's feeling lighter than he had in a long time even though he had a feeling things with Yanna were going to get ugly. He wasn't looking forward to it, but he was ready. After hearing his baby girl's heartbeat today, nothing was going to keep him from being a family with Cassie. He'd fucked things up royally with her, but hopefully, it wasn't beyond repair. She didn't give him the impression she'd never forgive him just that she was going to make him earn it.

He could do that.

Lucas slept the entire evening in Cassie's guestroom, not even waking when Luke carried him to the Challenger or when he tucked him in his toddler bed. God, Luke missed the days of being able to sleep through anything.

Ah, to be a kid again.

Unfortunately, being a kid also meant having no filter, and at breakfast the next morning, Lucas told his mama all about his madrastra and his little sister in her tummy and visiting Cassie's house, which was "in a big building in the sky," as well as his Tia Brenna and Tio Ron's house on the water where Rex was staying. Adriana clenched her jaw and shot him a dirty look but didn't let on to Lucas she was upset although she did set things down on the counter a little harder than necessary and muttered under her breath.

Adriana didn't speak to him the rest of the morning, and Luke didn't pursue a conversation with her until Lucas went down for his afternoon nap.

"Yanna," he said quietly behind her as she loaded the lunch dishes into the dishwasher.

She kept at her task, ignoring him, and refusing to turn around.

He walked over and shut the water off, gently leading her to the kitchen table. He wanted to be as kind as possible because he wasn't an asshole, but also because he wanted her to be amenable to giving him custody of Lucas.

"We need to talk," he told her then took a deep breath.

"Don't worry, we'll be gone by morning." Adriana's voice was quietly menacing. "I was hoping you'd want to be Lucas' father. I made a mistake coming here with my son."

"You mean, *our* son," he corrected with a growl.

"Your son?" Her cold smirk sent chills down his spine. "Your name isn't on his birth certificate. I will take him back to Mexico tomorrow and be out of your hair so you can be free to be with your new family."

That got his ire up, but he remained calm. He'd play her game until he got the DNA test and his lawyer to take care of the necessary paperwork solidifying his legal rights as Lucas' father. Then he'd ask her for a divorce.

He bit back anything nasty he wanted to say and even put his hand tenderly on her hip. He should get an Academy Award.

"I don't want you to leave, Adriana. You and Lucas are my family. You belong here with me."

Chapter Forty-Nine

Luke

He noticed the white delivery truck at the house next door to Brenna's when he and Lucas stopped by the following day to pick up Rex. He was bringing the pup home since his grand plans of moving out had been set back.

"Tia!" Lucas squealed when Brenna opened the door.

"Hey buddy," the older Sullivan sister said as she bent over and hugged him, asking him in Spanish, "Are you hungry? I'm baking Tio Ron's favorite cookies." Brenna opened the door wide, allowing his son past her with a smile.

"Is Rex here? We've come to take him home."

She tilted her head. "He's next door with Ron, helping Cassie with the furniture delivery and installing her garbage disposal."

Yet another thing she didn't rely on his help for.

Or couldn't.

"You don't need Rex to stay here?"

"No," he shook his head solemnly. "It looks like I'm not moving out right now after all."

"Oh, I see." Brenna pursed her lips in disapproval. "Why not?"

He took a deep breath, about to offer some token of an explanation when she stopped him.

"You know what? It's none of my business. I'm not the one you owe an explanation to. She's next door. Take your time, Lucas will be fine here helping me bake cookies." With that, she politely closed the door in his face. Well, as politely as one can close the door in someone's face.

Three men in coveralls were getting in the cab of the delivery truck as he walked through the grass and landscaping between the two houses. His baby mama was standing at the entry, smiling brightly at him.

"Hey, you! What are you doing here?" she called, stepping onto the front steps as he crossed the paved circular drive leading to her front door.

Rex came barreling past Cassie, followed by Zona to greet Luke excitedly, almost knocking her over in the process. He sprinted to cover the remaining distance, sliding his arm around her waist to steady her.

"Are you okay?" he asked gently before admonishing the dogs in a stern tone. "Rex! Zona! Inside, let's go!" he said, then snapped his fingers and pointed in the house. The two wagged their tails gleefully and complied with his command, oblivious to their offense.

"Are you okay, doll?" Luke repeated himself, pushing her hair behind her ear.

"Overprotective much?" She shook her head with a grin. "I'm fine. They've been roughhousing all afternoon. They're going to be inseparable when you and Lucas move in. I found some really cute furniture for Lucas' room I want to show you."

He slowly released her and ran his hand through his hair. Her expression fell at his gesture, recognizing he was about to tell her bad news.

Looking at the ground, she whispered, "You're not moving in, are you?"

He shook his head glumly, "Not yet, Cass," then reached for her.

She crossed her arms defensively in front of her and stepped out of his reach.

"I want to be with you, please don't doubt that, but I need to get some things squared away before I can ask her for a divorce."

Her disingenuous smile suggested she didn't believe him. He watched as she began the process of writing him off in her mind, her expression giving away everything she was thinking. He had no doubt, she was done with him. There would be no second—or in his case, fourth—chance without serious contrition on his part. Contrition he couldn't offer yet.

"Madrastra!" Lucas' voice squeaked, followed by the pitter patter of his little shoes on the asphalt, Brenna following close behind.

A single tear ran down her cheek, and she uttered to Luke, "You need to explain I'm not his stepmother," then wiped it away and kneeled down to greet his son with a hug and as real a smile as she could muster.

"Hi sweet boy," she murmured in his hair, hugging him close.

Lucas kept his arm weaved around Cassie's leg after she stood and chattered happily about the cookies they had baked for Uncle Ron, and how Brenna said he was the best helper she'd ever had.

"Tia said I can come back anytime and bake anything I want! She even gave me cookies to take home, Papa!"

Brenna stood back quietly with a small plate of baked goods, a sad expression as she watched the three of them.

"Be sure to thank Mrs. Brenna," he advised quietly.

His son didn't catch that Luke didn't refer to her as tia, but Brenna did, and she shot Luke the dirtiest look he'd ever seen by such a beautiful woman. Her pregnant sister silently weeping nearby might have contributed to her ability to form it.

Ron, dressed in old jeans and a black t-shirt with paint on it, appeared in the doorway next to Cassie. He was wiping his hands on a rag and silently surveying the scene before him when his arm went protectively around his sister-in-law.

"Hey, your garbage disposal is all installed. Go try it out." He then called to Brenna, "Darlin', I think we need a new one too. Check hers out."

Lucas followed the ladies inside but stopped and presented Ron with a cookie. "I helped Tia Brenna make these for you!" the little guy exclaimed proudly.

Ron smiled and took the cookie, making a production out of taking a bite and raving how good it was, making Lucas beam with pride.

"Are there any more?" the older man asked with a chuckle.

His son nodded enthusiastically and pointed to the plate Brenna was holding. "But those are for me. Yours are at your house."

Ron threw his head back and laughed. "Thank you for leaving me some. Go inspect the kitchen and see if you think Cassie will be able to make as good of cookies there." The trio disappeared inside and Ron's face turned serious.

"What's going on, Luke?"

Luke shook his head, not sure he wanted to share his dirty laundry with the lieutenant general.

Ron must have sensed his reluctance because he simply asked, "Do you love her?"

"Of course, I love her." The question was fucking ridiculous and Luke snorted his derision. "More than I ever thought I could love a woman."

"Then do something about it." Ron leaned forward to add, "Word of advice? Before it's too late. There are more than a few men who would do anything to be in your position. She's not going to wait forever."

Thanks for telling me something I already know.

"I know," he spit out through a clenched jaw. Luke knew the Marine was only trying to be helpful, so he tried to hide his annoyance

Ron seemed to understand Luke's frustration and smiled. "The ball's in your court, my friend," he said as he clasped Luke around the shoulder and squeezed.

Except Luke didn't think it was in his court anymore. It felt like he'd already lost the game.

Chapter Fifty

Luke

They were back to weekly, polite text exchanges. He fucking hated it.

She looked like the beautiful professional she was in her black skirt, tan blouse, and low-heeled black and tan pumps when he and Lucas showed up to her next appointment. The two males were dressed starkly different in their casual cargo shorts and polo shirts.

Luke didn't want Lucas to forget about Cassie or vice versa. That wasn't going to be a problem. She dropped down to her knees, and Lucas hugged her tightly around her neck the second they saw each other.

"I've missed you!" she told his son while she ruffled his hair. "I think you've gotten bigger since the last time I saw you two weeks ago!"

Lucas replied in stilted English to which Cassie replied with the appropriate fanfare of how impressed she was, causing the boy to grin from ear to ear.

Watching the two together made Luke's heart happy, and hopeful. She didn't correct Lucas when he called her Madrastra, but she did say through unmoving lips as she stood up.

"I thought you were going to talk to him about that."

He shrugged, knowing she wouldn't argue with him about it in front of Lucas.

Truth was, he knew Cassie was going to be a great step-mom even if he didn't know how he was going to make that happen. She was a lot chillier with her reception of Luke, barely looking at him and answering his questions in clipped tones. A vast contrast to how warm she was with his son.

So, Luke decided to play a little dirty.

"How late are you working tomorrow?" he asked nonchalantly.

"I usually get off around four these days," she replied, still not looking at him.

"Any way you could pick him up from daycare? I've got training that's going to run late."

"Why can't his mom?"

"She's got a part-time job now, so she works tomorrow until eight."

Lucas' English was definitely getting better because he seemed to understand what Luke was asking of Cassie and choose that moment to lean his whole back against her thigh and grab her fingers in his hand.

"He certainly got your charm," she muttered.

"You think I'm charming, doll?"

She shot him a mean look while replying, "I'm sure your wife does, too."

Ouch. Point for Cassie.

"As long as my future wife does, that's all I care about."

Her tiny gasp was exactly the reaction he was hoping for.

Tie score.

"So, can you, doll?"

"Please don't call me that, and yes, I can. Text me the address and make sure I'm approved to pick him up."

Her appointment went well. Their baby girl was developing on schedule with no complications. Every time

Luke saw her on the monitor, he was amazed he'd help create that little human. Cassie seemed awestruck, too, because she didn't balk when he held her hand as she lay on the table, and they looked at the screen together.

As soon as the display turned off, she was back to business as usual, short and to the point as far as Luke was concerned. He and Lucas walked her to her Lexus parked in the front row in front of the building.

"So, I'll pick him up about six—at your new house or the condo?"

"My beach house," she replied, unable to hide her smile when saying *my beach house.*

He hadn't seen the inside of her place the other day when he picked up Rex but imagined she'd been putting a lot of work, time, and money into it to make it exactly how she wanted. He wished that still included him and Lucas there with her, someday.

"I'll bring Figurino's."

She cast him a suspicious look.

"What? You gotta eat, plus it'll be my way of saying thank you for doing me a favor."

She bent over and kissed Lucas' forehead. "It'll be my pleasure to hang out with my favorite little man. Maybe we'll even run next door and say hi to Tia Brenna."

She didn't even seem to notice she'd referred to her sister as Lucas' aunt.

He was getting Cassandra Jo Sullivan back, no matter how dirty he had to play.

****

Cassie

She picked up Lucas around three thirty; she was looking forward to spending time with the little boy who was going to be her daughter's big brother. He was an easy kid to love, for sure. Whether it was because he was the spitting image of his handsome daddy or because of the charming innocence three-and-a-half-year-olds possessed, he had her heart wrapped around his finger. Like his handsome daddy had done at one point.

Not anymore, she admonished herself. Luke Rivas' days of dragging her heart through the mud were over. Cassie had again come to terms they were over like she'd done so many times already. Something this time was different though. A quiet resolve she really was done with all the bullshit, she didn't have the energy anymore. She had thought seeing him yesterday would be hard on her, but the reminder of the existence of their little girl made her realize she couldn't hate him, they were going to have to get along for the sake of their daughter. Lucas was an easy extension to accept and love.

So, she wasn't prepared for the dip in her stomach when he showed up at her doorstep in his SWAT uniform, looking hot as fuck as he greeted her with his cocky smirk. She hadn't changed from her work attire of the sleeveless, seafoam green sundress and long beaded necklace but was barefoot as she stepped aside to let him in.

"Hi, doll, you look beautiful," he said as he set the bag of Figurino's on the small table by the door.

She rubbed her stomach, not believing him, and lamented, "I'm starting to feel very pregnant."

He glanced at her feet and kissed the tip of her nose, pausing to lean down and whisper in her ear as his hand brushed her tit while making its way to her tummy.

"I like the feel of you." He brought both hands to encompass her belly. "Barefoot and pregnant with my baby, you're perfect."

Damn that man for being so sexy and damn her hormones for falling under his spell.

"Papa!"

He broke his hold of her baby bump and bent over to swing Lucas up in his arms.

Yeah, watching him adore his son wasn't helping her swooning situation.

"Were you good for your Madrastra?" he asked as he kissed the boy's cheek.

"Luke Rivas, what did we talk about?" she reprimanded.

He cocked his head as if giving her question serious consideration. "I think we talked about you marrying me?"

She scowled and turned toward the kitchen. "I'm not falling for that again."

With Lucas on his hip, he reached out and grabbed her around the waist, his green eyes pleading with hers.

"I've got things set in motion, doll. I swear, it's not going to be much longer until I can make things right again."

She smiled sweetly as she slipped out of his grip and patted his cheek with her hand.

"I'm not holding my breath."

Chapter Fifty-One

Luke

She was as fucking stubborn as she was beautiful. It was one of the many reasons he loved her. And why he was worried she was going to move on without giving him a second thought.

He'd upped his text game. Fuck polite and fuck weekly. As he'd shown before, he wasn't above playing a little dirty. He was flirting with her several times a day and looking for any chance he could to see her.

Things that week were crazy at work. He'd been on a callout every day for five days straight, including his days off, and he was going to be stuck at training again tomorrow. Since he would be late picking Lucas up from daycare, he naturally took the opportunity to ask Cassie for help again. Lying in bed, he fired off a text.

Luke: Hey doll, any way you could pick up Lucas tomorrow?

Cassie: I want Figurino's again, including cheesecake was her reply two minutes later.

He smiled as he adjusted his pillow behind his head and shoulders.

Luke: You got it.

At breakfast, he told Lucas Cassie would be picking him up again. His little boy's excitement at the prospect of seeing his *madrastra* made Luke's heart swell.

Soon, dammit. She would be his again, and they would be a family. Soon.

His lawyer promised him he'd be able to file the paperwork to name Luke as Lucas' father and solidify his paternal rights. Since he and Adriana were married when Lucas was born, it was easier to establish paternity without having to wait for the DNA results that were going to take several months to receive.

Knowing his son was being taken care of, coupled with the fact he was going to see Cassie later made it easier for him to relax while he taught that day's training class. He was at the podium going over the slides on the overhead when he felt his cell buzzing in his front pants pocket. Normally, he wouldn't have even pulled his phone out, but something compelled him to.

He saw Cassie's name as the caller, and he immediately excused himself. She rarely called him, only texted, and it was right around the time she was supposed to pick up his son.

"Luke! Where are you? Do you have Lucas?"

His heart dropped at the panic in her voice. His mind started reeling. *What day was it? Was it Adriana's day to work? What time was she supposed to take him to daycare?* It was Tuesday, Luke remembered Adriana telling him that morning she would drop their son off at preschool after lunch, and they agreed he'd be responsible for getting Lucas since she'd be working until eight. Why was Cassie calling him and asking if he had Lucas?

"No, doll, he's at daycare. You're supposed to pick him up, remember?"

"Luke, I'm *at* his daycare. He's not here. They said he never came today. Is this your idea of a joke? Because it's mean."

No! No, no, no. This wasn't right. Maybe Adriana stayed home today. The sinking feeling in his gut told him differently.

"I'm sorry, Cass," he told her, trying to keep his voice even so as not to let on he was alarmed. "I would never play a cruel joke on you like that and waste your time. I'm not sure why he isn't at school; let me call Adriana and see what's going on." He hung up and dialed Yanna's phone.

No answer.

He fought back a sense of panic. He kept telling himself there was a perfectly good explanation for why Lucas didn't go to school and Adriana wasn't answering her phone. Still, he let his trainees go and raced home. Rex greeted him at the door, spinning in excited circles and chasing him through the house as Luke raced from room to room looking for them.

All of her clothes were gone, along with Lucas'. Luke slid his back down the wall next to Lucas' toddler bed, landing with a thud on his ass as he buried his face in his hands.

He couldn't lose Lucas now. He couldn't.

Luke pulled his work phone from the breast pocket of his camouflage jacket. *Time to call in the cavalry.* Fortunately, the chief's secretary answered right away, instead of letting it go to voicemail and put him through to Todd immediately.

There were five officers at Luke's house by the time Cassie arrived. She was beside herself, and although he was feeling the same way inside, he needed to be strong for both of them.

She desperately wanted to help but seemed to quickly realize after answering the detective's questions, she didn't have anything to offer other than making coffee.

Brenna rushed through his front door about thirty minutes after her sister did.

"Ron's on his way home from D.C. He's getting on the next flight out, but said to let him know whatever you need, Luke."

Oorah. Ron was a three-star general in the United States Marine Corps, and Luke served ten years as a Marine. Although Ron's offer of help probably had more to do with Luke's association to Brenna than the Marines, he knew Ron always looked out for his fellow devil dogs, active or not.

"Thanks, Brenna. If there's anything, I will be sure to let him know." He lowered his voice, "Can you take Cassie home? I don't want her driving in her frame of mind, and she really needs to get her feet up. I can't worry about her too, right now."

Brenna snorted. "So, you're asking me to be the bad guy and suggest she leave? Not a chance, Rivas. I value my life."

He sighed. Fine, he'd be the bad guy. To his and Brenna's shock, Cassie didn't argue when he proposed she let Brenna take her home. The dark circles under her eyes indicated how worn out she was.

"We'll take Rex, too," Brenna offered as she rubbed the dog's ears.

"That would be a big help, thanks." One less thing he needed to worry about.

"You will let me know the second you hear anything?" Cassie asked as he got her situated in Brenna's front seat.

"You'll be the first call I make,"

She grabbed his hand, tears filling her eyes. "Find him, Luke."

Luke leaned down to cup her cheek. "I will, doll. I promise," he said before giving her a chaste kiss goodbye.

"Try to get some rest," was the last thing he told her before closing the door and tapping the hood.

She gave him a forced smile as Brenna drove off. He watched them down the street, then quickly turned on his heel to get back inside. He had to find his son before Adriana got him across the border into Mexico.

****

An Amber Alert had been issued for Lucas. Video footage from the neighbors' security cameras showed Adriana loading up her blue Kia and putting Lucas in his car seat, then a Hispanic man being dropped off and getting in the car to drive away with them.

At least Lucas looked happy and not scared. Luke knew Adriana would never hurt their son, but he couldn't have her fleeing to Mexico with him, not to mention he had no idea who the man with her was.

Command staff knew better than to tell him he couldn't be part of the investigation, so he was right in the thick of things—from going through surveillance video the detectives had gathered of the three as they made their way through town to chasing down leads generated from the Amber Alert to personally calling commanders at the border points of entry to be sure they were aware of the situation.

Luke didn't let himself have a moment to breathe. He knew if he did, he would break down. The thought of losing

Lucas was unfathomable, which is why he fought the captain when he told him to go home and sleep. He had to keep busy. The SWAT sergeant lost the battle with his superior and left.

Unable to face going back to his now-empty house alone, he found himself mindlessly driving to Cassie's. He knocked gently and checked the door to find it unlocked. He'd have to talk to her about that later.

Maneuvering around unpacked boxes dispersed throughout the house, Cassie was nowhere to be found, which he was glad for. That meant she was being taken care of by Brenna, helping to alleviate some of his guilt for not being with her.

The shower was hot when he stepped into it. As he washed his armpits, he thought about Lucas making muscles at breakfast to show him how strong drinking his milk was making him. He had fought back a smile as his son flexed, then made a big deal about how big Lucas' muscles were getting to his son's delight.

That's when Luke fucking lost it.

The sobs wracked his body as he leaned his head against his forearm on Cassie's brand new black marble shower tiles. His despair pouring out of him in waves.

Was Lucas alright? Was he asking about his papa? Did he think Luke had abandoned him? What had Adriana told him? Luke was supposed to protect his son, and he'd failed.

As the tears continued to flow, he was glad Cass was next door so she didn't hear his anguish over his missing boy. He'd never felt so helpless in his entire life. He cried until he had no tears left. It was cathartic, and he shut the shower off with even more resolve to find Lucas. His little guy needed him, Luke would find his son if it was the last thing he did.

He found a pair of pajama pants he'd left in one of Cassie's drawers and laid in the newly delivered guest bed alone, tossing and turning. The house was eerily quiet. Since it was so late when he got there, he'd decided not to disturb Cassie, but now realized he needed to hold her if she'd let him.

He used the key Brenna had given him when he was dog sitting to let himself into Brenna's house. He was hoping not to wake them but knew if the dogs heard him, that possibility would be null. Still, Ron and Brenna would forgive him.

Creeping into the guest room, he planned on slipping under the covers next to her but found the bed empty and made. He softly walked to the family room couch only to find it empty. Next, he tried the living room couch, also empty.

Maybe she was sleeping with Brenna?

He was sitting at the bottom of the stairs, debating if he should wake them up or go back to Cassie's alone when the dogs finally got wind of him and appeared at his feet.

They barked excitedly, causing Ron and Brenna to emerge at the top of the stairs. Standing in the dim light, Brenna reminded him of Cassie in her pink satin robe while Ron had bedhead and was tying his navy-blue terrycloth robe around his waist. Well, as much bedhead as the Marine commander could have with how short his hair was.

"Everything okay, Luke? Any word?"

He shook his head. "Sorry to wake you. No, no word. Where's Cassie?"

"Isn't she at her house?" Brenna furrowed her brow, obviously confused. "We came home from the airport, and she was gone. I assumed she went home."

Luke refused to panic. She probably fell asleep on the couch, and he had simply missed her. He was out the door and sprinting to her house with Rex and Zona hot on his heels, and Ron and Brenna not far behind. They searched the entire house, top to bottom, with no sign of her. Her Lexus wasn't in the garage because she'd left it at his house, and he'd noticed her purse had been sitting on the counter at Brenna's, but they discovered her phone and keys were missing.

Her phone picked up on the second ring, only it wasn't Cassie's voice on the other end.

"Luke, my friend, are you just now realizing your whore is gone? It's been hours, man! There's no telling what could have happened to her by now. Who knows which cargo container she's in at this hour," sneered a male's voice with a heavy Mexican accent.

"What do you want?" Luke asked. His voice remarkably calm for what he was feeling.

"Well, I want to use your bitch all night long. I've always had a thing for blondes. And pregnant ones? Oh, fuck yes. But my boss is determined to get the highest bidder for your baby girl, so he won't let me play with mamasita until the auction is over. Apparently, if the mama is bruised, it tends to deter bidders. Now, when we auction your bitch, well, bruises and welts just show how good she can take it."

"Why are you telling me this? Where is she? Where is my son?

"See, that's the thing." The caller's chuckle was ominous. "He's not really *your* son, is he? My boss wanted to make sure you learned a valuable lesson today about stealing what doesn't belong to you. When you steal from powerful people, bad things happen. Some lessons are best learned the painful way."

Luke gritted his teeth. "Lucas is *my* son. Cassie and the baby have nothing to do with this."

"They did the day you decided to try to pass a Guzman child as your own," the man scolded.

"What are you talking about? I'm not raising anyone else's son. Adriana is my wife, Lucas is *mine*. For fuck's sake, all you have to do is look at him to know he's my son!"

That seemed to rattle the man on the other end, because he stammered, "Yeah, well," before sneering, "I wonder if your daughter will look like you. Hehe, you'll never know," then hung up the line.

Luke roared, heaving a box of unpacked dishes at the wall. The sound of them shattering provided only a temporary moment of satisfaction. He wanted to tear the house apart, a poor substitute for ripping to shreds whoever took his family. Instead of raining down more destruction, he leaned his head back against the newly painted wall as he caught his breath. Brenna looked at him with silent tears streaming down her face, and Ron was already on the phone with the chief. There were two police cars in the driveway in less than six minutes with many more arriving quickly behind, and the mobile command center bus was set up in Brenna's drive less than an hour later. It looked like a fucking cop convention at the Sullivan sisters'.

Her new neighbors had to be wondering who the hell just moved in he thought with a mirthless laugh and realized he only gave a shit because Cassie would.

His resolve deepened. He was going to rip the motherfuckers who had his family, limb from limb. The caller had actually given them some good leads—the name Guzman meant they were obviously dealing with the cartel. By answering Cassie's phone, it allowed them to easily ping the geographic position the call took place. Her Lexus had gone mobile, and they were able to track it to a different location than her phone through the anti-theft device installed in the car.

Luke's team was now doing surveillance on both locales and developing a plan to storm them simultaneously. Luke was following the events from the command center. The chief refused to let him leave, citing Luke's personal involvement, coupled with his lack of sleep might cloud his judgment. His judgment wasn't so bad he disagreed, so he thought that had to say something.

Luke had known since Brenna's daughter's car accident in May, Ron was a fucking rock star, but he was seeing it in action tonight. Ron had helicopters available should the department need backup choppers and was a goddamn strategy genius, weighing in with his opinions on how to coordinate synchronized raids. Luke was feeling optimistic when Ron sat down beside him and diplomatically suggested he try to get an hour's rest.

"You're running on empty, Luke. You've been up for almost twenty-four hours straight, you're not going to be any good to anyone if you don't recharge, at least for a little while. Your guys have everything under control and are on standby for at least another hour until we make sure all the bases are covered and we get a little daylight. You're not thinking straight right now, go get some shut-eye. I will come get you personally if anything develops before you get back. You have my word."

Luke didn't know how it was going to be possible to sleep but knew he had to try. He had to have his shit together when his team breached the locations where her phone and car were if for no other reason than to be ready to leave to get to Cassie and his son.

"Good man," Ron patted his back when he made his way toward the door of the mobile police station. "I'll come get you in ninety minutes or sooner if something happens before then."

Luke gave a small smile and turned to his, hopefully, future brother-in-law. "Thanks, Ron."

"We'll find them," was the Marine general's stoic reply before turning back to the activity in the bus.

Brenna and Cassie's parents were at Brenna's, and he knew he should earn brownie points and go talk to them but didn't have the energy, so he went to Cassie's place instead. There were a few detectives still processing the house, but since they thought the abduction took place next door, there wasn't much to manage.

Luke whistled for Rex, and the two made their way upstairs to Cassie's bedroom. Luke sat down on her bed, realizing only then, he was clad in his pajama pants from earlier. He plugged his phone into her charger while Rex did three circles next to the bed and settled down with a loud sigh.

He laid down on her pillow, breathing in her smell. He was finally in her bed again, and he hated it, he thought with a bitter laugh. But her scent provided a bit of comfort and allowed him to relax if only a little. Rex understood things were amiss and let out a whine.

"We'll get them back, buddy," Luke promised before slipping into a fitful sleep.

Chapter Fifty-Two

Cassie

The handsome, uniformed officer smiled and waved at her when she saw him through the window at Brenna's door. Brenna had left to go to the airport to pick up Ron but only after Cassie assured her she'd be fine by herself. She didn't want to make her brother-in-law take an Uber. Besides, she was planning on lying on the couch until they got back. Or pacing. Or pacing, then lying down and getting up to pace again.

Rex and Zona were going ballistic at the man at the door, so she stepped outside to talk to him. Hopefully, he was bringing her good news about Lucas.

Cassie swatted her neck when she felt something like a bee sting the second she closed the door. She whirled around to find another man with a shaved head had appeared, probably from the bushes because she hadn't noticed him before. This one wore jeans and a blue button-up shirt fastened to the top but with no tie. He also was holding a hypodermic needle. She started to feel dizzy, and the man in the uniform put his hand around her waist, as if to steady her.

"Go to sleep, mamasita. Don't fight it," were the last words she heard before passing out.

****

Why was it so hard to open her eyes? Or even move for that matter? It was like her body was refusing to cooperate even though she was willing herself with all her might to wake up. Finally, her eyes fluttered open, only to find she had no idea where she was.

She was lying in an ornately carved four-poster bed in a bedroom suite opulently decorated in maroon and gold colors and antique mahogany furniture. The deep red paisley comforter was thick with gold corded piping and matched the heavy drapes covering the windows. An elaborate light fixture hanging in the middle of the room complemented the decor.

About the time she was appreciating the high thread count sheets was the same time the events of the day came back to her. It's also when she noticed the cameras throughout the room, and she was now dressed in a white cotton nightgown with a blue bow along the neckline. Fortunately, her bra and panties remained on.

She really had to pee and was praying one of the many doors in the room led to a bathroom, hopefully, without cameras. Unsteadily dropping her feet to the floor, she jumped a mile when a deep male voice with a heavy Spanish accent sounded from nowhere.

"Oh good, you're awake."

Cassie frantically looked around the room, trying to figure out where the voice was coming from, only to find she was alone. Was she imagining things?

"Hello?" she called out, tiptoeing toward the door that was her best guess as the bathroom.

The voice came again, "Please, have a shower or bath, Ms. Sullivan. My servants will bring you your clothes for today, along with breakfast. Unless you are hungry now?"

"What time is it?" she called.

"Time doesn't matter here," was his cryptic reply.

"I'm trying to figure out the last time I ate so I can decide if..."

She was interrupted by the heavy, wooden double doors opening and two middle-aged women in maid's uniforms scuttling in. One was pushing a cart of food while the other scampered to open the drapes, which brightened the room immediately and revealed a beautiful balcony where the morning sun was shining.

The woman pushing the cart asked in Spanish, "Would you like to eat inside or on the terrace?"

Cassie hesitated; did she let them know she could understand?

The voice said, "She asked if you'd like breakfast inside or outside."

Well, that decision was made.

"Outside, please," she said with a smile at the woman as she gestured to the French doors. Then with a questioning expression, asked, "Bathroom?"

The maid looked quizzically at her, then at the other servant who translated. The woman pushing the cart laughed and said, "Ohhh," then pointed to one of the doors.

"Thank you," Cassie murmured and started walking to where the woman had indicated.

Once inside the room, she closed and locked the door and looked around for cameras. Seeing none, she used the restroom and washed her hands, then quickly brushed her teeth with the new toothbrush still in the package sitting on the counter. Leaving the water running, she quietly went through all the drawers, unsure of what she was looking for but thinking maybe she'd know it when she saw it. There was nothing that stood out, not even nail clippers, just toiletries and cosmetics. All the brands she used, she noted.

Cassie didn't know if the servants were waiting for her, so she hastily shut off the water and ventured out to the balcony, briefly pausing at the open doors leading to the hallway, then remembering she was probably being watched.

Instead of sitting at the table set for two, she walked to the stone railing overlooking the grounds. She was at least three stories up, too far for her to jump in her current condition. The landscaping was magnificent like something you'd see in a movie. There had to be a full-time staff dedicated solely to maintaining the blooming flowers, immaculately trimmed hedges and trees, and the greenest grass she'd ever seen.

"Wow," she said with a small gasp.

"I'm glad you like it," the male voice said, only this time it was in person and not through a speaker.

She spun around and gasped again. The man standing beside the table could only be described as flawless. He was tall with caramel colored complexion and appeared to be in his forties. His jet-black hair had the perfect amount of grey to make him look distinguished, and he wore a suit that was obviously custom-made and tailored beautifully to his athletic body.

"Please," he gestured to a seat at the table with an outstretched arm, "join me."

Cassie tentatively walked toward the table. He pulled her chair out, then sat down opposite her.

"Are you able to eat or do you experience morning sickness?" he asked while one of the matronly servants set down a plateful of hot food in front of her. The other served him once Cassie's plate was put down, and he looked at the women with a smile and thanked them, telling them in Spanish, "That will be all." They scurried out, but the man barely noticed, his gaze fixed on Cassie, waiting for a response.

She glanced down at the plate full of piping hot food in front of her. "I—I'm usually able to eat. Although I don't know if I will be able to today, having been kidnapped and all."

"Yes," he sighed. "It is unfortunate how you came to be here but be glad you ended up here and not somewhere where you would have been treated... less hospitably."

"Who are you? Why am I here?"

"My name is Dante Guzman. You're here because my idiot nephew is seeking revenge against your boyfriend."

"I don't understand. My boyfriend? I don't have a boyfriend. Do you mean Luke? What did he do? Did he arrest your nephew or something?"

The man chuckled. "No, he is trying to claim my cousin's son as his."

"His son? Lucas? Your nephew thinks Lucas is his?" The idea made her start to giggle in disbelief.

"What is so funny?" he asked as he laid the cloth napkin on his lap.

Following his lead, she placed her napkin across her legs. "All you have to do is look at Lucas to know who he belongs to. He is the spitting image of his papa."

The man frowned but said nothing more than, "Hmm."

"How is me being here revenge against Luke? Are you going to kill me?"

It was the man's turn to chuckle. "My dear, Cassandra, if I was going to bother killing you, I wouldn't have welcomed you into my home to do it."

"Then why am I here?" She was getting agitated and took a sip of the orange juice in front of her.

"That part is not so pleasant, I'm afraid. You're here until your baby is born."

"You want me to give birth here? Why? Then what happens?" She was glad she hadn't eaten yet because it would have certainly come back up right now.

"Well, your daughter will go to her adoptive parents, and you will go to your new husband."

She felt like she was going to hyperventilate and put her head between her legs. Dante was immediately kneeling at her side, rubbing her back.

"Breathe," he quietly coaxed.

Cassie reared her head up. "*Breathe*?" she hissed. "You tell me you're going to put my child up for adoption and marry me off and your follow-up to that is, *breathe*?"

He sighed but kept his hand on her back. "First of all, it is not me doing this. I think it's a despicable practice, but it's one my family likes to use on our enemies' loved ones, so the best I can do is make your stay here as comfortable as I can." He slipped back to his seat, readjusting his napkin. "I promise you will go to someone kind."

"How can you promise such a thing?"

"I just can that is all you need to know," he said as he spooned sugar into his coffee.

"You could let me go," she whispered.

"I could, but I am too, what's the word? Selfish. I do not wish my father's wrath, which I would surely get if you somehow escaped." He stirred his coffee, then tapped the rim of his china cup with the spoon and set it on the saucer, looking very much like a regal gentleman and not a kidnapper.

"It doesn't matter. Luke will find me," she said defiantly, reaching for the butter on the table.

"I'm counting on it," he murmured in Spanish before taking a drink of his coffee, pinkie finger out.

Cassie didn't let on she understood what he said and instead, buttered the pancakes in front of her. They smelled delicious, and if she was going to find a way out of here, she was going to need her strength.

Chapter Fifty-Three

Cassie

Dante treated her like a guest over the next few days even taking strolls with her on the grounds and sitting by the pool while she swam. He had eaten with her for all her meals, and she actually found him intelligent and charming. He was a true gentleman, you know, except for the whole, holding her hostage and selling her and her baby thing.

She'd had a lot of time alone to miss Luke and thought about him constantly. She hoped they'd at least been able to find Lucas; the thought of Luke being separated from his little boy pained her almost as much as being separated from him herself.

Cassie should have told him she wanted to marry him the last time he asked her. She wanted that more than anything, but she had still been hurt, angry, and unable to trust him. She knew he was sorry, but somehow, it felt like it'd been too easy for him. Like he decided he wanted to be with her again, and *poof!*, she was just supposed to be on board with everything now that *he* was ready. It pissed her off how on board she really was, so she fought easily giving in.

She prayed he knew deep down, she loved him and wanted to be his wife. The idea of never seeing him again without him knowing consumed her.

It had to be Stockholm syndrome that made her trust Dante would make sure she and the baby were treated well, but she really did believe it. Besides, she was going to escape before the baby came, so it didn't matter.

An opportunity to set that plan in motion came on the third day of what Dante liked to call, her *stay*. One of the servants handed her a note he'd left when she was served lunch.

Cassandra,

Please forgive my absence today, unexpected business has come up I must attend to. I have arranged to have some more magazines and books delivered to you, and Raul will accompany you should you desire to go to the pool. Please let Maria know if there's anything you require. Staff has been instructed to grant your (reasonable) requests. I hope to return this evening for dinner.

Best regards,

Dante

Today would be the ideal day to plot her escape. There had to be more days he would be called away, she merely had to take in more details of her surroundings while out with Raul today to formulate a plan for the next time he was gone. Dante always watched her carefully, so she consciously made an effort to not appear interested in camera placements or where guards were positioned. She doubted Raul would be as concerned about her curiosity; the young twenty-something viewed any time he had to spend with her as a cakewalk babysitting job even going so far as to be on his phone, surfing the internet when he had to escort her on the patio when she had a snack or asked for a breath of fresh air when Dante was unavailable to accompany her.

She was floating on a raft in the pool when her sitter jumped from his patio chair, rushing to respond to a loud disturbance, leaving his phone on the glass table.

Cassie almost tipped over as she clambered to get the raft to the steps and out of the pool to the unattended cell. She had just reached the table when she heard a high pitched, "Madrastra!"

Spinning around, she saw Lucas running wildly toward her, his little arms outstretched as he did. Dante stood in the background observing. She knelt down and opened her arms to embrace the boy when he crashed into her at full speed, knocking her back onto her bottom.

"Whoa, buddy! You have to be careful of your little sister in my belly!" she told him with a laugh.

"I'm sorry! Please don't be angry."

His sweet, anxious face almost broke her heart, and she kissed him while soothing his hair. "It's okay, baby, I'm happy to see you. Have you been a good boy?"

It wasn't until she was hugging him tight, she realized she'd had her conversation with Lucas in Spanish. She looked over at Dante who had a knowing smirk on his face.

"I thought you might be keeping that from me," he said in Spanish as he took deliberate steps toward them. He stopped short when he noticed the phone on the table and narrowed his eyes at her.

She glanced over at the table where he had been looking, feigning surprise when she turned back to him. "I didn't even know it was there, I swear!"

The corners of his mouth turned down in a disbelieving scowl, and he walked over to pick up the phone, briefly inspecting it before slipping it into his suit pocket.

"Why is he here?" she asked in English as she looked down at Lucas, careful not to use his name and draw attention to the fact she was talking about him.

Dante sat down in the patio chair previously occupied by Raul and poured a glass of tea from the pitcher sitting on the table. "I told my father what you said about the boy looking like Lu...." He glanced at Lucas still in her arms. "His father. Apparently, someone else had the same concerns and voiced them, so a DNA test was done. He is not a Guzman."

"I told you. So, you're going to let us go?" she asked hopefully, squeezing Lucas a little tighter.

The older man grimaced and stated matter-of-factly, "I'm afraid not" while gesturing toward the pitcher as if to ask if she'd like some tea.

She shook her head no, and he suggested to Lucas he dip his toes on the front step of the pool. Once Lucas was out of earshot and Cassie seated opposite him, he continued in a quiet voice. "He is also going to be... adopted."

"*Dante! No!* You can't!" she gasped, reaching for his closed fist resting on the table.

He took her hand gripping the top of his. "I'm trying to arrange it so he goes with his sister, then he would be able to stay here until she's born. But to be honest, Cassandra, I'm not optimistic. He will most likely fetch a higher price by himself." He squeezed her fingers before releasing them.

Cassie snatched her hand back as if she'd been burned. She'd almost forgotten who the man in front of her was and what he did. His charming demeanor and easy smile had made it seem like she really was here on vacation. The reality was he was facilitating the sale of her children. *Children.* She loved Lucas as much as the little girl she was carrying in her stomach.

"Dante, *please.* I'll do anything." The look she gave him conveyed her meaning of *anything*.

He gave her a sad smile. "As beautiful as you are, Cassandra, I only fuck women who are willing and who want to be in *my* bed."

A tiny tear escaped the corner of her eye. She quickly brushed it away before Lucas noticed. He may not completely understand what was happening, but he would definitely understand her crying.

"You can't do this," she whispered. "You're not that cruel."

"While this particular unpleasantness is a part of my family's business I want no part of, you're wrong. I am this cruel."

"Why not just let us go?"

"Because I really am a selfish bastard, Cassandra. Don't be fooled by my good manners."

"I don't believe you. It's more than good manners. Why keep us here and treat us kindly if you don't want any part of this *particular unpleasantness*?"

"I have my reasons, and they have everything to do with my own self-interests and nothing to do with you. I saw an opportunity when my nephew had you taken, nothing more. Although I am glad I have been able to make this at least tolerable for you, comparatively speaking, I didn't do it because I am a good guy and can save you. I'm not the man who can do that."

No, but the man who could was out there, and if she knew Luke Santiago Rivas like she thought she did, he wouldn't rest until he found them.

Hopefully, while there was still time.

Chapter Fifty-Four

Luke

The raids where Cassie's phone and car were located proved to be less fruitful than he had hoped. The men taken into custody were more afraid of the Mexican cartel than the American justice system, so they refused to provide any information.

Still, Luke wasn't going to stop until he found his son, daughter, and future wife. Fortunately, the men on his team shared his determination and resolve and worked tirelessly alongside him.

He was leaving the station on the fourth evening Lucas and Cassie had been missing when Adriana appeared out of the shadows in what was supposed to be a secure parking lot.

"Luke," she said quietly.

He whirled around, pulling his off-duty weapon from his waistband as he did. He'd been on edge and what one could call slightly paranoid since his family's abduction. Recognizing it was Adriana, he lowered the gun to his side but didn't holster it.

"Where is my son, Yanna?" he snarled.

Luke knew he could easily take her into custody, but also knew she would lawyer up and remain silent like the rest of the people they'd already arrested. Right now, getting information about Lucas and Cassie was more important than arresting her.

"They took him, Luke," she sobbed. "You have to get him back."

He didn't exactly understand who the *they* were she was referring to but knew he had leverage, and she would talk, so he quietly escorted her inside to an available interview room. He brought Nathan Dickenson, the lead detective on the case, in the room to question her, but she refused to talk to anyone but Luke. Which proved to be a blessing and a curse because she told him everything. It took every bit of his willpower to remain calm and not throttle her in front of the cameras set up in the room.

She was married to Javier Guzman, the grandson of the brother of a high-ranking cartel member. The only power the man really had was the clout his last name provided him in the state of Sinaloa, Mexico. Adriana found him in bed with one of her friends and fled to the United States where she met Luke and proceeded to get pregnant. After marrying Luke—while still married to Javier—her first husband found her and demanded she return home to Mexico with him, not realizing she was pregnant with Luke's child.

Once she was back in Mexico, Javier quickly lost interest in her again. This time, she fled to her mother's home and managed to hide her pregnancy and Lucas, once he was born. Javi was content since she was in Mexico and gave her money from time to time. That coupled with the money she'd taken from Luke kept her from being destitute, but her funds were dwindling. Then the private investigator showed up.

"And you saw an opportunity to get more money," Luke wistfully remarked.

"I saw an opportunity for Lucas and me to have a better life," she lamented tearfully. "I thought we could be a family, and you'd take care of us. But I know you don't love me anymore, and Lucas told me about his madrastra picking him

370

up from daycare. I worried you were going to take him from me, so I called Javi in desperation. I let him think Lucas was his, but you were trying to claim him as yours so Javi would help me cross the border undetected because I knew you would have it guarded. I thought once we went back to Mexico, things would go back to Javier not having any interest in us, and we could at least go back to how it used to be. We were preparing to sneak back into Mexico when his grandfather demanded a DNA test. Once Javi found out Lucas wasn't really his, he took him from me. He's going to *sell* him on the black market, Luke." She burst into inconsolable sobs.

"Over my dead body," Luke seethed.

Nathan, who'd been quiet the entire interview, asked, "Do you have any idea where they might have taken him?"

Adriana wiped her eyes and nose with the department provided tissues stocked in every interview room. "The first night, after we left and were lying low, I heard Javier on the phone, telling someone they'd taken the girl to his cousin's compound in Ensenada until her baby was born." She turned to Luke. "I had no idea at the time they meant her, Luke. It wasn't until Javi was in a rage when he found out Lucas wasn't his that he started ranting about having to teach me a lesson like he had you. That I'd also learn what it was like to lose someone important. When they took Lucas, I heard them talking about *packaging* him with his sister when she was born." She started to sob again.

Nathan offered her comfort when Luke made no attempt to. He couldn't. He was too livid.

While his coworker comforted his... what was she? Ex-wife? Wife? Their marriage was never legal since she was already married when they tied the knot almost four years ago, so what did that make her? His son's mother?

His son.

Luke needed to follow-up with the FBI about the leads Adriana provided. They had gotten involved the night Cassie was taken since kidnapping is a federal offense. Cranston and Williams, the agents he'd been working with, were at the station within the hour. After telling them everything Adriana had admitted, the two men looked at each other.

Finally, Cranston spoke. "You thinking what I'm thinking?" he asked his partner.

"We need to get Kenny involved," Williams answered.

"We need to get Kenny involved," Cranston confirmed.

"Who's Kenny?" Luke asked.

"An agent who knows Dante Guzman better than anyone. He's the relative we think is keeping Cassie and your son."

"Well, what are you waiting for?! Call him!"

The agents chuckled, Cranston answering for them. "It's not that easy. *She* can be a little hard to locate."

"Well, can you try?" Luke was getting beyond frustrated.

Williams seemed to be finishing a text, then set his phone on the desk. "Done. If she's available, we'll hear from her shortly."

No sooner had he said that than his phone started vibrating on the desk. The agent picked it up, looked at the screen, and smiled.

"Speak of the devil."

**

The bio of Kennedy Jones, a.k.a. Keni was impressive, to say the least, especially when it came to the cartel. A former Marine, she knew their inner workings and hierarchy better than anyone, and it was rumored she'd been able to develop a relationship with a high-ranking member and get far enough in his inner circle to be able to kill him.

She'd been underground ever since, but when she learned about Cassie and Lucas, she was willing to come to San Diego the next morning and meet with the agents and Luke's team.

Luke went to Cassie's that night feeling more optimistic than he had since this whole ordeal started. Brenna had suggested he stay at Cassie's in order to be closer to her and Ron so they could help with Rex. He readily agreed; being there made him feel closer to his baby mama. With any luck, tomorrow night, his son and future-wife would be back home with him. When he got Cassie back, she was marrying him—he wasn't taking no for an answer.

He was up early the next morning, raring to go, even taking Rex for a walk on the beach at sunrise. He couldn't remember the last time he walked his poor dog. Thank God Brenna and Ron had been taking care of him.

Keni arrived shortly before eight in the morning and wasn't at all what Luke was expecting. She walked in with her flowing auburn hair perfectly coiffed and cascading below her shoulders, petite stature and features, and high heels that made her five-foot-five, tops. Her cleavage in her black mini-dress distracted more than one man in the room. As they discussed strategy, Luke quickly realized her appearance was part of her advantage—no one expected a beautiful, petite woman to kick their ass or worse.

His ego inflated a little when she seemed to be impressed with his resume.

"Former Marine, former sniper, and current sergeant," she said matter-of-factly, flipping through a stack of papers in a plain manila folder she'd brought with her, then looked up at him and smiled. "Glad we're on the same team."

They had a plan in place by eleven.

She knew exactly where Dante Guzman's home was located two hours away in Ensenada, Mexico and had a good knowledge of the layout of the house and grounds. She wanted to do surveillance that day and evening, learning how many guards they were dealing with and, hopefully, catching sight of Cassie or Lucas for visual confirmation they were there.

"Normally, I would insist on doing surveillance alone, but I think it's important you come with me, Luke," she said as they were wrapping things up in the conference room.

He was as surprised as anyone in the room, assuming he wouldn't even be allowed to go on the mission because of his personal involvement.

"Do you think that's a good idea?" his lieutenant asked. "I mean, he's..."

Keni interrupted him. "I think if anyone is motivated for this extraction to be successful, it's Luke, don't you?"

"I'm simply concerned he might not use the best judgment." His commander turned to him, "It's not an assessment of your abilities, Luke. You're one of the best in the department, but I worry you're too close to this and would be willing to take unnecessary risks to get them out."

"There's no way I would do anything stupid when it comes to my family's safety. If anything, I'm going to triple-check everything to make sure they're safe." Luke replied, his tone urgent. He needed to be included in this.

The lieutenant turned back to Keni. "If you think it's a good idea..."

"I do." She didn't waste any time and gathered her paperwork before heading toward the door. "Grab your gear, Rivas, but dress in tourist clothes—that's going to be our cover. Can you be ready in thirty?"

He'd have to make a quick trip to Target down the street, but he could be ready when she was. "I'll be waiting."

She nodded. "We'll update the rest of you when we're able," then breezed out of the conference room.

Luke watched the door close behind her. He was used to a strong woman, *but damn*. This one was a force to be reckoned with, and she was going to help him get his woman and kids back.

Chapter Fifty-Five

Cassie

Having Lucas actually helped her observe her surroundings easier when Dante was around because she could position herself to watch the boy while she figured out the guards' schedule and patrol routines, the servants' shifts, and when there seemed to be the least amount of staff on duty.

Unfortunately, that was late at night until early in the morning, before Lucas was awake and functioning. That might not be a bad thing, actually; she could carry him without him knowing what was going on.

She decided it didn't matter the time. When she saw her next opportunity, she was taking it. In the bathroom away from the camera, she experimented making a harness sling to carry Lucas, trying both the top sheet from her bed and a beach towel. The sheet seemed to work better even if was a little big. Maybe she could rip it.

Rosa and Maria were the quintessential Mexican grandmothers when it came to Lucas and were great about making a fuss over him. Every time Cassie and her boy sat down at the table, his juice or milk was ready, and the women quickly learned Lucas' favorite snacks to bring him throughout the day. They were wonderful about taking care of her too, making sure she stayed hydrated and fed and bringing her lotions and concoctions for her skin.

"For no stretch marks," Maria told her when she handed her the latest bottle while mimicking rubbing it on her own belly.

Cassie laughed and hugged the matronly woman. "Gracias."

They were having dinner on the patio by the pool. Although they were still always under careful watch, Dante had been a lot more lax about restricting her movements now that Lucas was there. She guessed he thought she wasn't going anywhere without her little man. He was right about her not leaving without Lucas, but he was wrong if he thought they weren't going anywhere.

Maria brought Lucas his food before Dante arrived for dinner. Cassie pulled the napkin from the table to put into her lap and a small piece of paper the size of the fortune in a fortune cookie fluttered between her legs onto her seat. She moved her thigh over it to hide it, then waited until Maria left before slipping the paper from under leg to read it, looking around first to make sure Dante was nowhere in sight.

Say you're having morning sickness and use the bathroom in the pool house, it said in feminine writing

She slipped the paper into her bra.

"Maria?" she called. The sweet woman appeared in her snug gray uniform, wiping her hands on her apron.

"Yes, Miss Cassie?"

She pushed her chair away from the patio table and stood, putting her hand to her mouth. "Would you mind sitting with Lucas? I think I'm going to be sick," she said as she rushed to the pool house.

Once inside, she approached the bathroom with trepidation and flipped on the light at the same time she closed the door. A hand covered her mouth and pulled her back into a hard body. She knew instantly by his smell it was Luke before he even spun her around to face him.

"It's me," he harshly whispered then turned her around, groaning, "Oh, doll," as he held her face in his hands. He searched her eyes with his beautiful green ones. "Are you hurt?"

She shook her head, and he urgently kissed her everywhere above her shoulders—hair, eyelids, cheeks, ears, neck, and finally lips. She wrapped her arms around his neck and clung to him.

What the hell was he wearing? He was dressed in tan cargo shorts and a black polo shirt. Not at all the normal bad-ass attire he wore to work.

Reaching between them, his hands moved to cradle her baby belly. "Thank God you're okay!" he hissed against her lips.

"I knew you'd find us," she whimpered, tears streaming down her face as she burrowed into his performance-blend polyester covered chest.

Luke pulled away, planted a quick peck to her stomach, then stood up straight with a serious expression and grasped her elbow.

"Listen to me. We don't have much time. Go back out there and finish dinner and act like everything is fine. What do you usually do after dinner?"

"We go back to our room and play or read before bed."

"Good. Okay, do what you normally do until it gets dark and things are quiet. Once it's dark, be ready—keep your shoes on and jackets nearby if you have them. A woman, Kennedy is going to come to your room and give you instructions. You can trust her—she's a federal agent, and you need to do exactly what she tells you. We're getting you and Lucas out of here tonight."

"The cameras..."

"Don't worry about the cameras, we've got it covered."

Cassie nodded her head and took a deep breath. Luke clutched her hands between his. "You can do this, doll," he reassured her.

"Damn right, I can," she whispered.

The front door of the pool house opened, and Rosa's voice called out. "Miss Cassie... are you okay?"

"Yes, I'll be right out!" she cried as she flushed the toilet and turned the faucet on, splashing her face with water as Luke slid into the shower to hide. She blew him a kiss then opened the door wide like nothing was amiss and shut the light off as she stepped out.

Offering a weak smile at Rosa waiting in the entry, she wiped the corners of her mouth with her fingertips and offered an explanation in Spanish. "I got a little light headed and felt nauseous."

"Are you okay?"

"I think maybe if I eat, I'll feel better."

"Dinner is ready. Mr. Dante is waiting for you."

They walked out of the pool house, and she found Dante sitting in a patio chair, helping Lucas eat his dinner. It killed her the little boy adored him. Part of her refused to believe Dante would actually go through with assisting in selling her children or even her, but there was no way she was risking it.

Now that Luke and federal agents were here, she wouldn't have to make her escape on her own.

"Are you feeling better?" he asked, his voice full of concern as he stood when she approached.

"I think I just need to eat," she offered, amazed at how normal she managed to sound.

He kissed her cheek before she sat down, something he had never done before. *That's weird.*

"Let's get you fed, then."

She didn't remember much regarding what they talked about at dinner, she was too nervous about what was going to transpire later. But she did remember he was exceptionally attentive, both to her and Lucas. They sat at the table longer than usual after they finished eating.

He knows.

She took a deep breath and exhaled slowly. *I'm being paranoid. He doesn't know.*

"Feeling better?" His question interrupted her paranoia.

She offered a smile. "Much, thank you."

He reached over and squeezed her fingers. "Good, I'm glad. Let me carry Lucas to your room."

"Oh, um, okay. Thank you."

Dante escorted them to her room, stopping outside her door, which wasn't unusual. He always made sure they made it into their room, then locked the door behind them once they got inside. He kissed Lucas' forehead before setting the little boy on his feet, then leaned over and kissed her cheek with a smile.

"Goodnight, Cassandra." Ruffling Lucas' hair, he said, "Goodnight, buddy. See you at breakfast."

A tiny part of her wanted to thank him for being so kind to them but knew that would be suspicious, so she responded, "Goodnight, Dante. See you in the morning," then stepped inside the room. Hearing the door lock behind them, she released a shuddering breath, but then remembered Lucas was watching her and tried to give an upbeat smile.

"Do you want to read a story?"

She pulled Lucas into her lap and started to read *Goodnight, Moon*, the book he'd chosen.

Now they wait.

**

She dozed off next to Lucas. Having no idea when to expect her rescuer, she'd made sure they left their shoes on when they slid between the sheets. She'd tried to keep him awake, reading book after book until Lucas started to whine he was tired, so she reluctantly put him to bed.

She shut the lights off before climbing into bed and hoped whoever was monitoring the cameras in her room didn't notice their lack of pajamas.

"We're going to play a game later, so let's leave our shoes on, okay? We're going to play hide and seek, and we'll have to be really, really quiet when we play," she whispered, in case they were listening too.

"Okay, madrastra," he yawned. He was asleep in seconds, and she was dismayed to say she was right behind him. Growing a baby inside you kind of wipes a person out.

Cassie was startled awake and sat up like a shot. Looking around and seeing no one, she started to lie back down when she heard a woman's soft voice say her name.

"Cassie, are you ready?"

She laid perfectly still when she responded, "I think so."

"Good," the voice said, and Cassie slowly sat back up, moving to set her feet on the floor.

A stunning, petite woman in black yoga pants, black t-shirt, and grey running shoes with an auburn ponytail pulled high on her head appeared out of nowhere at the side of her bed. It looked like she was picking Cassie up to go to spin class instead of rescuing her.

Kennedy wasted no time with pleasantries, instead launched right into her instructions.

"On my signal, you're going to follow me with Lucas down the back stairs, to the right, and through the kitchen. We'll wait at the back door and watch for the guard. When he walks by, the count will be fifteen, then we'll slip out the door and run toward the driveway. Luke will meet us at the second hedge and guide us the rest of the way. Do you think you'll be able to carry Lucas and keep him quiet?"

Cassie was already adjusting the top sheet around her center, creating the makeshift sling as the woman spoke. Quickly fastening it around her waist, she simply replied, "Yes."

Kennedy grabbed her arm to get her attention and look her in the eye.

"Under no circumstances are you to stop for me should something happen. I can take care of myself; you focus on getting out of here safely with the boy. Understand?"

Cassie nodded her acknowledgment, and they got a sleeping Lucas situated against her chest without even waking him, he was such a sound sleeper. The auburn-haired beauty began to pick the lock at the door leading into the hall. Cassie heard the lock click, but Kennedy made no attempt to open it, instead scrambled back as if startled.

She understood what surprised the agent when the door opened from the outside and Dante stood in the threshold, still dressed in his grey suit and open-collared white shirt from earlier.

"My little assassin, I knew you'd come," he murmured with a smirk as he stalked toward the woman with the ponytail who was backing away toward the middle of the room.

Without warning, Kennedy threw a punch, which Dante easily blocked then gripped her wrists and spun her around to pull her back hard into his front. The woman began to struggle, and Dante escalated his hold to a bear hug.

Without a glance toward Cassie and Lucas, he casually ordered. "You better go, Cassandra, Luke is waiting for you."

She was torn, shouldn't she stay and help the woman who had come to rescue her?

"Go, Cassie, *now*," the woman barked as she continued her struggle against Cassie's captor.

Cassie remembered the woman's edict and was out the door and down the stairs the servants used without a second glance back, precisely following Kennedy's instructions until Luke grabbed her arm and tugged her down to a crouched position next to him by the manicured hedges.

As if unable to resist, he grabbed her face and kissed her, then tried to take Lucas.

"It's okay, he's in there pretty tight."

"Can you handle him?" he whispered.

"I've got him," she assured.

Luke peeked over the shrub, then positioned himself closer to Cassie.

"Okay, on the count of three, we're going to make a break for the next set of hedges. Ready? One, two, three!"

They dashed to the next set of bushes, undetected.

"Luke! What about Kennedy? Dante has her!" Cassie exclaimed while Luke seemed to be preparing for the next step of their journey.

"She was crystal clear, Cass. Get you and Lucas out of here, no matter what. She assured me she could handle herself, regardless what happened, and I believe her. Now, get ready. We've got two more rows of hedges to cover this time, then we're home free."

They were safely off the compound and keeping in the shadows of the trees lining the road as they made their way to a waiting black Mustang convertible with the top up, when Lucas woke and yelled excitedly, "Papa!"

She yanked him to her chest, and they both shushed him at the same time, but the boy's little voice had echoed loudly in the quiet night. They started to run, Cassie half expecting alarms to sound and floodlights to inundate their surroundings.

But, nothing.

Once they were safely at the car, Luke took his son from her and hugged him tightly, kissing his hair and murmuring how much he'd missed him, then quickly got him fastened in the car seat in the back. Of course, Luke would think to bring a car seat to his son's rescue.

God, she loved him.

He had started the car and slipped it in drive when the adrenaline started to wear off, and she began to shake uncontrollably. Luke reached behind him, produced a blanket, and helped cover with it as best he could while driving. Once she was snuggled underneath, he gripped her hand and confidently told her, "It's going to be okay, doll. I've got you. I promise." He continued offering soothing words of comfort, stroking her face and hair with one hand, while his other hand steered the car.

As they drove, Luke filled her in on how he found them, and about his and Adriana's marriage not being legal.

"That's such good news, Luke," she murmured. "I'm glad she did the right thing for her son. Where is she now?"

"She's currently in jail, but I suspect she'll be out on bail by the time we get back."

Cassie nodded, closing her eyes, hearing his last words before slipping into slumber,

"I love you so much, Cass. I thought I was going to die without you."

She tried to tell him she loved him too, but the exhaustion took over before she could.

Chapter Fifty-Six

Luke

He wasn't sure if Kennedy's intention the entire time had been for the two of them to get Cassie and Lucas without backup or if she merely saw an opportunity and decided to take it.

They had been doing surveillance on Dante Guzman's mansion, and his lack of security seemed almost too easy. Luke had been convinced it was a trap the entire time until he was crossing the border into the U.S. with Cassie and Lucas in his car.

He'd briefed Cranston on his secure line about what transpired and how Kennedy seemed to have been captured by Guzman. Luke thought for sure he'd be returning with a team to get her as soon as he got his family home safely, but Cranston was evasive about coming up with a plan to rescue his fellow agent. Luke knew there was a big piece of that puzzle he wasn't privy to and decided he needed to focus his attention on making sure Cass and Lucas got home safe.

Rather than going to the station, Luke drove straight to the hospital to get his baby mama and son checked out. They both seemed in good health-both physically and mentally, but he wasn't taking any chances. His team, Nathan, his lieutenant, and the chief were there waiting for them when they arrived.

The hospital staff was great and whisked Cassie and Lucas immediately into an exam room in the E.R. where a doctor assessed their health and determined they were fine.

"I told you," Cassie chided Luke from behind a curtain while she got dressed.

"You can't blame me, doll."

She pulled back the blue curtain and smiled. "No, I can't. Thank you for caring."

There was a soft knock on the door, and Luke checked to make sure Cassie was completely dressed before opening it to find Nathan waiting.

"I'd like to ask you a few questions, Ms. Sullivan if that's alright?"

"It's fine," she took a deep breath and pointed at Lucas who had fallen back asleep on an exam table waiting for them, "but if he wakes up, we need to stop."

"Well, I need to talk to him too."

She narrowed her eyes at the detective and pointed her finger at him. "Under no circumstances is he to know he was kidnapped, do you understand? You're not going to talk badly about his mother or suggest she did anything wrong. As far as he is concerned, he was on vacation at his Uncle Dante's."

Nathan slowly nodded, which was not good enough for his Mama Bear.

"I'm not kidding. If you even insinuate something, your interview with him will be over."

"Well, technically, you don't really have the legal authority..."

Oh, fuck no. Squaring off with Cassie right now was about the stupidest move Nathan could have made. Luke wasn't quite sure what the hell the man was thinking. This was about to turn into a shit show of epic proportions, and Luke needed to put a stop to it.

"It doesn't matter, I do, and I'll do whatever she says." Maybe that made him sound whipped, but he didn't care. That was by far the lesser of the two evils right now.

Finally, Nathan seemed to get it, and his whole attitude changed for the rest of the interview with Cassie. She didn't actually tell them anything they didn't already know, except that she and Lucas were treated like guests of Dante Guzman's to the point they were almost pampered.

That was a huge fucking relief for Luke. He had imagined all sorts of terrible things happening to them during this nightmare and was thankful to learn that wasn't the case. He thought it was probably going to make Cassie's recovery from the ordeal easier although he was sure she was going to be jumpy and a bit paranoid for a while. He knew he was going to be overprotective as fuck.

Brenna and Ron arrived as Nathan wrapped up his questions. The older sister burst into the room and made a beeline to where Cassie sat, hugging her tight before going to where Lucas was still sleeping and picked him up to hold him in her lap as she sat down in a chair.

Softly rocking him back and forth, Mrs. Thompson defiantly told them, "I don't care, I need to hold my little guy," when they scolded her for disturbing the boy's sleep.

Ben arrived not long after Brenna and Ron, and noticing the officer standing guard outside the room, suggested he stay with them at the beach house for a while.

"I can stay with you guys until things settle down. Ya know, help with Lucas, make sure someone's there when you're not, allow you to let your guard down a little when you're home."

Luke grinned and gripped his friend's shoulder. "Aw, buddy, if you miss me, you can just say so."

Ben grinned back. "Nah, I'm just bored. My girl's out of town this week."

Brenna spoke up. "You know you can count on us to help too with whatever you need."

Ron nodded solemnly in agreement.

"Thank you, all of you. We're going to take you up on that, especially babysitting duties," Cassie said with a laugh while Luke hugged her shoulders.

Definitely the babysitting duties. he planned on seducing little Miss Cassie Sullivan while his son was with one of his aunts or uncles.

Luke appreciated the department stationing a guard outside the exam room even though being vulnerable and relying on someone else to protect him or what belonged to him went against every fiber of his being. Still, he valued the support of his Blue Family.

The chief came in, making the already crowded room that much smaller.

"I'm going to post a car outside your house where they have a good view of both your place and yours," he said, gesturing to Ron and Brenna. He turned back to Luke, "And I want you to take some time off."

"But..."

"A week, Luke. I want you to take at least a week. People will still be working the case while you concentrate on your family for a few days. Maybe take your son to Disneyland, plan your wedding, hell, take an early honeymoon."

Luke looked at Cassie for her reaction to planning a wedding or going on an early honeymoon. The woman should play poker because she had the blank face down pat.

"You'll keep me posted on any new developments?" he asked before agreeing. Not that he had a choice, given it was a directive from the chief of police, but he didn't really mind since he was going to be able to spend much-needed time with Cassie and Lucas.

"I will keep you in the loop with all of it. You absolutely need to know what's going on. Of course, I expect you to do the same if you learn anything."

"Ten-four."

Ben leaned over to Cassie and told her in a loud, sarcastic whisper, "That means, *okay*."

Luke flipped him off, and Ben started laughing. "Wait, what does *that* mean?"

Cassie did her own stage whisper. "He thinks you're number one."

That elicited a laugh from the whole room.

A man in a white lab coat with a stethoscope around his neck walked in, pushing the room past comfortable capacity.

"Enjoy the time with your family, Luke. We'll have someone there twenty-four-seven to keep you safe but think about checking into a resort or give the Disneyland suggestion some serious consideration." Chief Pearson turned to walk out the door, then hesitated and turned back around, handing his card to Cassie. "If you need anything, don't hesitate to call me."

"Ten-four," she teased.

Todd nodded his head toward her while addressing Luke with a wink. "I like her."

He kissed her temple and smiled at his beautiful baby mama. "Me too," he murmured as his boss left the room. She smiled back at him, but the worry over things not being over was evident on her face. He picked up her hand and kissed her knuckles while the doctor started to explain the discharge instructions.

Don't fret, doll. I take care of what's mine.

Chapter Fifty-Seven

Luke

The sun had come up by the time only Cassie and he arrived at the beach house. Lucas was going to stay at Brenna's so Luke and Cassie could sleep, and Ben got the hint to stay the fuck gone until later that night when Lucas returned. Luke wasn't sure where things stood between him and Cassie, but he wanted time alone with her to find out.

It wasn't until the drive home Luke realized he was starving. Nothing the greasy cheeseburger in the to-go bag in his hand wouldn't fix.

Cassie sat next to him at the table in the kitchen, looking longingly at his burger while she ate her bran muffin.

"Want a bite?" he asked, holding it toward her.

He expected her to politely decline, so he couldn't suppress his chuckle when she took a big, ravenous bite, wiping her mouth with her fingertips and muttering, "So good," as she chewed her food.

"We should've gotten you one too."

"No," Cassie shook her head. "It's one thing to steal a bite from you, it's quite another to eat a whole burger by myself."

"You need to let go, live a little. Indulge your desires."

He wasn't talking about breakfast, and he was sure she knew it because she countered with, "That usually leads to more misery in the end."

Luke dropped to his knees in front of her and began to massage her pregnant belly, gently laying kisses over her blouse as he whispered, "Not always, doll. Sometimes it leads to beautiful things."

Almost absent-mindedly, she began to play with the hair at the nape of his neck as she carefully watched him caress her stomach, not saying anything.

He pressed on, pushing her top up so he could stroke her bare skin. He'd missed how she always felt like silk and leaned down to rub his cheek against where his little daughter was growing inside her.

She let out a little whimper as she tugged his hair tighter.

"I love you, Cassandra Jo Sullivan," he whispered.

"I love you, too, Luke Santiago Rivas," she admitted.

He lifted his head to look into her eyes. "Yeah? Still?"

She made a disapproving face that would make any mother proud. "Of course. You're the love of my life and the father of my baby—and my hero. I don't know what would have happened if—"

He didn't let her finish her thought, wrapping his arms around her middle and planting his mouth on hers to keep her from saying anything more. Her response was immediate, slipping her arms around his neck and drawing him closer. His tongue sought hers, and soon they were deepening the kiss.

When they came up for air, Luke rested his forehead against hers and closed his eyes, taking in the moment. She was in his arms again. For good, if he had anything to say about it.

"Hero aside, baby doll, I'm sorry I fucked everything up before. If I could do it all over again, I would do it a lot differently. But, I can't. All I can do is ask your forgiveness and promise to do better from now on." He leaned down and kissed her belly again, continuing in between kisses. "You... Lucas... and Claire... are my world now."

"I haven't agreed to Claire, yet," she smiled.

Luke resumed kissing her stomach while talking. "I know. We can name her whatever you want, just promise me her last name will be Rivas. Like her mama's." He looked up hopefully, his lips still on her skin. Her face was unreadable as she returned his gaze while her fingers entwined in his hair again.

"What do you think about Sofia Claire Rivas instead?" she asked softly.

"I love it!" He immediately sat up, not wanting her to change her mind or think any more about it.

"It doesn't start with 'C' though, like you wanted."

He caressed her chin and kissed her below her ear, murmuring, "As long as her last name is Rivas, I don't care. We'll give our boys 'L' first names, and our girls will have 'C' middle names."

With both hands, Cassie drew his face to hers so they were eye to eye.

"Whoa. Slow down, cowboy. Let's get this little girl outta me before we start planning any more baby Rivases."

"Can we practice making them, at least?" Luke smirked.

Her face fell. "Let's take it slow, okay?"

"We'll go as slow as you want. But can I at least touch you? Hold you as I sleep next to you?"

"Of course, you can touch me."

She didn't answer his second question, and he was feeling brave. "I need to share your bed, doll. There's no way I can sleep alone now, I need you next to me."

"Me too. Every night we were away and Lucas slept next to me, all I could think was how much I wished you were with us. Not to be kidnapped with us, of course. But to be there so I could feel you next to me."

He pulled her to her feet, then scooped her up and started walking to the stairs toward her room.

"What are you doing? Put me down!"

The SWAT sergeant ignored her protests until he gently deposited her on the king size bed, lying down beside her and immediately unbuttoning her blouse.

"Luke! Stop it! What are you doing?" Even as she protested, she bowed her body up to help him manipulate the buttons easier.

"I'm going to show you how grateful I am you're home safe and sound, and how sorry I am for hurting you. I'm going to make my apologies to your body, over and over, every day until you forgive me."

She tried to suppress a giggle. "But I've already forgiven you."

He opened her blouse, staring at her beautiful figure. "I still need to make sure," he said as he began to kiss his way from her stomach to her tits.

Her front-clasping bra made removing the pesky material easy. Her boobs were fucking awesome before she got pregnant, but holy hell, they were spectacular now. He kneaded them in his hands, feeling the weight as he pushed one up into his mouth. Cassie gasped softly when he took a nipple between his lips, swirling his tongue around the stiff peak before gently biting down. She held his head to her chest, her eyes closed in ecstasy, and he wanted nothing more than to escalate things, but he needed to prove to her he respected her wish to take it slow, so he continued his apology to her tits but didn't go any further.

Which was obviously not what she wanted as she pressed her hips against his.

He lifted his head to look at her. "Doll?"

Her chest was heaving when she answered him. "Hmm?"

"I thought you wanted to take things slow?"

His question seemed to anger or embarrass her, and she shoved him away as she sat up, attempting to fasten her bra.

"I don't know what I want anymore, Luke Rivas. These pregnancy hormones make me so goddamn horny, and I've missed you like crazy. But I do want to take things slow with you. But I also want to fuck your brains out."

She was having trouble securing her bra in the position she was in, and he gently put his hands on hers to stop her from continuing.

"Lie back," he quietly ordered.

"Luke..."

"Lie back, Cassandra," he said in a sterner voice as he eased her back onto the pillows.

She did as instructed, and he methodically began to undress her. Every time she started to protest, he'd put his fingers to her lips to silence her. When she was completely naked before him, he paused to take her in.

He didn't know what he would have done if she'd have been hurt or worse. This beautiful creature carrying *his* baby. This stubborn, sassy, sexy as fuck, gorgeous woman loved *him* and his son, and he was going to make a life with her. A life he could have never even dreamed up, his imagination wasn't that good. He didn't think it was possible to have his heart so full, but it was overflowing with how much love he felt for her.

"I've missed you so much, doll," he murmured.

Starting at her feet, he massaged and kissed the tops reverently and worked his lips up her calves. He took his time, making sure to kiss every inch of her skin as he made his way toward her baby bump. Her sharp intake of breath when he sucked the skin on the backs of her knees made him smile slightly before he massaged her inner thighs, planting little hickeys on her skin along the way to her hips. He could smell her arousal when he licked the crease between her thigh and hip, and he inhaled the delicious aroma deeply. He'd fucking missed that scent.

Luke purposefully bypassed her pussy, kissing along her pubic bone to the other side of her body only to lick the matching crease on the other thigh. Cassie shifted her hips slightly as if to encourage him to move a few inches to her magic center.

Instead, he continued his ascent up her body with his lips and hands. Her sides, which were usually ticklish, were covered in goosebumps as he swirled his tongue over her skin. Her nipples were little pebbles when he kissed the underside of her breasts. He took his time pleasuring her tits. Probably because he just fucking loved her boobs, but also because her whimpers and moans grew loudest when he was tending to them.

His lips meandered up her chest to her neck where he buried himself between her ear and shoulder. This was another one of his favorite scents, and he could get lost kissing her neck and never want to be found.

Finally, he reached her face. Cupping her cheeks between his hands, he kissed her eyelids, under her eyes, making a path with his lips to her mouth, which he caught with his in a slow, sensual kiss. He poured every bit of love and affection of his being into that kiss, wanting it to be the culmination of his exploration of her body.

Well, not quite the culmination.

"Please, Luke," she whimpered while grinding her hips against his clothed body.

Again, he placed his fingers to her lips with a "Shhh."

He slid down her core to nestle between her legs, her pussy glistening with desire. Running his finger up and down the length of her labia, he murmured, "You are so wet for me, doll."

She moaned in response, spreading her legs a touch farther.

Normally, this would have been when he made her beg for him to continue, but he was smart enough to know now was not the time, so he decided to forego that game and satisfy her until she was seeing stars.

Delicately spreading her with his fingers, he dipped his head between her legs and slowly licked her from her clit to her ass and back.

"You taste so fucking good," he growled as he lapped up her pussy. "So. Fucking. Good."

She started to move her hips against his mouth, and he looped his arms around her thighs, pinning her in place as he began to fuck her with his tongue

"Oh, God, Luke. Yes, just like that," she moaned as she tried to thrust off the bed.

He pressed her against the mattress, forcing her legs to remain open so he could continue attacking her pussy with his mouth. He moved his tongue furiously around her clit as she began to pant. Sliding one finger inside her pretty, pink pussy, he began to finger fuck her as he continued to devour her.

Cassie was fisting the bed sheets, gasping his name while trying to thrash about as he held her in place. Her cunt started getting wetter, then began to quiver, and she gripped his hair to hold his head in place as her whole body shook from her orgasm.

Luke didn't stop until she was squeezing her thighs around his head, begging him.

He crawled up her body, feeling pretty fucking proud of himself. Nobody knew her body, knew how to satisfy her, like he did. She wrapped her arms around his neck and pulled him in to kiss his mouth. He knew she tasted herself, and it made his cock even harder when she didn't hesitate to kiss him passionately.

"That was incredible," she purred. "I hope you haven't been practicing."

Smirking, he brushed her bangs from her forehead as he stared into her eyes. "Only on you in my mind, baby. I haven't been with anyone else since our very first date, and I don't plan on ever being with anyone else. I love you, Cass. I want to marry you and spend the rest of my life with you." He dipped his head to kiss her again and felt her contented sigh.

"I love you, doll. Please marry me."

She turned over so he was spooning her. "You can't ask me that while I'm in the afterglow of a mind-blowing orgasm," she scolded.

"It's the best time to ask, are you kidding?" he grinned. "How can you say no to a lifetime of coming like that?"

She rolled over to face him, giggling as she did. "You're insane." Her face got serious, and she leaned over to kiss his jawline. "And sexy." She continued kissing down his neck, pausing in between kisses while telling him, "And gorgeous. And funny. And smart. And you make beautiful babies."

He chuckled at her last comment and tilted her chin so she was looking at him.

"I know Sofia wasn't planned, but I thank God every night that you got pregnant."

Her mouth turned upward. "Me too."

Her admission she was thankful to be pregnant made him so damn happy.

She leaned over to whisper in his ear, "Do you wanna practice making another one?"

"I thought you wanted to take it slow?"

"Mmm, I want to take it really slow," she muttered, reaching down to stroke him firmly over his cargo shorts.

"Fuuuuck," he hissed.

"Now, you're getting it," she teased.

A squeal escaped her when he flipped her onto her back. "*You're* going to get it."

The little vixen bit her fucking lower lip and looked up at him through her eyelashes. "Promise?"

"Guaran-fucking-teed."

****

Cassie

They slept all day after their morning of making love and woke up to have dinner like old times—her clad only in his shirt and him in nothing but his boxer-briefs as they ate from delivery boxes on the couch, feeding each other and stealing kisses while they talked nonstop.

God, she'd missed this.

Lucas was coming home after he ate dinner with Brenna, Ron, and Dee who had come home from college when she learned Cassie and Lucas were safe. Cassie knew when Lucas came back, things would be different than they had been but in a good way. She and Luke were now a real couple, openly in love and living together. A thought occurred to her.

"You are moving in, aren't you?"

"You'd need more than a gun and a deadbolt to keep me out now, baby doll," he growled, placing the Styrofoam containers back in the bags they were delivered in.

She shimmied her way next to him, curling up against his side on the couch. "Good," she murmured as she tried to get even closer to him.

He pulled her into his lap, keeping his arms wrapped around her. He didn't say anything else, just stroked her hair while he kissed the top of her head.

This. This is what she wanted every day for the rest of her life. To feel this wanted, this content.

Annnnnd, she started bawling.

"Cass, baby! What's wrong?" His voice was filled with panic.

"Nothing. Nothing at all. I'm pregnant, so my hormones are all over the place. I'm so stupidly happy right now, but then I think about if something had happened to me and Lucas.

She felt him smile against her hair as he held her tight.

"Hey, nothing is going to ever happen to you or Lucas as long as I'm alive. I'm glad you're happy, that means I'm doing something right."

She nodded her head while brushing her tears with her fingertips, murmuring, "So, so right."

Luke pulled her tight against his chest and continued stroking her hair, resting his cheek on top of her head. She felt the vibration of his voice in his chest when he asked, "So, does that mean you'll marry me?"

She pulled away to look at him while shaking her head. "You're relentless!"

"Yep. You should know that by now. So, will you?"

Cassie snuggled back against his chest and quietly teased, "Yes, probably. I'll think about it."

His arms stiffened around her and he dropped his ear to her mouth. "Say that again. I want to be sure I heard you correctly."

"I said, I'll think about it."

"No, no, the first part. One more time, I didn't quite hear you," he teased.

Putting her lips to his ear, she murmured, "I will be your wife and the mother of your children. And your lover, and your friend, and..."

He held her face in his hands to stare into her eyes before breaking out into a huge smile, then kissing her soundly.

"I love you, doll."

She stifled a yawn while returning the sentiment. She hated how the exhaustion seemed to hit her out of nowhere, but loved that Luke always seemed to notice and take action, making her rest the minute he thought she was tired. This evening was no exception.

"No take-backs," he uttered as he pulled her down to lie next to him on the couch.

"No take-backs," she agreed, nestling against his body and closing her eyes.

Chapter Fifty-Eight

Cassie

She woke when she heard their little man scamper loudly through the patio door, Brenna, Dee, and Rex following close behind, a female voice calling, "Hello?"

Cassie had been snuggled against Luke when she fell asleep on the couch but found herself alone with a blanket tucked closely around her.

"Hey," she said groggily as she up on the couch, setting the throw to the side.

Her niece, Danielle, squealed and ran to sit next to her and hug her tight. "Aunt Cassie, thank God you're okay!"

"Hey, Dee. It's so good to see you."

Lucas backed himself against Dee's legs, then proceeded to lay upside down over her thighs like a little monkey.

"I see you've met my son," Luke's deep voice was filled with humor when he walked in from the garage in jeans and a navy Marine Corps t-shirt, taking in the scene before him.

"Lucas and I are best buds," Dee said in Spanish, flipping the little boy over in her lap and tickling his sides.

"He's a charmer, like his daddy," Cassie murmured.

Brenna sat on the other side of her and brushed Cassie's hair from her shoulders. "How are you feeling, sis?"

The younger Sullivan sister cast a glance at Luke and smiled brightly. "I'm good. Really good," she answered, then turned her attention back to Brenna. "Thank you for watching Lucas."

"Anytime. It was my pleasure, you know that. Although I am going to sleep good tonight. I sometimes forget how much energy little kids have."

Luke joined them in the family room, unwrapping one of the new chairs still encased in the plastic packaging.

"Did he take a nap today?" he asked as he sat down.

"A short one," Danielle answered with Lucas still wiggling around in her lap.

"I think someone has a crush," Cassie said with a grin.

"Can you blame him? Cousin Dede is awesome!" her niece said with a smirk, then blew a raspberry on the little boy's neck before setting the shrieking kid down so he could run to his papa for protection.

"Hey, do you want some help unpacking?" Brenna asked as she glanced around at the dozens of boxes.

"Actually, I would love it." Cassie sighed with relief.

"Let's have brunch tomorrow at our place, then afterward, we'll come back here and get started?"

"Perfect, thank you so much," Cassie replied, then focused on her niece. "When do you have to go back, Dee?"

"I'm home for two weeks. I talked to my professors and explained what was going on, so they were cool with me taking next week off, then the following week is my spring break."

"Oh, terrific," Cassie exclaimed with a smile, followed by a yawn.

Brenna leaned over and kissed Cassie's cheek. "We'll get out of your hair. So glad you're back, baby sister."

"Brunch at our place tomorrow at eleven," Danielle ordered as she stood up.

"We'll be there," Luke said, walking the ladies toward the door. "What do we need to bring?"

"Just you guys, we've got everything else covered," Brenna responded.

"Okay, but we're having you over for dinner this week," Luke conceded.

"Who's cooking? Your housekeeper, Kristen?" her niece teased.

Cassie came to stand with the group in front of the patio door and shot the college girl a look. "Ha ha, Smartass. I can cook, ya know."

Luke came to her defense, slipping his arm around her waist and pulling her to his side. "She really can, and I'm an excellent sous chef."

"Oh my God, you two are sickeningly adorable," Dee said, rolling her eyes and stepping over the threshold onto the patio.

Brenna grinned and winked at the couple. "You really are. See you in the morning, neighbors."

Dee peeked her head back in the door and called to Lucas in Spanish. "See you tomorrow, cutie! Keep practicing your English!"

Brenna kissed her fingertips, then waved at them. "Love you guys. Sleep tight."

"Goodnight," Cassie and Luke called in unison. He stepped onto the patio and watched the pair until they walked into their own house.

"Hey!" Cassie called to Lucas. "You wanna build a fort?"

The boy jumped up and down with glee, clapping his hands. Luke cocked his head, a questioning look on his face.

"I thought Lucas could sleep in his fort," she explained.

"And I'm assuming this fort is going to be in our bedroom?" he said with a smirk.

"Is that okay? I want him close to us tonight."

Luke gave her a skeptical look. "I don't want this to become a habit, Cass. He needs to sleep in his own bed."

"I know," she sighed, "but I'm not going to sleep very well if he's not near us and considering his bed isn't set up yet..."

With a small smile, he said, "He can sleep in a fort in our room, *tonight*. Tomorrow, I'm scheduling an alarm installation, and we'll get his bedroom furniture ordered. Will that make you feel better?"

She kissed his cheek. "Yes, thank you. But, um, I already ordered his furniture. It's in boxes in the garage," she confessed.

He shook his head with a grin at her admission. "Come on, buddy," he called to Lucas. "Let's go build a fort!"

Luke could talk tough all he wanted, but it was he who ended up putting their sleeping son between the two of them in the king-sized bed.

He saw her smirk and defended himself. "It's just for tonight."

"Just for tonight," she mocked.

"It is. I have plans for his madrastra tomorrow he can't be in the room for."

"Oh my," she purred.

He leaned over the sleeping boy and kissed her gently. "You have no idea," he winked.

Cassie caught her breath, her toes curling at the thought.

"Goodnight, baby doll. I love you. I want you to sleep in tomorrow, don't worry about getting up with us, okay?"

Could this man be any more perfect?

****

Luke

His mandatory week off flew by. With the help of Brenna and Dee, they got the boxes unpacked and the house organized, and he had an alarm and cameras installed so even though the threat of the Guzmans still hung over their head, it wasn't looming as large anymore.

His baby girl was getting bigger inside her mama, much to Cassie's chagrin, and his little boy was learning English— thanks in part to his future niece-in-law. She was amazing with Lucas.

"Do you think she'd be willing to be his nanny this summer?" he asked Cassie one night after dinner as they cleaned up the kitchen.

"I don't know. I can ask her. She usually comes home once school ends, it's too hot to stay in Tucson. I'm sure she would if the price was right."

He nodded absent-mindedly, lost in thought. There was a lot he wanted to talk to her about. In addition to picking a wedding date, they hadn't discussed what was going to happen after the baby came, and he had been apprehensive about approaching either subject with her, in the event he didn't like her answers.

As she wiped down the table, he asked, "How long are you planning on taking off work?"

She slowed the rag and replied, "I've talked about it with my boss, and I was planning on three months, then going part-time for a year. Which, most likely, will still translate to full-time, I'll just be doing a lot of work from home."

"Is that what you want?"

She sat down in one of the high-back chairs around the table, scrubbing an imaginary spot on the new wood before answering.

"It is. I love my job, Luke. The money is great and my company is amazing. Look how supportive they've been since I got back. I'd be crazy to quit."

It was true, her boss had stopped in the first day she was taking visitors to make sure she was okay and to see if there was anything she needed, telling her to take all the time necessary to recover from her ordeal. The company had sent four-course catered dinners twice that week and paid Kristen's salary for the month so she was coming five days a week, instead of two. Between Luke, Brenna, Dee, and Kristen, Cassie hadn't had to worry about much.

"You're right, they've been great," he agreed and sat down next to her.

"What about you? Were you planning on taking any time off? FMLA says you can take up to twelve weeks."

"Well, I have more than enough accumulated sick and vacation time..."

She smiled at him. "But..."

"I think I'd go stir crazy," he confessed. "I need to be there for my squad, make sure shit is getting handled and they're safe. But I know I need to be there for you and the kids, too."

Cassie grabbed his hand in both of hers. "You will be. We'll be fine, baby, but promise you'll take a few weeks when she comes. We'll get a nanny—not a hot one—when Dee goes back to school, and maybe after this month, we can increase Kristen to three days. The point is, we'll have tons of help, and if you want to go back to work, you should. Or if I want to go back, I should. I don't ever want us to feel guilty doing what we love because that leads to resentment, and resentment leads to unhappy marriages."

She provided him the perfect segue. "So, when are you marrying me, doll?"

"Ugh, Luke." She flopped back against her chair. "I'm as big as a house. Let's at least wait until she's out of me and I've had a few months to get in shape."

"You're not as big as a house, you're beautiful, and I want to marry you before our daughter is born, Cass. I know it's unnecessary and old-fashioned, but I want our daughter's parents to be married when she's born. I want her birth certificate to say, *Mother: Cassandra Jo Rivas*. Just a small ceremony. We can go to the Justice of the Peace or have it here on the beach. We'll have a big party on our one-year anniversary. Please, Cass."

Her expression was sad. "I know it's important to you, but I'm sorry. I don't want to get married while I'm pregnant. I'm wearing your ring, and I promise I'll marry you but later. We can even set a date. I think sometime in August will be perfect."

"August?! That's over five months away. I can't wait that long."

She sighed. "Can we talk about this later?"

Can we talk about this later? was her old standby when it came to discussing things she wanted to avoid, and frankly, it was starting to piss him off.

"No, I want to talk about it now."

"Please, Luke? I'm too tired right now."

He looked at her skeptically, then leaned over and kissed her cheek before standing up. "You're lucky you're so damn adorable."

"Thanks, baby." Cassie batted her eyelashes and smiled. "I swear, we'll sit down soon and pick a date. On another note, what do you think about taking another week off and getting out of town next week for a few days? Maybe take Lucas to Disneyland? Take advantage of having Dee here to help."

As he loaded the dinner dishes into the dishwasher, he couldn't help but feel offended.

"I don't need help with Lucas. I'm perfectly capable of taking my son to Disneyland without a nanny, Cass."

She smirked and gestured to her baby belly. "Well, *I* do need help. Have you been to Disneyland lately? It's insane, Luke. Besides, Dee's feelings would be hurt if we didn't include her."

He thought about it for a second and shrugged. "I'm sure I can take another week. When do you want to leave? Saturday?"

His baby mama shook her head. "I thought you have that golf thing with Ron Saturday morning?"

"Oh, yeah, I almost forgot. It'd probably be hard for him to find a replacement with this short notice. How about Sunday?"

"Let me check on hotel availability."

Chapter Fifty-Nine

Cassie

She had so much to do to get ready for this weekend. She hoped Luke was going to be surprised and happy. The thought of him being upset she tricked him caused her momentary stress.

"He'll love it," she whispered to herself as she walked out of the dress shop late Friday afternoon.

It had almost taken an act of Congress for Luke to let her go out on her own. San Diego P.D. had recovered her stolen Lexus, and since the cartel had put less than ten miles on it, there had been no damage. Still, Luke had insisted it be cleaned and detailed and double-checked for any tracking mechanisms other than the one installed with her anti-theft device. Cassie felt like a teenager being allowed to take the car out alone for the first time when she slid behind the wheel.

"I want you to call me after every stop," he demanded as he stood at the driver's side window before she pulled out of the garage.

"I will, baby. I promise."

"I wish you'd let me come with you."

"Luke, you can't be with me every second. I just have a few errands to run, then I'm going to stop in at work to make sure there aren't any fires I need to put out. I'll only be a few hours, and you can call me anytime, and I promise I'll answer."

He pursed his lips, then leaned inside the window and kissed her mouth softly. "Hurry back, doll. I love you."

As she placed her dress carefully inside the trunk, she smiled, imagining the look on his face when he came home tomorrow.

Maybe because she had been lost in her daydream or simply hadn't been paying careful enough attention, but she failed to notice Dante Guzman in her backseat until she buckled in and started the car, her purse and phone on the passenger seat.

"Keep driving, Cassandra," he instructed, his tone low.

"What do you want, Dante?" It couldn't have been her or Lucas, otherwise, why would he have let them escape?

"I came to let you know you have nothing to worry about from my family. It's over."

She slowly pulled into traffic. "Why are you telling me this?"

"I don't want you worrying and constantly looking over your shoulder for the rest of your life. I'm sorry my family put you through that, but I've taken care of it. You have nothing to fear from us, for you or your children."

A weight she hadn't realized was crushing down on her, lifted and her eyes began to water. "Thank you, Dante," she whispered emotionally. "You didn't have to come here, and I want you to know, I appreciate it. I appreciate your hospitality and kindness to me and Lucas in that horrible situation."

"So you know, Cassandra, I would have never let them separate you from your baby or from Lucas, for that matter."

"How could you have prevented it, Dante? I thought it was out of your hands."

"I was prepared to buy you myself," he said softly.

His revelation almost caused her to rear-end the car in front of her.

"You would have done that for us?"

"If my little assassin hadn't found you in time, yes, I would have. I was counting on her to be as good as I know she is though."

"Did you—I mean, is she..."

"Kennedy Jones is alive and well although I'm fairly certain she is plotting my death as we sit here. She is not nearly as cooperative a houseguest as you were, I'm afraid."

She looked at him through her rearview mirror. "You're in love with her." It was a statement, not a question.

Dante looked past her out the windshield as he answered. "At one time, I thought I was in love with the woman she pretended to be. I found out too late that woman doesn't really exist."

She didn't think she believed he didn't still love her.

"What are you going to do?" she asked quietly, scared of his answer.

"That's the million-dollar question. I don't have any idea."

"You're not going to..."

"Kill her? No. Although that's more than likely going to bring a war within my family once they find out I have her. And I wasn't joking about her probably planning to kill me."

They stopped at a stoplight, so Cassie was able to meet his eyes with hers. "You agreed to keep us, thinking she would be the one to come to our rescue, didn't you?"

The corners of his mouth lifted in affirmation, but he didn't verbally answer.

"Why did you do that?" she asked.

"So, then I'd know for sure."

She tilted her head. "Know what?"

He winked at her, his smile growing wider, and reached for the door handle.

"Take care of yourself, Cassandra Sullivan. If you should ever need my help, you know where to find me."

With that, he exited the car right before the light turned green. Cassie knew better than to search for where he had disappeared to and didn't hesitate to hit the gas once the light changed.

****

Luke

Thank fuck the golf tournament with Ron was only nine holes. They arrived at Brenna and Ron's just before noon and hadn't even gotten out of the car when Brenna was at the driver's door.

"I need you two to go pick up some ice, beer, wine, and, well, here," she said, handing him a long grocery list.

"What's that for?" Luke asked.

"Your housewarming party in three hours. The caterers should be arriving anytime."

"What are you talking about?" the SWAT sergeant asked, totally confused.

Brenna clapped her hands. "Chop, chop. No time to explain. Go!"

As Ron drove, Luke texted Cassie.

Luke: Um, we're having a party?

Hot and Beautiful Mama: Yeah, I'll explain when you get back.

She had come home from running errands yesterday and told him about seeing Dante. Part of him was livid with himself for allowing her to be so vulnerable, but seeing the worry gone from her expression more than made up for it.

Of course, he still called it in and an alert was sent department-wide to be on the lookout for Dante Guzman although Luke knew the probability of one of the cartel's most influential members being found was next to zero. That didn't upset him too much. From what Cassie had told him, Dante had been good to her and Lucas, and the ease in which Luke was able to help them escape struck him as suspicious.

But a party the very next day the threat was alleviated? One thing he had learned over the course of this week, Cassie, Brenna, and Dee were dangerous when left to their own devices.

An hour and a half later, with a trunk and backseat full of booze and ice, they pulled into Luke and Cassie's driveway and parked next to a white van with *Karen's Catering* written on the side. As they were unloading the car, Brenna met them outside again. Her clothes hadn't changed from earlier, but her hair was now styled and her makeup far more dramatic.

"Oh, good. Take everything to the patio. The caterer has coolers for the beer, wine, and soda, and there's a bar being setup."

"Shouldn't the caterer have taken care of the alcohol then?"

"No, she doesn't have a liquor license, so this circumvents that. Go! They're waiting for you," she barked.

She pulled Ron aside, and Luke could hear her hissing at him, but only caught bits and pieces of the conversation.

"Told you to keep him gone longer," was the most suspicious part of the discussion he understood.

He noticed there was activity going on at the beach while depositing the booze and ice with the young man setting up bar on his patio and went in search of Cassie and Lucas. Catching a glimpse of Dee chasing Lucas through the kitchen, he began to look for Cassie, finding her in the bedroom. She was sitting on the edge of the bed in her bathrobe, but her hair and makeup were also done dramatically like Brenna's. She was absolutely stunning when she looked up and smiled wide when he entered the room.

"Doll? What's going on? How long have you been planning this party?" he asked as he walked toward her.

Cassie stood and held both his hands in hers. "A few days." He looked at her suspiciously, holding in a growl when she cryptically told him, "Wait here, I'll be right back," then disappeared into the hers of the his-and-hers bathrooms in their bedroom suite.

She didn't come right back, and he was about to barge in on her and find out what the hell she was up to when she appeared, causing him to take in a sharp breath.

The strapless, floor-length, white, satin and chiffon gown with a rhinestone band right under her tits had to be a wedding dress, and she was fucking gorgeous. He blamed how gorgeous for why he was unable to process what exactly was going on. Why was she showing him this dress?

"You look incredible," he murmured, crossing the room to her in three strides. She gripped both his hands in her trembling ones and smiled.

"So, I was thinking about what you said earlier this week. You know, about getting married before the baby comes, and I was wondering, would you marry me today?"

Everything clicked into place—the party about to happen downstairs, her dress, the women's fancy hair and makeup—and a slow smile spread across his face.

"You sneaky little girl," he said with a chuckle. "I thought you didn't want to get married until August."

"I might have been playing a little dirty trying to throw you off," she confessed.

Luke yanked her against him, his hands caressing the satin material on her ass before squeezing and snarling in her ear, "I'm going to have to punish you for that."

"Promise?" she breathed.

"Guaranteed, doll. Guaranteed."

****

Luke

Serious. Fucking. Bliss. That was his life right now.

Their guests had gone, Lucas was spending the night at Brenna's, and they were sitting on the patio in their wedding clothes, holding flutes of sparkling cider while watching the sunset. Cassie got up, telling him, "I'll be right back," only to return a few seconds later with her phone.

She scrolled until she found what she was looking for, then set her Samsung device on a patio table and wagged her finger at him in a *come here* motion. Etta James' voice singing "At Last" filled the night air as he took his wife in his arms and began to sway with her on the red paver bricks.

She'd used a different hairspray than usual, so her hair had a new smell, but when he nuzzled into her neck, he caught her natural scent and let out a deep sigh, squeezing her a little tighter.

He didn't know what he'd done right to deserve this moment, but he never wanted it to end. Damn the song for only being three minutes long.

"Come on, Mrs. Rivas," he whispered softly as he tugged her toward the house. "I want to make love to my wife."

"I thought you'd never ask," she teased,

Luke growled, "I'm not asking, doll," and she let out a little gasp.

He smirked. Exactly the response he was hoping for.

Epilogue

Cassie

Luke's voice bellowed from the kitchen, "Any child not in the car in exactly five minutes is going to miss out on Disneyland!"

Feet scampered through the second-floor hall, followed by the thunderous rumble down the stairs.

Lucas was first to arrive at the car with his suitcase, followed by Charlotte, then Sofia. Little Gabriel had on his backpack, but Cassie had already packed and delivered his suitcase to Luke to stow in the back of the Expedition.

They were celebrating their tenth anniversary like they always did—in Disneyland with the kids, followed by a getaway for the two of them.

Their drive to L.A. was spent reminiscing about previous trips, and Cassie privately reflecting on her life.

There was no way she would have ever predicted this life. Before she met Luke, she just assumed she'd be married to her career, childless with the occasional boyfriend for the rest of her days. Now, she was going to turn forty-five in a few months with four kids and two dogs and a house on the beach. Her career was still important, and she'd continued to rise up the ladder in her company as did Luke who was now Lieutenant Rivas, but it no longer was most important. That distinction belonged to her husband and children.

They decided right after Adriana was found guilty and put on probation to still allow her visitation with Lucas. Cassie had just given birth to Sofia, and there was no way she would feel right about keeping a mother from her child—even though she considered Lucas her son, too.

She often wondered about Dante—if he and Kennedy had their happily ever after or if Kennedy actually succeeded with offing Dante like he had predicted.

The day Cooper Johnson called and asked to have a playdate with Lucas, you could have knocked her over with a feather. When he showed up with a little boy around Lucas' age, she was intrigued, but tried not to make a big deal out of it. For whatever reason, she worried doing so might spook him, so she treaded lightly.

But probably the most surprising thing in her life was the man next to her. The first time she saw him, he was getting out of a topless Jeep in worn Levis and a tight grey t-shirt with Aviator sunglasses. She'd described him as sex-on-a-stick. Now, he was driving his wife and kids to Disneyland with a Barbie doll on the dash of the SUV he had to buy to seat his entire family comfortably.

He had streaks of grey in his jet-black hair and more lines around his eyes and mouth than when she first met him, but that only made him sexier.

She still received punishments in the bedroom and had yet to be in charge when it came to sex between them, but she wouldn't have had it any other way.

Cassie looked back at her brood and smiled.

Domestic bliss. Who would've thought that would be the result of playing dirty?

****

Cassie and Luke make another appearance in Ben's story, *The Heiress and the Mechanic*. Get it here!

https://tesssummersauthor.com/heiress-%26-the-mechanic

Get Cooper's love story, *Cinderella and the Marine* here:

https://tesssummersauthor.com/cinderella-and-the-marine-1

Want to know what happens with Dante and Kennedy? Read their story, *Inferno*, here:

https://tesssummersauthor.com/inferno

Cinderella and the Marine
San Diego Social Scene Book 4

One night. No strings attached. What could go wrong?

Cooper

I was pretty happy living the carefree life of a successful bachelor. Money to spend, a revolving door of women, no commitment, no relationship troubles—it was perfect. At least that's what I thought until I held my friends' newborn baby in my arms, and she smiled at me.

That was the moment I realized what life was all about. That was also the moment it occurred to me that I needed a baby mama—stat.

So...the hunt is on for the perfect candidate. But first, I might have to have one last fling—you know, go out with a bang. Literally.

Kate

Thanks to making a few wrong decisions along the way, I'm now busting my ass waiting tables while putting myself through college. It's not ideal, but I'm determined to stand on my own two feet and take care of my responsibilities the best I can.

But I'm still a woman. I have needs. I just don't have the time for any kind of commitment. Naturally when a smoldering hot Marine offers me a no-strings attached one night stand, I'm all on board.

Turns out...he wants more than I'm willing to give.

Inferno

Agents of Ensenada, Book 1

Kennedy Jones

I'm a special agent with the CIA, and I'm good at what I do. In fact, I'm considered one of the best. I can play the role of anyone and eliminating bad guys without them seeing me coming is my forte—which is why I was chosen to take down the head of the Guzman family.

Dante Guzman is a ruthless, sexy, cold-hearted cartel money-man. And now it's my job to study him, learn his likes and dislikes—in and out of the bedroom—so I can gain his trust and access to his uncle, the head of the Ensenada cartel.

I just didn't count on falling into Dante's clutches.

Every second I spend with him he manages to pull me further and further into his world. And the more time I spend there, the deeper I slip into the darkness with him, the more I realize...

I like it.

Dante Guzman

Don't let my good manners fool you—I'm one cold-hearted SOB, and I control the family's monetary affairs with an iron fist. There's no place for weakness in my world. Show weakness, and you die. As simple as that.

So when a petite, feisty, hot-as-hell bombshell storms into my life, I didn't stop to think about the consequences of keeping her. I wanted her, and I always get what I want. Period.

Turns out, the stakes were too high...for the both of us. And there's going to be hell to pay if we're going to be together, to one form of the devil or another.

https://tesssummersauthor.com/inferno

Other Works by Tess Summers
Free Book!

The Playboy and the SWAT Princess

BookHip.com/SNGBXD Sign up here to receive my newsletter, and get SWAT Captain Craig Baxter's love story, exclusively for newsletter subscribers. You'll receive regular updates (but I won't bombard you with emails, I promise), and be the first to know about my works-in-progress. (Like when Ben's story is coming out!)

She's a badass SWAT rookie and he's a playboy SWAT captain... who's taming who?

Maddie Monroe

Three things you should not do when you're a rookie, and the only female on the SDPD SWAT Team... 1) Take your hazing personally, 2) Let them see you sweat, and 3) Fall for your captain.

Especially, when your captain is the biggest playboy on the entire police force.

I've managed to follow rules one and two with no problem... but the third one I'm having a little more trouble with. Every time he smiles that sinful smile or folds his muscular arms when explaining a new technique or walks through the station full of swagger....

All I can think about is how I'd like to give him my V-card, giftwrapped with a big red bow on it which is such a bad idea because out of Rules One, Two, and Three. Breaking the third one is a sure-fire way to get me kicked off the team and writing parking tickets for the rest of my career.

Apparently my heart—and other body parts—didn't get the memo.

Craig Baxter

The first time I noticed Maddie Monroe, she was wet and covered in soapy suds as she washed SWAT's armored truck as part of her hazing ritual. I've been hard for her ever since.

I can't sleep with a subordinate—it would be career suicide, and I've worked too damn hard to get where I am today. Come to think of it, so has she, and she'd probably have a lot more to lose.

So, nope, not messing around with Maddie Monroe. There's plenty of women for me to choose from who don't work for me.

Apparently my heart—and other body parts—didn't get the memo.

Can two hearts—and other body parts—overcome missed memos and find a way to be together without career-ending consequences?

Operation Sex Kitten
San Diego Social Scene Book 1

Ava Ericson thought she had her life planned out: graduate with her Ph.D., marry Brad Miller when he finished law school, have 2.5 babies... and mediocre sex for the rest of her days. But when Brad dumps her upon learning he's passed the bar, citing new "opportunities" available, she has to rethink her future. Believing her lack of experience was the reason Brad broke up with her, she launches Operation Sex Kitten (OSK), a plan to become a vixen in bed and get Brad back. Things might go astray when she meets the notorious attorney, Travis Sterling, the bachelor who she is sure can teach her a thing or two in the bedroom.

As she enjoys putting OSK theories into practice, she realizes the real 'operation' will be for the two not to fall in love. Fun and romantic, *Operation Sex Kitten* turns up the heat with explicit scenes while you root for love to conquer all.

The General's Desire
San Diego Social Scene Book 2

Falling in lust is easy but falling in love is more than they ever imagined.

Brenna Roberts hasn't had the best luck with men—from her deceased philandering husband to most recently being stood up for a date and having it announced in the gossip section of the newspaper. She's beginning to doubt that good guys still exist. Then she meets decorated Marine General Ron Thompson. Stoic, handsome, and all alpha... he's literally her hero when he saves her from a bad situation.

Decorated Marine General Ron Thompson isn't looking for love. Lust maybe, but not love. As a military star on the rise, he'd rather keep his head down and his focus on the prize—promotion. But when the widow of professional baseball player Danny Roberts sits down at his table at the Sterling wedding reception, everything changes. Lucky for him, he's always been the type to go big or go home, and he's going big when it comes to her.

But she's not sure she's cut out to be with a military man for anything more than just a fling. The sex may be amazing, but the long periods apart and his inability to discuss his work might be too much for her to handle. Except he keeps saving the day, making it impossible for her to stay away.

The General's Desire is a feel-good romance featuring main characters in their forties with open-door scenes and romantic touches that will melt your Kindle and your heart.

This is Book 2 in the San Diego Social Scene series. Each book is a stand-alone with an HEA and no cheating.

A Note From Tess

Thank you for reading *Playing Dirty*. This was a tough one, and I gained ten pounds writing it (that have since multiplied... sigh). When I first started writing this book, my intention was for Cassie to end up with Cooper—but as usual, the characters had other plans. Which was a good thing because I really loved how it turned out. Cassie and Luke were meant to be together.

I hope you will leave me a review for *Playing Dirty* on Amazon, Goodreads, and/or Bookbub. Reviews are so important for authors—especially newer ones like me.

Follow me on social media-I'm fun! You can find the links in the Contact Me! section.

xoxo

San Diego Social Scene

Operation Sex Kitten: (Ava and Travis)
https://tesssummersauthor.com/operation-sex-kitten
The General's Desire: (Brenna and Ron)
https://tesssummersauthor.com/the-generals-desire
Playing Dirty: (Cassie and Luke)
https://tesssummersauthor.com/playing-dirty
Cinderella and the Marine: (Cooper and Katie)
https://tesssummersauthor.com/cinderella-and-the-marine-1
The Heiress and the Mechanic: (Harper and Ben)
https://tesssummersauthor.com/heiress-%26-the-mechanic
Burning Her Resolve: (Grace and Ryan)
https://tesssummersauthor.com/burning-her-resolve-1
This Is It: (Paige and Grant)
https://tesssummersauthor.com/this-is-it
Sloane: (Ashley and Sloane)
https://tesssummersauthor.com/sloane

Agents of Ensenada

Ignition: (Kennedy and Dante prequel)

> https://tesssummersauthor.com/ignition-1

Inferno: (Kennedy and Dante)

> https://tesssummersauthor.com/inferno

Combustion: (Reagan and Mason)

> https://tesssummersauthor.com/combustion-1

Reignited: (Taren and Jacob)

> https://tesssummersauthor.com/reignited

Flashpoint: (Sophia and Ramon)

> https://tesssummersauthor.com/flashpoint

Boston's Elite series

Wicked Hot Silver Fox
https://tesssummersauthor.com/wicked-hot-silver-fox-1
Wicked Hot Doctor
https://tesssummersauthor.com/wicked-hot-doctor-1
Wicked Hot Medicine
https://tesssummersauthor.com/wicked-hot-medicine
Wicked Hot Baby Daddy
https://tesssummersauthor.com/wicked-hot-baby-daddy
Wicked Bad Decisions
https://tesssummersauthor.com/wicked-bad-decisions-1
Wicked Little Secret
https://tesssummersauthor.com/wicked-little-secret-1
Wicked Grumpy Heart Doc
https://tesssummersauthor.com/wicked-grumpy-heart-doc
Wicked Little Thief
https://tesssummersauthor.com/wicked-little-thief

About the Author

Tess Summers is a former business woman and teacher who always loved writing but never seemed to have time to sit down and write a short story, let alone a novel. Now battling MS, her life changed dramatically, and she has finally slowed down enough to start writing all the stories she'd been wanting to tell, including the fun and sexy ones!

Married over twenty-eight-years with three grown children, Tess is a former dog foster mom who ended up failing and adopting them instead. She and her husband (and their six dogs) split their time between the desert of Arizona and the lakes of Michigan, so she's always in a climate that's not too hot and not too cold, but just right!

Contact Me!

Sign up for my newsletter: BookHip.com/SNGBXD
Email: TessSummersAuthor@yahoo.com
Visit my website: www.TessSummersAuthor.com
Facebook: http://facebook.com/TessSummersAuthor
My FB Group: Tess Summers Sizzling Playhouse
TikTok: https://www.tiktok.com/@tesssummersauthor
Instagram: https://www.instagram.com/tesssummers/
Amazon: https://amzn.to/2MHHhdK
BookBub https://www.bookbub.com/profile/tess-summers
Goodreads - https://www.goodreads.com/TessSummers
Twitter: http://twitter.com/@mmmTess

Made in the USA
Middletown, DE
04 August 2024

58472514R00266